Watertight

Jez Evans

Published in 2015 by FeedARead.com Publishing

Waypoint Publishing. All rights reserved.
For enquiries: Ambrose Swift, SWCC, 13A Hill Street,
Saffron Walden, Essex, CB10 1EH.

Front cover design Shutterstock, 2015.

A CIP catalogue record for this title is available from
the British Library.

For my sister, the sailor.

Glossary
AIS – Automatic Identification System
Epirb – Emergency Position-Indicating Radio Beacon
GRP – Glass (or glass-fibre)-reinforced plastic
'Oppies' – Optimist – child's sailing dinghy

Chapter one

The boat ploughed down an unseen trough and met the next wave at speed. The bow slammed hard water and shuddered so that hissing salt spray showered the air. It cascaded the length of the deck and drenched me. But I didn't care; *Ocean Gladiator* was doing 22 knots in 36 knots of wind. She was tearing through the black of night with sails tight as drum skins propelling me towards my first major win in offshore racing.

From the cockpit, I caught sight of my sailing partner below decks. "I owe it all to you, Josh Lewis," I shouted. The wind swallowed my words but I knew he had heard it.

Faint red light from the cramped interior of our Open 62 cast a warm, candle shadow on him. His youthful features were caked in salt, he was unshaven and wearing the same clothes he had put on three days before. His shaggy blond hair and boyish good looks also made him our poster boy. His expression broke into an exuberant smile.

"You do," he said. "Oh, but, you do." He came to the entrance so that only his head was exposed and the blasting wind whipped his hair across his eyes. His grin was broad. In the maelstrom of the storm, he was in heaven. "I'll remind you of that when the sponsors ask us what we want to do next."

"I know. Better than begging them for money."

I turned to the sea and it took a few seconds to acclimatise to the blackness of the night; seconds when my senses were nothing but the sound, smell and feel of the roaring wind, the salt taste of the sea and the motion of the boat as it rolled to the ocean's rhythm secured under my feet. I held onto the stainless steel rigging with cold-numbed fingers and stood with feet wide apart.

I ran my eyes over the black and white of leaping waves in the darkness as *Ocean Gladiator* surged through the foaming swell. My knees flexed as the bow rose, dipped and shuddered and water cascaded down the foredeck like white-foam blood that spurted from the wave backs as we fell, crash-landed and sliced our way through. I searched ahead of the speeding race boat looking, just looking for dangers. I could see nothing. Of anything. The night was black on black.

"How's our track?" I called behind me.

"Fine," said Josh. He turned to the computers, his body too big for the space. "We've got commercial vessels all around. Gramm and Stosur are one hundred and fifty nautical miles behind. Finishing line is eighty miles thataway. Keep pouring it on." Josh was excited. We both knew that we had to stay cautious and not lose the rig or hit something so close to the line, but we were on our way to glory. It was in our sights. Stosur and Gramm were a long way behind and we wouldn't give them the chance they were desperately hoping for.

There could be no off-watch. We would just keep pushing for the finish and keep our eyes on the AIS and radar that tracked the clutter of shipping as it headed for the Channel. Never mind that we were both exhausted after fifty-plus days at sea. Exhilaration had replaced fatigue. We were so close. The finish line was off Brest in France and once we were safely over it, we could pull in for one huge party. Our first major win. The big one. Unbelievable.

Josh said from the companionway: "I'm gonna clean myself up for the cameras. I'll let you know if anything comes too close." He ducked inside. Josh had about six feet of space to work in in the cramped interior of the big, racing boat. Inside, he was surrounded by all the computers and electronic navigation equipment of a modern race boat.

Bang. Bang. A third bang.

The boat moved through the water exactly as she had before, but that sound was wrong.

"What the hell?" I said. I was standing in the cockpit and I felt my neck muscles tense, my arms twitch.

Josh looked up at me with anxious, sleep-deprived eyes. "I don't know." He stood very still, listening for something more.

I indicated the big flashlight and he reluctantly moved towards it.

"I sort of felt…" he said.

"What do you mean?"

"I don't know."

I took the torch from his gloved hand and headed out on deck. Josh followed.

We clipped on to the safety lines and searched in the sails, running the beam of the torch over the rigging. In the shadows we could see nothing. We walked the deck looking for cracks. Something might have parted. We covered the entire deck swiftly and thoroughly checked each fitting.

"Nothing," I said. I felt the blackness of the night and the surging seas all around *Ocean Gladiator*. We were crashing ahead into big waves that we could barely see.

7

"I'm going round again," said Josh, nervous now that something we couldn't find would spoil our dream.

I stepped back into the rolling cockpit, feeling the boat's progress in every pore. After two months at sea, I felt she was me.

"Speeds dropping," I said. I turned to the instruments to see what I had felt from *Ocean Gladiator*. That nagging sensation that we were sluggish was real. "We've dropped under twenty knots."

"But the wind's still holding up…"

Josh slipped past me and into the boat, his heavily muscular body tensed.

"There's water," he said. "Something must have snapped."

I thought it might be a chainplate or something welded to the hull that had cracked and made those loud bangs. They sounded as loud as gunfire with a sort of dull thudding echo to follow each one.

We ran through the boat checking for strain in the most likely places. Nothing. All the seacocks were good and all major fittings looked normal. We had lost twenty minutes' race time searching but we had found nothing. There was a slosh of water over the sea berth and the sole boards as we rode a wave.

"Here," said Josh. "Look."

I followed his out-stretched hand. He pointed to the outer hull, halfway up the topsides. "Bloody hell," I said. "What are they?"

Three neat holes were visible in the GRP along the port side above the berth.

"There are two more on the starboard side."

"And one here in the nav station." One hand steadying myself against the seas, I pointed to the fitting that was bolted into the centre of the boat's cramped interior.

We followed the lines between the holes, judging; three holes to port about an inch diameter and dipping under water with each wave; a hole in the nav station table; two holes on the starboard side. They'd gone clean through.

"What sensation did you have when you heard the bangs?"

"It felt like something passing me. In the air…"

I dug into the nav station with my knife and drew out an object: a metal pellet as long as my thumb.

"We've been shot at."

"In the Bay of Biscay?"

"In Biscay," I said.

Josh looked down at the water around the sole boards. "How's our speed?"

I glanced over, conscious of the boat's toxic smell of sweet, sea-time decay. "We'll limp in. Look, get the coastguard onto it. There must be a vessel nearby. Someone just tried to nobble our chances of winning." I hurried on deck and into the rolling, pitch black and silver spray.

I stared at nothing but surging black waves in a black sky punctuated by thick, grey cloud. The boat, like a hungry salmon coursing and weaving, pitched and thundered through colliding white capped seas and pressed on relentlessly.

I ducked below and started the task of plugging the five separate holes in the hull with sicaflex.

"Get the bilge emptied," I said. "We can still win this race."

Chapter two

"The winner's trophy for the inaugural double-handed *Vendee Globe A Deux* goes to," there was a pause for the audience's benefit, but they knew what was coming; "Tom Shepherd and Josh Lewis aboard *Ocean Gladiator*."

There was wild applause, mostly from our sponsor and their army of employees who had been sent out to fly the company flag. A massive image of the boat flashed on the big screen in the glory of her orange *Gladiator Tyres* logo on its modern green background. The colours were an eyesore, but the boat had been superb.

If you want to feel deliriously happy, try bringing an Open 62 home after fifty-six days at sea with an average four hours sleep in any one day.

Through the crowd, Josh's big muscular body almost fell on me. He slapped my back, giddy with champagne and looked anxiously about him with a troubled grin.

"Where's Jenny?" he asked.

Four giddy hours later I fell into a deep sleep on a real bed and woke sixteen blissfully dream-filled hours after that.

I dressed ready for food. There was a knock and I opened the door to my plainly furnished hotel room.

"Where's Josh?" I said. "I need to tell him I'll do the next race with him. I'm going to stay in the partnership after all. I had a dream we win the mini-transat and go on to defend the *Vendee Globe A Deux*."

At my door, a handsome and tanned man in a sharp suit stared back at me. He was vaguely amused at my over-excitement. He seemed to bare his teeth as he said: "He's gone back to Cornwall to be with his wife. Apparently, she's gone into labour."

"You're kidding?" I took in the American's expensive corporate suit. I'd never seen him in the same one twice. This one was summer blue despite the time of year. His chin was so smooth he could have stepped right out of an advert for shaving razors and his hair as neat as if he had just come from the salon. He had caught me out with his message; I had wondered why Jenny hadn't been at the finish line. "Is that okay? How far gone is she?"

"Only 30 weeks. It's all the excitement. I'm sure she'll be fine." He smiled, all west coast slick.

"Isn't 30 weeks really premature?"

"Jenny's tough," he said. I knew he was Josh's friend and one of the sponsor's big guns. In truth, I didn't really like him. His name was Patrick Colt and amongst other things, he was in charge of Josh's PR. My girlfriend Amy worked for him. I guessed Josh and I would need an entire PR company now that we were big time.

Sixteen entrants, thirty-two competitors, five abandonments, one lost vessel and two limping home late, eight had crossed the line, and we had won. I was elated. Completely, bloody elated. Even the news about Jenny didn't stop me feeling like I'd just sky-dived from Mount Everest.

Patrick Colt greased a smile. He slapped me on the back with a light touch and directed me out of my hotel room and down the nondescript hallway. "Well done, ace. You've done the corporation proud. The old man's been on the phone, he wants to talk terms about a new deal taking you beyond the next *Vendee A Deux* and up to the end of the decade."

"I'll have to talk to Josh…"

"Sure."

"Has there been any news about the gunshots?"

"Nothing… Hold on," he said. He raised a manicured hand and pulled a mobile phone from his inside pocket. "Josh is on the phone now."

"Congratulations!" he said. He nodded to me as he spoke, his slick smile wide across his face. "So, what Mr Drax was thinking…" He was interrupted and immediately his expression changed. He started to look doubtful. "I see…go on," he said. "But Why? Are you sure?" He frowned staring down at my chest and caught my eye without conveying any explanation. "Alright. Alright. I will. Thanks for letting me know."

Patrick pocketed his phone and smoothed his suit. He turned to me; all of his good humour had evaporated. "Josh…" he said.

"Is everything alright with the baby? Is Jenny okay?" I could see he was suddenly floored. The sardonic smile had gone.

"They're fine. They've had a boy and called him Rory. Jenny is doing well."

"That's great. So what's wrong?"

"Josh is giving up on the partnership. He never wants to sail with you or anybody else again."

"Because of the baby?"

Patrick Colt shrugged and his neat suit rippled at the lapels. "He didn't say."

Chapter three

Amy met me in the lobby of the hotel. I had barely managed ten minutes with her before leaving the party early and even then we had a chaperone of seven including Patrick Colt who talked over us the entire time.

The lobby was 1980s glitzy and there were dozens of yachties milling about. A film crew with a pushy, if attractive, journalist had made some arrangement to shadow me for the next 12 months. News to me, but I let them tag along. They stood beside Amy and me, as awkward as any gooseberry on a date, as far as we were concerned.

I put my arms around Amy and hugged her to me. She smiled awkwardly and gave the camera an uncomfortable glance.

"Could you give us a minute, please?" I asked.

The dark-haired journalist, Kate Hutchinson, made a sign to cut the throat and she and the Slavic-faced and neatly dressed cameraman wandered off towards the dining room. Kate Hutchinson was wearing a tight-lipped look of exasperation at odds with her softly warm complexion.

"So how are you, sweetheart?" I put a hand on Amy's shoulder and squeezed. "It's been a long couple of months without you."

Amy sighed and I could see she was troubled by something; probably the excessive workload they had

13

her under. Amy was gorgeous; she turned heads. It was especially apparent in this male-orientated world of offshore sailing and the weeks we spent away. A tall and strong woman with long legs and muscular, bony broad hips, she was pale and blond and Nordic-looking. Originally from Leeds, she had that sort of no-nonsense attitude that I admired in the northern Brits. And she was ambitious, like me.

"I'm good," she said quietly. She shook her head. "It's been a really busy couple of months…"

"I know!" I said laughing.

She smiled. "For me, as well," she said. Her straight, blond hair had grown longer and she had tied it back in a tight ponytail. Her long, soft and pale neck seemed open and exposed. Two tiny moles, one above the other and low on the right side of her neck just above the collar bone were the only blemish against the whiteness of her Scandinavian skin. I remembered them with nostalgic pleasure and watched as the two dark pinpoint moles rotated as Amy turned her head and the long muscles in her throat contracted and expanded. "I've had all this stuff going on," she said. "Work has been crazy, P. has been on… on at me all the time to stay focused, and get all your PR done. It's been mentally exhausting. I don't know if I can carry on doing it."

I tried not to look irritated when she mentioned "P"; the shorthand she used when talking about Patrick Colt. I focused away from my daydream of her long, cream neck and to her eyes. "What? Of course you can carry on, sweetheart. Hey, don't worry, we just won." I took her arm and drew her hands into mine so that she was also forced to look straight at me. "You're not worrying about the crank shooter, are you?"

14

Amy's dark pupils grew large in surprise. "No, but who would do something like that? They could have injured Josh."

"I don't know; crazy people everywhere. Look, let's get something to eat. Tell P. – Patrick - you're working. You're looking after the sailor-man. P. is just a smooth-talking exec, pay no mind to him."

I drew her along with one rough, salt-water damaged hand through the crowd of sailing staff and journalists. Her own delicate skin felt soft and cool. I had missed the youthful touch. Other hands were thrust out to me and I shook them and moved simultaneously. Amy followed me reluctantly towards the cafeteria.

I placed a hand on her soft neck, feeling the cool warmth of its alabaster veneer and the rising heat of her body. "There's a lot of... stuff," she said, and she gave me a worried glance. Her dark eyes – where the Nordic image retreated – were troubled.

I was probably too excited to take her concerns seriously. "You're not thinking of changing jobs, are you? Don't leave the team. Remember what we always said, follow the money and we'll find a sponsor. We've got one. We're about to go global. There'll be a whole PR company doing our – stuff - from now on."

We entered the cafeteria.

"No..." she said doubtfully. She stepped left and my hand came away from the porcelain white of her skin, the two moles drifting into obscurity. "I'm just..." She spotted the journalist Kate Hutchinson and her cameraman and we changed direction towards a corner table.

"We barely see each other as it is," I said. "And I had hoped to see more of you last night... one minute I was dancing and the next I was out like a light. Where did you go? I thought you would come to the hotel room."

"You went to bed at six. You slept for sixteen hours. I've been working, silly." A strand of straight blond hair fell across her eyes from the ponytail and she flicked at it.

We sat down at the table but were over-taken by other people. More hands were thrust forward between us, people looking to shake my hand. People I didn't know. Amy looked on with a gloomy smile as each new visitor turned and walked across the dining room to stand in front of us with a beaming smile. Her head dropped and her neck seemed to retract into the sailing jacket. I needed to give her more of my time, I realised, but the world had gone crazy. My world had gone crazy.

I saw Gramm and Stosur across the crowded room. They were sitting at a table in the corner furthest from us, deep in conversation. Their own PR guys were also hovering and no doubt discussing the race with them.

"Hold on a minute," I said. I got up and crossed the dining room to congratulate the runners-up. So far, we were the only two boats in and on dry land. We had survived and made history. The first boats back from this murderous double-hander. I grinned as I put out a hand to my mentor, Bernie Gramm. We had a future now. We were celebrities.

Celebrity is awful. From the outside, it looks exciting. People follow what you say and ask what you do in your spare time. Then they take up your time asking the same questions as the last person and then they follow you with their eyes, or worse with bolder and more intrusive questions, and hang around too long for more. According to Patrick Colt, I have to write a Twitter entry daily even when I'm on shore and they want to make a documentary about my preparations for the next race and follow-up with a book. There goes the peace of the sailing life. Twenty-four hours on land, and I wouldn't mind getting back out on the water and fast.

I must have been half an hour. When I turned back, Amy had gone. I saw her only in passing throughout the day. She was shadowing Patrick Colt everywhere and taking notes as she went. She stood behind him, head bowed to the iPad while Patrick Colt talked to a lot of people. I couldn't help but think that the handsome, tanned executive was a slimy piece of work. Patrick Colt must be in his early thirties. He was tall with light brown, coiffured hair and he was slim and muscular; the generous description would be debonair or as I would describe it, trying too hard. He looked pretty much the pin-up; the smart, squeaky-clean version of Josh. Josh with his blond, shaggy locks and his cheeky smile was more natural. No doubt, the sponsors would have loved to swap Patrick Colt for me. I don't suppose they were too delighted to have a wiry little tough guy with a weather-beaten face and the look of the devil carved on it for some God-knows-why reason that nature had decided to play tricks on me with.

I never did much wrong in my childhood, but everyone always took one look at us kids and said: 'Him, Tom Shepherd, he did it'. I just have that look; an odd sort of cross between an English schoolboy, a Mexican bandit and the forces of darkness. I knew what they saw when they looked at me: a devil child. I worked every day at proving myself trustworthy, loyal and determined. It made no difference, I looked guilty.

They assumed it was me. I don't need any sympathy for it. I didn't then, I don't now. I work for myself. Up until Josh persuaded me, I always worked alone.

It was sink or swim, and I am a swimmer.

Outside the hotel room's window, the wind was whistling and grey clouds scudded over head. I dropped into the single, high-backed chair and put my feet up on the double bed. Looking out at the marina and the boats swaying to the high wind, I picked up my mobile and called Josh. He rejected the call. I gave my mobile a long look of puzzlement. I couldn't believe that he wanted to give up on the partnership after we had won the biggest double-handed race on the entire planet. We had the chance to go on and make a fortune before either of us hit thirty.

And it had been his idea that we sail together. I had been quite happy doing my own thing. I am the loner. He came to me to ask if I wanted to team up. Bernie Gramm had suggested it. Three years in the making, he had been the driving force behind us doing the *Vendee Globe A Deux.* And we had won. Surely, he wouldn't throw that away.

Things must have changed since he had seen Jenny, I decided. I guessed the baby was a big shake up for him. I don't do babies, nor does Amy. Maybe he had found the change… good.

There was a moment in the Southern Ocean, we had dipped into the biggest wave I have ever seen in daylight and he had been standing on the deck. I could only watch in disbelief as he was engulfed by the entire wall of water that came over us like a shift in reality; as if we were entering another dimension and going underwater whilst still heading horizontally. Josh slipped inside the water, the boat lurched to a halt, and the wave cascaded down the decks dissipating as it washed away over the cabin and the cockpit where I stood and then it was gone. It must have stood ten feet over the deck and it had made us into a submarine.

When I picked myself off the floor, I saw Josh spilling across the foredeck, grasping onto his life-line attached to the port-side runner. He flailed in the scattering water like a beached fish until the ocean released him. After a few seconds prostrate, he drew himself up onto one knee and heaved out the sea water from his lungs.

I helped him back into the boat's compact interior and he spent the next couple of hours sleeping it off. He certainly looked humbled by the experience, by the power and ferocity of the unyielding rogue wave. The next day he was back to his old self, with a glint in his eye that told you he had seen his maker and he wouldn't forget it. Maybe things had changed.

I left the room and passed quickly through the warm hotel. Outside, I drew my green race jacket with the orange flash across it close against the chill of a northerly breeze. I walked the short distance around the front of the hotel and turned down behind it to the harbour. It took no more than a minute.

I stood on the quay and watched the tourists ogling the race boats. *Ocean Gladiator* and *Swiss Time* certainly looked powerful in their bright company livery and with their massive rigs and flat, driving shape.

Patrick Colt appeared and came to stand by my side. His hair fluttered in the strong breeze and he settled it back to perfection with a steady hand.

"Mr Drax wants a private word with you," he said facing forward. The American accent was smooth.

"I'm a lucky man."

"He'll be here in an hour. He's coming by helicopter from Truro."

"Truro?"

"Yes, he's been to see Josh and Jenny at the hospital."

"Oh, right." That didn't sound like our sponsor the self-serving billionaire and sometime offshore sailor who enjoyed what we could do for *Gladiator Tyres* and other associated products.

"Yes," said Patrick turning towards me. The wind whipped at his lapel and shook out his hair. "Well, he couldn't let Josh just walk away like that. We've got an amazing product in you two now." He indicated the tourists around the boat with a sweeping hand as if their presence told us something.

He couldn't miss this trick, I thought. O*f course it was too much business to lose.* Josh was an important ingredient. Tony Drax wouldn't let him go just because the man's son was in hospital.

"The French love him," said Patrick. "Josh speaks the lingo with a Breton accent because of his mother and that gives the locals here a kick. All that Cornish-Brittany camaraderie between fishing folk of old, I guess." He smiled with a broad grin that I imagined anyone else might only manage to reproduce after eating a whole tin of sardines in thick, olive oil. "We've got to get him back," he said without warmth.

"I'd love to, but he's not taking my calls," I said.

"Tony'll have an idea how you can persuade him." He smoothed his hair down once more and turned back towards the hotel.

20

"I see," I said. I put my hand on my mobile in my pocket and walked down to the boat. From the edge of the quay, I took a look round the big ship with a quick, practised eye. It needed a good clean up.

Tony Drax walked into the conference room talking and with his hand held out directly at me. He was a rotund man of fifty-five with a deep tan and an easy smile. He exuded confidence and a warm personality. Every time I met him over the years, I had thought that I could really like him if he just stayed himself... but then he always seemed to want something.

Maybe it was my kicked-in-the-face childhood that made me wary, I had thought he was a genuine advocate of offshore sailing until I realised he was principally a player. In everything. At least Patrick Colt was an obvious slime ball, Amy and I had said that to each other the first time we met him, when he came onboard as her new boss from across the company hierarchy (he'd done something 'monumental' in the States for Drax Holdings). No, Tony Drax disappointed me because every time we met I couldn't help but believe in him until the chubby cheeks expanded in confusion, the brow furrowed and then the face cleared like the arrival of fresh innocence and Tony Drax had somehow won.

"Tom," he said in a long drawn-out way. He walked towards me stepping out of the light from the window and with the view of the harbour behind his almost completely bald, soft-skinned head. "Fantastic achievement. Wow. I can't tell you how delighted I am for you. Brilliant stuff." He shook my hand and I blushed. He was chubby and charming. "You are an amazing young man. How old are you?"

"Twenty-five, sir."

The Australian billionaire had a bellowing voice. He seemed to project through me as he said: "Twenty-five? And Josh only twenty-six. You've done something men like me couldn't do in fifty years. Fifty-five in my case. Well done! Well done."

He led me back past the large round table surrounded by hard-backed chairs and across to the window. We looked down on *Ocean Gladiator* in prime position one hundred yards from the building and below our vantage point. Patrick Colt stepped alongside us smiling ferociously. Tony's own smile widened and I couldn't help but return it.

"What do you say, Patrick? Hell of an achievement, don't you think?" He beamed at Patrick whilst he held on to my shoulder with his pudgy hand.

"Yes, sir; I think these boys will go far."

Tony gave Patrick a smile and his eyes twinkled. He lowered his voice to a soft tone. "Now Patrick, you know Josh has pulled out…"

"But, sir," interrupted Patrick, "surely he's just anxious about his wife and child…" A studied concern spread across his handsome face. His brow furrowed.

Turning, Tony looked doubtful. His rounded shoulders and big belly gave him the appearance of a soft toy, almost comical.

"It's very difficult…" he said, equally tactful in his concern. His volume level remained unusually low. "There is a lot of emotion in childbirth and winning a major race. It can be just as daunting to win as it can be humiliating to lose, you know. First, we must help him to get past this moment of tremendous change, and respect his wishes."

"We could help him transition?" said Patrick.

"Yes," said Tony warmly, "that's right…"

"Alright," I said, stopping them. "Before this double-act gets any more painful, I'll talk to him. I'm sure he'll change his mind when things settle down. We aren't due to do our next race until May. We've got four months preparation time. I'll deal with all of that. Let him go to the hospital with his wife until the baby comes home and then I'm sure he'll want to continue."

"There you go," said Tony brightly. The soft toy was always looking for the angle. His big puppy eyes shone.

"He's probably just playing hardball for more money," said Patrick laughing.

I grimaced. I doubted a new father really saw his child's premature birth as an opportunity to increase his pay packet.

"It'll be fine, I'm sure," I said.

"Marvellous," said Tony. His booming voice had returned. "I'll have my helicopter drop you in Truro this afternoon. Thanks for doing this."

"Wait a second," I stammered. "I didn't say I would go now… besides I want to spend some time with Amy first; we've hardly had a moment alone."

"Take Amy with you," said Tony. He squeezed my shoulder. "Spend a couple of days in the sunshine and meet baby Rory."

"I need Amy here," said Patrick. "We've got a hell of a lot to do, there are journalists crying out for background information, and future plans to put together."

Tony sighed. "The media don't know about Josh's decision to pull out, I take it?"

"Not yet."

"Good," he said. "So you'll go? Tom? Just a couple of days in Cornwall, then come back and take Amy to the best restaurant in town – on me."

I started to answer.

"You know Josh doesn't want to pull out really," said Tony. "He asked you for this, didn't he? Go and support them. Jenny will be relieved to see you aren't upset with him. Go and help them get back together."

I shot a glance up at Tony. "Did you see them? Are you saying something was wrong between them? What exactly do you mean 'get back together'?"

Tony shrugged cautiously. He stepped away from me, taking his plump fingers from my shoulder for the first time since he had taken hold of it. "Nothing serious, she's just had a baby. Her nerves are a bit jangled. When you've seen them, come with Amy up to the estate. I want you to stay a few days with me. We'll talk about your next move and defending the *Vendee Globe A Deux*."

"Yes," I said brightly. "I'd love it if we could defend the title…"

Tony guided me to the door. "Chopper will be ready to go in thirty minutes. You can be back here in two days' time. What do you say?" He smiled with bright and expectant eyes.

I hesitated. "No," I said finally. "I'd be intruding on their time. I'll call and see how they are. That's all."

"Think about it," said Tony. His smile turned to one of sympathy. His thick chest sagged as his shoulders came round. "Don't let a little emotional hiccup stand between the two of you and glory."

They stood in the room waiting for me to leave, watching my reaction. I stepped backwards self-consciously.

"One thing happened," I said. "You must have heard about it."

"What's that?" said Tony. He stood upright, shoulders back.

"Someone shot at us."

"Yes," said Tony, his smile disappeared and he again frowned with concern. "I had heard about that. The world has gone mad. There are some crazy people out there, don't you agree, Patrick?"

"Crazy," said Patrick. He smoothed his suit pockets. "Probably Gramm's mother. Have you met her? Phew, what a harridan. Talk about the mean Swiss streak."

Tony leaned in like an overly-sincere politician. "Patrick will look into it," he said with gravity.

I hadn't heard of the 'mean Swiss streak' and I left feeling foolish. Maybe I should have said 'yes' to going to see Josh, after all he had been desperate to put this team together; he was the one who had really wanted to enter the *Vendee Globe A Deux* in the first place. I decided to ask Amy what she thought.

"Tom, you should go. It's the right thing to do. I'll see you in a couple of days' time."

We were sitting in the taxi at the little airport. The helicopter was standing quietly on the concrete dais. The silent blades were dipping limply in the breeze. A wintry front was blowing across the grass and the helicopter seemed exposed out on the landing bay.

"Will you be okay on your own? I only just got back."

"Don't worry," she said. She took my rough, salted hands in her thin, pale fingers and rubbed the cracked

25

skin. "You've both worked so hard for this. We all have. Try to sort things out…"

I saw the seriousness in her pale face. There was that same anxiety that caused over-work and the same driving ambition that I had. She dropped her gaze. Her pale neck and the two minute moles disappeared from view as her chin fell. "I don't want to let you down. I know how everyone's career could be made on the back of this…" I squeezed her hands, feeling their smoothness as I spoke.

"Josh wanted it," she said. She bent her head timidly and then raised her eyes. "He's just having some… understandable issues at home."

I leant in to kiss her and she kissed my cheek and sat back. "It'll be fine," she said.

I hated disappointing her like that.

"Alright," I said. "I'll go. If you think it will help."

"It *will* help," she said.

I stepped out of the car. "What issues?"

"You'd better ask Josh," she said.

I stood in the cold wind. My sailing jacket flapped against my arms. "He didn't say anything to me. I just spent two months at sea with him."

"P. thinks… Look, it's not for me to say…"

I turned onto the concrete and walked across to the helicopter. I threw my hold-all in, turned and waved and saw that Amy was already talking on the damn phone to some reporter or more likely to Patrick bloody P. Colt.

Chapter four

I arrived in Truro an hour later. It was raining and I wished I hadn't come. Amy had arranged for a taxi to take me from the helicopter to the hospital because Josh and Jenny were spending all their time on the ward watching over little Rory Lewis.

I'm not particularly comfortable in hospitals. They make me feel sick. Or at least, make me start worrying I might be. And the old people wandering around like lost souls living out small, collapsing lives fills me with terror. If anything made me want to get back out racing, it was the thought of how we all end up in a bath chair having someone else wash us because we can no longer do it for ourselves or worse we can't even remember if we have or haven't taken one.

I found the paediatric ward with relief and was directed by a healthy-looking, young nurse to a small out-building that looked like a Nissen hut. Inside, tiny, fragile babies were fighting for life in miniature greenhouses.

I took a deep breath and went in through the outer door. I could see Josh on the other side of a second security door. He was standing close and he placed his large muscled arm around Jenny's lean shoulder as they stared down into one of the greenhouse cocoons. There were a lot of gizmos and electronics coming out of the clear box and I could see several other baby stations with anxious parents looking on.

I took another deep breath and pressed the buzzer and noticed Jenny move aside so that Josh's hand fell away.

An older, plump and senior-looking nurse in a green jacket came to the door and opened it.

"Yes?" she said briskly, obviously busy. She pushed her glasses on to the top of her head. The lines of her skin were etched deep around ruddy cheeks.

I noticed Josh turn to look round. I indicated and waved past the nurse to him.

"My friend," I said.

The senior nurse turned and Josh said something to Jenny. I waved again and she glanced up. Jenny's hand fluttered briefly and her eyes descended. Her expression was weary but not too horrified, I thought.

Josh pressed her arm and came out and closed the door.

We walked slowly inside a sickly green and pastel-painted corridor and made our way towards the cafeteria. Josh needed a coffee.

"How's little Rory?"

"He's doing fine," he said with relief in his voice. "He's nine weeks three days early, but he'll make it. I know it. You should see some of them. It's under thirty, under twenty-eight weeks, they are the scary ones..." He trailed off.

"How much does he weigh?"

"Three pounds and eight ounces."

"Is that good?"

"It'll do." He was looking inwards. He looked up at me again through deep eyes and too-long hair. "It's all good," he said and his tired eyes said more.

After a pause I said: "I'd like to meet him."

Josh put out a muscled arm and his thick fingers took hold of my elbow. He directed me into the cafeteria. "Of course," he said. "Now, let's get the sponsors off our backs: what did they say?"

I grinned and his exhausted, youthful face broke into a weary smile for the first time.

"They told me to change your mind," I said.

"And can you?"

The cafeteria was busy. We stood in a broken queue. I saw the confusion of trouble and real life all around; bandaged bodies and concerned faces. It was why I preferred the uncomplicated ocean. People were full of intractable, long problems.

"I don't know," I said. "Perhaps we could talk about it later. I'd really like to meet Rory."

"He's amazing," said Josh and he began talking about the new love in his life.

We stood over little Rory and made silly faces. Jenny gave a tight smile. "I'll go for a quick toilet break," she said. She looked pale and drawn despite the bump of flesh that still clung to her middle. Her long, black hair had been quickly tied in a ponytail and the stray strands were tucked in behind her ears. She stood with anxious eyes looking down on her newborn son, as if she were unable to leave.

I rubbed her arm.

"Congratulations," I said.

"You, too," she said with a strained positivity. She gave Josh a dozen instructions as she went.

Josh said: "There's a coffee on the side in the parents room for you."

"Okay," she answered, but she didn't look back.

We watched her exit through the swinging door with heavy legs that confirmed her exhaustion and then we turned back to the helpless infant who lay on his back, swaddled inside the clear plastic box. He seemed to have screwed up his sleeping face under a tiny, sky blue, home-knitted hat and a feeding tube was taped into his nose. "Is everything okay?" I asked. "Between you and Jenny, I mean. You both seem tense…"

"Yes," he said, but it was enforced. Something wasn't right at all, and it wasn't just Rory. As far as I could tell, little Rory was doing very well for a premature baby.

"What is it?" I asked.

Josh and I were sitting in the parents' room and Jenny was back in and feeding Rory.

Josh suddenly sat upright and looked at the ceiling, head tilted like he had a neck strain. "I did something crazy… before we left…"

"Oh, no," I said. A premonition of what he might say flashed through my mind. "Josh, are you insane? Look at Jenny – she's amazing, beautiful, talented, and smart as a fox. What were you thinking?"

"I know," he said, blushing with embarrassment. The bags under his eyes were dark. He shook his unruly, blond hair and I was reminded how powerful his muscular body seemed. "It was a terrible mistake. I don't know what I was thinking. She was, I don't know, young – and she pushed herself on me."

"Josh!" I said. "How old was she?"

He seemed out of place in a small room. He was too energetic for it. He fidgeted awkwardly in his seat as if it was his first experience of furniture. His eyes took in everything but mine.

"Nineteen."

"Barely an adult," I said. He caught my eye for a moment at this. "When… did it happen?"

"Last year. And then I stopped it…" The shifting boy stopped grinding against the chair.

Go on."

He leaned towards me, suddenly intense. "We saw each other before the race and… it started up again. A one off, I mean. If it hadn't been for that, Jenny would never have found out. The day before the race, she confronted me."

"Dear God," I said. "I must be the most blind man in the world. Why didn't you say something? We've just been round the world together."

"What was there to say? Besides, it's over now." He pressed workman's fingers together so that the thick muscles of his forearm tensed.

We sat opposite each other not speaking for a moment. I drained my cold coffee. The little room with its depressing array of coffee cups and personal effects to do with long-term visitations by anxious parents reminded me of a Tracey Emin bedsit. The cheap chairs and labelled bottles that said "Wilkins" or "family Smith" were reminders that there was no money in premature birth.

"Is that why you're not sailing with me any more?" I said after I could no longer stare at the depressing little room.

"I don't want to lose Rory," he said hurriedly. "I got in over my head. I'm afraid of what might happen."

I looked at him, face distorted with doubt. "It's only a woman. She's not a pyscho, is she?"

31

"She got a bit upset but, no, she's a very sweet girl, even if she is young. No, it's her dad."

"Who's he?"

Josh gave another awkward glance around the room before settling on me briefly. He turned away to stare at the ancient fridge in the corner. He muttered: "Tony."

"*Tony*? Our Tony? Tony Drax?"

"Yes," he said and Jenny walked in.

Out in the corridor and alone, I peered through the glass at the two of them pacing in front of the cot. Rory had looked terribly small but he appeared normal in most other ways. Apparently, his lungs were yet to fully form and he had to stay until his technical birth date, his due date, in nine weeks' time, but there was a low anxiety about Rory's chances compared to many of the other little blighters. And Rory looked to me like he was a fighter.

Jenny turned to peer up at Josh for a moment and they exchanged a relieved and exhausted hug. Jenny's fragile shoulders in the blue sweater disappeared in his big arms. It looked very stressful and I was glad that Amy and I had a normal relationship without complications like affairs with teenagers and children.

Jenny released Josh first. She pushed a stray strand of dark hair behind her ear and took a big breath in. She had clearly had enough of emotional shocks and was privately reeling. Not least, she had only given birth two days before and her world had been spun about her. But she was mentally tough. I knew her will power would pull her through.

I had known Jenny only through a few brief contacts when she had accompanied Josh to France to see what progress we were making. She had always been very friendly and encouraging but she admitted to being phobic about the dangers of offshore sailing and to being seasick on the boating lake at Totnes.

She was as attractive as Josh was; they made an ideal-looking couple. Where he had curly blond locks, she had thick, shiny dark hair that might, like Patrick Colt's, have been straight out of a hair conditioner advert. They were young, she was lean and he was muscular and athletic, and both of them seemed vitally healthy and alive. I was cursed by living around all these beautiful people. I know some women found my appearance compelling. I knew I wasn't strictly ugly, I knew it was more a demonic, slightly unnerving thing that I had. I was too intense. I stared at people a little too keenly; I intimidated the weak and bashful but it was only an outer shell. And, although that could be useful at times, on the inside I was soft as ice cream. Jenny was the same but different: she was soft as ice cream inside and out.

She wouldn't have come to me for sympathy about Josh's infidelity. One thing I knew, she had come to accept my slightly odd appearance but she certainly wasn't one of those who fell for the devil. She had always been a little wary of me. I knew I didn't do it for her at all. Josh was who she dreamed of.

Amy, on the other hand, had gone for the risky. We had met at a college ball in Plymouth. I had been doing my Yachtmaster Ocean Astro-Navigation class and she was a third year Events Management undergraduate. We danced across the ballroom in a state of drunken enthusiasm and woke up lying side-by-side in my, then, Corribee 21.

I had just met Josh and started the first round of talks about our *Vendee Globe A Deux* dream. I suggested she help us with the campaign and wangled her a job with Drax Holdings PR department. Her then boyfriend took it badly, and occasionally he turned up asking her to take him back. He was a lot older than Amy and it never could have gone on anyway. He was practically bankrupt and was going bald. Three years later, Amy was doing well at Drax Holdings and working as Patrick Colt's personal assistant and although that sounds low level, I was led to believe it would help her to move up in the company when the time came.

Amy's pale and Nordic appearance was a little haunting in itself. She looked a bit like she had just seen a ghost all the time, beautiful as she was. I joked it was because she had just seen me. Her eyes were always dark as if she had been working all night. She stood an inch taller than me at five ten and tended to wear flat shoes because of it.

Josh came out of the room and breathed out.

"God, it's tough," he said.

Josh was worrying about Jenny as much as anything, I could tell. She was sort of half there and half not there with him. She had admitted that she had told her mother about his affair. It kind of suggested her trust was back with mum and not with her new husband.

"It's going offshore, Josh. Things were a little flat between Amy and me when we got back as well," I admitted. "You sort of imagine a great reconciliation and what you get is awkwardness, a kind of need to rediscover each other."

"But Jenny and I have always been so easy in each other's company," he said despondently. "We've been

34

together since school. I'd never been with anyone else other than this... fling."

"Is that why you got married? To smooth it over?"

"That's not exactly how I'd describe it, but it sort of brought things forward a bit, yes. And she was pregnant... but we were always going to get married."

It sounded pretty lame, but I'm sure it was true enough. They had had a pretty rushed wedding in her parents' garden a week before the start of the race.

"I'm not going to make the same mistake with Amy," I said.

Josh flinched. He stood squarely in front of me. "You self-congratulating arse," he said.

I winced and shook my head. I struggled for the right thing to say. I am a loner. I don't do team talks. "Sorry... Josh. Look, it'll die down."

We both looked away. Josh bit at his damaged nails and I felt like walking out of the room. It was easier to be alone, no-one to get it wrong with, no-one else to make mistakes, no-one to upset. But Josh was a good team mate. He had been right to put this team together. I owed it to him to try.

"Is that why you are breaking off the teamwork? Because we could find another sponsor other than Tony... I guess."

"It was hard enough getting Drax in the first place." Josh seemed dismissive.

"But now we're famous we can ask for sponsorship from any of the big players. I know they'll at least *listen* to us."

Josh shrugged his thick shoulders. "Just forget it, will you? I'm sticking by Rory and Jenny for now and the immediate future. You're right, I want to avoid Tony Drax and his daughter but more importantly I want to stay close to my family. Who the hell is that?"

I turned to follow his line of sight over my shoulder and through the internal window that had a view down the pale corridor.

"Oh, hell," I said. "Go back in. I'll head them off. It's the journalist who's supposed to be following me for a year. She must have got wind of where we are."

I passed through the outer door as Josh went in the opposite direction and through the inner secured door to Rory. I met Kate Hutchinson walking purposefully towards the ward. Her long, dark hair and warmly rich complexion made me think of Italian chocolate. Her fixed expression of journalistic neutrality seemed at odds with the softness. There was something hard in her manner, a ruthless persistence.

"Why didn't you tell me about this angle…?" she said with a frown that crossed her striking, televisual face.

"Because it's not an angle, this is real life," I said. I took her by the arm and marched her away from the prem baby unit. "Come with me," I said. "I'll give you an interview right now."

Chapter five

I agreed to do a piece to camera about Rory on the understanding that they stayed out of the hospital. I agreed it with Josh. He accepted that giving a secondhand interview through me was the best way to fend off the intrusion of media attention from them.

I did the piece. It was late when I had finished. Eleven in the UK and it would be midnight in France. Kate, alone this time, her cameraman remaining in France, seemed satisfied with what she had got. She packed up her little camera into a black hold-all. I left the empty family room and went down the echoing corridor. I rang Amy as I walked towards the front reception. I wanted to hear her voice, even if I woke her.

She sounded hassled.

"You busy?" I asked wearily.

"No, I'm okay," she said breathlessly. "I can talk. Are you alright? You sound exhausted. Where are you?"

"I'm on my way back."

"Here?" I could hear the usual scrabbling sound of her bundle of papers and the ubiquitous iPad being scooped up.

"Yes. I'll be there in a couple of hours. I'm heading back to the chopper now."

"Right," she said with an odd tone to her voice. She sounded relieved. The scrabbling sounds stopped. "What did Josh say?"

I could hear a voice in the background asking a question. It sounded close but muffled. I couldn't quite make out what was being said.

"He said: 'he'd be fine,'" I answered. I felt a sick sense of foreboding that seemed to crawl across my face. I couldn't help but feel that the conversation was going wrong. My face seemed to burn across the left side.

"Fine?" said Amy sounding confused. "Does that mean he's still onboard or is he leaving the team?"

"'Fine' means," I said irritably, "that Rory is likely to make it into normal childhood."

"Oh, I see. Look... I didn't mean to seem uncaring..."

"I'll stop you there, Amy," I said. "The penny's finally dropped."

Back in France, I crossed the tarmac to my hotel room. Amy was not there but on the bed's grey blanket was a plain hotel envelope with my name on it in her handwriting.

I threw the white envelope on to the sideboard and dropped onto my back on the bed.

"Bollocks," I said. "Bollocks."

In the morning, a cold north westerly poured itself down the estuary and sent *Ocean Gladiator* jumping against her lines. She didn't want to be tied to the quay when there was a strong blow like this to take her on a wild ride out at sea.

On the dockside, I stood facing into the stiff wind and felt it buffeting me. I didn't like the feeling of being static repulsing the wind. Just like my boat, I wanted to be free, blown along by the wind's power like one of the big, grey-white clouds that were thundering across the sky over my head and building into angry mountains in the sky inland.

On one of the racing boats, a head appeared. Bernie Gramm was on *Swiss Time*. He beckoned me to go over to him. The old boy looked fit and agile even if he had the lines of ages across his face. He was probably the only old person I knew who had my complete respect. In truth, old people unnerved me, I found them an irritation. Bernie was different. He was an energetic sailor, someone making his life into something exceptional, even though he was in his late fifties. He wore a red jacket with the boat's name on the left breast and he came out of the companionway like an athlete.

"Goot to see you, Tom-ass," he drawled in his country Swiss accent. "Congratulations, by the way."

"Thanks," I muttered. I was feeling pretty deflated for a man who had just won his first big race.

"Where is Josh-ua?"

"Gone to visit his wife and their new baby."

"Ah, yes. I heard this." Bernie rubbed the side of his big nose. He had the look of a farmer, rather than a sailor, with his big facial features and his rough hands and weathered and lined face. "Tom-as, may I broach an awkward subject with you?"

"Is it about Amy Mackintosh?"

"No," said Bernie, slightly taken aback.

"Oh," I blushed. *Damn it*, I thought. *Now Bernie thinks I'm a fool as well.*

"No, it is your sponsor, Ton'ee Dr-ax, I want to speak about."

"What about him?" I stood on the quay shivering in the cold and blustery wind. I put my hands in my pockets. My t-shirt and my own sponsor jacket were not enough alone to protect me from the blast of Arctic air.

"Come aboard." He beckoned to me and I went down below gratefully.

His partner, Stan Stosur, was not onboard.

Bernie waved towards his laptop computer. "I found this in my email account this morning. It's from Josh."

"From Josh? Josh Lewis."

"Yah. From Josh."

I stepped across the tiny, damp cabin that was chaotically untidy. I stared down into the bright screen.

I read the email quickly. There was an attachment.

'Bernie, you were right. I know why you pulled out of the deal now. I've seen his stuff.'

"What stuff?" I asked. "Whose stuff is he talking about?"

"I'm going to show you, Tom-as." Bernie pressed a hand against my chest so that I stared up at him. "Promise me you'll keep it to yourself. I didn't tell you before because I knew you desperately wanted a sponsor but now you can have anyone... hold on, Stan is back."

Stan Stosur, Bernie Gramm's racing partner, was walking along the quay towards *Swiss Time*. We could see him through the porthole taking long, lazy strides towards the boat.

"He doesn't know. I'm not going public. It's just between me, you and Josh-ua, okay?"

"I'm not even sure what you're saying…" I protested.

"Later, Tom-as. Meet me tonight at the front of the hotel. You're in *La Bellevue*, aren't you?"

"I am," I said. He pronounced the hotel name so melodically, it distracted me.

"Not a word," he said. "Ten-thirty out the front."

"Very well," I said.

"Go, go." He shoo-ed me from the boat and I took a hand from Stan Stosur as he arrived on the dockside. Stan hauled me on to the quay with a practised swing and he grinned down at me from his lanky six foot three.

"Great bit of wind," said the Australian. "Shame we're stuck here."

"Last boat is due in this evening around ten-thirty," said Gramm.

"Yes, okay," I muttered, annoyed at his cryptic posturing.

"Must be having a hell of a last day plugging into this headwind," said Stan and he ducked into the cockpit. "See you around, Tom Shepherd, *Vendee-A-Deux* winner!" He yelled it back cheerfully as he disappeared below.

I walked away but I had no purpose in my stride. I had no idea where to walk to. Josh was out of the team. Amy had obviously decided to move on, too. Blind, I had certainly been. Up ahead, I saw Kate Hutchinson turn the corner of the harbour building. All I had for my efforts was a trophy and Kate Hutchinson's icy glare to look forward to.

"Kate," I said, as she paced down the quay on long, slender legs in expensive stockings and high heels that were as inappropriate for the day and the location as they were striking. "Good to see you."

41

I didn't mean it, but somehow I had ended up with an impartial judge as my closest confidante and a camera recording my every move. I must not give them the satisfaction of seeing that the little boy who had been kicked down all his life had been kicked again in his moment of triumph. I buried all the recent bad news and smiled my most winning, devilish smile.

The camera's red light flickered on and Kate Hutchinson's toothy, red-lipped smile illuminated in front of it.

Chapter six

"Come on, Bernie," I urged.

It was cold on the steps of the hotel. I had had the equivalent of three pints of beer – something I wasn't used to after more than two months abstinence – and I consoled myself by pretending to be happy.

On the steps of the hotel, a small, thin man stopped in front of me. He had on a creamy brown overcoat and an unfashionable cap. He must have been past ninety and he looked doddery. He shivered in the blast of wind that eddied around the building.

I had yet to see Amy, and the envelope she had left me remained sealed inside my jacket pocket.

I touched the paper of it, conscious that when I finally opened it, I would have to face the inevitable *Dear John* contents. I was also aware that I had not yet opened it because I was holding on to an irrational and clearly unjustified hope that it was something else, like an invitation to meet for moonlit sex.

Well, not on a night like this. There was fast-racing cloud passing over a milky moon and anyone out in the fields getting a frisky lay, was desperate.

I shielded myself against the wind. Everyone else had gone to await the arrival of Mercier and Foyer in last place. It had not passed the French media by that their boys were last. Nor that the American all-girl team had beaten them into last place by a full sixteen hours.

The old man was facing towards me. He placed a pair of black gloves on his hands deliberately, as if preparing for a long wait. He checked his step as if waiting to speak to me and I tried to ignore him. No doubt, he was after my autograph and was trying to pluck up the courage. I was in no mood to be nice but I couldn't think of any suitable French expressions for 'leave me alone, I've had a lousy day.'

I checked my watch. It was ten-forty already. Bernie was nowhere to be seen. The little, old man crept closer.

"I've done the Atlantic meself," he said in a steady, Yorkshire accent that instantly made me think of Amy. "Not in sail boats, mind," he added. "I was in convoys."

"Oh, yes," I said. I was hoping he would get to the point quickly. The beer had gone down smoothly and I was desperate for a pee.

"Johnnie Walter," he said, offering his hand.

He removed a glove. I peered at the old timer's silkily-smooth, paper-thin hand that was covered in large, purple age spots. I didn't want to but I reached out to shake. Despite my misgivings, the touch was smooth and warm. He had a small, fantastically lined face with bright, watery eyes. I wondered what the little man was doing in France. As if guessing my thoughts, he began speaking. I sighed; I clearly wasn't going to get away quickly. The old bugger was going to tell me his life story.

"I'm here for the Normandy Landings. I wasn't actually in it, to be honest." He grinned with what must have once been a cheeky glint in his eye. "I did the Atlantic run. I'm just here with a friend who can't walk. I push his wheelchair for him."

I could hardly imagine the old man pushing anything more than a Zimmer frame but there was something about the way the bent and wizened, old sailor spoke that made me ask: "What were you transporting?"

"All sorts of stuff from the Americans. Food, clothes, arms. You name it. Cigarettes and silk stockings!" He laughed. "I did eight runs and got bombed twice."

"Twice?"

"Yes," he said. His mouth flipped as he said it and I saw a pair of false teeth re-settle on his gums. He put his gloves back on and he wiped at his mouth with an unsteady black-gloved hand.

"Cold, isn't it?"

"Very," I said, trying to forget the image of his multi-faceted mouth. "How long did it take you?"

"We ducked and dived around but a slow convoy could take twenty days. What did you do the entire world in?"

I laughed. It was his first indication that he knew who I was. "Fifty-five days and seventeen hours."

"We would have taken three hundred and that under power."

I searched above the old man's head for Bernie. There was no sign of him and no-one much else about. The old man fell silent. A tear formed at the corner of both eyes and he wiped at them with a white handkerchief.

I had to wait and he didn't seem like he would go. I rubbed cold hands together. "What happened when you were bombed?" I asked.

"Well, the first time, a U-boat put a hole in the ship and we lost half the crew." He stepped alongside me, warming to his subject. "I swam to another ship. We

45

were lucky – it wasn't rough weather – and most of us managed to get up the rope boarding ladder. The second time, we wasn't badly damaged and we limped home. The U-boat was destroyed by one of ours."

I saw someone from the corner of my eye coming towards us and turned to them. I expected Bernie but it was just another spectator hurrying to the quay.

I checked my watch again. It was five to eleven. I could hear a cheer and saw flares going up.

"I've got to go," I said. "Nice to meet you, er, Johnnie."

"And you, Mr Shepherd." I felt bad for having had only half an ear out for the old man. I passed him one of a dozen little *Ocean Gladiator - Vendee Globe A Deux Winners* leaflets that Patrick Colt had stuffed in my pockets.

"If you're ever in the Royal Cruising Club we would love to hear you give a speech about your racing," he called.

I stood on the last step. "Do you still go sailing?"

He grinned and the teeth wobbled. "Not very often these days, I have to admit," he said.

I waved to him. "And nobody bombs you, either!" That was what he had really wanted, I thought, a speaker at the club. I could probably find time to talk to the Royal Cruising Club some time in the future. They were a big organisation and I would like to go. I would catch up with him later, I decided. I hurried round the building and down to the quay. Bernie must have waited to see *French Foundations* come in after all.

I tripped down the dockside, a little drunk. A few stragglers passed me on their way to see what was going on and someone with a heavy bag going in the opposite direction pushed past them heading back towards the hotel. I really needed a pee.

I stopped at *Swiss Time*.

"Bernie?" There was no answer. I stepped down and put my head around the entrance to the little unit that made up the crew's everything, their world.

Stan Stosur turned around sharply and stared at me with wide, horrified eyes. His mouth dropped open at one side as if he might scream but he spoke very quietly.

"I just found him like it…" he said unnaturally.

I shot a glance beyond him at the crew's berth. Bernie was on his back, mouth open, eyes unblinking. There was no mistaking, Bernie was dead.

Chapter seven

The French coroner's office consisted of a sober group of five, grey-coated men. I would have trouble remembering what they looked like in the future, so similar and bland were they.

The two detectives who ducked under the tape and walked towards me at eight a.m. the following morning were much more interesting to look at.

The first, Rene Pignol, had a Breton moustache to rival any I had seen and shoulders as wide as a car. He stood about six feet tall but looked as if he had been taller than that at one time and that his neck had been shoved down on his shoulders to squash him down a bit. Probably an ex-rugby player, I thought.

The other detective was a woman in a stylish outfit under a thick, winter coat that, despite the cold sharp wind, she seemed comfortable enough in. She had good legs and wore her hair in a floppy, rather unfashionable hat which put me in mind of the one worn by Johnnie Walter.

I shook Pignol's meaty hand and the woman, Sylvie Melville, stepped up, clicking her high heels on the flagstones of the quay with a military step as she did. She clutched my hand in thin, bony fingers and then with both hands she smoothed her stray blond hair behind her ears.

Both detectives seemed a little sheepish and then I realised that they too were sailing enthusiasts. Pignol admitted to having a racing dinghy and Sylvie Melville said she sailed with friends in the summer on cruising boats. They congratulated me on the race win. They were clearly a little star struck themselves.

"I understand," said Pignol once his professional composure had kicked in, "that you entered the cabin to discover Mr Stosur standing over Herr Gramm."

"Yes, that's right," I said cautiously. "I mean, I don't think he had done anything wrong... he was checking on Bernie. They were good friends, sailed together in three races."

"Quite so, Mr Shepherd," said Sylvie Melville. She bent her head in a gesture intended, I thought, to suggest empathy. She had a pleasant, thin face and had a faded suntan as if she had been in the winter sun a few weeks before. "We are not concerned at this point about Mr Stosur's actions," she said. She waved a slow hand across her body. "We must first await the results of the post mortem examination."

"I wasn't aware of any illness," I said.

"Perhaps," said Pignol softly, "it was a heart attack. These things happen. You had just returned from a rigorous sailing race, to the Southern Ocean, no less, and Herr Gramm was nearly fifty-eight." He caught my look. "Not old," he said. "But even young athletes can become ill just like that. It is the unknown of life, is it not? Anyway, we shall see in due course."

I nodded. Pignol's French accent was thick Breton but his English was good enough. There was a faintly sweet and noxious smell to the big detective carried by some tarry cigarette he must prefer.

"Is there anything you would like to tell us?" asked Sylvie Melville. Her English was excellent, with only the trace of an accent. I had revised my initial opinion of the policewoman. Although not strikingly beautiful like Amy, she had a poise that was attractive; that special French 'something' people speak of. Her figure was excellently trim in a way that made me consider it for each part; every angle seemed just right and almost controlled. She moved in a deliberate, precise manner as if each step, each turn of the head or hand gesture were entirely separate from others and considered.

I thought for a long moment how to answer her question. "No," I said slowly. I wasn't about to start mouthing off about the note from Josh. Bernie had wanted to keep it to himself for some reason. I could always ask Josh about it first, until then I would keep my mouth shut. Besides, what did it say? Nothing. Bernie was about to tell me a story. I think he was going to show me the attachment to Josh's email on his laptop computer before Stan arrived, but I had nothing to say about it yet.

Rene Pignol appeared to be embarrassed.

Sylvie rotated minutely towards him and gave a sideways glance from wide eyes that suggested exasperation. I noticed the brittle cheekbones and rose-pink colour of her winter skin under a fading tan. She said: "I understand you were waiting for someone yesterday evening. Outside the hotel."

"Yes," I said and then I lied: "My girlfriend, Amy."

"Then when you didn't see her, you came to see Herr Gramm or Mr Stosur? Did you imagine your girlfriend, Amy, was on the boat?"

I took a second long look at Sylvie Melville. She was a polite, well-dressed and poised French woman in her early thirties, and she was to the point. I thought, this woman doesn't suffer fools gladly. She rubbed her cold hands together methodically. I noticed the wedding ring with a slight disappointment. There was something quite attractive about her no-nonsense approach and the features of her face that were almost sharp. She pressed delicate, pink lips against her hand slowly as if to kiss her own fingers, and her pale grey eyes studied me.

I held her gaze aware of the intensity behind it. Pignol followed my eye movements. He had probably registered my fraction of a second glance at the ring.

"We split up," I said. "I was going to look for her down at the quay as *French Foundations* arrived back but I had had a couple of drinks and decided to ask Bernie for his advice and his toilet. He mentored me in my last year of junior racing - and Josh; he mentored him the year before."

I see," said Sylvie. She took a sideways step across the flagstones and back again for warmth with steady, precise feet.

Pignol nodded approvingly. He was just happy to be this close to a famous racing sailor. He clapped big hands together vigorously and let his shoulders loosen.

Sylvie gave him an irritated look. Pignol, I realised, didn't want to find anything murky in the sailing world. These sailors were his heroes. He would have nodded approvingly if I had spoken the alphabet backwards just then.

And Sylvie Melville wasn't bothered that I was a free agent. No flicker crossed her impassive face. I laughed at myself. I was a fool. Twenty-five going on sixteen. The three of us were doing separate things whilst standing together talking about poor Bernie. I was thinking about my dead love life and wondering if the first woman I met would have me after Amy's sudden and unexpected exit. Sylvie was conducting an investigation into the death of my former mentor, and Pignol was hanging out with his heroes, thinking about what he would tell the guys back at the sailing club when he returned.

"Something funny?" asked Sylvie.

"No," I said. "I just felt embarrassed. An awkward laugh, that's all. I'm not good with these things, never have been. I guess you deal with it all the time."

"All the time," agreed Pignol. "All the time."

"We'll be in touch," said Sylvie Melville and we shook hands again.

Pignol put both his big, bear hands on mine. "Congratulations again, Mr Shepherd."

Sylvie winced.

"Please," I said. "Call me Tom."

My mobile phone buzzed loudly in my ear and woke me. I was lying on my bed in the dreary hotel room. It was four p.m. My sleep was still all over the place. I either slept too long, fell asleep in the day or woke too early to stare at the ceiling in the shadows.

I was due to check out in the morning. I rolled to a sitting position and stared at the envelope where I had dropped it on the floor next to my discarded jeans.

I checked my phone. I had missed a call from Amy.

I picked up the envelope. I would have to read it before we spoke, I realised. I carried the letter into the bathroom and cleaned my teeth holding it up to the light to see if I could read the words through the exterior, too much a coward to have a look inside.

The phone rang again.

It was Amy.

I tore open the letter and read it and answered the phone at the same time.

"Hello," I said looking down at the words. The note wasn't brief. *Dear, Tom, Sorry to put this in a letter. We haven't had much chance to talk on our own...*

"Hi, Tom," she sounded nervous. "How are you?"

"I'm alright," I said. *...I really want to congratulate you...*blah blah... *It is difficult to write this...* blah blah... "How are you, Amy?"

"I'm okay. I just wanted to check on you."

The main reason for this letter is to apologise for what has happened. I didn't mean to... Patrick says – I dropped the letter on the floor. It hit a patch of water and the ink began to dissolve into pools.

I could see there was more written on the other side of the page but I couldn't take the long-winded apology. It hurt more than a swift 'goodbye'.

"Tom, are you still there?"

"Yes," I said. I put my hand on the sink and lowered my head. I held the phone to my ear, unable to say anything to her. I was surprised that it hurt like that, I had been kicked plenty of times before by women who thought my face meant I could take it.

She said: "I'm sorry about what I said about Bernie."

"Bernie?" I stammered. "What did you say about Bernie?"

There was pause. "Did you get my letter?"

"I just opened it."

Another pause and then she said quickly: "Throw it away. I wrote more than I meant to say..."

"You mean you're not leaving me?"

There was a pause of pure silence.

"Don't worry," I said. "You've already gone, I know that. Are you taking Archie?"

"He is my dog."

"Be out of the house by the time I get back tomorrow," I said. I terminated the call.

I raised my head and stared at my fearsome features in the mirror. I laughed painfully at the ugly, tough face and turned away to pick up the letter from the floor.

Back in the bedroom, I sat down on the bed and read the rest. My heart was racing in my chest. She had made me angry and she had given me pain. Three years and I had got the same swift treatment that the last boyfriend had suffered. She had moved out and moved on. I flicked over the page, not wanting to see the words but fascinated by the intense pain.

After mentioning that the dog would in fact be going with her, I got to the part about Bernie. I read it again. *You should know, Bernie tried to touch me. He's a creepy, old man. He has things on his laptop that would make you sick. You think he's great, but he's horrible. Don't trust him any more.*

I screwed up the letter and threw it in the bin. *Bitch*, I thought. If I got back first, I'd throw her things out in the street and give Archie to my neighbour. He was the one who cared for the dog most of the time, anyway.

I walked down the street and away from the quay. I found a quiet bar and went inside. It was empty. I started drinking.

Two demis of French beer later and I was surprised to see Sylvie Melville walk in to the bar.

Chapter eight

I woke up with a start. My head ached and it was pitch black in the room. It wasn't my hotel room. It was Sylvie Melville's apartment in the centre of town. Memories flooded in. I remembered the night before. Sylvie had taken off her long, woollen coat and stood there briefly with her long, slim legs. It was enough to imply. At least, I imagined it was. And then the admission that she wore a wedding ring only to avoid the inevitable unwanted interest from those she was investigating.

A brief conversation about Bernie's initial post mortem in which she said the coroner had mentioned a heart attack, and then a lot of questions about sailing, followed by some surprisingly shy questioning about Amy and my love life.

Celebrity was, at last, having its benefits. It was obvious that just like Pignol, Sylvie Melville was a little star struck by our encounter in a way that she wouldn't have been had she met me two months earlier. She had hidden it well, or maybe Pignol had done enough gushing and blushing for the both of them. I wanted the intimacy and I took every opportunity to follow up her delicate leads.

Several drinks later, we walked arm-in-arm to her apartment and lay together in her white-sheeted bed, the window allowing a stream of moonlight to fall onto one corner of the room, enough for us to see bodies in the shadow of night.

Sylvie stirred and turned to me in a languid stretch. We kissed thickly and she dragged her tousled, blond hair out of her eyes. I smelt the warmth of her body odour; a tang of French perfume and sex. I ran my hand down her naked flank to remember the curve of her body from the night before and touched the flat stomach, allowing my hands to wander across to her belly button. I kissed her neck and regretfully slipped out of the single sheet to pad across the wooden floor to the bathroom. She murmured with a lover's sigh.

The room was cold. I wished I had not left the hot, dishevelled bed. The en suite was colder, condensation against the window. I rinsed my face in water and then took a pee shivering. I heard Sylvie on her mobile phone but she was speaking too quickly for me to interpret her French.

There was silence for a moment and then the light came on. I closed my eyes against the glare with the image of Sylvie's almost-thin and naked body at the door holding her mobile as if in explanation.

"I have to go," she said awkwardly. Her brittle cheekbones were coldly pink and the grey eyes confused. Goosebumps appeared on her skin.

"It's okay. I am due back in England today myself," I said. "I have to get back and prepare the yard for *Ocean Gladiator* to come in."

The grey eyes appraised me. "You may not be able to leave," she said. "We have found in Herr Gramm traces of cyanide."

Down on the quay, I stood with Stan Stosur. We faced the wind whilst we watched the forensic team going over *Swiss Time* for a second and much closer inspection.

The anonymous-looking men had already slipped on their white over-alls and were picking their way systematically across the topsides before entering the cabin of the red and white yacht.

Stan had a haggard-looking, drawn expression. He was probably afraid and he looked like he was feeling sick.

"What are they saying?" he asked.

"I just talked to the detective, Sylvie Melville. All she said was that they had discovered cyanide in his toxicology tests. They had initially thought it was a simple heart attack, but now they are considering alternatives."

Stan turned to me, dragging his eyes from the race boat and the white-suited operatives gathering samples from it.

"What sort of alternatives?" He stooped and his neck twisted to see me.

"I don't know," I said. "I think they would be considering murder. Why else would there be cyanide in someone's blood."

Stan grabbed my arm and dug his fingers into the flesh until I yelped. "Why would anyone want to murder Bernie? He was a great guy. He helped everybody. He looked after you and Josh. He gave me my break ten years ago. Everybody in this fleet got some sort of support from him. Everybody loved him."

He released my arm and I shrugged away the sharp pain where his fingers had been. "I don't know," I said lamely. For some reason, Bernie had not wanted to share with Stan the information he had had from Josh. I kept that to myself. I stole a glance at him; Stan's bloodshot eyes were anxiously following the movements of the forensics officers aboard the boat. How did I even know whether Stan had murdered Bernie? It seemed impossible. But it also seemed impossible that Bernie had been murdered at all. Except it wasn't impossible; there was cyanide in his blood.

I glanced away from Stan and caught sight of Amy. She was walking down the quay towards us in her thick sailing jacket that had my name and Josh's splashed across it, orange on green.

They were brash colours.

I gave a deep sigh and felt Stan pat my arm soothingly. He would know I was devastated to lose Bernie, but I had to confess that at that moment my love life was painful, too.

"Hello," said Amy. She held her iPad and notes to one side against her hip. The wind whipped at her hair and blew strands of straight, blond across her eyes. She held my gaze.

"Hello," I said flatly.

She turned to the tall Australian. "Hi, Stan. I'm sorry about Bernie."

I felt the sick feeling in my throat that Stan must be feeling for his long-time friend and racing buddy. I saw the desperation in him. I pulled myself together. My love-life was irritatingly awry, but Stan's best friend and my mentor was dead.

"Thanks, Amy," said Stan. He hung his head. "Poor, old buzzard. I can't believe this happened to him."

"No," I said. "It's all wrong. We'll get to the bottom of it, don't you worry, Stan. The police will work out what happened."

Amy cleared her throat. She had the sailing jacket zipped high to her chin so that nothing was exposed to the bitter wind except her face.

"I've got some news..." she chased the hair from her eyes. The dark circles and the paleness of her skin made her seem vulnerable in the cold, Breton weather. The clouds were building as if this was the place where every cloud would eventually finish its days and it looked like it would soon rain.

Stan glanced towards Amy, dragging his eyes from the taped-off boat. He seemed to be surprised by her pale, white bueaty.

"Tony says *Ocean Gladiator* should be taken back to England now." She shifted her feet. The dark eyes also shifted. "No need for you to go ahead to the yard. He's organised everything for you."

"When? I'm not sure I can go anywhere just yet. The police wanted me here."

"Why? You're not involved, are you? They can't stop you unless there's a reason." She crossed her arms and pressed the tablet computer to her chest.

"There's no reason, Amy," I said, annoyed. I realised Sylvie Melville had no right to stop me going. "I just feel like I should be here," I said.

She looked coldly at me, dark eyes critical, perhaps really seeing my devil-face for the first time.

"Where's Patrick?" I said.

"He's in Brazil. He went this morning. I'm to go after him tomorrow. You're to take the boat to England. Tony has asked Josh to come out and help you."

"I don't need any help. He can stay with Rory."

"Apparently, Josh has agreed. Jenny wanted him to come away for a bit."

"Oh, God," I said.

Amy shifted her feet again and a small, complicated smile developed at the corner of her mouth. "Tony and Mrs Drax are flying to Brazil tomorrow and they have suggested I go along with them."

I said nothing for a moment. She turned away and then turned back to stare at me, curiosity in her grey-white expression and dark eyes.

"You always said to follow the sponsorship money."

I saw her defiance, her independence from me. "Yes," I said. "I did say that." I turned to Stan and touched his arm. "Come on, Stan. I'll buy you a coffee."

"I don't want to go…"

I took his arm. "You do," I said.

Chapter nine

I spent the evening onboard my boat. *Ocean Gladiator* was familiar and I needed that. I didn't fancy going back to the hotel room with its four big, cold and white walls. Stan Stosur joined me. *Swiss Time* was in front of *Ocean Gladiator* and we avoided looking at it.

We had a couple of drinks and talked about Bernie. When we were too drunk to talk, we slept bent into the cramped little bunks. I hadn't heard from Sylvie Melville and I didn't feel like contacting her. It would only confuse things. She obviously wanted to investigate Bernie's death without my involvement. She probably felt foolish to have slept with me before knowing what had actually happened to Bernie. No doubt, sleeping with a potential suspect is as foolish as it gets for a police detective.

I woke in the middle of the night. There was a moon under heavy cloud. The wind had dropped to a whisper for the first time in a week and light rain was falling in a drizzle. I sat up. Stan stirred.

"It's okay," I said. "I just need a drink of water and a pee."

A patch of light from the quayside picked out the shadows. I got out of the sleeping bag, stood up in my long johns and found a plastic bottle in the dark. I drank thirstily from a minor sponsor's mountain spring drink. The cold water trickled down my throat. A noise alerted me that someone was outside.

I put down the water and it crossed my mind that in the half-light I had no idea what I had just poured down my neck, and I poked my head out into the mizzling rain.

I turned 360 degrees but I couldn't see anything on *Ocean Gladiator* that looked out of place. I relieved myself from the back of the boat and turned back. Two boat-lengths down the quay I could make out the shape of *Swiss Time*, nudging against the wall.

Ocean Gladiator wasn't moving. The dock was still. Somebody must be aboard the Swiss boat for it to be bobbing like that; a police officer, perhaps.

I wondered if Sylvie Melville was on the waterfront. I pulled on jeans and my orange and green sailing jacket. I stepped onshore, slipping on deck shoes.

The rain began to fall in thicker sheets and I cursed my sex-drive for hoping to bump into the French detective. *Swiss Time*, in the traditional red and white and with black lettering slashed across her, rode silently against her warps.

The movement of the boat was falling back into a still calmness, almost at rest. I searched on the deck from outside the police tape, but could see nothing of interest from the bow. I wondered why the police hadn't left someone to keep an eye on the big racing boat, but there was no-one.

The large and imposing wall behind me sheltered the dockside from rain and the westerlies that would sweep through on stormy days. I walked alongside the wall and stepped towards the stern of *Swiss Time*, peering forward, thinking I should have brought the torch with me.

I thought about going back for it, but now I was here it would only take a second to check up on the cockpit and see if the boards were in place in the companionway.

I stepped further down the quay. I heard a sound and looked up. A figure was disappearing towards the conference building and the exit from the marina.

It was a woman wearing a long, dark coat and a hat. I thought it might have been Sylvie Melville. If it was, she hadn't wanted to see me. I hesitated before following. It would be very awkward if it was her and especially if she had intended to slip away unannounced.

I turned and went back to *Ocean Gladiator*. It wouldn't work out with Sylvie. It had been a one night stand. It was already over. At least it had given me something to think about other than my disappointment at Amy's leaving. It had just been consolation sex.

I climbed back in through the companionway. Stan stirred. A noise disturbed me from behind. I turned to look up into the rain and a winch handle hit me in the face.

There was blood on my cheek when I woke. I wiped at it, but it had dried. I knew it was blood, and my own, because I could still visualise the winch handle coming at me like a horse's hoof striking out in the night.

I sat up groggily, wondering what had happened to Stan. Why hadn't he done something for me? I must have been laying there for hours, because there was already a crack of dawn light in the sky and the rain was pelting down on the roof.

I sat up. Stan was still in his bunk. There was blood on his sleeping bag. I stood up, banged my head on the coaming and cried out with pain as my head shuddered with the new impact on my already throbbing skull.

I sat down holding my head in my hands. My cheek was thick with my own blood and Stan Stosur was dead.

Chapter ten

Pignol's moustache twitched as he regarded me. This time his sympathy was still in place, but now the reticence and the star-struck demeanour were gone.

I sat inside a dull room in the police station with my head bandaged. An x-ray had revealed no fracture to the skull, but there was a massive bruise just ahead of and above my ear, and spreading to my eyebrow. The right side of my face had swollen and blood had seeped under the skin giving me a bruise that turned the man with the look of a devil into the devil himself.

I held my face in my hands because although it hurt like hell to touch it, it felt better to sink forward onto the desk to be alone with my thoughts.

"We wait for Sylvie," said Pignol. He sat down with stiff knees. "Then the questions."

"Fine," I said without looking up. I tried to rest my eyes. I had taken several pain killers but they had not helped with the dull thudding.

Sylvie walked in.

She seemed harassed, probably she was feeling exposed by the fact of our tryst two nights earlier.

She took off her overcoat carefully and placed it over the back of a metal chair so that the creases were right. She sat down opposite me in the tiny room. I raised my head and gave her a despairing look.

"Talk," she said. Her thin cheek bones, wire pulleys under her skin, were strained by the muscle around her mouth. She firmly clamped her delicate lips together and apart as she said: "What do you know?"

I dropped my head into my hands and then looked blearily into her eyes. I told her about waking, getting up, seeing the woman and then going back to the boat.

"Who was the woman?"

"I thought it might have been you..." I said.

Pignol glanced between us. He sensed that this statement had stirred some question in the air and he shifted his big bulk uncomfortably as Sylvie's rose pink cheeks glowed.

"I thought you had been to *Swiss Time* for something," I said by way of explanation. "I thought I saw you leaving. So I went back to bed. I was going back to bed when someone hit me."

"Did you get a look at them?" Sylvie shot a sideways glance at Pignol and carried on. He had a severe, almost embarrassed expression on his face and continued to search hers for a moment before turning back to me.

"No," I said. "They must have been waiting for me when I got back to the boat."

"Is anything missing? Did they take anything?"

"Not as far as I know," I said. "But the paramedics took me away. I didn't look around."

Sylvie sat upright so that her shoulders drew back. Her thin features were gaunt now, her fading suntan almost gone. Her chest was tight against the thin sweater. There was something about her. Her smell, a real body odour not perfume, I sensed its depth and complexity across the room.

She said: "Stan Stosur is comfortable... but in a coma."

"He's not dead?"

"No," said Pignol, sitting up himself. He pulled a cigarette from a packet, rolled it in his fingers as if measuring it, and then he lit it and sucked in smoke. "No, Mister Stosur survived."

The relief I felt was immense. I had imagined Stan was certainly dead. I could think of nothing to say, but stared ahead. The last image of Stan was just like Bernie. I shuddered. I really had thought…

"Joshua Lewis is here," said Sylvie at right-angles to the conversation. "He's in the station waiting to take you to a hotel room."

Nobody spoke for a moment.

Then she said: "He says his laptop computer is missing from the boat, your boat. Do you know where it is? Did you take it away before last night's incident?"

"No," I said.

Pignol sat up in his chair although he didn't seem able to get fully straight. He was just hitting middle-age and his bones were creaking and flecks of grey touched his thick, black hair. His thick neck and shoulders were like one single block that moulded into a padded roundness. Big as he was, he was stiff where the damage had occurred. It left a sense of fading dominance; a once magnificent beast fading from glory.

"Then they must have taken the laptop with them," he said. "Why did they do that?"

"I don't know."

"Perhaps," said Sylvie Melville. She turned in her precise manner to gaze at Pignol surrounded in a haze of sweetly noxious cigarette smoke. "Perhaps we had better ask Josh Lewis."

This time the journalists and media were not slapping me on the back and wishing us well. They were not asking excitedly for an in-depth interview 'some-time' in the vague future. This time they camped-out outside the police station and mobbed us as we left. The clamour for autographs had been replaced by the ferocious fascination with blood.

Josh arriving at the police headquarters had only added to the frenzy.

I'm not sure what we expected as we emerged from the station, but as we ducked out of sight and into a waiting car, the situation became chaotic. Two men shielded us as we got in, but God knows who they were.

Inside the car, Amy sat opposite me and her dark eyes shone with astonishment. The cameras flashed through the blacked-out windows and she blinked and shielded her eyes.

I looked forward into the front seat. There was the Slavic cameraman who had followed me. Sitting in the passenger seat, and smiling beneath her outer calm, sat Kate Hutchinson.

"Drive," said Kate with a hint of relish. "Drive!"

Josh, Amy and I were back in my hotel room.

"What are we going to do?" I asked.

Josh stood by the window, he crossed thick arms over his sternum, resting them against the faint bulge of a six-pack stomach. Behind him, the curtains had been drawn so that the reporters and camera crews who were right outside were at least screened away. Amy, pale skin drawn with concern, sat very upright in the hard-backed chair.

"Tony wants you to fly out to Brazil to his place. You can hide out there for a while until the commotion dies down." She held her iPad on her lap and her white iPhone on the top as if awaiting the next call. "P. thinks we should…"

"Yeah, well P. can kiss…"

Josh held up a hand. "Someone's at the door." He stepped across and opened it minutely. "It's Kate."

He pulled the lock aside and let her slip through into the room.

She was the oldest amongst us, she must have been nearly forty and she had on a mask of thick make-up at all times. She was striking to look at. She had a strong face, long and protruding. She was handsome with an Italian cream-coffee complexion and was pleasantly reminiscent of an exotic animal. I could see why the television people had given her a job but it worked better on the telly, here the thick make-up made her seem false.

"I've been speaking to the French police," she said, business-like. She took off a long coat similar to the one Sylvie Melville owned and placed it over the back of the chair. She wore a grey skirt and I could see she had very good legs. "It seems that they have no direct reason to keep you here. You're not under suspicion of anything. They have requested you remain to help them with enquiries but they won't stop you leaving."

"Well, that's one thing," said Josh.

Amy, using his real name for once, said firmly: "Patrick thinks you should take the boat back to the UK. It will get you some distance from the press and… everything else."

"Won't they be waiting for us at the other end?" I said.

69

"Tony's other suggestion was to bring the boat to Brazil…" said Amy doubtfully.

"We couldn't," I said. "She needs loads of work before we do anything else. She's still got holes in her, for one thing… The police have probably impounded her…"

"And I'm not leaving Rory for three weeks," added Josh. "Look, let's patch her and take the boat back to Falmouth. We can take our time until the heat goes out of this story."

"That will take a while," said Kate. "The media are ten deep out there." She turned to me. I found myself surveying the make-up considering how it had been applied. She was surveying the bruise. "Should you be offshore sailing with a head wound like that one? What if you have a black-out? I'm sure concussion is a risk for sudden, spontaneous death, isn't it?"

"That's what the doctor was trying to say. I couldn't make out his French too well, but I think he did suggest I should be monitored for 24 hours."

"Well, we'll leave the day after tomorrow. We can spend thirty hours in here." Josh peered around the room. "It's bigger than any boat's saloon I've lived in. You'll have thirty hours to recuperate and Amy can work on the police. Then we can get back to the West Country ASAP."

It felt like a risk to go offshore so soon if I could have a sudden brain haemorrhage but I could understand why Josh was desperate to get back to Rory and Jenny. Thirty hours to him was a big loss.

"Okay," I said slowly. "It sorts out a few problems all at once, I guess. Gets the boat back to England, gets you back to Jenny, and I can recuperate a bit first."

"You could come with us, Amy," said Josh.

I glanced up at him quickly and then to Amy. She put a hand on her neck as if to relax the muscle at the back.

"I'm flying to Brazil later today," she said, and the words hung in the air.

"Didn't you know?" I said. "She's going with Tony and Cecilia Drax. To be with Patrick."

"Patrick?" said Josh. "What's this?"

"Nothing," said Amy. "I just work for Patrick. He wants me in Brazil to arrange the Portsmouth-Rio race. Things are very difficult, very tight. You've only got four months to prepare for it. The boat needs a full over-haul. You two need to rest and then get back into training. Tom's got a head wound. You've said you're pulling out. Bernie died and now Stan's been injured. Tony is on to me all the time about… It's a mess."

Josh waited until the list was finished. He turned to me with an expression of confusion.

Amy slapped her iPad and white iPhone down on the desk and walked over to the bathroom. She leaned against the door frame facing away from us. The nape of her neck, where the small hairs rose into the ponytail, dropped forward. Her skull hung down. She sounded like she was crying.

"And Tom and I split up," she said, still facing away.

Josh looked both awkward and puzzled. He knew I had been pretty keen on Amy but because she was crying, he was trying to work out why I had broken it off. I put him in the picture.

"Amy sent me a *Dear John* letter the day after we finished the race."

"Oh," said Josh. He looked between us with an even more awkward expression. "I'm sorry," he said. "I've been out of action because of Rory. I didn't know

71

about any of this." He turned to me, thick muscle flexing on awkward arms as he opened his palms as if in holy communion. "You didn't say anything at the hospital."

"I'll tell you about it on the water," I said. "I'm going to have to have a sleep now because my head is pounding. Amy, could you arrange for some food and water to go aboard, and we'll need a tow-out for *Ocean Gladiator*. Someone will have to get up early to take us into deep water before the press get wind of what we're doing." I felt my eyes closing as if hypnotised by the mere idea of sleep. "For now, we'll just have to hide out in here."

Sylvie Melville came to see us the following morning at ten am. She gave my bruise a silent inspection and winced. I guess it looked worse than it did the day before.

"Are you okay, Mr Shepherd?" She removed brown leather gloves one finger at a time.

"Yes," I said. "Don't worry about me." She had business to attend to and I wanted her to know our secret was safe with me. "I know you have a lot to do, Madame Melville." I purposefully referred to her in the married tense. "Don't let me stop you investigating the murder."

She dipped her head in acknowledgement.

"I understand you wish to take *Ocean Gladiator* back to England."

"Yes," I said. "Unless the police have any further need to do forensic examination."

"Sailing boats have so many nooks and crannies," said Sylvie. She held the gloves almost self-consciously. "You wish to leave in the morning?"

"Ahead of the press," said Josh from the window.

"Very well. If anything changes my mind, I will let you know."

"Thank you," I said.

Josh took in the forced formality of our conversation. He said: "Did you find my laptop?"

Sylvie stood to go. She straightened her coat so that her shape was perfected. Her suntan had all but faded. I had forgotten to ask her where she had been on holiday in the heat of the one-night stand, but just then I realised that it must have been fake tan, sprayed on in winter. She blinked as she prepared to leave.

"Yes," she said. "We did find your laptop."

Josh waited a moment and then said: "Can I have it back?"

"No, Mr Lewis, not yet."

She placed her leather gloves together in one hand and I opened the door for her.

"I will send a message to clear you and your boat to leave. Do nothing before that time." She stood in the doorway. The corridor remained clear of journalists for the time being. "We will need to speak to you both again," she added.

She stepped away quickly with her expression fixed in neutral and, with purposeful strides, she hurried down the corridor. For a moment I watched her hips moving rhythmically from side to side as her feet seemed to measure the length of the hall. The coat was well-cut and accentuated her neat proportions. She reached the corner and turned. She did not look back.

Chapter eleven

Four days later, stir crazy for fresh air and more claustrophobic than I had ever felt in a boat's saloon one tenth the size of that room, we finally got the go-ahead to leave.

I breathed a sigh of relief. The only change had been Josh's invitation to an interview with Pignol the day before. He was gone all afternoon and came back and went straight to sleep.

Tony was furious. He had also delayed leaving whilst Amy had organised our passage out and every day he had cursed the French and their 'damned bureaucracy.' He and Mrs Drax had been forced to idle a few days in the blustery French resort that was all but closed for winter. Only the brief flare of excitement caused by the race coming home had reignited the town, and now it had gone back to that dreary winter place. The only company were the hordes of journalists looking for the angle and the story to explain the extraordinary events post-race in the *Vendee Globe A Deux.*

The race itself was a sideshow. It was as nothing to the journalists compared to the gunshots in the night that remained unexplained and the murder that had occurred since our return to French soil. I read the papers, not surprisingly what they wanted to know was what connected all these things together. But they had no answers, only questions. *Same as me*, I thought. And from what I could tell, these were exactly the same unanswered questions as the police were considering.

In the small hours of the fourth night, I followed Josh down to the quay. The semi-permanent rain had slowed to an intermittent scatter. The cloud had shifted high above Brest, and the moon had sunk low over the horizon. It was a perfect morning to get out to sea.

Josh was full of nervous energy. Being four days away from his newborn son was too much for him. He rubbed his eyes and slapped his own face and darted looks across the entrance and back to the hotel.

Escorted by a bleary-eyed and limping Pignol, we passed the vans of sleeping reporters and crept away from the melee of interest. We passed down through the wet and cobbled streets to the harbour careful not to slip in the half-life of early morning.

We walked unimpeded past *Swiss Time*, still taped off, and now protected by a young, straight-backed and uniformed officer.

The bear-like Pignol, swaying on a stiff left knee, waved a familiar hand to ward the policeman off and we went by silently.

We crept into the cockpit of *Ocean Gladiator* and Amy arrived to help us load our box of stores on board.

Pignol handed Josh his laptop in a case and then removed the police tape from around *Ocean Gladiator* moving awkwardly on the locked left leg. The young policeman stooped to pick up and pass the boxes of stores out to us.

The tow came chugging through the glass-flat water of the harbour. The rain stopped and stillness came over the marina. The sounding of the gulls in the distance was the only melancholy call over the soft pounding of distant waves.

Pignol stood back. His thick moustache seemed to quiver as he allowed cigarette smoke to circle from his lips. "Sports..." he said with a shrug. He waved and stepped into darkness towards the hotel, crushing the cigarette butt under his leather shoe. I saw him swing the locked, left knee as he disappeared into darkness.

The deep-sea smell of fish and crab meat was powerful from the early morning fishing vessels as men began to arrive and prepare for the daily haul.

"Tony's in bits waiting to get away," said Josh when Pignol had gone. "I just saw him." He tucked the laptop inside the cockpit as he spoke.

"At this time?" I checked my watch. "It's four-thirty in the morning."

"He wanted to know what time we were leaving. He says his plane goes as soon as we do."

"Why's he waited for us? Amy could have flown out on a commercial flight later. She's only a minor employee." I turned my gaze her way. Amy was busy correcting her notes on the iPad.

From the quay, she put one hand on her broad hip, and stood holding the ubiquitous papers and computer in the other. "That's everything you asked for," she said.

I felt that this might be the last time we saw each other, at least before we became real strangers to one another. I guess the race had already put the physical distance between us; I couldn't help but remember the shape of her body now that she stood opposite me in the fashionably-tight trousers around her womanly hips and her strong thighs. Even with the sponsor jacket over the top, she looked pristine with her hair tightly tied in the ponytail. She always did pay close attention to her hair and make-up, and even at four-thirty in the morning there was no exception. The jacket was open at the

76

collar this time and I saw her exposed neck from the collar bones to the straight jaw.

"Did you make some sort of deal with Tony?" I asked.

The little fishing-style towboat came round making a gentle wash in the calm water. The small, weathered and silent harbourmaster was at the wheel. He nodded to us in recognition and then Josh helped him to put a line on *Ocean Gladiator's* bow and run it back to the motorboat.

I cast off our lines.

Amy stood with her hands on her powerful athlete's broad hips, papers tucked against her side. Her ghost's pale skin and tender neck were exposed to the night. Her facial features seemed skeletal, dark at the bone.

"No answer, Amy?"

She shrugged. "Patrick and Tony have their master plans as they call them. I just do the leg work. Tony said he would wait for me to come to Brazil so that I wasn't stuck here fending off the media and the police on my own. He was being thoughtful."

"Well, that was generous of him," I said. "How did Mrs Drax last so long without a large drinks cabinet and her usual circle of girlfriends?"

Amy smiled at me for the first time in a week so that her lips showed colour. "Very badly," she said. She pushed at the shroud of the racing yacht as it lifted away from the quay and the harbourmaster gunned the engine giving the Open 62 a quick turn that brought it expertly into clear space. *Ocean Gladiator* was heading towards the marina entrance and the sea.

"Goodbye, Tom," said Amy. She smiled; relieved, I imagined, that I was going out to sea again and that she would be in the sunshine in Brazil within twelve hours and into the arms of her new lover.

It's hard not to feel a little self-pity at times. I wished that Sylvie Melville would turn up and wave me off with a wistful French 'au revoir, ma cherie' but that was a fool's day dream for another life. I nodded without words to Amy, unable to think of any last rejoinder that would give me the moment. Josh gave a short salute to her and then turned his back and concentrated on the job of leaving.

Ocean Gladiator spun through the tight basin and began to move steadily out of the port. Behind us, we saw the lights and movement, as one, two and then a dozen reporters suddenly realised that they had missed a trick.

My phone rang and I saw Kate Hutchinson's name come up on the display.

"Where's your launch?" I asked.

"We're just ahead of the tow," she said brightly, as if four-thirty a.m. was the time she always got up.

I glanced ahead of the boat. "Keep out of our way. Get your shots and I'll see you in England," I said.

"Yes, boss." Kate Hutchinson was being obliging now that she had the scoop of the year.

Chapter twelve

As the dawn light grew from the grey in the west, a light drizzle fell and then faded away and the high cloud began to dissipate. A cold, still February day awaited us. *Ocean Gladiator* struggled to find a fluke of wind to carry her safely out to sea and away from the dangers of the jagged Finistere coast.

Josh was on the phone to Jenny while we still had a good signal. Rory was doing well. Jenny said she felt a calmness from being left alone with him. Josh found this a confusing statement and he finished the call with a disappointed and dark frown.

"What was it that Pignol wanted you for yesterday?" Josh had been in the police station for three hours.

He shook his head and the shaggy blond curls twisted. The sun lifted over the edge of the horizon and its warmth spread across his troubled face.

"I've been cautioned," he said, laughing as if something were ironic. He blinked long eyelashes.

"Go on…"

"It's a very long story," said Josh.

"We've got all day," I said. "At this rate, we won't be getting there until the early hours tomorrow morning."

I checked the log. Distance run: two nautical miles; time taken: one hour fifteen minutes.

"Tide'll have us on the rocks soon enough," I said. "Engine on?"

"Bit noisy," he said. "Let's give the wind a chance to build." He drew the sleeves of his thick, fisherman jumper up his muscular forearms and fine blond hairs reflected the sunlight.

I checked behind us. "What if the journalists start hiring motor boats? They could be out here in twenty minutes."

"I wouldn't put it past them."

We could see the motor launch carrying Kate Hutchinson heading back towards the harbour entrance. The early, bright sunlight and lack of cloud gave fantastic visibility.

"Falmouth is getting on for a hundred miles. Hell, we could be here for days. What's the weather forecast?"

Josh pulled out the laptop that Pignol had returned to us and he consulted the weather gods of the internet.

"Heavy weather for Friday," he relayed. "Today and tomorrow light south westerlies. Then going south easterly before backing north westerly and hitting F8."

"Everything! At least we'll get there…" I glanced at the glassy water and the long swell, "…we'll get there, eventually. Do you want to tell me your long story?"

"Not really. It's been trouble."

We sailed away from the coast at one knot and although we were buzzed by one reporter in a fast rib, he got bored and went away after ten minutes of watching an empty boat sail itself with Josh and me sitting below decks cooking and then eating breakfast with curtains closed.

The languid day passed and we made twenty nautical miles with the help of a strong east going tide and a bit more wind once the tide turned.

We plugged out to sea following a breeze that kept shifting us away from the continent. We were travelling on a course about seventy degrees off our intended track to avoid getting snarled in the small islets that made up Ushant. The last of which, the Ile d'Ouessant, we passed as the sun dropped over the horizon.

We were almost three miles off the tiny rugged island as the wind died to nothing. We trailed through the night going nowhere fast and took turns at the night watch. I saw the dawn on the second day begin with a haze in the skyline and consulted the laptop. Wind would be here by the end of the day, we'd make Falmouth quickly once the weather came in.

I pressed on for open water. Ushant was still an object in the near distance behind us.

Josh poked his head up.

He looked around and his hair fell in his eyes.

"Still here?"

"We made about six miles over the ground last night."

"Thank God we're not racing. Perhaps we should start the engine." He pressed his hands together and his fingers popped noisily.

I gave an exaggerated frown. "Not the pig," I said.

He shrugged. "I think I'll ring Jenny," he popped his head down again.

By lunchtime we had a trickle of breeze and I could see a great swathe of cloud; a front crossing the Atlantic and heading for the UK and for us.

"By the way, the radar has packed up."

"Really?" I said.

"Yeah, everything else is working fine. AIS is on."

"Keep an eye out for anything without a signal." We couldn't rely on the information coming from the AIS alone; that was just for the ten per cent who broadcast their position on it.

"How was your phone call to Jenny?" We were back in the cockpit.

"Ok," he said but without great enthusiasm.

We began to get sailing, by the time it was dark at five pm, we had a F5 and rising. The traffic in the Channel was heavy, as it always is. We kept staring ahead into the gloom of evening.

When the darkness was complete, rain began to fall. Then that stopped and the wind blew hard. The waves started to build in the Celtic Sea. By now we were on a line west of Falmouth, so we turned for home and set a course of 010 degrees to put the Lizard directly on our bow.

We reefed down and *Ocean Gladiator* started to roar off with the wind on her port quarter.

We grinned to each other: this was what we went sailing for.

Whatever hit us was not ahead. It did not give off an AIS signal and it struck like a concrete slab. *Ocean Gladiator* stalled as if she had ploughed into a rogue wave head first.

Josh lurched across the cockpit body-checked by the impact. He crawled up to his knees and looked behind the boat, dazed. I looked over my shoulder and could see in the dark that the bow of a large fishing trawler was about to crash down a second time onto our port side.

It struck with a violent force that mangled the guardrails and ripped a hole in the hull and deck. *Ocean Gladiator's* GRP screamed. It ripped with a sound like an animal that had been slashed and mortally wounded and the racing boat fell back towards the trawler dropping as if immediately sinking under. Her mast struck the bow of the powerfully-built fishing boat and the port side shroud snapped, parting with a loud and metallic gunshot. The mast was now unstable and loaded with main and genoa and plenty of wind. It would come down.

I grabbed my knife and ran forward to the life raft attached on deck. There was no hope of saving the boat, only a chance to escape. I worked my way under the boom. I kept checking above, fearful that the mast would land on me as I worked. The deck was heaving against the forces of wind, water and the terrible damage.

Josh went back through the cockpit to the cabin for the grab-bag. We knew *Ocean Gladiator* was fatally wounded. We had to get out.

I saw Josh, upper body swinging in a gym-toned arc as he threw out the epirb - the emergency beacon - and it flashed as it disappeared into the sea. It began to transmit our distress to the world. The trawler dropped back and I forced off the life raft, slicing my fingers as I did and dropping my knife.

The trawler, I couldn't understand, began to come towards us again. It had no lights on and in the darkness it crashed onto *Ocean Gladiator* once more, the steel bow tearing into our soft, plastic hull.

Ocean Gladiator slid sideways and then shot back upright sharply. I stumbled onto my knees, Josh fell into the sea.

"I'll get you," I yelled. I scrambled across the deck towards him.

The life raft was slippery in my hands. I shoved it off the deck towards Josh. I could see that the waterline was rising dramatically against the hull. In no time, *Ocean Gladiator* would sink. I followed the life raft into the water, gasping as the cold ran up my body and I gripped the line that kept the raft attached to the boat.

Waves rolled *Ocean Gladiator* and the heaving water inside made her pitch and lurch violently. The power of the water exerted all its forces on the boat and the mast snapped two-thirds up. Sail and mast together fell to starboard. I saw with relief that the life raft had begun to inflate out on the big sea swell.

I looked up behind me, fearful of the boat. The mast swung downwards, falling from the deck, and I ducked under the water, the steel mast towering and then crashing down over me. I protected my head with my hands and then burst out of the water. The mast had landed on top of the half-inflated life raft.

I gasped for breaths of air between surging waves that had spumes of salt spray flying from their tops. Drinking in sea water, I swam forward and clung to the dangling mast with one hand. With the other, I clawed at the life raft, trying to drag it out from underneath the heavy mast. The life raft continued to inflate underneath it.

Flailing at the shrouds hanging from the mast that were still attached to *Ocean Gladiator*, I turned round in circles looking for Josh. The wires were entangling my legs and I felt panic as they knotted around me.

Josh was swimming around the stern of the boat as waves surged him forward.

He swam alongside me and together, without speaking, we tried to lift the top section of mast away.

My boots were full of water and my jacket was fully water-logged, the energy was already sapping out of me. A wire snaked around my leg. Without my lifejacket I would have already gone down, I realised. I held onto the mast and took a breath. The boat rose in the swell and the mast rested, bent and damaged, on top of the life raft as if this had been intended. For the moment, things seemed strangely secure in the heaving sea.

I felt the wire unwind from my leg. Calmness came over me. Although far from safe, there was a moment when no further damage occurred. The trawler had begun to go astern.

"Promise you'll keep it to yourself until it can be proven."

"What?" I yelled. The trawler was moving away silently. I could see it reversing out of the remnants of the great yacht. "Is this your long story, Josh?"

I clung to the wreckage of our former formula one racing boat and he held on alongside me to the life raft. The wind flogged at the tattered remnants of the main and headsail that had settled into the sea around us, shredded and useless.

"Are you talking about your message to Bernie?"

Josh gave me an odd look. I realised that he was suddenly suspicious of me. "What do you know about my messages to Bernie?" he yelled.

The epirb was blinking in yellow strobes and illuminated the darkness as it bobbed slowly away from the crash-site. It would bring help.

I put my hands under the mast, feeling for damage to the life raft that was wedged underneath. I tried to protect the plastic from being ripped by the sharp metal, but it cut at my hands like shards of glass. It would rip into the raft at any moment.

"He showed me an email in which you claimed to have proof about something," I said. "He didn't get chance to say what that was. He said he knew it and that you knew it, too, but that no-one else did."

"That's right," said Josh. He helped me to shift the mast six inches towards the bow of the boat. A wave came powerfully through between boat and life raft and water cascaded over us, filling my mouth and nostrils.

"Not a soul," said Josh as the water receded.

I was getting too tired to try to survive. Two minutes in the water and my clothes were such exhausting weights. Everything was so heavy. My head pounded from the blow I had taken days before. I blew out the foaming water from my throat and nose.

"Tell me now, Josh," I gasped, as the next wave came towards us, breaking. "Otherwise whatever it is *will* be lost forever."

Josh's head disappeared and then returned from the spume of the breaking wave top, only his pretty face was above water; the powerful body was below. He was a poor swimmer, built for hauling ropes, winding winches and climbing masts at speed. In the water he was thickly awkward, arms out of control.

"I'm not going to die here," he shouted. His eyes flashed with determination. "I'm strong enough for this. I want to see Rory. I must get back to Rory."

I breathed in deeply because the wave had passed over. "Had you agreed with Bernie that you would tell me?"

Josh looked away, towards where the trawler had been. His arms circled quickly. "No," he said. "That must have been Bernie's decision once I told him about the images I had. The ones the police found on my laptop." He turned back to me, awkward and suspicious even though we were in the black of night, holding on to a sinking ship in the expanse of the sea.

"What images?"

"The police wiped them from my computer, but they accepted my explanation. It didn't matter, though, they gave me the caution anyway. They had to. I couldn't prove what I was saying."

"*Which* is?"

"I was given the images to prove what I knew about them."

"*Who* Josh? Tell me who. What images?"

He seemed to have ignored my question and then said: "Horrible images. Images of young girls. Terrible things."

A wave washed through and crashed against the mast, dowsing us in foam.

"You've got to tell me." I was getting angry. This had gone on long enough. I gasped for breath. "Either tell me now or stop. I can't make sense of half a story."

The life raft came free.

The mast disappeared quickly and *Ocean Gladiator* tilted down towards the weight of it to her starboard side.

"If I do tell you, you'll be a target, too." Josh stared at me, eyes wide. "I have been fearing for my life, for my family's life, since I found out. That's why I didn't tell you before."

"I'm already in danger," I yelled. "Look at my head! Look at what's happening now!"

"Alright," he said. He was beginning to tire, too. The sudden burst of power had begun to dissipate in him. The cold, February sea was biting. We had very little time before hypothermia would set in.

A wave swallowed us again. We ducked below and then swam out from behind it following the life raft as it buffeted away down the wind. We swam as if we were out for a leisurely dip, but truth be told, we had no energy to move faster. Josh's big shoulders seemed to weigh him down.

"How come you told Bernie?"

"I confided in him about my affair…"

"The daughter. Jesus, Josh, you're talking about Tony, aren't you?"

"I can't tell you."

"But I know. Everything you said tells me you're trying to say that Tony Drax has done this."

Josh shuddered. He got a hand hold on the life raft and he held out his other hand to me. We rested in the water, numb fingers apparently holding on, although the sensation was of nothing. "Tell nobody what I am about to share with you," he said.

I could barely nod. "Go on."

"The short story; I started seeing Helene Drax following a party at Tony's house. It was stupid, I know, but there was something about her I couldn't resist. If you ever meet her, maybe you'll understand.

"We spent several nights together when Jenny thought I was offshore. We slept at Drax's house in Brazil where she grew up and at Drax's holiday home in St Tropez last summer. That was it."

He rested for a moment.

Wearily he continued: "One night he turns up when we thought he was in England. He isn't with Helene's mother, Cecilia Drax, he's with two young girls and a minder of some sort. The girls are no more than teenagers.

"Helene is in bits, crying and upset, but we hide from him. He must have done something pretty hideous to the girls because they both leave in tears. The minder is given a wad of money to keep it quiet.

"We creep out and get away unseen. Helene wants to tell her mother. I want to keep quiet because of

88

Jenny. Helene and I stop seeing each other and I think it is over, even if there is no real agreement between us about keeping quiet or exposing him, or anything. We just walk away from each other."

"And you said you had a second meeting with Helene."

"Yes," said Josh. He looked back at *Ocean Gladiator*, dimly illuminated by the strobe light from the epirb. The boat was almost gone. "I saw her in August last year. We had an argument; then we got drunk and slept together. The next day, Jenny told me she was pregnant. Two days later you told her we had come in on Thursday and not Friday.

"It's not your fault, don't get me wrong. We had been doing sea trials and I didn't expect Jenny to speak to you that week. It was one of those freak accidents. She's not stupid; she knew there must be a reason why I didn't mention I was on land for twenty-four hours before I spoke to her.

"My world fell apart about then." He raised himself in one clean movement and lifted up into the life raft with what little strength he had left. He lay out on the raft breathing shallowly. He turned over and let his head sink wearily down so that our faces were close together. "I confided in Bernie before the race and he said he also knew about it. He had been given other stuff, even worse pictures of... bad stuff, Tom." He drew in a long, lung-aching breath and blew it out sharply. "Helene contacted me. She said she had photographic evidence of Tony's activities. The day we got back. About three hours before I left for the hospital to go to Rory and Jenny, Jenny was..."

"Jenny had had a premature birth..."

Josh's face darkened further. "I asked Jenny to keep it quiet but there was a reason she went into labour

89

early. Somebody attacked her in the street. He grabbed her and knocked her to the ground. He told her that I must keep quiet, mustn't tell a soul about what I knew."

"Oh, Jesus," I said. "You mean someone threatened Jenny and Rory to stop you from going public?"

He held out a hand. "Ready?"

I tried to climb but despite Josh's help, I fell back meekly into the freezing water.

"Hold on," I said between deep breaths. "I'll try again in a minute."

He nodded and he too breathed hard. A wave washed over me. "You can't stay in there too much longer or you'll start to go into shock."

"Just to catch my breath," I said. My breathing was quickening. I knew I was beginning to suffer, my heart was racing against the freezing water's attempt to stop it beating permanently. Any moment now the thumping speed would begin to recede and slow the heart to an irregular beat to nothing.

A hissing sound behind us was the sound of boiling air bubbling out of the boat. We turned to see *Ocean Gladiator* sink into the water. Her transom rose and then slowly edged below the surface, air bubbles expanding.

"So you can't tell anyone, understand?"

"Of course," I said. "I'll keep it entirely with me." I looked around us, feeling paranoid. There were no other vessels nearby. I couldn't see the trawler. "What are you going to do?"

"I've lost the evidence. Bernie has been killed; Stan badly injured. My laptop was stolen from me and then whoever it was handed it to the police. The pictures didn't implicate them but it made me look like I had them for... pleasure."

90

"Did you tell Pignol and Sylvie Melville?"

"Definitely not. There wasn't any proof. Jenny was knocked down in the street. I'm not going to the police."

"Then we're on our own." I stared into his face. Anxiety and fear creased lines across his forehead as if the youthful man had aged to one hundred in a single moment. "We have to get some new evidence against him before we can do anything more."

Josh seemed to falter. "I don't know if I can carry on. Rory, Jenny… I just want to protect them."

"I understand," I said. I felt a little faint. My vision swam briefly. I was numb in the water staring up at Josh's pale, desperate face in the darkness.

Ocean Gladiator was gone. The life raft rolled and shifted in the waves and the current. It moved as if dragged.

"It's still attached," I said urgently. Although my head was spinning, I was suddenly alert.

Josh turned round. "The knife," he called.

Ocean Gladiator dropped into the depths and the life raft followed, attached by a line. It started to be sucked downwards leaving me in darkness alone.

A moment later, the line must have snapped, and the life raft shot back up, Josh inside.

It was almost thirty feet from me. I started to swim breast stroke towards the raft once more. I couldn't feel my feet or anything past my knees. My hands were numb. The only thing I could feel was my heart bashing in my chest as I swam. I was so damned tired. I wanted to close my eyes.

Then I looked up. I could see the black shape that was the trawler.

It came alongside the life raft at low revs.

At last they have reacted, I thought. *They took their bloody time*. I felt tearfully angry but relieved.

But as I started to stroke towards them, I saw a black-suited figure step to the rail. They looked down over at the liferaft and pulled something up. I focused as if seeing something impossible. The black figure held a semi-automatic weapon in their hands. They leaned over the rail and, as Josh put up a hand for salvation, they pulled the trigger. Bullets struck Josh from above.

A moment later and the trawler was reversing back and ploughing away into the night.

In disbelief and without thought, I swam laboriously to the life raft. I could feel nothing physically; I was just cold-numb all over.

The life raft had collapsed and would end up a semi-submerged plastic mess with the dead body of my friend and sailing partner lying half inside it.

Moving as if I could never arrive, I finally put my hand out to Josh. There was no response; only the broad and dense muscle twitched but without the response of life. I put both hands on his chest and shook him. A moment later, a wave rolled us entirely over for the first time.

On the third occasion, Josh's body broke free from the ruined life raft and my numb hands clasped only flowing water. In the dance of black and frothing sea that was strobe-lit only by the flashing of the epirb and obscured by the breaking waves hunting in gangs, I saw nothing of him. He was gone.

Chapter thirteen

The Swedish captain of the 20000 tonne shipping vessel, *Rotterdam Maid*, gave me a large mug of hot chocolate laced with rum.

"I am just glad we were here to help," he said in lilting English.

"Thank you," I murmured. I sank back against the hard bench seat. I probably looked washed out, in truth my mind was racing. Within the space of a week, two out of four of the first finishers of the biggest double-handed yacht race on the planet had been murdered, and a third was in hospital. And, it seemed, it had been done in response to the passing over of documents relating to some seedy sex images that belonged to the race's biggest sponsor.

"What do you want me to do?" asked Captain Thornberg. He walked quickly across the expansive bridge. The big windows behind him were high above the deck and the navigation equipment covered the consoles between us. He stopped and put a hand on the bulkhead to steady himself. Thornberg was a big man with short blond hair and a neat, blond beard. He sported a chunky sweater and an affable demeanour, as if he picked shipwrecked yachtsmen out of the sea on a daily basis. "I have a French police officer on the satellite telephone; a Sylvie Melville."

"Tell her I'm dazed," I said. I pointed to my bandaged head. Luckily for me, the First Officer had excellent First Aid skills and he had cleaned me up, dried me out and re-bandaged my head wound with fresh tape.

Captain Thornberg nodded and the seaman on the satellite phone relayed my message. I sat at the Navigator's table and noted our position. We were steaming up the Channel, close to the Sangette Bank and were en route for The Hague, *Rotterdam Maid's* first scheduled port of call.

I took long pulls on the mug of chocolate. For someone who had raced to the Southern Ocean and back, I was quite clear that I didn't enjoy falling into the sea in winter even in these familiar latitudes.

Next time I went offshore, I'd remember how quickly the whole thing turns into disaster. *If I hadn't dropped my knife,* I thought. *Would Josh still be alive? Or maybe I would be dead, too.*

Captain Thornberg interrupted my worries.

"We can contact someone to meet you at The Hague. There is no formal arrangement for who collects a shipwreck survivor once you're through customs. Do you have someone to come for you?"

"No," I said. My life was the sailing world. Bernie, Stan, Josh and Amy. Even Tony and Patrick were my closest associates. My parents might come for me, if my dad's golf handicap wasn't in doubt. My brother was doing his gap year in Australia. Besides, I didn't want to involve them any more than I had to. Someone had murdered half the racing fleet and the less people around me the better.

"Now there is a Kate Hutchinson on the phone," said the captain gently. He raised his eyebrows. "Could she be asked to collect you?"

I nodded. "Yes," I said. "I'll speak to Kate."

By the morning, *Rotterdam Maid* found her way into the tight spaces of the shipping quay and was inched perfectly alongside into her berth and made secure. Under anonymous, grey cloud I thanked Captain Thornberg and stepped ashore in my own clothes that the crew had dried out for me.

The Dutch police met me at the quay and escorted me across the cold, damp dockside. I gave a statement about the loss of *Ocean Gladiator* and I told them about the collision with the trawler without lights. I left out the gunshots and the assassin who had killed my partner. I knew I couldn't call in family and friends, and I had to protect Jenny and Rory by staying silent for now. Someone wanted us all dead, and Stan and I were still clinging to life. If I blabbed about the murder, it could only make the killer more desperate. Who knows what they would try then?

If it really was Tony coming after us to protect himself from a scandal about some sordid videos then clearly he would stop at nothing to protect his freedom. I couldn't quite tally the man I had known for the past three years with that image, but then what does a killer actually look like?

Like me, I thought. *He looks like me.*

I could honestly give no more idea about the trawler than the colour, which I thought was dark blue and the length, about fifty feet, and the direction it was heading when we hit, roughly north east. I had not seen a nameplate or any identifying serial numbers normally associated with a fishing vessel.

The two dutch policemen scratched their heads, wondered what else to ask me and finally stood up.

They were both very tall and young. They looked like policemen should: handsome and athletic.

Despite what I had assumed, they didn't simply let me go. They opened the door and stepped out. A minute later and I was moved to a second small, cramped room. Green paint peeled from the ceiling. Sylvie Melville and Rene Pignol were already in the room.

Sylvie stared at her paperwork and then at me.

The two Dutch policemen walked out closing the door on us silently.

"What's going on?" asked Sylvie. Her skin was pale, the old, fake suntan long-since washed away.

I thought about Rory and Jenny in the hospital.

"There was an accident," I said. "*Ocean Gladiator* was hit in the Channel. Josh was killed."

"Killed?" said Sylvie. "Not drowned? Or were you thinking murdered?"

I kept quiet. I had to choose my words more carefully. She was right: with Jenny and Rory in danger I didn't want anyone else involved. I had to protect them first. No loose words.

I looked around us. I took in the untidiness of the little room. It was more like a sparse staffroom than an interview suite. It seemed a funny little room for this, an interview with a foreign police force.

"Do you have jurisdiction here?" I asked.

"Co-operation," said Pignol. He sat with his left leg out straightened and to the side of the table.

I stood up. "That's a 'no', isn't it, Rene?" I crossed the room to the door. "You've pulled in a favour."

The two plain clothes French police officers remained seated. They could not have been dressed more differently from the smart young men of the Dutch police force. Pignol had on a cheap black leather jacket and loose jeans. He smoked one of his foul-smelling filterless cigarettes that twitched under his big moustache. His eyes remained steadily fixed on mine. One hand touched the sore knee. Sylvie was silent. She had a file of papers on the desk and she closed it cautiously as if an unseen wind might remove the pages. She looked up slowly and humourlessly, wrapping her big coat around her in the pinch-cold of the room.

I opened the door and grey light seeped in.

Sylvie said: "It could only have been the friends and family boat."

"What?" I held on to the cheap ply door, hesitating.

"The three shots fired at *Ocean Gladiator* on the finish line could only have come from the friends' boat."

"I see."

"And the trawler just now, Captain Thornberg followed it on radar. It headed back towards Brest before he lost it." Sylvie glanced at Pignol who raised an eyebrow.

With only a quick look back, I stepped out into weakly bright sunlight that like a single, cataract eye burned dully from thick, low cloud and reflected from the tarmac and puddles of the port's vast container terminal.

Sylvie Melville called out to me: "They are taking us off the case, Tom."

On the last step, I turned back to Sylvie inside the little room; they were both still seated. Pignol fingered his big moustache where the stain of persistent nicotine had coloured it a rich hazel. His intelligent eyes flickered to the ashtray.

Sylvie's hands were pressed down on the dossier. One hand rose to the side of her face and she pressed stray hair behind her ear.

Pignol's cigarette smoke curled around them. He inched the foot to soothe the knee.

"We can't protect you if you don't help us," Sylvie said.

"I... I don't know what you mean," I answered. My head was pounding again. I wanted to go back to the ship where I could rest and accept cups of hot chocolate and sympathy from Captain Thornberg and his well-behaved crew.

"It's got too big. The media are in a wild frenzy. Two out of four of you are dead, Tom." Sylvie looked pained. "The other two badly injured."

"I know you're trying to help," I said, "...but you can't."

I took the step down and away from them. The grey and weak sunlight returned from water lying in cracks in the inlaid block paving of the expansive car park. I cautiously stumbled across to the terminal building. The great lorries rumbled by with the coloured containers of export and import goods. I was careful to keep out of their way as they sped across the concrete and flooded paving.

I pressed my back against the terminal building and rested against a wall for a moment to catch my breath. I found a door and entered. It was warm inside the building and I felt sick with even this minimal exertion. I stumbled with heavy legs into the interior space. I found Kate in the main hall. Her warm coffee-coloured face stood out from the winter of other people. There were other journalists with cameras held limply. They hovered around Kate, no doubt figuring that she was their best link to me.

Kate suddenly looked up and was walking with long strides towards me before anyone else saw my arrival. Then the crowd surged my way. Kate came close and with a tight smile, she took my weak arm and led me through the hall without a word.

Then the journalists awoke into a din of questions. Kate put her arm around my shoulder and dragged me through a mad crowd of comments, questions and flashlights. I couldn't see beyond them and my head thundered.

At some point I must have fainted, because when I came round, I was on the floor. I stared blankly into Kate Hutchinson's impassive and animal, coffee-cream face, then the flashing lights began again.

"Stop that! Get away from him!" she hissed angrily.

Kate elbowed the journalists away with sharp bones and helped me to my feet. She glared at the pack with a face full of indignant anger, and then she was pushing her way out of the building and into the same car that she had bundled me into once before. Our cameraman didn't wait, this time he shoved his foot down hard, squealing the tyres as he drove away without needing to be told.

Chapter fourteen

We drove out of the port and I kept looking behind checking for the journalists who would doubtless be following. The roads were empty but for long, dirty puddles. The sky was overcast. It was a dreary northern European winter's day like any other and the pattern of sky unique and bland.

"Where can we go?" I asked. The road was quiet now but a dozen vans had started to reverse out of parking spaces behind us.

"The British consulate have agreed to provide you with a replacement passport. They will deliver it to us here and then we will get you home to Devon on a ferry."

I took a second look at the TV woman. Her expensive clothes and groomed dark hair and the movement of her jaw were all I could see. She must have been busy this morning sorting all those things out for me.

"Thank you, Kate." I spotted a small French hot hatch. "I think that little Peugeot is staying with us."

"Slow down, Pete," said Kate and the cameraman did as he was asked.

"It is," I said. The little red car eased back to stay in our shadow.

"It's inevitable that someone will manage to keep up. There must two hundred journalists in the port who were out looking for you."

Pete's Slavic features were calm and his pale skin creamy-grey. He put his foot down again. We pulled away. The red hot hatch left the crowd of vans behind as it broke free of the following pack.

"What time is the ferry?" I said, staring through the back window.

"We call them when we are ready. It's an hour's drive." Kate held onto the dash and diverted glances from front to back, holding steady against Pete's erratic driving so that her face came and went across my groggy vision.

I turned to the little, red car. Two people were up front. The back seat seemed empty.

"Was there something else?"

"I'd like to do an interview with you about what happened."

I turned to her. She held my gaze. Her thick make-up and bright red lipstick were ready for the camera.

"I've been patient," she said steadily.

"And helpful," I conceded.

"We'll pull in to a hotel and get a room. Pete can set up the camera and equipment. We could stay the night and go to England tomorrow. The consulate will bring your new passport to us."

I checked on the small, red car.

"Alright," I said. "But can we lose the Peugeot?"

Pete was a very good driver. He took a complicated set of turns and did his best to remove our tail but although they hung back a fair way, we could not escape them.

"They are determined."

"Professionals," said Pete softly.

Pete might have been enjoying the driving game of hide-and-seek but I was beginning to feel sick from the constant, swerving motion and the pounding headache I already had.

"Forget it," I said. I tapped Kate's shoulder. "At least we've lost the others. Let the red car book into the next room. They can't do anything, can they?"

Kate's nostrils flared as if she wanted the flight, but her brown eyes relented. "Just go to the hotel," she said. "Tom looks like he might throw up." Pete relaxed his driving style and took a couple of backward glances at me.

"Sorry," he said and it was the first time he had directly spoken to me since we had met. I took a quick look at him. He wore grey trousers, a pale green v-neck pullover and a dark green tie. He was non-descript. His hair was fair and his eyes probably blue. He was average height and weight. He had strong Eastern Bloc bone structure. I realised that normally I hardly noticed him against the dynamic and domineering personality of Kate Hutchinson who stood slightly too close when she spoke. She also spoke at you, as if she was always in interview mode.

Forty minutes later, we pulled into the grounds of a luxury hotel.

The chateau was surrounded by a private park of rolling, green lawns as if it were attempting to recreate an English country garden. It was expensively private and grand.

"You're paying, are you? Because all my possessions have been destroyed," I said. I might be hot property but I was yet to see any actual money.

"Yes," said Kate. She opened my door for me and I stepped out gingerly. "The TV company are paying."

A receptionist came out to meet us. The young woman wearing a very smart suit seemed concerned when she saw me. Probably, she was wondering if I might die and stain the hotel foyer. Together, she and Kate helped me in through the front door. An hour later I was asleep having eaten a small lunch in my very grand room.

Before I lay back on the bed, I took one quick glance out of my window which faced down towards the gravelled entrance, but the little red Peugeot was nowhere to be seen.

At four pm, Kate woke me with a doctor. I was examined and the plump man suggested I went to hospital.

"What for?" I asked him.

"Just to observe that you are okay. With your head wound and the exposure, you are very weak. I suggest saline for a day or two." He was matter-of-fact, and ready for retirement.

"I'm fine," I said. "Fluids? I'll drink plenty of water."

I refused any further help and the doctor left showing his gravest face and appealing to Kate to change my mind.

She closed the door on him and turned to me.

"We're all set up next door," she said. "We can do the interview tonight after dinner or in the morning."

"Tonight," I said.

"I've reserved a table for us for seven pm. As soon as we've eaten we'll do an hour's interview. Okay?"

She could be nice when she wanted something, I thought, but I said: "That's perfect."

She put her hand on the door knob and turned it. "It's brave of you to go through with this," she said. "I admired you for going to the Southern Ocean, but

103

you've lost a lot of friends this week. I can't imagine how hard that must be for you to deal with." She opened the door and peered out. "Why didn't you agree to hospital like the doctor suggested?"

I studied her face. She was sincere.

"Because I'm afraid to," I said.

I turned away and heard the door close with a small click behind me.

I picked up the telephone and asked for an outside line. My mobile had gone to the deep. I rang Jenny.

"Hello," she said and her voice sounded small. Her emptiness resounded down the telephone line.

I told her how sorry I was. I told her how good a father Josh had wanted to become. I told her that he loved her more than anything; that his last words were to say those things about Rory and Jenny.

She listened and she thanked me and then she hung up.

I stared out of the window for a long time. I watched a single raindrop as it slithered down to the sill, and then the rain fell more heavily and obscured everything and I closed the curtains and went into the bathroom.

My face was the same ugly mess of bloodied bruise. It had turned purple and would no doubt go on to sickly yellow before it finally faded away.

I satisfied myself that there was nothing more that could be done to improve the gargoyle in the mirror and I shaved for the sake of decency.

After a shower, I put my only set of clothes back on. I would need some more things. I was desperate to go back to Devon and go to the house. There was normality there. I felt a pang of pity as I thought about poor Archie the dog living with my next-door neighbour for so long, but he was probably ten times happier for it.

I went down to the lobby. It was six-thirty and dinner would be at seven. I went out for a stroll in the grounds for the sake of some fresh air. It was dark and cold and it reminded me that my twenty-eight minutes in the English Channel in February had nearly killed me. Thank God for the quick thinking of Captain Thornberg's crew.

I sat with my back against a big oak tree and watched as a smart saloon car pulled in to the hotel grounds and a lean man got out. He walked with a brisk, long stride into the hotel. He had a large envelope with him and I guessed this was the consul with my papers.

I waited a few minutes until I saw him leave the hotel. Kate Hutchinson stood at the door and waved him goodbye. As she went back inside, the consulate car's lights came on.

I was about to get up and follow Kate as she disappeared back inside when I noticed the lights of the consulate's car pass over the small, red Peugeot parked at the furthest end of the hotel building, almost out of sight.

I walked in the dark shadows of the garden and crossed the gravel path behind the Peugeot. I held my hands up to the windows and stared into the rear and then the front seats. There was an unfashionable, floppy hat on the driver's seat and a French newspaper on the dash.

I walked back to the main house and went inside to the restaurant.

Wherever they were, Pignol and Sylvie Melville did not come in to the dining room for dinner.

In Kate Hutchinson's room, I closed my eyes against the harsh glare of the lights that they had set up. Pete was behind the camera in semi-darkness and Kate sat to my right, exposing mostly my undamaged side to the camera so that the viewers would only get glimpses of the injury except for the moment when she asked me to turn my left side for a proper inspection. She knew that the preliminary glimpse would keep people watching in the hope of seeing the whole, ugly mess which she would reveal only at the end of the piece.

I concentrated on the chintzy bedspread and tried to appear as normal as possible, although in truth I felt quite sick and very tired and not a little crazy.

Kate was extremely professional. She seemed to discover some inner strength of character once the cameras rolled and I felt the force of her concern and the sincerity of her interest.

Half-way through, we had covered Bernie's tragic death and Stan's hospitalisation as well as the race, something that now seemed a distant memory lost behind a very real nightmare, and we came to the trawler and the accident in the Channel. I gave Kate only what I had given the police.

When the interview was over, and Pete was packing up, I felt the grogginess come at me in waves.

"Pete," I said. "Could you give us a few minutes? I need to ask Kate something."

"Sure." Pete opened the door with a quick flick of the wrist and stepped outside. "I'll get a night cap and

106

take a look around for les flics," he said, using the French slang for the police.

Kate looked up so that her long eyeslashes flickered. She was distracted by the edit she would do on the raw footage, but I could see she was curious and focused.

"I need your help with something," I said.

"What's that?"

"I want you to find something out for me. Find out all about Patrick Colt. He works for Tony Drax…"

"I know who Patrick Colt is," said Kate shortly. "He was the exec who contacted me about this year-on-the-circuit film we've been making about you." She stared at me. A crease appeared at the corner of her eyes as she scrutinised me. The warm colour of her skin was soothing. Her animal appearance on alert. "What are you saying about Patrick Colt? That he is implicated in these deaths?"

"Kate," I said. "You can tell no-one about this. It has cost two lives already. I just want your help to find out what's going on. I'm going home to Devon so that I can patch myself up. I want to see Jenny and Rory, make sure they are alright. After that I'm going to Brazil to find out the truth."

"Brazil? What's in Brazil?"

"My ex-girlfriend and Patrick Colt," I said.

"What about them?"

"I don't know," I said. "I think Colt has a lot to do with all of this, and I'm going to find out what that is."

Chapter fifteen

Kate escorted me the three metres back to my room and checked no-one was around. I locked the door behind me and sat down on the end of the bed, alone.

All I ever do is hang around hotel rooms these days, I thought. I couldn't think of anything better than getting home to my own bed for a few days. Not even sailing would entice me away from its comforting, heavy depths.

Moonlight fell across the room through the open curtains. Kate had wanted to know more, but I had nothing yet to say. I felt bad about naming Colt, but he had stolen my girlfriend and I needed an excuse to go to Brazil. When Kate discovered that Patrick Colt and Amy were now an item, she would put two-and-two together and realise I was a boyfriend scorned. But it gave me an opportunity to go to see Tony and Helene Drax and learn for myself what it was that Josh had discovered. I wanted to hear exactly what Helene Drax had found out to her horror in St Tropez that night. I could do that without putting Kate in danger if I didn't name Tony as the man Josh thought was after him. I could do that by blaming Patrick Colt for now. And that would also keep Kate busy for a few days, keep her from bugging me.

I slipped out of my clothes, brushed my teeth, and grimaced at the face in the mirror. I decided the bandage would go in the morning. There were stitches but they would for the most part disappear under the hairline. Only small children would be frightened of me from tomorrow, I decided. At least, once I had cleaned myself up a bit more.

I flicked off the bathroom light and padded back into the bedroom and felt a blast of cold air touch my skin. I glanced up quickly. Sylvie Melville stood by the window, breathing heavily from the climb. She delicately closed the window behind her and smiled weakly.

"Surprise," she said.

I stood naked as I had no night clothes, and said nothing.

Sylvie remained stock still opposite me. I wondered at her agility to climb up the front of the hotel and climb into my bedroom still wearing her long winter coat.

The cold made me shiver.

After a moment, I got into the bed, under the smooth, linen sheets.

Sylvie said nothing. She took off her winter coat and I watched her undress. Neither of us spoke. She placed the coat on the back of the chair and slipped off her shoes. She drew her blouse over her head, unclipped her bra at the back, stripped off her skirt and when she was fully naked, in an unhurried, sexless manner, she slipped into the bed beside me.

Her hands touched my sensitive skin and her mouth found my own. A moment later she was on top of me; her hands softly brushed my face, and her pelvis, with slow movements, instinctively found mine.

The sensations were soft and tender. She knew I was in pain. I remembered a time when I had fallen off a horse a year before and Amy and I had made love. That time, Amy had given me no quarter, she had

109

openly enjoyed my discomfort and the moans of pain I exclaimed at the touch of my bruises and it had only excited her. I was relieved to find that Sylvie Melville was a gentle lover when gentleness was called for.

Chapter sixteen

"I am taking two weeks off," said Sylvie. "I will nurse you back to health."

I smiled, whether ghoulishly or shyly as I felt, I didn't know. In the half-light of the small hours, we were both lost in shadows.

I touched her skin with my fingertips and kissed the lean, muscular flesh of her shoulder. "That would be… very kind; but what about the case?"

"I told you, I'm off it." She flicked her hair out of her eyes with an irritable shrug that was out of character in its imprecision. "Paris has sent the top team, our equivalent of your MI5. It's way too high profile for a Breton girl like me to take charge."

She turned her head to look at me in the darkness and rolled onto her shoulder, body under control once more. Despite the cold night, the clean, white sheets in the shadows covered only her legs. She was obviously still smarting at the insult to her skills, and the pink in her cheeks glowed.

"It's international," I said. "And the media are like flies around me. Kate, my journalist friend, says there are two hundred TV crews following me."

"I can believe it," she said. She kissed me in the darkness and touched my face and cheek bone with slow finger tips.

I enjoyed the sight of her nakedness reaching out to me from the pale grey of night. Her breasts softly brushed my chest.

"Ow," I said, gently.

"Poor baby," she murmured. She kissed my lips and the swollen cheek bone with her own soft lips. Tenderly, her hand slipped down to me once more.

"Again?" I said. "I'm supposed to be resting."

Sylvie caressed my face with a single, light kiss. "Nurse knows best, Cherie."

In the morning light, I opened my eyes to see Sylvie slipping into her skirt. She had brushed her straggling, blond hair and tied it into a bun at the back.

I sat up and felt my cheek and temple.

"How is it?" she asked.

"Getting better," I said. "I think it's time to do without the bandage."

Sylvie's expression melted and she giggled, her body convulsing with cruel amusement. "You do look like something out of a cartoon," she said.

"Thanks."

I padded through to the bathroom, took a look at my purple bruise that now had the tinges of yellow and green I had been expecting and which I took to be a sign of healing, and I noted that the swelling that had made me look like a freak show main attraction, had reduced significantly. It did not, however, make me look like a young Marlon Brando.

I cleaned myself up, dabbing tentatively at my wounds, and I dressed in my one outfit. Sylvie was standing at the window, staring out at the rain. I took her hand in mine.

I closed the door behind us and we went down to breakfast. We didn't speak but walked in the silence of newness, side by side.

Kate and Pete were at a table set for three. They were drinking coffee and had obviously finished their breakfast. There were no other guests, only the remains on breakfast tables with discarded napkins.

Pete seemed surprised to see Sylvie Melville, but Kate gave her a cynical smile, one that touched the corner of Kate's mouth cruelly. The small lines that gave away the hint that she was no longer youthful, although not yet old, defined her lips.

I could see that Kate was a little jealous. Not, I suspected, at the thought of us as a couple, but professionally jealous. She would know that Sylvie Melville would now be the first to learn anything about my life. Kate, I was sure, had been hoping I would confide in her. Sylvie Melville had stepped into that driving seat.

I pulled up an extra chair for Sylvie and we sat down.

The two women smiled to each other without warmth on either side.

From the look on his face, Pete was still trying to figure out at what point Sylvie had arrived. Was it just now as I passed through reception, or had we been together all night?

"We are pretty much packed up to go when you're ready," said Kate.

"Sylvie is going to tag along," I said, unfolding my napkin and taking in the brightness of the room.

"As a professional…?"

"No," said Sylvie. "As a friend. I am on leave. This case has gone to the highest authorities."

"So you're just coming along to keep us company?" Kate raised an eyebrow.

"Tom and I have spent some time together and I intend to... help him."

Kate leaned forward. "To do what?"

I shrugged to Pete. He ducked as if to say 'I'm staying out of it'. He was odd-looking as ever. He was slim and with strong features on pale skin attractive, at least compared to me, but he was again dressed like an ageing grandfather. He had swopped his nondescript green v-neck sweater for a similar one in pale blue and the same dark tie. He pushed a pair of thin-rimmed spectacles up his nose and turned to Sylvie.

"Whatever needs doing..." said Sylvie as a vague answer to Kate.

The waitress came to the table speaking in fast but awkward English and we ordered a breakfast.

When she had gone, Kate said: "Does your partner know?"

Sylvie said nothing for a moment and I turned to her.

"Know what?" she asked. She poured coffee into a small, white cup and passed it to me.

"Know that you are here with us?"

"Yes," said Sylvie and she smiled to me brightly. She poured her own coffee with precise simplicity.

I took a glance between the two women and wondered what Kate was getting at. I sipped the coffee quickly and then stood up and went over to the large wooden sideboard where the compots and fruit, and the breads and cereals had been laid out.

A moment later, Sylvie was at my side.

"What is she suggesting?" I asked.

"I don't know," said Sylvie. She shrugged with Gallic exaggeration.

114

"Were you and Rene in a relationship before...us?" I asked. "Is that what she means to imply?"

Sylvie stepped towards the bread bowl and away from me. She collected a croissant, turned and headed back to the table without speaking.

I followed her.

Finally, she said: "It's over."

"How over? Does Rene know it's over?"

Sylvie put the bowl down, and the croissant fell on the tablecloth. She smiled with cold eyes at Kate and turned to me in front of them. "Eight months over."

I felt a sudden embarrassment at standing in front of Kate and Pete discussing Sylvie's past relationships. It had nothing to do with the rest of us.

"We'll discuss it later," I said.

"Yes," said Sylvie. She dipped her croissant into milky coffee and kept her own counsel.

I glanced up at Kate; her smile had been replaced by the TV expression: aloof, determined and inscrutable.

Half-an-hour later, Sylvie went out into the grey daylight and crossed the gravel, heels pressing in amongst the stone. She walked to where the Peugeot was parked in the middle of the turning circle, engine running. Pignol had driven over from a lesser Chambre d'Hote a mile down the road in the centre of the village.

Sylvie leaned in and took a bag. She spoke briefly then stood back.

Pignol turned the little red car sharply, gravel slipped out from beneath the wheels and he shot away.

Sylvie picked up the light rucksack and momentarily stood watching the car's retreat.

As we waited, Kate said: "Keep her close, Tom. You don't know if you can trust her motives."

I turned to Kate, my eyes on the little Peugeot and the dust rising from the displaced gravel. "No," I said, glancing at her. "I realise that."

The ferry terminal is an exciting place to me. I love to watch the ships coming and going. Even the short hop across to the UK gives me a thrill because I love being at sea, even on a short ferry ride.

Unfortunately, I got a lot of strange looks on the boat and eventually went to the shop and bought myself a baseball cap to hide my injured face. No doubt, people were trying to remember where they had seen me before and how I got the ugly bruise.

One or two people, I noticed, had begun to figure out who I was. Luckily, the ferry crossing is short.

On the other side, we drove in silence for over an hour.

Kate was upfront alongside Pete who was driving.

Kate abruptly said: "The only boat that was in the right place to shoot at you and Josh when you finished the *Vendee A Deux* race was the friends and sponsors launch."

"Who was on that boat?" I asked.

"Tony was there," said Kate. "Helene and Cecilia. Pete and I were there. Amy and Patrick, the crew – only two of them, I think - and Sylvie Melville was onboard."

"You were?" I turned to Sylvie in the backseat next to me.

"I was there with the mayor," she said. "As his guest."

"You didn't mention that before."

Sylvie shrugged. "Why should I have?"

"Because someone on that boat shot at us."

"Yes, I know." Her delicate pink cheeks and soft mouth were in profile.

"What did you see?"

"Nothing but hands."

"Hands?"

She flashed me an irritated glance. "I spent the entire time fending off the mayor."

Sylvie fell back into a cold silence.

I avoided Kate's eyes expecting a knowing glance.

We drove for five hours straight. The journey was tiresome and as I took my turn at the wheel for the last hour, it was a relief to have something to do.

It was dark by the time we arrived at the house. The little flint cottage was gloomy and the curtains were open.

I stepped up to the front door and pushed in my key and it felt as if I had been away many years.

The door refused to budge.

"Is there a problem?" asked Kate.

"It's locked from the inside."

I looked up to the dark windows upstairs and the closed curtains. The whole street was dark. My house seemed darkest of all.

"Shall I go round the back?" said Pete.

"Don't worry, my brother's a locksmith. I can break in," I said.

I took my credit card and edged it into the lock. Eventually, the door swung open.

"I'm a bit rusty," I said. "But we're in."

I switched on the light. The room was a mess, possessions scattered. I stepped in amongst the papers and household objects up-turned on the floor. I groaned.

I hurried through the house. Kate, Sylvie and Pete remained downstairs as I ran up to the two cramped bedrooms.

I came back down the stairs wearily.

"My old laptop is missing but otherwise everything else is here. Except Amy's stuff has gone. I am assuming she took that before this happened."

Kate switched on the kettle. "We better clean up," she said.

I looked down at the chaotic belongings of my home. Nothing really damaged, I noticed, more discarded.

An hour later, we went to the pub for a drink and ate fish and chips at one of the long tables. My neighbour, Seth, dropped Archie in and we stroked his wiry hair. Several people I knew wanted to talk and I eventually gave up and went home to the peace and quiet of the cottage.

Sylvie and I went to the main bedroom and we left Kate and Pete to work out how they would sleep downstairs as there was no bed in the second bedroom. In the night, the dog whined to go back to his new home.

The following day, I handed Archie back. Seth looked delighted and so did the dog. Amy had said she had wanted him; well she would have to sort that one out herself.

I drove in my car, an old Volvo Estate that had survived the lay-off due to the continued generosity of my over-burdened neighbour, and hurried across the county border and out to Truro's hospital wearing my new baseball cap as a disguise. I parked and hurried across the car park in light rain. I buzzed to be let through into the premature baby unit. Jenny came to the door and led me inside. Her red eyes were sleepless from crying in the night and worrying about Rory in the day.

I took off my hat and held it in my hands. After checking on Rory's health, which was good, I asked: "Why didn't you tell me you were knocked over?"

Jenny wiped her nose with a large tissue, drying the ever-present tears.

"It all happened so fast," she said. "Besides Rory came along and…"

"Did you report it?"

"No,"

"Why not?"

"Josh said not to. He thought it might cause more trouble."

"What sort of trouble?"

"He didn't say." She blew her nose and her cherry cheeks and red eyes made her look as if she had been through a month-long storm in the Southern Ocean. No doubt, that would have been preferable to this. Somehow, she still remained extraordinarily beautiful.

She took my arm. "Come outside," she said. She motioned to the nurse that we were leaving.

Out in the frigid air, she said: "Did it have something to do with these…" she struggled to say what she wanted, "…these images on Josh's computer?"

"No," I said. "I don't think so." I didn't want her to have any suspicions. It was best if she remained innocent and the lie was easy to make to protect her.

"It's disgusting," she said. She looked about her, searching for the right words. "I can't believe I married a man like that."

I stammered. "It's not like that at all," I said.

"You know he slept with that girl, don't you? I can see by your expression that you do. Men!" said Jenny. She turned to face me, defiant. "Do you all think it's okay to look at pictures of defenceless girls? They're not even adults some of them. They are often drug addicts and some of them are illegal immigrants, slaves to these men who…"

"Jenny," I said. I grabbed her arm.

"Ow, you're hurting me."

I drew her against the wall.

"I can tell you only this," I lowered my voice and relaxed my grip on her pinched flesh. "Whatever you think right now is not true. Josh was involved in stopping these things…" she started to interrupt. "He was about to expose a very powerful person. The images were copies, proof of what he had seen. Jenny," I shook her arm once more, "don't believe anything you hear to the contrary, do you understand?"

She rubbed her elbow where my fingers had pressed in and she turned a furtive glance up at my battered, fearsome face.

"Okay," she stuttered. "I'm not sure what to think now." The tears had stopped and her face was salt-dry. "If there is someone, who is it?"

"I can't tell you. They are still out there." I glanced down the corridor but there was only a nurse turning a corner much further down the sickly green hall. "The proof has been derailed." I spoke gently. "They'll now say it all belonged to Josh, you see, and they will have destroyed the originals. You have to stay completely quiet, tell no-one. You know nothing, okay? Whatever I find out, I won't tell you. Do you see?"

"Why won't you tell me?"

"To protect you," I said. "From them."

120

She looked doubtful. She held a fresh tissue halfway to her face. "Is this the truth?" She brushed at her eye with the back of her hand and caught a single tear that clung there.

"Think back for me, who knocked you over in the street, Jenny? Can you tell me what he looked like?"

Immediately, she took on a haunted expression. "You think that that was somebody coming after us because of these pictures? It wasn't just a street robbery? He did say something strange to me. It made no sense. 'Make sure he drops it.' What does that mean?"

"It was them," I said. "I'm sure of it. Josh believed it. I believe him. He was frightened for you. I know he screwed up, but this was something different. These are dangerous people."

Jenny turned towards the hospital baby unit. She flashed a glance back and then to me. "What about Rory? Is he safe?"

I wanted to answer quickly, but I stuttered as I said: "I'm sure he is. They…"

"Oh, my God." Jenny pushed away from me. "Let me go, I need to be with Rory."

Jenny began to run down the corridor. She pushed my hands away.

"Was he good looking, Jenny?"

I caught up with her and held her arm. She elbowed her way out of my grasp. An old couple shuffling down the corridor stopped to stare at us.

"I don't know," she said. "He was wearing a balaclava." I watched her go. She ran back to the baby unit and turned the corner out of sight.

So much, I thought, *for keeping Jenny safely in the dark.*

121

I drove out of Cornwall and back into Devon. It had been a joke between Josh and me that we were from rival counties. I had forgotten that we used to laugh a lot and I remembered that Josh had been a good friend as well as my sailing partner. I pulled up outside the house, weary from the drive and with my head pounding again. My mood was grim; the long drive had given me too much time to think and brood over the death of my friends.

Back in the dark, flint cottage, I saw the others had re-assembled the house so that it looked normal again.

"Sylvie," I said. I dropped the baseball cap on the sofa. "We need to talk."

"I can't tell you."

I slapped my hand down on the bed. Sylvie stood by the window in my bedroom and faced me. The sunlight streamed in at us and the dark, little room shone in one beam of dusty light.

Sylvie clasped one hand in the other in front of her. "Why do you want to know?"

"My friend is dead," I said. "His wife thinks he is some kind of pervert. I just want her to know that the police believed him when he said the computer images weren't his."

"I can't say that."

"Why not?" I shook my hand angrily. "Who gave you back the laptop?"

"I'm sorry," said Sylvie. "I am not allowed to share this information with you."

I stood up and kicked out at the wardrobe.

"Two people have died because of those images, and Stan is in intensive care. The real culprit was in the original images but spliced out of the ones on Josh's computer after you got it back."

"How do you know that?"

"Josh told me. He said they were proof and you haven't got a name. They must have been doctored." I stood and glared at her. Still she remained silent. "Why are you following me, Sylvie? It's not for my dashing good looks. You just can't bear it that your bosses took you off the case, can you? Is that it?"

"That's not the truth," she said. She remained steady, hands together across her midriff. "I'm trying to help."

"Then help me by sharing what you know."

At the window, she turned to the sunlight. Her face disappeared in the dazzling brightness.

"An old man gave it to me," she said, "an Englishman called Johnnie Walter." She turned through the sunlight to face me. "But you didn't hear that from me."

Chapter seventeen

"So what do we do now?" asked Kate. She sat back into the deep sofa.

Standing in the low-ceilinged room, I stared out the window. I fixed the baseball cap firmly on my head and tugged it down low. Outside the cottage, a weak sunlight broke through low, rumbling storm clouds and shards of light filtered through the window and across the wooden floor. I took in a deep breath. "I'm going to Brazil. I have some investigating to do."

"We'd better all go," said Kate. She drew out her phone. "I'll book some tickets."

"I'll get my own ticket," said Sylvie. She sipped tentatively from a cup of steaming tea and her grey eyes followed the sunlight's rays as they made patterns on the floor.

"What will we find in Brazil?" asked Pete from the darkest corner of the room.

"Amy, Patrick Colt and Tony Drax. Maybe even Helene Drax."

Pete nodded. "I'm going for a walk." He stood up and smoothed his green jumper. "I've arranged to go for a dog walk with Seth and Archie."

I watched him go.

"We must prepare for the worst," I said. I turned to Sylvie. "Do you carry a gun?"

"I can't take one on a plane to Brazil," she said. The sunlight caught dust in the air that swirled in random particles.

"No," I said. "I guess not."

The plane ride was smooth. Kate had arranged for the two of us to have first class tickets courtesy of the TV company. Ostensibly this was a way to get an informal interview with me, but in truth it was merely so that I could get some rest. Sylvie and Pete were back in economy.

Once we left the mainland behind, the stewardess brought us drinks.

Kate said: "I've done some checks. Tony for example, he has an alibi for all the attacks. He was with lots of people every time. One time he was with Cecilia, me and Pete, so he couldn't have killed anyone himself."

"I'm not surprised to hear that."

"Me neither." Kate rubbed at the window and looked down on the sea far below us. "Who is Johnnie Walter?" she asked.

"He's a ninety-seven-year-old ex-seaman I met in Brest."

"What's his connection to all this?"

"I have no idea," I said. "Unless he's the world's first nonagenarian serial killer." I glanced out of the window at the Atlantic Ocean below us, aware that the old man had traversed it a dozen times during the Second World War. "Perhaps he works for Patrick Colt."

Kate smiled and her radiant face glowed. "You don't think I really bought your story about Colt being the killer, do you?"

I shot her a quick glance and turned back to inspecting my coffee cup. "I don't know," I said.

Kate waited as the stewardess passed by and then said: "Sorry, I'm no longer a cub reporter." She watched the stewardess as she served coffee to another passenger. "I know you think Tony is involved, I'd like to know more." She waited only briefly because she knew I wouldn't say anything in response. "I hear Sylvie has come up with something for us."

I turned to look back down the plane but saw only the closed curtain. "Oh, yeah? What's that?"

"She just said she's been doing some digging around." Kate smoothed down her skirt and settled back into the comfort of the big plane seat. It was my first time in first class and it was a lot different from low-cost economy.

Kate closed her eyes, a seasoned air traveller. "I called the hospital this morning," she said. Her eyes remained closed as she spoke. "Stan is still in intensive care. He is still in a medically-induced coma."

"How long will that go on?"

She opened her eyes briefly. "They didn't say."

During the second hour into the flight, Sylvie walked down the aisle into first class. She handed me an iPad. "These are the images that we found on Josh's hard drive." She drew up the lid of the protective case. As if in response to my questioning look, she added: "Rene sent them to me."

I wondered what risks Pignol had gone to to steal this information. We took a glance at the graphic photos of young girls. It was disturbing and I felt myself flushing uneasily. "Are there none with the man's face in it?" I asked.

"No," said Sylvie. "They have been very carefully removed, I'd say. But it's obviously not Josh; couldn't be more different, in fact. Whoever the man is, he is older, fatter and he has dark body hair."

The obscured male in the background of the photos had thick black hair on his forearms and was probably middle-aged. I couldn't be sure, but it certainly could have been Tony Drax. As Sylvie had said, it was, without a doubt, evidently not Josh Lewis.

"There's so little of him," said Kate.

"Kate, could this be stills from a video?" Sylvie glanced towards her and back to the film. "Rather than time-lagged stills?"

"I'm certain it is. They may have removed the incriminating sections and kept these ones." Kate leaned over and closed the iPad resting in my lap. She had seen enough. "If we could get hold of the original film, I imagine it would tell us exactly who this is."

"Whoever he is," said Sylvie, "this man has been very incautious to allow this to get into our hands."

I shot a look between them. "He wanted to implicate Josh," I said. "He wanted the police to think Josh was purchasing the images for the sexual content and that the male person in it was of no consequence. A lesser crime, but still deeply unpleasant."

"You know that for sure?" asked Kate.

"No," I said. "But Sylvie let Josh off with a caution and he told me that they believed him. That you believed him, Sylvie."

Sylvie took the iPad. She closed the fastener on the black case that surrounded it and stood in front of me for a moment.

Kate and I waited for Sylvie to respond.

127

"For the sake of argument, we told Mr Lewis that we accepted what he was telling us was his version of the events. These images are extremely graphic, they represent a borderline position. Having them is not necessarily an offence. We do not know how old any of the young women in them actually are. They are not published material and that is different, too. We cautioned him and then we let him go. We told him we were not planning to pursue him further at that stage. He did not offer to get more proof to show his innocence. He did not say he knew who these people in the pictures were. He did not have a reason for holding these images."

"I'll get that proof," I said quickly. "I'll go to Tony's place and then I'll break in and search Patrick Colt's room."

Sylvie frowned slowly. "Why do you keep saying Patrick Colt is the man in this picture? I would say he is older, and he is plump. I would guess shorter, too."

Kate nodded, her creamy make-up emphasised the contours of her face. "It doesn't look like Colt."

"Perhaps they were taken a few years ago," I said trying without expectation to continue my lie at least for Sylvie's benefit.

Sylvie shifted her torso to rest against the seat. "I don't think so. In the background, there was an iPhone 6. That only came out in 2014."

"Truth is," said Kate, "we all know that that is not Patrick Colt. You're not out here chasing him."

I swivelled in the expensive seat. I knew that that charade was up. It didn't take a genius to figure out that I was really following Tony Drax. "Could we enhance the picture, see what's on that phone?" I asked.

"We did do that," said Sylvie. "My colleagues in special branch tried." She leaned in to us and spoke

128

softly. The stewardess squeezed past her. "I have a contact there who told me off the record; the phone is off. The screen is blank."

"Did you see anything unusual? Was the room French or English?"

Sylvie dangled the iPad in one hand and watched as the stewardess moved down the plane. "We did see a couple of things." Sylvie was close to me and I caught a scent of her perfume. "The iPhone in question has a protective casing. It's mostly black with a white patch in one corner. We thought that maybe if you flipped the phone over, you would then see the rest of the design on the back but so far they've had no luck matching it to a known product."

"We could look for the phone in Brazil," I said.

Sylvie nodded with a deliberate, slow nutation. "Secondly, the trousers discarded on the floor are expensive corduroys. They are common enough to look at, but the label is just showing. It is only a red corner. It could be a high street label but there is a very expensive London tailor who uses that particular colour. Forensics are particularly pleased to have matched it up."

"You could go to see them."

"I already did," said Sylvie.

Kate glanced at me with a knowing smile at this revelation and then turned to Sylvie.

"My colleagues had already been," Sylvie continued. "As I am only unofficially interested I couldn't ask the tailor too much. They sell only to very high-class clientele. My colleagues might have got a name but I did not."

"Can you ask your contact?"

"I'll call him when we have more questions. I don't want to waste my opportunity with him. Eventually, he'll dry up."

"Any more?" I asked.

Kate leaned across. There was a lot to take in and she was concentrating. The animal instinct for story attracted her so that she seemed to apply herself fully, her face thrust out and searching.

"There was a third possibly incriminating object. On the door, there is a sign. This suggests it is a hotel room."

"What does it say?"

Sylvie glanced between us. "It is the fire drill."

"Not very helpful," I said.

"It's in Portuguese," said Sylvie. She seemed grave. "Which is why when you said you wanted to come to Brazil, I suddenly became interested."

Sylvie stood fully upright, contemplated us for a second, then she turned on her heel. She walked down the plane. I leaned out into the aisle and watched her go. There was the swaying elegance to her movements; the French thing. As she stepped lightly through the cabin of the plane, her hips swayed to the deliberate cadence of her footfalls and the passengers followed her with their eyes. She disappeared behind the curtain.

I turned back to Kate.

"What do you think?"

Kate glanced out the window and then back at me. "Your bruise has cleared up," she said.

Chapter eighteen

The taxi ride to Tony's house was a riotous affair. The driver pulled in and out of the traffic as if we had immunity from danger. Perhaps he did, I knew all too well that I did not.

I called the house and first spoke to Amy. She had sounded cold, as if the distance we had gone from each other was enough to protect her emotions. I didn't tell her where I was when I rang. I just asked to be put through to Tony. She could find out that I was thirty minutes away by crazy-cab when her boss got off the phone.

Tony sounded surprised when I said I had just landed in the country and was getting a taxi to his house. He had initially sounded a little flustered, but he accepted my excuse that the press were trying so hard to tail me that the only way I could keep free of them was to give no advance indication of where I might be to anyone.

I had considered going to Tony's on my own, but arriving with my entourage would somehow give me a distractingly busy appearance, I thought. I could explain away Kate and Pete as they were Patrick Colt's idea in the first place. I would explain Sylvie Melville as my new girlfriend, which she kind of was. And besides, I reminded him, it had been his idea in the first place that we hide out there. I should have taken him up on the offer to come to Brazil before Josh was killed; too late for that now.

As the gates opened, the taxi driver took in a deep breath and whistled.

We nodded to him and he grinned so that a large pink scar on his cheek elongated. "That's one hell of a house," he said.

The car swept into a gravelled courtyard that had a fountain in the middle. Water cascaded. Four guards were outside the two-storeyed classic mansion and apparently they were waiting for us. We stepped out of the taxi and two house boys scurried out to collect our bags.

One of the guards escorted our party around the house onto a sun-drenched terrace that had a luscious view down to the ocean. We could see the famous statue of Jesus in the distance and the city stretching below it. From this vantage point, the clean air cooled us. We stepped onto the lawn and Tony met us with pudgy hands out and welcoming as ever, and his wife, Cecilia, smiled through thickly gruesome make-up with drink in hand, and behind them were Amy and Patrick Colt, standing together like they might be Tony's son and his daughter-in-law and we had arrived for the wedding.

"Tom," said Tony. He pumped my hand. "It's fantastic to see you. I said you should come out and here you are. It's great. I like your tactical arrangements- tell no one!" He laughed, and I liked to think that the laughter was a little brittle even for someone as calculating as he was. "You know my wife, Cecilia, don't you?"

The thick make-up on Cecilia Drax's face was like a literal mask. Her thick eyelashes were monstrously over done, her rouge so heavy as to create a pantomime.

She sloshed a little of her cocktail on the patio as she held out her hand to me.

"I didn't get much chance to congratulate you in France, Tom." I kissed her hand as she slurred and her knees seemed to give way momentarily. "So much trouble," she added in a throaty whisper. She still had a Portuguese accent, but her English had a faintly-Australian twang taken from Tony's bellowing voice.

"This is my friend Sylvie," I said. I wondered if they recognised her at all from France. "And you know Kate and Pete from *Race Sailing TV*."

"Yes, of course," said Tony amicably. "It is my company after all," he added awkwardly. It was taking him longer than I expected to relax and I found myself enjoying his discomfort.

Amy scowled at Sylvie Melville and equally darkly at Kate.

Tony shrugged and laughed again. After a moment, I stepped forward and shook hands with Amy. She was wearing a scarf at her neck and light, flowing trousers of the type popular in the 1930s. She smiled stiffly.

I nodded to Patrick Colt in his sharp suit.

Tony turned towards us. "Come on now, Tom," he said enthusiastically, re-asserting his dominance. "Things change. We all move on." He shot a glance at Amy and back to me. "You play nicely with each other. Besides, Tom, you have a beautiful, young lady at your side in Madame Melville."

So he does remember Madame Melville, I thought. I had only said 'Sylvie'. He had remembered exactly who she was.

"Have you been taken off the case, Madame Melville?"

"I am afraid so, Mr Drax," said Sylvie without emotion.

"Always the way with high profile cases…" Tony called the house boy, turning away disinterestedly.

"Drinks?" he asked with wide eyes, and we sat around the large garden table and enjoyed the view down the terrace to the landscaped garden. The eye followed the lawns to the small fountain, passed on to the private woodland and then went out towards the deep blue of the sea.

I lay on the bed in our room. Sylvie stood at the dressing table preparing for dinner. She placed pearl earrings in to each ear carefully, staring at herself critically in the mirror.

"How long do you need?" she asked.

"At least two or three days," I said. "I need to get to know the place a bit. We'll swim in the pool and be sociable until a chance comes up. Whoever gets the opportunity goes in. The study, a computer, anything that looks like it might have private information."

"And who are we really after, Tom?"

I shot a glance up at her and saw her looking back at me in the mirror.

"Tony, of course," I said.

Sylvie fitted the second earing.

"Why?"

"There's a plump man with dark hair and two young women in all of the pictures. It's got to be him but it's not good enough to be evidence, is it? And Josh implicated him. He told me that he had a contact who could prove the connection."

"He didn't share that with the French police. Why not?"

"He was afraid of what Tony might do to protect himself."

Sylvie applied lipstick, stooping to the mirror. "He should have trusted the police. You both should have. Who is the contact?"

"You'll meet them later."

Sylvie watched me fumbling with my tie and came over to help.

I shrugged. "What I can't understand is why Tony would allow us to get access to any of the images. He has killed to protect himself and then the images get to us anyway and point straight back at him."

Sylvie placed the lipstick into a purse that matched her dress.

"We have to talk to that old Englishman again," she said turning round. "Find out where he got the laptop."

The borrowed dress was pale and figure-hugging. She looked good in it. I should have commented but I was distracted.

"Do you mean Johnnie Walter?"

"Yes," she said. "Who is he and where is he now?"

"I have no idea," I said.

We went down to dinner. I was wearing black-tie that Tony had arranged for me and Pete was dressed the same. Sylvie and Kate wore the dresses loaned and apparently available on demand in the twenty-five bedroom colonial house.

We stepped into the sitting room and took more cocktails; no wonder Cecilia barely managed to sober

135

up with the amount of socialising she and Tony did. There were eighteen of us for dinner. Some business associates of Tony's had already collected in the sitting room and I recognised a few faces of sponsors and shook hands in condolence from a few genuine and some simply intrigued members of the Rio business community.

As we sat, the last two guests arrived. I found myself trying to get a first glimpse past the shoulders of the business elite as they themselves began to take their seats. A young man, a dashing Brazilian racing driver named Phillipe Tourenasi, shook as many hands as he could, grinning widely to the money men. He had just started his first year in Formula One. I remembered that we had been compared in an article about emerging sports stars of the future. I would have been delighted to meet him in other circumstances.

On his arm, he escorted Tony's daughter.

I stared at her longer than was appropriate. To say that Helene Drax was beautiful was to describe the sunset as the moment before night. The young, timid woman seemed to be shy in the face of all the admiring glances that came from every member of the male contingent of the room. Half of them could not help but complement Tony on his daughter's exceptional beauty. There was no detail about her that was not flawless, from her delicate nose to her unblemished skin. And what's more, it all seemed completely natural.

Most of the men realised a little too late that their dinner companion was not amused by their sudden interest in Helene Drax, even if the women were equally impressed by her radiance.

I turned to Sylvie. She was staring at me with a cool expression.

I coughed awkwardly. I guess I was one of those men who had been momentarily utterly distracted by this tender young girl's intense beauty.

"Josh had an affair with her," I whispered to Sylvie.

She leaned in to me. "And that means you need to stare at her to do what?"

"She knows about the photos."

"I realise you are trying to deflect me, but what does she know?" Sylvie's face came close to mine. The thin, brittle nature of her bone structure and the delicate line of her soft lips were very close.

I turned to look down to the opposite end of the table and felt Sylvie's warm breath against my cheek. The perfume of her body had a tang of sweetness.

Helene Drax's parents were sitting side by side, smiling and laughing as if on the throne of a historical court surrounded by courtesans. Amy was to Tony's left and beside her was Patrick.

I noticed Amy's scarf had been replaced by a black neck choker. It made her haunted face seem paler and more regal-looking. She raised her chin defiantly.

"What does Helene know?" asked Sylvie again, glancing down to the girl. She was seated between Patrick and Phillipe and she continuously turned to the racing driver with timid glances. He grinned back at her.

"That the man in the photo is Tony," I said. "She's the contact."

Chapter nineteen

I spoke to the driving ace, Phillipe Tourenasi, for half-an-hour. We had a lot in common and I gave him some feedback on what it is like to win your first major competition. He was very appreciative and I liked him for it. There was none of that brashness that you might expect from a rising star in a glamorous world where money comes easily.

He turned to look at the party. He had an easy smile and immaculate teeth. We saw that the old men had surrounded Helene.

"You're a lucky man," I said. "All eyes are on your girlfriend tonight."

"Yes," he said, waving his drink. "The old men are certainly weeping but Helene is, in fact, an old friend. We grew up together. I help her to keep unwanted men away. The way she looks attracts a lot of male attention, as you can imagine. No, my parents live about two hundred metres over that way. My dad is his lawyer; although he mostly seems just to play golf with Tony." He grinned. "My actual girlfriend is in Italy, she's a model. You know driving racing cars helps… what can I say?"

I nodded, glancing over to Sylvie. "I know, I've been a lot luckier with the ladies since I won the *Vendee Globe A Deux*." I caught a glimpse of Amy. "And not so lucky." I added.

"And there was some awful killings," said Phillipe. "Your partner was killed?"

"Yes," I said. "And Bernie Gramm, too, one of the crew of *Swiss Time*."

"What do you think happened?"

"I don't know," I said. "I'm waiting for the police to work it out. So far, nothing."

"Not even a lead?" He smiled warmly, just like Tony.

Now that I was in the serpent's den, I would trust no-one. Not even this nice young man from next door. "French Special Branch are on to it and they haven't told me anything. In fact, they haven't even contacted me."

Phillipe nodded. He knew there was no more to be learned.

"It was good to meet you." I shook his hand. "I hope we see each other again some time. You can tell me what it's like to win your first Grand Prix."

He laughed showing his pearly teeth. "From twelfth to first is a long way," he said. As I stepped away, he added: "But I will let you know," and he laughed again.

I found Sylvie, but she was talking to Patrick Colt and so I moved on. Kate was talking to Tony Drax and some other guy. Cecilia appeared and she took my arm.

"Come with me," she said. Her drink in one hand, she linked arms with me and drew me into the sitting room. She flashed her big, black eyelashes, and the bags under her eyes hung thick with foundation.

The rest of the party behind us, Cecilia stood opposite me.

"I'm not sure I like Patrick Colt and Amy Mackintosh," she said. "Nor does Rex."

I grunted in agreement.

"They are thick as thieves and Amy is always here." Cecilia stood under the gleaming chandelier. "They – she - seems to have a lot of influence over Tony's decisions these days. Can't you… take her back?"

I laughed and stopped myself before she became offended. She was serious.

"Cecilia, Amy left me. I have no influence over her any more and Patrick Colt and I didn't talk much before and definitely won't be talking now."

"Why not?" she asked and she staggered slightly. Her vodka sloshed up the side of the glass and nearly over-flowed. A wine waiter stood close by, clearly instructed to protect Cecilia from herself.

I frowned at her. The main group followed us into the sitting room.

With difficulty in pronouncing the words, she said: "You know how much I have always loved sailing. It was my influence that got Tony interested." She shot a glance up at me. "And Bernie Gramm was a good friend to me."

"I'm sorry," I said. "I really didn't know…"

Cecilia took a second long look at me and then said: "I'll discuss it with you later." She spun away from me and found one of her girlfriends walking towards her. She raised the glass again and her friend dodged the spillage with a practised manoeuvre.

Tony caught sight of Cecilia's drunken sway as he crossed the room and his face darkened. He came to stand with me and his smile broke through.

"Tom, let me present my daughter, Helene," he said loudly.

Helene offered a timid hand and I shook it carefully. Her skin was dark olive and her hair jet black. She wore a simple brown dress and little jewellery. Her

140

eyes were a deep hazel. I admired the strong bone structure of her exceptionally beautiful, half-Brazilian and half-Australian features, and the smallness of her frame, though womanly and curved, seemed almost doll-like. I could understand, as Josh had said, why men found her irresistible.

I realised she didn't particularly like being looked at. It was probably the curse, I thought, of being naturally and exceptionally beautiful and that she probably felt scrutinised all the time. It wasn't so different to being as fearsome-looking as I was. People found themselves staring at both of us for too long. It always made me feel exposed by their continued watchfulness, no doubt she felt something similar but for the opposite reason.

It occurred to me that I had also taken a moment too long. I was other people.

"It's very nice to meet you," I said.

She nodded politely as if she didn't want to stay speaking to me or maybe my devil's face scared her, too. *At least my ugly bruise has finally disappeared*, I thought.

Tony was distracted.

"I'll leave you to chat," he said and walked towards a group of laughing men.

Helene took a quick glance around the room in the hope, I imagined, of spotting Phillipe and salvation.

"You must get invited to a lot of parties with boring people to entertain."

Helene smiled. "A few," she said.

"Don't worry," I said. "I'll try not to be too dull."

Helene twisted her mouth into a disapproving smile. "How long shall I give you?" She asked.

Across the room I saw Sylvie was talking with Pete. I leaned in. "I guess only until I mention Josh Lewis," I said, careful not to be heard.

Helene was following my line of sight. Her hazel eyes shot me a look of alarm. "What do you mean?"

"I know about the two of you."

Helene stepped closer to me and bowed her head. "What do you *think* you know?" Her eyes were dark and her expression more devilish than my reflection.

I laughed for the benefit of anyone watching and caught Cecilia's eye, she was not so drunk that she wasn't watching over her daughter. I leaned back in close to Helene.

"I know about you and Josh. I know about the fight. I know about what you both saw."

Helene Drax stepped back from me. Her hand went up to her face as if I had slapped her hard. She stepped backwards and tripped and her ankle buckled in the high heels she wore.

As she fell hands went out to her, but she righted herself untouched and the men's hands retreated disappointed.

The room's conversational tone dropped to a murmur as all eyes followed Helene as she gave me a long and pained, silent stare and then she stumbled out of the room followed by Phillipe who shot a confused and angry glance my way as he went.

For a moment, I stood in the centre of the room and dodged the awkward, indignant faces of every other guest. Cecilia's expression soured and she turned away from me. I looked about for an exit. Pete had left Sylvie Melville standing below an expensive-looking landscape painting and with her glass in one hand poised in front of her mouth, she gave me a quizzical smile; she turned her head to one side and waited patiently for me to join her.

I walked to her as calmly as I could manage, deeply embarrassed.

"You're good at this," she said and I frowned.

I had blown my chance to learn from Helene Drax. I had not got her on my side. In fact, I had scared her away.

In bed that night, I couldn't help but think about Josh and Helene Drax. I had made love with Sylvie, but my thoughts were on what Josh and Helene had found out. I lay back on the bed contemplating what to do next.

I felt Sylvie's irritation rather than saw it.

"Who or what are you thinking about?" She too had drunk too much and her speech was a little slurred.

"Helene Drax," I said.

Sylvie turned to me in the shaft of moonlight that fell on to her side of the sumptuous bed. She placed her head on her hand. Her face was set with lips forced together.

"You admit this?"

I cottoned on. "No, Sylvie, not like that. I was wondering about she knows."

"That's not what it seemed like just now."

"I was distracted. I could never attract a woman like that any way. Look at Phillipe in comparison! And Josh was equally as handsome."

Sylvie pursed pink lips and opened and then closed her delicate mouth. Her grey eyes narrowed and then she turned her back to me.

143

I lay in the dark considering the possibilities. How could I get an audience with Helene again where we could talk without interruption?

If she was still in the house at breakfast, I would ask for her help.

"I can't believe I scared her off, I was trying to make her understand…"

Sylvie said nothing.

I knew I would struggle to get to sleep. I said: "Good night," but Sylvie did not reply; she must already have dozed off.

Next morning, neither Tony, Cecilia or Helene was at breakfast. Only we four outsiders were there.

"Any news?" asked Kate. She had on perfect television-ready make-up and her coffee-cream complexion shone.

"Nothing," I said.

Sylvie sipped her coffee. She had been very quiet all morning. She wore only a touch of make-up and remained withdrawn, her pink cheeks were cool with rose and ice cream paleness.

"There's a little study on the left underneath the main staircase," said Kate. "I would imagine a man like Tony keeps it under security surveillance. You'll need to find out where the cameras are and cover them."

"What's the chance he might have something arranged for this week that means he won't be here all the time?" asked Pete. He settled his glasses on his nose as he spoke, blinking behind the spectacles.

"If he goes into town," I said, "will you follow him, Pete?"

"Yes, sure." He had removed his pullover and was wearing a casual, short-sleeved white shirt and no tie.

I went over to the breakfast table laid out like one of the best hotels.

Pete looked up and readjusted his glasses a second time. I turned to see Amy enter the room.

She was wearing a different outfit but she had the colourful scarf around her neck again.

"Good morning," she said. She put her iPad and phone down on a table across from us.

We glanced at the phone. I was aware that it was an iPhone 6 that she had. The cover was white. I remembered it from before, when we had lived together in Devon. That seemed a long time ago now.

"We've found a replacement boat for you to take a look at," she said, stepping alongside me. She chose from the long breakfast table what to eat. "We can acquire it by next week." She turned to me. "You'll need to see the boat first, of course."

"Where is it?"

"The Caribbean. Berscolini's yard."

"Berscolini's? In Antigua? Who will I sail with? It was Josh's idea to team up."

"You'll find someone, Tom. You're a winner; that will attract plenty of offers. All you'll have to do is say the word and they'll come running to you."

I took in the solemn faces of my companions around the table. I turned back to Amy who was smiling. "I still feel pretty raw about what happened two weeks ago," I said. "I'm not sure I'm ready…"

"You mean getting run down in the Channel?" Amy ladled yoghurt onto fresh fruit.

"All of it," I said. "Bernie, Stan and Josh. Being shot at in the first place, in Biscay. You leaving didn't help."

Amy nodded. "You need time. Of course you do." She took a long look at me with an almost amused expression.

"Do you want me out of here so badly?" I asked her.

"Tom," she laughed. "Enjoy a few days with Tony and then get back on with your life."

Her phone rang. I stood by the long table and she went to her things. She took the phone, said: "Hang on," and, with a quick glance at me, she stepped out of the dining room into the hall.

I stared at the door.

Kate stood up. She pointed to Amy's iPad.

"What are we going to find in there?" I asked.

Kate shrugged. She waved me forward, and I went to the door. Amy was in the hall speaking into the phone in a low voice.

I waved to them behind my back, whilst keeping Amy in sight. Kate snatched up the iPad. She spun it to me to show it was still on. She began to look through the icons. She flicked the screen, and glanced up at me as she did.

"Back," I said. I stepped into the room and Kate turned off the iPad, repositioned it and went over to the long table before Amy returned.

I stood in front of the big canvas on the wall by the door and admired the paint work.

Amy came back in and glanced up at the painting and then at me. "Too insipid for my tastes," she said.

I looked up at the seascape and the circling sea birds that were depicted calling in the wind.

"I like it," I said.

"You would," said Amy. She collected her iPad and the papers underneath it. She spooned a mouthful of fruit and yoghurt into her mouth. She swallowed and

146

wiped her lips. "I have to go," she said. I noticed she was wearing high heels, something she never used to do around me. She had grown much taller. "Think about what I said. There's a boat waiting for you. You can resume your career."

It might be a relief to go offshore, but I couldn't leave right then. I had to get some proof of what Josh knew.

Amy stopped at the door. "Oh, Helene apologises, she has had to leave for a few days."

"How long?" I said quickly.

"A week." Amy gave me an inquisitive look. "Was there something you wanted...?" She glanced over at Sylvie who had her back to us and was eating a croissant that she dipped into her coffee whilst otherwise seemingly lost in thought.

"Yes," I said more slowly. "I wanted to speak to her. I wanted to get to know Phillipe a bit more."

Amy smiled with a raised eyebrow. "Fame is going to change you, Tom," she said. She turned to the corridor and spoke over her shoulder. "Power always does."

"Was there anything on the iPad?"

"There was an icon I didn't recognise called 'P' and she was surfing an estate agents. Looking at apartments, that's all."

I sat and stared at my hands clasped in my lap. The breakfast room was empty but for the four of us. My mood was despondent. I didn't really want to know about Amy's new love life or where she now planned to live.

"What are we going to do?"

147

"About Helene?"

"Yes."

Kate took in the sombre expressions of both Sylvie and me.

"Shall I go after her?" she asked.

I looked up moodily.

Kate appeared animated. Her animal features, coffee-cream and Italian with eyes big and brown were suddenly enthused. "Pete can stay with you. I'll go after Helene. Soon as I see her leaving, I'll beg a lift. Don't worry, you and Pete and Sylvie can stay here and work out how you can get into Tony's study without being seen. Besides, I'm bored sitting around…"

"Very well," I said. Pete nodded with a murmur of agreement. I turned to Sylvie. She gave me a silent frown. "Are you alright?" I asked her.

She nodded but with a certain disinterest.

"What's the matter, Sylvie?"

"Nothing," she said. Her brittle cheeks were pale rose and her tender lips were pursed so that she bit at the soft pinkness. She pushed her chair back and went out into the hall.

I looked up into Kate's questioning eyes.

"I don't know," I said. But I did, maybe Sylvie wasn't trying to use me after all. She seemed genuinely put out.

I found Sylvie in the bedroom. She was staring out of the window. With a slow rotation of her head, she turned to me. "I just saw Helene Drax getting into a car. Kate managed to talk her way in and they have gone down the drive and turned towards the city."

"She's good. Where's Tony? Any idea?"

"Pete is going to scout around." She placed her hands on the window sill. "If he can, he'll try to keep with him and let me know by text where he is."

"As soon as you get his go-ahead, you text me and I'll break into the study."

"Do you know how?" The grey eyes were curious.

"My dad was a golf nut," I said by way of explanation. "He spent every day practising for the big games. He never made it out of his club tournaments, though. His best finish was twelfth. He had a handicap of seven. He never was going to make it but he kept going and he still thinks he can do it, even now.

"My brother and I got bored being left hanging about. We broke into the boatshed down by the river when I was ten and my brother was eight. We got caught, but the guy who caught us was the club sailing coach. He watched us pretending we were out on the high seas in one of the Oppies, it's a kids sailing dinghy, and he says: 'I'll teach you to sail and one day you can sail off to Antarctica'."

"And you did," said Sylvie.

"I don't think any of us expected it at the time or for several years after but I guess I showed some aggressive tactics for winning races. I was club champion within two years."

"Your dad must have been proud."

I half-laughed and it came out sounding like I had been choked. "He was furious. I got the strap. He belted me for breaking into the shed but mostly I got it for being better than him at winning."

Sylvie gave a tight-lipped smile so that the tender pink flesh cooled white. "Well, at least you learned how to break locks."

"My brother Dan was better at it than me. I'm afraid he was a bit of a cat burglar in his youth. Since he finally grew up, he made it a professional trade. He has this little device…"

Sylvie drew out set of lock picks slowly and her grey eyes showed amusement. "Something like these?"

I took them from her. I nodded. "That's the ones."

Sylvie's mobile bleeped and she glanced down.

She read out loud from her phone: "'Tony's at Rex Tourenasi's house next door.' Pete saw him go in. He says: 'I'll text you when he's coming back.'"

I took the lock picks from her soft fingers and headed for the door.

"Make sure your phone is on silent."

I nodded again and went out into the hall and walked down to the main stairs taking casual strides. I could hear the maid was in one of the bedrooms behind me, otherwise no-one was about.

I slipped down the stairs. I could make out one of the guards outside the front door. Inside the house was silent. I passed under the stairs and felt for the door handle of the study.

The door was locked. I felt around the pot plants for a key and found nothing so I pulled out the lock picks and began to work on the lock. A few uncomfortable seconds passed whilst I fumbled inexpertly. Dan would have already been in. Eventually, there was a click and the door opened a fraction. I stepped through and immediately spotted a camera that was fixed in place and facing towards both the desk and window.

The room was relatively small compared to the rest of the house. A computer on an ornate table caught my attention. Behind the desk was a big, metal safe with a large number lock on the front.

I began to pull a handkerchief from my pocket. The camera was pointed from the corner of the room inwards. The angle of the camera was set up to cover the window and desk rather than the door in the expectation, presumably, of a break-in from the outside.

A guard outside, obscured behind the tall net curtain, passed in front of the study window. His shadow moved across from right to left. I felt my mobile shake in my pocket. I pulled it out swiftly and saw a text from Sylvie. Tony was on his way back.

I cursed, stepped backwards, and inched back into the hall. As I closed the door to the study, I heard a noise. There was no time. I left the door unlocked and walked swiftly back to the main staircase and headed back to my room hiding the lock picks in my pocket as I went.

I slipped inside my room as Tony walked through the front door. I heard him striding through the house. He wasn't speaking, but he sounded like he was in a hurry.

I turned to Sylvie and winced.

"I didn't manage to relock the study door."

Sylvie nodded and stepped away from the window.

"We're in trouble, then," she said.

Chapter twenty

I took Sylvie's arm and we strolled brazenly down through the house, across the terrace to the lower garden and onto the main lawn that stretched out impressively to the park that was full of mature trees. The woodland disappeared over a steep descent and down the mountainside out of view. In the line of sight, the ocean spread out below.

From here the colonial house was elegant, frankly regal and we gave it admiring glances whilst keeping an eye out for guards coming after us with guns.

After fifteen minutes we began to relax and then we saw Tony walking down the lawn with Patrick and Amy close behind him. No guns and no guards.

"Tom," he said with both chubby hands out. Patrick and Amy struggled to keep up.

"Hi, Tony," I said. I could understand why Cecilia found the ever-present duo so irritating. Amy shadowed Tony everywhere, and Patrick Colt was almost as present.

"I've had an idea," said Tony. "In fact, my neighbour Rex has had a fantastic idea. He wants to go out on the *Christina* for a trip up the coast. We wondered if you would skipper her for us." He glanced between us. "If that suits your plans..."

"Yes," I said. "Does that offer include all of us?"

Tony's face darkened in mock disappointment. "I would love to but... do you mind if we keep it small?

Why don't you and Sylvie come," he waved his hand towards her, "and we can ask Kate and her cameraman to wait for us here."

Amy looked between us keenly. She stood ahead of Patrick and he seemed to peer over her shoulder as if in the back row. "I'll call the boat. Who shall I say will be coming, Tony?" Amy glanced up at him with ruthless enthusiasm.

Tony smiled with bared teeth. "There will be me, my friend Rex Tourenasi, Tom and Sylvie, and Rex's son Phillipe."

Amy had already dialled the number. "Shall I come along, too?" she asked, putting the phone to her ear and shaking her blond hair away from the receiver.

"Yes," said Tony quickly. "That's a good idea." He turned a chubby, innocent face towards Patrick but said nothing.

"When shall I say you will be going onboard?"

"Tomorrow morning," said Tony.

"Oh," said Amy. "Helene is coming back early and I said I would go into town with her. I can't come after all." She began speaking quickly into her mobile phone.

Tony nodded. "Very well," he said. He seemed disappointed, I thought. He probably enjoyed having such a beautiful woman working for him.

Patrick Colt said nothing. These days he seemed more lackey than boss. That was the trouble with taking on a girl like Amy, I thought, she had already taken charge of both of them.

That evening, Tony excused himself from dinner and went to his study early. Helene Drax didn't come back from her trip into the city and Kate came back alone when we were already on to the dessert.

She carried shopping that she left in the hall.

"Wow, I spent a couple of very expensive hours with Helene," she said.

Amy gave her a moody look. Amy had been very quiet at dinner. "That's not like Helene," she said. "She's normally a thrifty shopper." She held her spoon in front of her as if accusing Kate.

"With a billionaire for a father?" I asked.

"Thrifty for a girl with a billionaire for a father," Amy conceded. She put the spoonful of cream in her mouth.

"You used to shop like you did have a billionaire for a father," I said.

Amy made a sour face. "Winning still everything?"

I ignored Amy and turned to Kate who appeared flushed. I hoped she had found out something useful from Helene after my complete failure.

Kate took a seat, placing herself between Pete and Amy. Pete shifted across. The houseboy brought her through a main course.

"No Tony?" asked Kate.

"He's in his study," I said, letting the sour exchange with Amy fade from my mind.

"Mrs Drax has gone to stay with her friend in the next village. They are having a bridge party. Ladies only," said Amy. "I'm afraid tonight it's just the six of us." She flicked a quick glance my way.

Patrick Colt eyed Amy. He wiped his lip with his napkin. "I've got some business to attend to myself," he said. His confident American demeanour was subdued.

Amy gave him a sharp look of irritation.

Patrick dropped the napkin lightly on the table. He stood and nodded to the group courteously. His phone rang. As he walked away, he pulled the mobile from his pocket. I got a good look at it.

It had a zebra pattern on the back, and the stripes over-lapped the edge. It was Patrick Colt's black-and-white coloured iPhone 6 cover we had seen in the photos. It was a perfect match.

We took a stroll on the veranda so that we could talk. Pete leaned across Kate and said under his breath: "Tony came back pretty sharp-ish this morning. He must have known someone was in the study."

Kate's expression said she wasn't surprised. She flicked her long and brown hair aside with a quick turn of the head.

"He has a lot to hide," she said. "We need to be careful. He wants you to go sailing with him? I suggest you stay vigilant. Just make sure he's not planning to throw you over the side."

"That's reassuring," I said. "Anyway, there will be other people on board; the staff will be there. The neighbour Rex Tourenasi and his son, too. Sylvie as well."

"Just be careful, that's all." Kate glanced away, taking a sideways glance at Pete's unfashionable shirt. "What's the weather report?"

"Nothing too strong. A Force five from the south."

Kate fell silent.

Sylvie tucked her hair behind her ear. She glanced up at the house that was lit by outside lights in the early evening. "What did you find out from Helene?"

Kate groaned. "Something and nothing," she said. "She was very cagey. Tom's intro startled her. She thinks he's trying to scare her off."

"Oh, God," I said. "She thinks I'm working for Tony…"

"You are working for Tony," said Sylvie. Her grey eyes ran over us in sequence. "All three of you work for Tony. *Race Sailing TV* belongs to Tony's company, Drax Holdings. You race his boat. You are all his employees."

"We are… I do, that's sort of true," I said. "But Tony wouldn't scare his own daughter with a threat from an outsider like that, that would be preposterous."

Sylvie and Kate both seemed untouched. Kate's red lips pouted and the deep cream cheeks elongated. "Who knows what motivates a penniless kid to become a billionaire?"

And who knows what they would do to get there and stay there? was what she meant.

Sylvie led us through the garden's little paths between flower borders until the trees. I followed her measured strides and the sway of her hips. We turned back towards the magnificent splendour of the great house. We took consciously casual strides trying to appear as if we were not conspirators amongst our enemies.

"Tony mentioned he was your boss the other day," I said to Kate.

"Never mind that," said Kate. Now her soft but heavily made-up features showed a hint of irritation. "It's not important. Tony has never been my direct boss. I only ever met him through you. The important thing is that Helene does have some information for us."

"She does?" I stopped pacing. "What is it?"

"Something and nothing, remember? She didn't say exactly. We spent half the day talking about how useless her ex-boyfriends have all been."

"Well, that's not very bloody helpful." I was irritated myself.

"Hold on," said Sylvie. We followed her gaze.

One of the houseboys came out to the veranda and he was hurrying down the lawn to the path amongst the azaleas where we were walking. I pulled out my phone like a tourist and asked him to take our picture. He discreetly waited with hands behind his back and then stepped forward.

"Would you?"

The picture was slightly too far away, we all looked awkward and at the wrong moment Pete turned away.

"Was there something else?" asked Sylvie.

"A call for Mr Shepherd. It is the French police. They insist on speaking to him."

"Of course," I said. The houseboy went ahead. I turned back to the darkness where the others were waiting in the half-light. "Can you find out any more, Kate? Is Helene coming back to the house?"

"In a couple of days' time. She's hoping you will have gone. Like I said, she thinks you were told to scare her off."

I stepped back and whispered, but the houseboy could not have heard because he was already on the terrace waiting for me by the French doors. "Scared off by someone working for her own father?"

Kate peered at me from the gloom of dusk. "You've never seen Tony do business, I take it."

"No, I didn't think you had either."

"No," she said quickly. "But bosses of mine have come and gone on the back of some pretty minor viewing figure dips."

I hurried after the houseboy.

The French police officer wanted to see me in France. I told him there would be a delay before I could do that. He insisted I should get on a plane and despite my suggestion of an interview conducted over the telephone, he said he wanted me to return to see him face to face.

I took his name and a number and said I would call him as soon as I was back from the business trip I was taking aboard the *Christina* and that I would arrange something with him.

As soon as I had seen what Tony had, I wanted to get out of Brazil and fast. Going straight to France and the French police would suit me fine.

Sylvie had waited for me on the terrace in the warm evening and the light coming from inside the house. Kate and Pete had gone ahead and were already inside. Sylvie suggested we also went up to bed.

I took her arm and we strolled up the flagged steps, onto the wide veranda and into the house through the main sitting room. In the hall, I could see the lights on in Tony's study.

"Go on up," I said.

I knocked and waved Sylvie to go on without me.

Tony came to the door.

"Tom," he said with less than his usual good humour. He held on to the door handle as if he didn't want me to enter. "What can I do for you?"

I could hear Sylvie climbing the stairs above me.

"What time do you want to leave tomorrow?" I asked, conscious that the door was being held only partially open.

"Not early," he said distractedly. "Ten o'clock?" He smiled in a tired way.

"Of course," I said. "Look, Tony, do you mind if I come in for a moment? I'd like a quick word."

Tony looked awkwardly about him. "I'm a little busy right now," he said.

I suddenly realised that Tony was wearing brown corduroy trousers like the ones in the photos. I also sensed that someone was in the study with Tony, behind the door.

I hadn't heard their voices as I walked past. Perhaps he was paranoid enough to have the room sound-proofed. It didn't seem so impossible.

I moved position and shot a glance around the small part of the room I could see. The study looked as it had when I had taken a quick glance inside earlier in the day. Whoever was inside with Tony remained silent and out of my line of sight.

"Of course," I said finally. "We can talk in the morning on the way to the boat, can't we?"

Tony smiled stiffly. "And we will have two days on the yacht," he said.

"Goodnight, Tony."

"Goodnight, Tom." He smiled curtly and closed the door.

I walked around the staircase and climbed for my bedroom. At the top, I crouched down and turned my phone onto video mode and left it running, pointing down towards the hallway. The person leaving Tony's room would either come out and turn towards the rear of the house and go unseen or turn right towards the main stairs, the sitting room and the front door. As long as my phone kept recording, I had a chance of seeing the person who turned to the front.

I returned to my room. I put my head against the door and listened for the sound of Tony's study door opening and closing. Sylvie watched me and kept quiet.

159

She sat at the window. She alternated between watching the stars appear in the night sky and looking over at me as I lay by the door frame, and she threw quizzical glances to me. I held up a quietening finger to my lips.

After ten minutes, I heard a sound that I thought might be them. I waited a few minutes more and then when it seemed to go quiet again, I stepped out, retrieved my phone from its precarious position over-looking the hall from the landing, and darted back in.

In my room, I switched off the recording and told Sylvie what had happened.

I scrolled through the video clip until the sound of the door could be heard. A head passed under the camera and both the person's shoulders and hair were clearly visible but not the face.

I turned to her. "Is that who I think it is?"

"Yes," she said. "It's Pete."

Chapter twenty-one

I could hear Patrick Colt's clear LA tones in the hall. I could tell he was pacing back and forth in constricted circles as he spoke into his mobile phone. He continued for a long time and I realised it was about the Open 62 that was available in the Caribbean yard. He was trying to delay things so that we could go out for a viewing the following week. It sounded like somebody else was also interested.

As Patrick finished his call, I heard Kate say goodnight to him as she passed and she began to climb the stairs. His footsteps retreated.

I waited until the house was silent and left Sylvie in her night clothes perched in the moonlight by the window, where she appeared ephemeral in the growing pale light. The wind fluttered the curtains and a cool breeze ran through her hair and distracted her chemise and I felt a pang of desire for her.

"I'll be back," I said. I slipped out into the now empty hall and tiptoed down to my left and away from the main stairs.

At Kate's door, I knocked quietly and slipped inside. Kate was undressing, slipping out of her skirt as I entered the room.

To her right was Pete, already in the bed. I realised I had never thought to ask what their relationship to each other actually was. In the hotel room in Holland, they had been in the same room for the interview I did straight after Josh died, but it had never occurred to me that they were sharing that room for the night. At my cottage in Devon, I had simply left them to find a sofa figuring Pete would be on one and Kate the other.

"I'm sorry," I said. "I…"

"It's okay," said Kate. Her Italian warmth had cooled. "We keep it quiet because the profession is so fickle."

"Of course," I said. The trouble was I had come in to explain to Kate what I had just seen. I had intended to tell her that Pete had been talking privately to Tony. I changed tack quickly.

"What else did you and Helene discuss? You mentioned there was something - something and nothing."

Kate pulled her skirt back on. She took out a cigarette and lit it. Another little fact I hadn't known about. I realised I wasn't really very observant at all.

"Nothing very useful," said Kate drawing in a lungful of smoke. "She clammed up entirely about her father. I didn't push things. I just told her that you hadn't meant to scare her; that you were a genuine friend of Josh's and that you wanted to help."

"What did she say?" I glanced over to Pete. He put his spectacles on and slipped below the covers. He was wearing a neat pyjama set. He watched but he said nothing.

"Helene said she'd think about it. She said she might be back for a few days but not to bank on it. She also said to take a good look around the boat." Kate was trying to seem casual but she was bothered that I had seen the two of them together.

"The boat? Okay," I said. I shot a glance at Pete and decided not to say anything more. I put my hand on the door handle. "I just overheard Patrick Colt talking to the boatyard about me coming out. I'm going to have to go next week once this sailing trip is over. They'll start getting suspicious if I choose to hang around here instead of going to see the new Open 62."

I shot a second glance towards Pete and said: "Do you two have anything else for me?"

"Not yet," said Kate. Pete remained silent. He had pulled the cover high to his chin and his expression was empty.

"OK," I said. My mind was going round any possibilities about why Pete would have been in the study with Tony and how come he was remaining his usual tight-lipped self. I said nothing because that would only invite him to think up a lie if he needed one; but if he kept quiet, maybe that told me even more.

I opened the door and slipped out. A sound on the landing made me check. I turned to my left. Someone was slipping into a room further down the hallway. They kept their back to me, probably having heard the door to Kate's room opening. But I caught a good glimpse of them. It was Phillipe Tourenasi from next door.

"He must have been going in to Helene's room," said Sylvie. She had her arms around her knees and sat in the bay of the window seat, close to the window. Moonlight shaded her in the low light of the room.

"But Helene isn't here and, besides, these are the guest bedrooms. All the master bedrooms are off the second balcony; they have views over the lawn whilst we've got the car park and the driveway." I took a glance past Sylvie's shoulder out of the window and then dropped into a chair by the desk. "Of course, these

163

rooms are good for snooping on who's coming and going but Helene has the grand view of the parklands from over there."

"He can't have a room here of his own, can he?" said Sylvie. "I mean, he only lives in the next property. It's two hundred metres beyond the fence."

Sylvie glanced out at the stars in the night sky.

I put my feet up on the desk and settled back in the chair. "How does Phillipe get from his house to here?"

Sylvie kept her eyes on the night sky for a long time.

"He goes across the lawn on the other side of the house. Tony came that way when Pete was keeping tabs on him. Pete told me."

I had told Sylvie that Pete had said nothing about his visit to the study. I rubbed my face with my hands and wisded I was out at sea and not playing some silly-cat-and-mouse game with a murderer. "Can we really trust anything Pete says now?"

"Can we trust either of them?" said Sylvie turning towards me. "If Kate and Pete are an item and Pete is talking privately to Tony… and they both work for his company…"

"He didn't say anything at all just now about being in with Tony. That bothers me."

"Pete barely speaks…" said Sylvie.

"That's true, but even so…"

I got up and went into the bathroom. I stared at my devilish face in the mirror. As ever, I looked the guilty one. Trouble was, now I couldn't be sure about any of the people who had offered to help me.

Sylvie seemed to be on my side, but she could just be following her policewoman's instinct and using her female charms. Kate appeared to be genuine, but she had a mask-like covering of perfect make-up and an

164

inscrutable mind underneath it. What about Pete? He was as quiet as a church mouse most of the time, but he had been sitting with his employer in his office late at night and his employer didn't look too happy when I had interrupted them. And Phillipe Tourenasi was sneaking around in the night.

Was someone after me? The first four competitors in the *Vendee Globe A Deux* had been attacked. Two of them were dead. I stared at my battered, wild face. For some reason, only now as I stood in the relative calm and safety of the bathroom, did I feel that my own death might be the only truth that I finally discovered.

Chapter twenty-two

At breakfast, I waited for Pete, or even Kate, to give an explanation why Pete had been in the study. They said nothing on the subject. Perhaps Pete hadn't even told Kate he had been in there, either. In which case, she didn't know and I wasn't going to tell her. We discussed Phillipe Tourenasi's late night movements instead.

After a while, I said as casually as I could manage: "So how long have you two been an item, then?"

It was just the four of us again.

"Only six months," said Kate. "Since Pete joined us from a Russian TV company."

Pete sat stiffly. Kate put a finger to her lips. I guess she wanted to change the subject, because she leaned in and whispered. "I know whose room Phillipe went into last night."

"Really?" I said. "Whose room was it?"

"Patrick Colt's," she said. There was a hint of pride in her journalistic skills.

"Patrick?" I must have looked as surprised as I sounded. "Was Amy there?"

"Amy's room is the next one down the hall, around the corner. It's you two in the first room, us next and then Patrick's room. Then there is a corner and Amy is on the next section where the hall continues beyond the stairwell."

"I thought that Amy and Patrick…" but I trailed off.

I walked over to the breakfast table and my eye was caught by the terrace and the distant sea. I went to the French doors and gratefully stepped out into the light.

Behind me, I heard Amy enter the breakfast room with her iPad and her white-backed iPhone and papers. She was finishing a call. She walked to the breakfast table. She was beaming with a big smile across her face. The scarf had gone and there was a faint smudge of something on the right side of her neck.

She hadn't seen me and I held back.

"Good news?" asked Kate.

I saw Amy grin as she turned away from me and towards Kate. From behind, I realised that it was an old bruise that I could see low on Amy's marble-white neck. It had almost faded away but the darkness of it still clouded the fine definition of the two little moles.

"You just seem pleased," said Kate. "It must be good news."

"What?" Amy seemed distracted. "Well, in truth I just bought my first house," she said. I caught a glimpse of her cheek and could see embarrassment. She scratched at her neck and then put down her things.

"Got a picture?" asked Kate.

"No," said Amy quickly. "It's just a one bedroom apartment. On the coast."

"Lucky you," said Kate. "Where is it?"

"Where?" said Amy. It was clear she didn't really want to answer. "The South of France," she finally said. "It's really a find…"

"A bargain on the coast? That sounds too good to pass up," said Kate.

I walked in from the terrace.

167

"I hope you've been given a decent raise, Amy," I said.

Amy turned and looked directly at me as if seeing me for the first time and her smile faded to a scowl.

"I discovered you and Josh," she said. "Tony's saying I'm worth investing in. He's promoted me. And yes, I have got a raise, actually. I can afford it."

"No need to justify yourself to me," I said. "I'm no longer picking up your bad debts."

Amy's expression turned to anger. Her pure, white flesh and make-up free complexion with the haunted beauty was creased by distaste.

She had never liked me reminding her to be thrifty with our money. Now, she just didn't like me being around.

"I've moved on," said Amy. "I thought you had, too." She turned away from the breakfast table and walked out of the room with irritated, quick steps in six inch heels.

She had lost weight, I realised. She was thinner than ever.

Kate beckoned me towards her. She held up her smartphone for me to see. "That's what she was looking at on the web yesterday."

I stared into the screen.

"Two million Euros? For an apartment?"

"A little bit more than a one-bed," said Kate.

I thought back to my little stone cottage. Amy had come a long way in a short space of time.

Chapter twenty-three

Patrick Colt was standing on the veranda speaking into his mobile phone. The black Rolls Royce's engine was purring waiting to take me down to the *Christina*. The wide door stood open, with Sylvie already inside.

I went over towards Patrick but as I did, he terminated the call and turned towards someone coming from the French doors. I got to the corner of the house and saw Amy crossing towards him. She was gesticulating and speaking quickly and crossly. As I hesitated, she caught sight of me and immediately began to speak more appropriately to her immediate boss.

Patrick saw me and he looked embarrassed. He had become more and more subdued since the end of the *Vendee Globe A Deux*. It seemed probable to me that Patrick and Amy had already split up.

I had never seen them kiss, hold hands or show any form of direct affection. Perhaps they were discreet to avoid me seeing them, but it seemed that they were no longer sharing a bedroom. I wondered how long that had been the case. Did she drop him as soon as they got to Brazil or had it been before that?

I thought about the faint bruise on her neck. Patrick Colt must have assaulted her. When I had arrived at Tony's she had been wearing a scarf, then a choker in the evening and the next day a scarf again. She had kept it covered for two days. The bruise was now almost gone, but she had taken off the scarf a little early. Did she want us to know what he was really like?

No wonder he was sheepish. She had probably told him she would expose him for being a girlfriend-beater. He was being good because he wanted to stay out of gaol, and she had conned two million euros out of him for that apartment. I had it all worked out in my head. As I turned back to the car and got in beside Sylvie, I realised I was an unreliable witness. I was ready to tell Sylvie everything I had surmised, but the car was already full.

Tony was in the Rolls opposite Sylvie and next to Rex Tourenasi. They faced backwards, Sylvie forwards. I got in and shook hands with the neighbour and dropped into a seat beside Sylvie. The two men were about the same age and build and they could have been brothers anatomically, so similar was their squat plumpness. Facially, they were quite different. Rex Tourenasi had a long nose and heavy jowls and he was the more refined. He gave off an air of flabby royalty. Tony was a typical Aussie, all matey and classless and he had a round, child's face with doleful eyes.

The two of them were in their sailing togs, sweaters draped over the shoulders, and they made me laugh inwardly. Sylvie had her hands on her knee-length skirt and I noticed both men take a furtive glance at her slender legs and healthy, young body.

Noticing my eyes on him, Tony said: "Youth is so wonderfully tantalising, Tom. You don't know it yet, but it is. Distance only magnifies the beauty."

I made no comment but Rex murmured agreement.

As we pulled away I saw Patrick Colt standing by the house, back on the phone. His neat silver-blue suit was made to measure and smooth. Rex gave him a hostile glance. He didn't seem to like the slick young man any more than I did.

Once we were moving, Rex and Tony traded jokes and Sylvie and I listened and smiled badly. The big car turned the corners with a satisfyingly smooth motion. At the dock, the Rolls Royce drew up to the ten-million-dollar-plus gentlemen's sailing yacht, the *Christina*, and her liveried crew who stepped forward and lifted our bags on board. They were deeply respectful.

As the tourists watched in envy, Rex and Tony made a big show of stepping onto the yacht. The two heavyweights gave the boat critical glances as they stepped along the pitch pine deck that had been varnished and scrubbed to within an inch of its life. The brass work on the funnels and the deck gear sparkled blindingly in the full Rio sunshine. This boat was an awesome treasure, a historic beauty sadly lost on these perfectionist voyeurs.

This ship wasn't built just to be admired for her looks; she was a genuine offshore sailing vessel and possibly the prettiest of her type in the New World.

A main and mizzen mast held gathered cream sails, and the big gaffs were like hefty trees, to be lofted high over the deck by men working with hand power and basic blocks alone.

Each aspect was clearly lovingly tended, from the hull and topsides in their cream-white and the varnished boot top and sturdy hand rail, to the waxy mottled rigging and the thick girth of the varnished masts, booms and gaffs. I was already in love with the ship.

The captain, a man who looked the part in his white, sleeveless shirt with captain's bands and a weather-beaten, tanned and bearded face, passed under the mizzen boom and touched it with a caring hand as he did. He came to meet us and we shook hands.

"I believe we're handing her over to you, Mr Shepherd, these next few days," he said amicably. His beard was short and neat and turning grey; his eyes were bright blue like the sea itself.

"Captain, humour me." I leant in close. "Don't take your eyes off what I'm doing with your beautiful boat."

He laughed. "Don't you worry," he said. "Famous sailor or not, she's still my precious girl."

Tony ignored us and went into the ship with Rex. In truth, Tony didn't really like sailing. It was just what billionaires did with their money. I had a feeling Rex was the same.

"Shall I show you round, sir?"

"Thank you, Captain. I would love that." We passed down the starboard side towards the stern and the magnificent helmsman's seat and the golden-sheen of the wooden wheel.

Away from any other crew or passengers, I dropped my shoulder and came close to the captain's greying chin.

"Captain Johnson, right?"

"Yes," he said; his smile faded to the barest glimpse. I was too physically close and something about my demeanour foreshadowed my question. Up close, his face bore the inflcited scars of time and sea wind. His eyes had a piercing quality like distant water.

"Does Tony ever bring girls on board this boat? Young girls?"

Captain Johnson turned away for a moment. The colour of his tanned face seemed to turn to a tarnished red and then quickly to an ashen grey, as if the sailor suffered seasickness tied alongside the dock. He swallowed and then turned back. There was an expression of doubt on his face that accentuated the lines being written there. It was mixed with fear.

"I don't know what you mean," he said finally.

"Come on, Captain. I already know it's true. I'm here to collect the proof. What do you know?" I stared into his face.

He tensed and flashed a glance beyond me towards the companionway and the saloon below. "Can I trust you, Mr Shepherd?"

"I am only here to catch him." I followed his gaze. "He killed my friends."

Captain Johnson looked confused. Some of the colour was returning around his grey-white eyes and the piercing blue remained. "But he didn't," he said. "I read in the paper that Tony Drax has a cast iron, watertight alibi for both of the murders in France."

"I know that," I said. "He's not the type of man to do these things himself. He would have paid someone."

"I don't know," he said.

"Have you got kids, Captain?"

For a while, he simply stared at me with an expression of doubt. His body was locked into a position as if he were momentarily frozen moving forward. "No," he said and his shoulders relaxed and his body became free from the sudden stasis. We held each other's gaze for a moment longer. His steel-blue sea eyes flickered towards the saloon where Tony and Rex had gone. He seemed to make up his mind. He scratched his short dark beard that was flecked by patches of white-grey. "I might be getting a bit long in

173

the tooth, but one day I'd like to marry and maybe have some."

I nodded. I felt my hands cupping as if to draw the rest from him.

Captain Johnson coughed into a raised and loose fist. "When you leave, ask me again," he said into his hand.

"Tell me…" I said. I had to hold my anger in check because he knew.

"Nothing until… safety," said Captain Johnson.

My own hands had involuntarily clasped into fists and they relaxed only in staccato moves. I had to be patient and give him the two days. I understood. He had the answer. Just a few days more and the proof would be in my possession. It was like fire inside me, burning through but he wanted something, too.

Captain Johnson put a hand on my shoulder and held it for no more than a second. "Protect my crew and me," he said. He coughed again, physically shaken by his own admission that there was something to tell.

"I will," I said.

I allowed him to show me around the *Christina* but his good mood had dissipated. Having this moment's hottest offshore sailor onboard had not turned out at all the way Captain Johnson had envisaged.

Eventually, I followed Sylvie, who was on the sun deck and about to go down into the saloon by way of the large, open companionway.

"Sylvie," I called.

She had taken her shoes off and was holding them in one hand. She turned to me with a deliberate and almost balletic spin on small and high-arched feet.

I saw her quick, small steps and came close to her cheek. I whispered in her ear. "The direct approach has

174

worked better this time. I think I can get what we came for."

Chapter twenty-four

"One time we sailed to the next bay," said Captain Johnson in a low voice. Sylvie and I stood close to his side at the wheel so that we could catch what he was saying. "Mr Drax had a launch come out. We sailed out to sea like a regular sailing trip."

We were under sail now, with a pleasant breeze blowing and the main and two headsails drawing handsomely. The *Christina* leaned over into the wind and made a solid course through the water. Her heavy-displacement was so different from the skittish racing boats I was used to, and it was soothing.

"What happened?" asked Sylvie.

Glancing up from the wheel, I could see through the companionway that Tony and Rex were sitting at the saloon table below decks. They were themselves in an earnest conversation. Tony was talking swiftly and Rex, intent on his words, wore a severe expression. Rex's eyes were wide with double bags under them, puffy like miniatures of his big, heavy body.

"A launch came out," Captain Johnson continued, "there were young models in it. There was a cameraman. We were under strict instructions to tell anyone who asked us that Mr Drax and Mr Touranesi had been onboard alone the entire time; including if it was Mrs Drax who asked."

"And what happened?"

176

Captain Johnson kept a distant-blue eye on the crew as they hoisted the gaff topsail, a complicated little sail that sits above the mainsail. They tensioned it into place with a practised skill.

"They took some still photography of the young ladies." He called forward: "Tie her off!" satisfied that the gaff topsail was in place.

"Is that all?" asked Sylvie fiercely.

Captain Johnson turned to her and frowned. His reddened cheeks seemed suddenly unhealthy on his tanned skin. He was sweating. His piercing eyes bulged towards the saloon and, from the relative dark below, I saw Rex staring back up so that their eyes met. Rex's face purpled as if containing an unspoken rage. His long nose raised high as his head titled back and he drew in a sharp breath that made the regal nose shudder.

Captain Jonhson's eyes diverted around the yacht's familiar scenes, away from the danger. "Then the launch took the young girls back," he said in quick words. "Nothing..."

I turned my back to the saloon, facing the captain and the stern, covering my questions. "Did you or your crew see anything else that happened to them?" I asked.

Captain Johnson stepped aside. "Here, Ms Melville, take the wheel," he said. His skin had greyed again and his eyes continued to shift distractedly like waves.

Sylvie stepped forward. She was a competent sailor and she soon felt the yacht's slight weather helm in her delicate hands.

The ocean rose and fell with a short wave pattern that was dappled with soft indents so that the sea seemed to fracture into light-reflecting shards. The wind was warm and smoothly rose and fell as if a mirror to the water. The great ship leaned and groaned pleasantly and her belly sank, sprinted over the sea and repeated. How perfect it would have been in any other circumstance - the *Christina* drawing powerfully with her cream sails full and the wind trade-like on the quarter – and yet it was the glass that covered darkness.

"Some of the crew raised questions with me after the girls had gone." Captain Johnson placed a steadying hand on the big pedestal that the wheel was attached to. He stood on the leeward side and leaned up the deck of the ship towards us. He turned his face away from the saloon's peering eyes. "I admit, I warned them against looking further into it. I feel ashamed of that."

"What else might the crew have seen?" asked Sylvie, her eyes fixed on the motion of the great yacht. Fully canvased and surging through the sparkling blue seas, a cascade of spray rose and fell in a sudden shower of light around us.

Captain Johnson, a man who had looked away before and who was now telling us some cock-and-bull story, looked pale as if he had sea-sickness.

I stood on the high side of the *Christina*, upwind.

"Why didn't you do anything about it?" asked Sylvie from the wheel. I could see she was furious; the delicate pink lips were held together, her brittle bones tight like wires and he hands clutching the wheel with thin anger.

"I was afraid for my job and what they might do to me. I am only a sailor, Ms Melville. I was given my dream job as captain of the most beautiful sailing boat I have ever seen. I know nothing."

"Were these girls… injured?" asked Sylvie with an expression of open incredulity.

Captain Johnson turned his back further and stepped quickly to the ship's polished rail. He threw up into the pretty and pure, azure sea behind the boat.

Below in the saloon, I saw Tony turn from his serious conversation with Rex at the ornate inlaid table, so that both men stared out at us with mouths slack.

Tony came to the companionway entrance as Captain Johnson righted himself, wiping the spit from his chin.

"Is everything alright, Captain Johnson?" asked Tony, his puppy-dog eyes shifted across the captain assessing him.

"Yes, yes," the ill man answered. "I just ate something that didn't agree with me last night. Nothing to worry about, Sir. I'm fine, thank you."

"At least we have Tom Shepherd with us if we need him, hey Sylvie?" Tony said brightly. "We'll be up soon," he said. With a short wave he went back into the saloon, his face clouding over as he departed.

"I am afraid I can only say," said Captain Johnson returning to our conversation, "that I know of no films or cameras on board." I could see he was trembling.

I turned to see Sylvie's deep anger. Sylvie let go of the wheel as if she cared nothing for the ship and she walked up the deck so that her body conveyed her disgust in swaying arms and heavy feet. The yacht began to turn to the wind. Captain Johnson took hold of the wheel's shifting spoke and righted the ship's course. I turned from his blue, unseeing eyes and followed Sylvie.

At the bow, the great yacht was rising and falling into the deep ocean of regular, smooth waves and she moved forward, beautifully balanced. Hot sunshine beat down from a clear creamy-blue sky and her bowsprit danced over the waves.

"What do you think, Sylvie?"

"We have to work on him," she said. "Because he knows everything."

The anchor dropped into six fathoms of crystal clear water. The mizzen sail, the last to be carried, was sheeted tight, and the deck was prepared for lunch.

Captain Johnson had neatly tucked the *Christina* into a bay where only one other yacht swung to anchor in a long swell. The wind was dampened by the headland but the rising peaks sent gusts skidding down and the *Christina* twisted on these occasional flukes making it an uncomfortable anchorage at times despite the stabilising effect of the mizzen sail.

I took the binoculars and made a sweep of the bay. There was no beach and there were no other craft in sight. The one other lone sailing boat was less than half our size and silent.

Within a minute, the *Christina's* crew had set up a dining table in the cockpit area and the four guests sat opposite each other. A bimini was raised over our heads and a bottle of champagne was popped open.

Tony turned and took the bottle from the youthful waiter who had the look of an amateur boxer. Tony read the label and handed it back and waved him on to serve.

The glasses were filled and Tony held up his flute for a toast.

"To Tom," he said with little enthusiasm. "Congratulations again. I admire your tenacity to get round the world. And to Josh and the crew of *Swiss Time*. I only hope, Madame Melville, that your colleagues finally catch this terrible killer."

Sylvie dangled her glass and then sipped at the champagne.

"I thought Phillipe was to join us on this trip," she said.

"He couldn't make it," said Rex. "Something with his racing car…"

Sylvie said slowly: "Patrick Colt doesn't come on the boat?"

Rex seemed to snarl. "Not when I'm onboard."

Sylvie turned her glass and looked into the bubbles of the champagne. "You don't like him much, do you?" She turned to Tony, not waiting for an answer. "What do you think happened, Mr Drax?" she asked. "What is your theory?"

Tony smiled as if he had expected the question and wanted to answer it. He put his glass of champagne down untouched and gestured with his hands out wide.

"Well," he said. "My theory is a little outlandish."

"Go on," said Sylvie.

I put down my glass. Rex Tourenasi had not raised his champagne for the toast. He watched us passively, saying nothing now.

Sylvie drank and waited for Tony's reply.

"I think the French were humiliated by losing to every boat, and the crew of *French Foundations* wanted to kill the winners," he said.

He laughed alone.

Tony sobered up. "Ok," he said. "A little bad taste." He turned to Rex. "We had problems in France," he said. "Someone tried to frame me for some sick photos. I don't know where they got them from and some of the racing crews were injured. Two were killed."

Rex looked over to the stern of the boat where the ship's compliment of crew sat. Captain Johnson and the three sailors were at a separate, smaller table set up behind us and under the swaying mizzen sail.

I saw Captain Johnson's shoulders stiffen as he listened in to our conversation. Under the hot, midday sun, the shadow of the sail crossed and re-crossed him as the *Christina* swung to a jostling wind.

I saw Rex contemplating the captain. Rex's jowls were slack but the muscle under them stiffened. He scratched his long nose and turned back to us.

"Mister Shepherd, Madame Melville," he said.

The young waiter had descended and now he came back on deck through the saloon companionway. Rex glanced up. The man stood quietly to his side and I noticed the sinew of muscle under his waiter's jacket.

"It seems someone betrayed us," said Rex turning back to face us with his purple-blotched skin and long, regal features cold under down-squinting eyes.

Tony quickly stood up as if this statement had triggered a response in him. The young boxer of a waiter held out something. I too stood up carefully. Sylvie put down her champagne glass and it fell sideways, spilling the rest of the contents. She re-set the glass.

Tony held the item. It was a USB stick and he drew a tablet computer across the table.

"Tom," he said. "Explain yourself."

Behind Tony, I saw Captain Johnson's shoulders as he flinched with anxiety. He said nothing and kept his mouth firmly shut and he remained facing the stern of the ship away from us. The back of his head was rigid, forced away.

"What are you and Sylvie planning for me?" Tony continued speaking as he pressed the USB home.

"What is it... you think has happened?" I asked carefully. I searched the faces of the two men but they remained enigmatic, staring at the screen.

"You told Helene you knew something terrible about me. Isn't that so?" Tony slumped towards the laptop and typed with thick, quick fingers.

From the stern the crew and Captain Johnson took uncomfortable, furtive glances towards us. I looked their way and Captain Johnson immediately turned to stare away again.

"There is a gentlemen's way to do these things," said Tony peering into the screen like a mechanic at work.

"How is that?" I asked.

He carried on pressing me without looking up from the screen. "Why didn't you ask me yourself?"

"About what, Tony?"

He turned the tablet towards me. "This," he said.

I looked down and saw the image on the tablet computer. It was similar maybe even the same as the ones Sylvie had shown to me and Kate on the plane.

"Where did you get that?" said Sylvie. She leaned over the table. The waiter poured her a second glass of champagne as she did and she brushed his arm.

"It was given to me by a friend," said Tony. "As you can see, it incriminates me in some pretty unpleasant things."

"Are you saying that that is you?" I asked.

"I'm saying this photo is doctored," he said quickly. "That could be the leg of any middle-aged man. That could be a hotel room anywhere."

"Whose is that iPhone on the side table?" said Sylvie. "The one with the black and white cover?"

183

"I don't know," said Tony. He gave Rex a sideways glance. "This is not a picture of me, so how could I know?"

"You were never in this film?" I said.

"It could be any middle-aged man," Tony said again. "Half the world has legs like Rex and me. You can't see anything else."

Rex nodded. His fatty jowls seemed to move independently from his long and haughty nose as he spoke. "It is a case of mistaken identity."

"So why was Bernie Gramm murdered?" said Sylvie.

"A mystery," said Rex and he launched into what sounded like a lawyer's speech. "There are witnesses who can prove that Tony was somewhere else when Bernie was killed. There is irrefutable proof that he was with Cecilia and the film crew when you and Stan Stosur were injured."

"You were on the boat that shot at *Ocean Gladiator*," said Sylvie.

Tony smiled. "So were you, did you see anything other than the mayor?"

Sylvie ignored the jibe. "So you don't make movies with young girls?" she said.

"No," said Tony with a serious twist to his mouth. He smiled through discomfort, as warmly as he could manage. His round and soft cheeks emphasised the depth and warmth of his puppy dog eyes. "Trust me. I have a daughter about the age of these girls, you know. I am afraid, however uncomfortable this may be to hear, Josh Lewis may have been part of a paedophile ring. He had these photos on his computer. It might be Bernie's legs we're looking at."

"Bernie? That's a lie," I snapped. "Bernie was a soft-centred man. Everybody loved him."

184

"It wouldn't be the first time someone had pulled the wool over the world's eyes. I think of celebrities who have been secretly doing this sort of thing for years on end." Tony looked between us. He waved an uncertain hand towards me. "Look, I wasn't going to say anything, but Amy said…"

"What?"

"Amy said that Bernie touched her. He tried to seduce her before the race." Tony looked down towards my champagne glass.

I turned away. I caught sight of Captain Johnson's tensed, straight back. He looked round. He appeared doubtful, the piercing blue eyes dropped to the deck. He was closing up.

I couldn't believe they were turning the story on its head; claiming that Bernie could be the man in the images, the terrible criminal.

"Had you heard that?" asked Tony.

I remembered the accusation in Amy's *Dear John* letter to me. She had said as much. I wouldn't believe it.

Rex put his hand forward and tapped the table with a finger. "You know that in this matter I am acting on behalf of Tony."

"As his lawyer?" I asked.

Rex nodded. "I am and have been his lawyer for over thirty years. I am asking you politely, but we can get a court order if you persist, not to harass Tony. He has done nothing wrong."

I turned to Sylvie.

She shrugged with a small movement of her shoulders that sank her down low into her chair and she drank from her fresh glass of champagne sulkily.

"We have done nothing to imply Tony was at fault," I said. I sat down heavily in my own chair.

185

Rex sighed through his long nose. A trickle of sweat ran down his temple and he brushed it away with the back of his hand. "You broke into his study two days ago and you accused him to his own daughter of having something to hide.

"We repeat, contrary to what you wish to hear, Josh Lewis had indecent images on his computer that the police cautioned him about. He had been involved," he coughed politely towards Tony, "in a sexual relationship with Tony's daughter when she was only nineteen and whilst he was engaged to be married to someone else who was pregnant, and he passed these images to his friend and mentor Bernie Gramm.

"They appear to have been doctored in some way to imply that Tony was the subject of these images. We are not stupid; we know what he attempted to do – implicate others when things turned sour with Bernie."

"You're saying you think Josh killed Bernie because they were paedophiles who fell out?"

"Didn't he?" asked Rex with a raised eyebrow that emphasised the contrast of fat at his cheek and the thinness of his long nose. "Who knows what lengths those sorts of people might go to?"

The crew at the next table tried to ignore our conversation, but they could not. As the mizzen sail flicked over their heads, passing shadow and sunlight alternately across them, they squinted into the fierce light and then the shade and heard parts of the conversation drifting across the wind.

"I have witnesses that I have asked you not to pursue me." Tony turned to Rex and the single, tough little steward. Both men nodded. Rex's creamy jowls wobbled. The waiter's tense, boxer's face barely moved as if he knew never to speculate only absorb. "I feel sorry for Jenny and little Rory in that hospital in

Cornwall," said Tony turning his attention back to me. "They are the real victims."

The tone of his words didn't make it sound like the threat that it was. I hated that he had even mentioned their names. I turned to Sylvie. The answers that I had been so sure of seemed to have been turned completely upside down. And Tony had just sent me a message that Jenny and Rory were in danger.

"You're saying Josh tried to frame you?" I said, my voice no doubt sounding desperate. Tony was quiet. He avoided my gaze by turning the champagne bottle in its ice bucket. "Who killed Josh if Josh killed Bernie? Are you saying the trawler that killed Josh was just an accident?"

"It may have been," said Rex. "That is one possibility. The fishing industry has had its fair share of disasters over the years. That is not what we believe, however. We think," Rex glanced at Tony who contemplated the thick bottle's neck as if uninvolved, and then Rex turned back to us, "we think that Josh was murdered by whoever runs his film-making ring. They turned on each other. These people are ruthless; we know that from television news…." Rex trailed off.

"I made a deal with Josh," said Tony. He fingered the ice bucket and looked up at me. "That he leave my daughter alone. I didn't want someone with those tastes near her."

We stared across the table at each other.

"Look, let's finish our lunch," said Tony after the long empty pause was too much for him. His humour returned almost instantly, as if switched on. "We have fresh, local crab."

Sylvie held up her glass, asking for more champagne. The waiter poured for her, eyes on the glass. Sylvie looked away into the distance with the champagne held to the light.

I took a slug from a glass of water.

Sylvie sat back in her chair with the drink and I slumped back into my own. Tony sat up looking hungry. The waiter brought starters of dressed crab as if nothing had happened. Tony put his knife and fork into his meal and dissected the innards of the upturned crab.

Sylvie watched them eat. "So you would like us to leave here with the knowledge that you are privately investigating Josh and Bernie Gramm as potential paedophiles?"

Rex contemplated his meal and then looked up at Sylvie. He took a long breath in that drew his nostrils wide. "We're not investigating anything," he said. "And we don't think you should, either. Tom is not a detective and you are out of your jurisdiction. We await the French police's report."

"Moi, aussi," said Sylvie.

Sylvie knocked back her champagne with a quick imprecise gesture like she was throwing back a shot, and then she held up the glass again.

For some reason, she no longer wished to stay sober.

We took the *Christina* on a longer passage down the coast and slipped into the mouth of a fast-flowing river. Captain Johnson motored us up the churning, muddy entrance until we could anchor in a sheltered spot. We had passed only thickly tree-lined shores with a few shanty buildings dotted in amongst them. Now, we were anchored amongst a wilderness backdrop of green over-hanging trees on brown, flowing water.

"We'll set a guard tonight," said Tony. "Be careful on deck, someone may try to board us. Our man with a gun should deter them." He turned to Captain Johnson. "Have someone march up and down with a rifle so it's obvious we're not in the mood to be robbed."

Captain Johnson nodded nervously. "Yes, sir," he said. "I'll do that."

After dinner, in which there was a strange sort of unspoken truce declared, Sylvie and I went up forward. I lay back against a thick, cream-coloured sail bag. Sylvie lay against me. The foredeck was peaceful and we watched the colourful birds circling and diving into the muddy river. A single guardsman stepped slowly around the boat. He came to stand with us and then moved on.

"Do you think they will kill us in the night and blame it on local bandits?" said Sylvie watching the man's back as he moved away.

"Surely another death so close to Tony would make it seem only too obvious he was the killer."

The wind had hushed to a silent trickle and the sound of the birds' wings could be heard as they swooped across the water. Their calls sounded over the gentle lap of tide against the hull. Early stars in a dark blue sky winked through patchy cloud in the deepening glow of sunset.

"I would guess," I said eventually, "that he had intended to satisfy himself to our intentions, put us off our guard and send someone to kill us at a later date."

Sylvie looked puzzled. Her wiry strength knotted. "Why did Helene tell Tony that you had interrogated her?"

"I don't know. Perhaps he guessed, or maybe Cecilia told him. Helene may have told her mother." I looked around at the hills surrounding the bay. It was magical in the last light of the day. "We are certainly becoming exposed. He will be forced to kill us eventually."

"Let's hope you are right when you say he will wait." Sylvie stroked my arm with a languid hand. She took in the gentle sounds and lilting movement of the boat that was now peacefully at anchor. "It would be lovely here if we were alone."

I drew her closer to me, felt her slim warmth and breathed in the sweet aroma at the base of her neck. "Yes," I said. "Perhaps we could come on our own one day when all of this is over."

Sylvie looked up at me with a small smile on her pale pink lips. "I'd like that," she said.

We kissed and she drew away.

I looked up.

"Captain?"

Captain Johnson was standing on the foredeck. The guard was making a new circuit and Captain Johnson waved him away from us.

"I haven't looked at them, but one of my crew did once," he said abruptly. He wiped his chin with a handkerchief from his pocket. His blue eyes gleamed diamond-like in the half light.

"Full films?" I said.

He nodded.

"Where is this crewman?" asked Sylvie. "I need to speak to him."

"He died in a bar fight two days later."

"I see why you are scared," said Sylvie. The hard, slightly-built policewoman's jaw softened. The pink lips closed doubtfully.

Captain Johnson said nothing for a moment. He checked behind him. The darkening deck was clear but for the one guard.

"There were full films, not just photo stills. The film gets copied and stored on USB sticks onboard ship. There is a safe built into the woodwork, very difficult to find unless you know where to look. There are at least thirty that they have made. I don't know what the actual content is, but the crewman told me he saw them both in it. Both Mr Drax and Mr Tourenasi. The photo stills are nothing in comparison…"

I looked down the ship. No-one was there in the shadows but I felt paranoid nonetheless.

"What's in the films?"

Captain Jophnson hesitated. "He causes pain," he said. His blue eyes were steady. "That's all I know. The safe is in Mr Drax's stateroom." Captain Johson turned away from us. "That's all I'm saying. Get me to safety when we get ashore."

He walked away from us and did not look back.

"They must be stopped," I said.

Sylvie clutched my arm.

"They can't be allowed to do that ever again," I said. I wished, not for the first time, that Sylvie was carrying her gun.

"Jamais," she said switching to French unconsciously. "Mais, non."

"My head is pounding from all that champagne at lunchtime," Sylvie said as we passed down inside the cabin by the forward hatch.

"You drank a lot."

191

"You must have noticed," she said, unsteady in the dim light.

"What?"

"That I always drink too much once I start."

"No," I said. Then it occurred to me that we had first gone to bed together quite drunk, she had left Tony's dinner party tight and now she had had too much champagne.

"A curse of my profession," she said. "I'm afraid if I have one drink, it is always followed by another. There was a time when I…" She trailed off.

I took in the deliberately steady precision of her hand movements as she corrected the stray hair that fell across her cheek. It was the only thing about Sylvie that was not precise; this straggling, lost-control hair. It stood out against her otherwise controlled mannerisms. And now an admission to weakness.

"When you what?"

"Well, let's just say, it's been a long time since I filled coke cans with vodka to get me through breakfast."

"Sober up for tonight," I said. "I might be wrong but we may need to defend ourselves."

There was a loud bang. I woke up. It was dark and our berth was an extravagantly perfect wood-carved stateroom. In the end, the thought of making love with Sylvie in the place where young girls had been harmed, put us both instantly out of the mood.

We had eventually fallen asleep watching the darkness and hunting for shadows.

I got out of bed and pulled on my jeans.

192

I could hear others rousing, voices low and troubled.

Lights came on as we padded through the boat. Outside, I could see members of the crew leaning over the port side of the *Christina*.

I followed their movements and stepped to the rail. They had hold of something in the murkiness of the half-light. Together, four of the crew heaved, and slowly they turned a body towards them. A rigid face stared up at us blankly.

The heavy, sack-like corpse fell to the deck.

"Bandits," said Captain Johnson. I turned to see the man shivering in the warm night. Tony was standing in his boxer shorts behind him.

"What happened?" he asked.

"A boat came out from the shore," Captain Johnson was speaking slowly but he sounded breathless. "It was a fishing dory with two men. Raul was on deck patrolling. One man came on board. He had a knife. Raul fought with him and shot him and he fell overboard again."

"Nasty for him," said Tony. "Better luck for us, hey, Captain?"

Captain Johnson held onto the rail, swaying slightly with a rhythm contrary to the sway of the boat.

I caught his eye. The piercing blue rose and fell in a storm. He shook his head with long arcs.

I turned to Sylvie. She gave me a grim shake of her head and hurried below. I followed.

"We've lost him," she said. "He won't talk now."

Chapter twenty-five

En route back to Rio, Tony stood by the helmsman at the wheel. I stood alone on the port side watching the coast as it rolled by. Sylvie was on the bow.

The *Christina* surged powerfully through the ocean's great swell. She leaned against the dark blue water, sails drawing. The ship felt strong in her thick timbers and urged on by her broad expanse of cream sails on the big gaff rig.

I followed the froth of white water as it fanned out from under the ship. Sunlight refracted from the sea and spray.

I turned to Tony.

"This deal you made with Josh. When did you make it?"

Tony glanced at me. He came close to me. "When? Before the race. Helene came to me in tears. Josh had a fiancé and a baby on the way."

"And what was the deal?"

"I told him," said Tony. The amiable salesman had disappeared. His face was rigid. "If you ruin my child's life then you will also ruin your own."

"That's more a threat," I said.

"Yes," he said. "It was."

Tony walked along the slanted deck to stand ahead of the mainmast. He stared out to sea.

The police met us as we re-entered the marina in Rio. They stood on the quayside, almost a dozen of them. The media were waiting at the fence that protected the boatyard.

Amongst the crowds, Sylvie pointed. "Over there. That's Cluzon, my contact in Special Branch."

I didn't interfere as the crew brought the yacht back alongside the dock. They knew their jobs even with the Captain looking dazed. Whatever Captain Johnson had decided twenty-four hours earlier, he was now barely able to function. His lower lip trembled as he gave timid orders to his crew.

We tied alongside and the police immediately stepped on to the boat. Cluzon came towards me.

"Tom Shepherd?" he asked in a nasal French accent.

"Yes," I said.

"I have an international warrant here for your arrest. Josh Lewis's body has been recovered from the sea. We have reason to believe you killed him and destroyed your boat. Come with me."

The police station was ultra-modern. Inside a small, overly bright room, Cluzon sat opposite me. A large mirrored wall on one side broke up the bland newness. Beside Cluzon was the Brazilian police officer, Chief Romana, who was in charge of the local investigation into the killing of the bandit.

"It's been quite a month for you, Mr Shepherd." Cluzon flicked through papers. His English was impeccable. "Bernie Gramm dead where you found him. Stan Stosur seriously injured on your boat with

195

you. Josh Lewis shot three times and then subsequently drowned as your boat was destroyed. And now a local thug shot here in Brazil whilst you were on board. What do all these people have in common, I ask myself?" He shot a glance at the Brazilian for effect. "Tom Shepherd, I answer."

I pulled a face. "That's hardly grounds for a conviction, is it? Just because I was there, doesn't mean I did it."

"It's a little too much of a coincidence for my liking," said Cluzon. His dark suit was neat and his tie was as thin as he was. Dark eyes betrayed his long hours.

"It's not a coincidence," I said. "It's simply a fact. I am one of the people caught up in this nightmare."

"So," said Cluzon with a faint smile, "why aren't you dead?"

The heavy-set Brazilian policeman grunted with amusement. He placed a delicate, fat hand on the table.

"I'm not sure," I said glancing between them. "I guess there must be an explanation." I had an idea what I thought that explanation was. This story was getting huge publicity. I was the biggest thing in the media right then. Tony's sponsorship was getting the same huge publicity. He was never going to let the chance of race success and all the associated publicity go begging. The more people died, the more he probably wanted me to survive so that I could sail on, the name of *Gladiator Tyres* emblazoned across me and across the world.

I could tell Cluzon what I thought, but I had to keep Tony's name out of it until I had evidence. It was too much of a risk to expose him without it. If he got free, he had already indicated that Jenny and Rory were in his thoughts. I wanted to keep them safe. He must not think I could or would betray him, not until I knew I had him for good. As soon as I was in that position, I had to have Jenny and Rory somewhere protected. How we could transport a premature baby to a safe house, I had no idea.

I stuck with my original plan. It seemed that Patrick Colt had got his come-uppance for running off with Amy already; she had started to despise him. I decided to continue sending anyone who asked his way. If he was innocent, then he was safe enough.

"Have you spoken to Patrick Colt?" I said. "I don't trust him. He's too slick. I think he's the serial killer in our midst."

"That's his phone in the unpleasant pictures, isn't it?" said Cluzon. "It's okay, Rex Tourenasi identified it for us."

"He did?" Rex Tourenasi seemed to have something against Patrick Colt, too, I thought. Patrick Colt's iPhone implicated him directly with them.

"But why Colt?" asked the Brazilian policeman without a great deal of curiosity. His heavy, fat face was bronzed and weathered.

"He ran off with my girlfriend and he tried to frame Josh with some lewd photos on his laptop."

"That's hardly a reason to suspect him of murder," said Cluzon. His thin shoulders disappeared inside a baggy, white shirt.

"He was there, just like I was."

"Not in the Channel when you killed Josh Lewis." Cluzon held my gaze. "And not on this sailing trip you just took with Tony Drax."

"Why would I kill Josh? We had just completed a major race together. We won it. We had our entire careers ahead of us." I felt only the bitterness of our moment of triumph. It had lasted barely a few hours. Josh had been called to Jenny's side in Cornwall.

Within a day, Bernie was dead. Then Stan and I had been attacked. I put my head into my hands and rested my elbows on the table, staring down.

"Josh turned out to be someone other than the man you thought you knew," said Cluzon. "You found out about his interest in young women, you spoke to Bernie and that made you even more angry; so then you killed Bernie. Bernie was your mentor. He had fooled everyone into thinking he was some kind of a kindly father figure. In reality, you had stumbled on to a paedophile ring." I looked up. Cluzon indicated the two of them with a thin finger. "It's okay, Tom, we understand. We respect your reasons."

He smiled sympathetically. It was another double-act and it reminded me of Tony and Patrick Colt trying to convince me to go to Truro to see Josh in the hospital. And the ideas sounded like those of Tony and Rex. "We know why you wanted to kill them." Cluzon's voice became a whisper as he spoke. "We'd have done the same."

The two men nodded to each other, conspiratorially.

Ignoring the chumming up, I said: "Do you think it was Bernie in those pictures?"

"Did you?" Cluzon said quickly.

"It was a question," I said. "Because I don't see a resemblance to him even if there are only legs showing."

Cluzon smiled. "Tell us about it, Tom."

I said nothing. The only thing I could think was how to get out of there so I could get the evidence I needed on Tony.

"Have you searched the *Christina*?" I asked.

"The Brazilian police are in the process of doing that right now," said Cluzon. "If you've nothing more to tell me, we'll have to stop there. Or are you asking me to consider someone on the *Christina*? Your boss, perhaps? Tony Drax."

I said nothing.

"Mr Drax was having dinner with his daughter, Helene, on the night of Bernie Gramm's death in a public restaurant and…" he consulted some papers, "…and an interview and dinner with Kate Hutchinson, her cameraman Pete Dunleavy and Cecilia Drax the night you were injured." He turned a thin and pale face towards me and his eyes were black from the night shift of his work.

"I didn't mention him," I said. I sighed and sat back, dropping my hands into my lap. "What happens now?"

"We are taking you back to France," said Cluzon suddenly indifferent. "You will stand trial."

"I want to speak to Sylvie Melville."

"You can have a lawyer," said Chief Romana standing up. His big belly rolled over his belt. He tucked a flap of shirt inside.

"I'd like Sylvie Melville," I said.

"Very well," said Cluzon. "I'll fetch her."

Alone in the room, I held my head in my hands. Sylvie entered the small detainment suite and glanced about herself furtively. Behind me was the large, mirrored wall and it bothered her.

"They are watching," she said. She turned her back to the mirror and sat on the desk as if anchoring her body.

"Cluzon knows you didn't do it," she said.

"Then why is he taking me to France?" I stood in front of her so that Sylvie shielded me from their view.

"He has to be seen to be doing something. You appear to be as close to the source of the information as anyone. He wants you somewhere he can contain you. That way, you won't be killed without him knowing about it first."

I laughed without humour. "He wants the killer to show his hand in front of him. I get to be the bait?"

"Precisely. The other thing he admitted to me is that he doesn't understand why you are protecting the killer."

"How does he know I'm doing that?"

"Because he figures you must have seen who shot Josh when you were out at sea."

It was true that I had kept the gunshots to myself. I had told no-one, not even Sylvie or Kate.

"Why didn't you tell me Josh was murdered?"

I turned my face up to Sylvie's. She looked tired. We had barely managed two hours sleep before bringing the bandit's body back to Rio. I'm sure I looked worse. I said: "I didn't want to involve anyone else until I could catch the killer."

Sylvie was as impassive as if I was looking at Kate; but the latter would never have allowed her hair to tangle and her make-up to wear as Sylvie's had. She looked like she needed protection, like she was done in. Even so, I couldn't help wonder if this was a bit of theatre and that Sylvie had been sent in by Cluzon to get me to talk.

I had been holding information inside me so long, the things I knew; I was beginning to feel physically damaged by the knowledge and like I just wanted to say it all. Just once.

But I held back.

"It was planned," I said, going back to our conversation. "Our radar was broken. It stopped us being able to see the trawler in the dark. That must have been done in advance; before we left Brest."

I felt dizzy from tiredness; more tired than I had ever felt working through months of sail racing and the broken sleep that came with that.

Sylvie waved her hand in expectation of more.

"In truth," I said, "I didn't see the face of the gunman. Whoever did it drew the trawler alongside *Ocean Gladiator's* life raft after they had disabled us. They shot Josh from the boat but they were dressed all in black and they were wearing a balaclava. I'll never know for sure who it was."

"Were they fat, thin, tall? What did they look like?"

I took a long look at Sylvie. "You're talking like a detective," I said.

"I am a detective." She peered down on me from her place seated on the table, her expression was questioning. The glare of the strip lighting was behind her head. I sat on the thin chair below her, under her shadow and squinting up.

"Is that why you've been with me, Sylvie? To find out who killed these men?"

"I want to know," she said. She raised her head. She tidied the strands of unwashed hair behind her ear. She was about to say more, but she hesitated. Her rose cheeks and delicate mouth were cool. "Just tell me, what did they look like? I might be able to help you if you co-operate a bit more."

I sat back and felt the disappointment. My love life was falling apart on me a second time. It was of no consequence; just a minor betrayal within the bigger picture.

I said: "They were slim, and they appeared to my fuzzy mind at the time, like they were fit and healthy."

"So not Tony, then?" said Sylvie.

"No," I said. "Definitely not a short and fat, old man." In fact, just the opposite.

She seemed disappointed. "How can we implicate him?" She stepped down from her perch on the table and stood in front of me. She smoothed down her top. With my eyes, I followed her as she took a short walk around the unpleasantly modern, little room. Her mouth was squeezed tight as she contemplated her shoes and each step that she made.

I realised she thought that I had just lied to her.

"I told you, detective, whoever it was, it wasn't him on the trawler." That much I knew.

I agreed to go back to France. There was nothing to be gained by staying in Brazil. I had failed to get information from Helene, failed to get the original films and failed to get cooperation from Captain Johnson. I had failed, full stop.

The police chief left us at passport control and Cluzon escorted me onboard the big Boeing aircraft.

The flight back was bumpy with a lot of turbulence midway. I had slept fitfully but the rough air woke me and I jangled my wrist against the bindings that held me trapped. Cluzon, sitting calmly beside me, opened a lazy eye and smiled.

"Almost home," he said. He was a little too tall for the seat and he half lay and half sat in it awkwardly.

"I think that when we get there, I'll be asking for that lawyer," I said. I could see Sylvie Melville's arm poking out from behind a seat ahead of me further down the plane. She looked over her shoulder and when our eyes met, she turned away quickly.

Probably the scowl on my face made me look like the murderer they would like me to be.

Rene Pignol welcomed me back on to French soil with a simple nod of the head. As I was working out what was going on, he took Sylvie's bag, and I realised he was only there to escort her back to Finistere.

Sylvie took a quick last look at me and then disappeared within the crowd of passengers and was swept into the main terminal building. I watched her go following the precise movements of her retreating legs and caught a backward glance from Pignol as he walked alongside with his own heavy, knee-locking strides.

I didn't know if I was going to Brest or staying in Paris. Nobody spoke to me unless they had to. Eventually, I was cleared entrance and put in a car. We started driving out of the city, and I guessed we were going back to the scene of the original crimes.

"Stan Stosur has come out of his coma," said Cluzon. "I am going to interview him this morning at the hospital in Quimper. You're going to the local police station. I can arrange for your lawyer to meet you there, if you give me his name."

"I'll have to ask someone to give me one, I don't know any lawyers," I said.

Cluzon frowned and dropped into a grim silence. The long journey to Brittany was only interrupted for one short comfort break.

When we arrived, it was raining steadily. I was placed in a police cell and given a sandwich and a strong coffee. I never could get used to the French version and I preferred a good cup of British tea. The thought of it made me homesick for the first time in my life. The fear of being locked up on dry land made me feel indescribably trapped.

Cluzon woke me the next morning early.

The little cell was bright with morning sunlight. The noisy drunks of the night before were sleeping it off in the next cubicle. We passed down the corridor and went into the interview room, an ugly grey little room with the same intimidatingly bright lights and a sparse desk.

"I've asked for Sylvie Melville to suggest a lawyer for me," I said.

Cluzon murmured something I didn't catch. He left the room and returned fifteen minutes later with another man.

"Your lawyer," said Cluzon.

We shook hands.

"Michael Staithe," he said. He was tall and very thin.

"You're English."

"Married a French girl. We live in Rennes. I came over as quickly as I could."

"That was good of you…"

Staithe winced as if he were feeling guilty. "This is the biggest case in France today, if not Europe, I couldn't pass it up. No lawyer could have, Mr Shepherd." He smiled awkwardly. "Don't worry, though, I will get you out of here - today."

I turned to look up into his aquiline face and took in his earnest expression. "Can you do that?"

Staithe held up a hand.

"Have you spoken to Stan Stosur?" he said turning to the French police officer.

"Yes," said Cluzon.

Michael Staithe was a little over thirty and thin almost to the point of malnutrition. His suit hung from his shoulders. He was tall and he looked very British. The two men were both as thin as each other and looked to my mind, like they could have been winners of some gruesome diet competition.

"What information did you get from Stan?" asked Staithe. I had the impression he already knew the answer to the question.

Cluzon said moodily: "He said he saw Tom Shepherd being hit across the head as he woke and sat up. He doesn't remember anything else."

"Then my client is free to go," said Staithe. "You cannot suspect him of murdering Bernie Gramm on that evidence."

"I still have an ink stained letter from Amy Mackintosh accusing Bernie Gramm of touching her. A letter that she tells me Tom read as they spoke on the telephone only two hours before Bernie Gramm was killed."

"And as I understand it," said Staithe, "the couple had split at this point in in time."

"And it may be that Mr Shepherd blamed Herr Gramm for that fact."

"Another problem you have," said Staithe. "Tom was waiting outside the hotel Bellevue when the murder took place. Stan Stosur found Bernie dead. There are witnesses who place Mr Shepherd in a public place at the time of the death."

"He could have killed him and then stood outside the Bellevue expressly for the purpose of being seen in public."

"That is… far fetched," said Staithe.

A uniformed police officer came in and whispered into Cluzon's ear. Cluzon immediately stood up, threw an irritated glance at the mirror and walked to the door.

"Well?" said Staithe.

"It seems that Stan Stosur has given you a reasonable alibi for his injuries." Cluzon turned to the mirror. "Of course, you could have killed Herr Gramm and somebody else struck the two of you in revenge. That seems to have been ignored." He turned back to me. "But you're free to go," he said. Then he added with typical French ambiguity: "Even if you are the tiger masquerading as the lamb." Cluzon opened the door, went through, and slammed the door behind him.

I thanked Staithe.

He smiled. "Only round one," he said, "but at least you're out of the police cells… a bit too easily, in fact." His expression turned doubtful. "Can we spend some time together? I've been briefed by Ms Melville, but I would appreciate some more of your time."

"Ms Melville thinks I am the bait and that they have arrested me and then are letting me out in France on purpose."

Staithe took my arm, his expression dark. "Not here," he said. "We can talk outside."

"Yes, okay," I said. "Then I must go to the Caribbean."

"The Caribbean?"

"Yes, strange as it may seem, right now, I need to buy a boat."

206

Chapter twenty-six

I wanted Tony to think everything was normal. At least, as normal as possible. If I acted as if my life was consistent with the old reality, then he might let me get close to him again. Then I would get another chance to find genuine proof of his guilt.

Right then, I had to remain calm. I had to have a plan that could get me what I wanted most: evidence. Long distance tactics were supposed to be my speciality. I was a marathon sailor and my ability to see the long view was supposed to my best attribute, I'd read that in a sailing magazine. I needed to think it through. Sailing must be my answer. It's what I do.

If the boat in Antigua was good enough, I'd sail it through the Caribbean. I could use my boat against their boat. Capture what I needed by stealth, by sailing stealth.

On the way, someone could join me. I drew up a shortlist of sailors I thought might fit the bill. The effect was more depressing than I had anticipated and I thought only of Josh being murdered at sea and how I didn't want to team up with anyone ever again. There was no way I could invite someone into what might be a death trap.

I screwed up the list and binned it. There were only two people I could ask to accept the danger. I wrote down their names on a fresh sheet of paper.

I called Sylvie. "Would you and Rene help me bring the boat back from Antigua? You'd be doing me a favour…"

"I would be honoured," she said.

We arranged to meet in a café.

A few minutes later, I had an excited call from Rene. He was in. I figured no-one else could be placed in that danger, alone at sea with a murder target, but police officers could accept it. It was their world, something they would understand. They would sail a thousand miles to chase down a suspect and to retrieve irrefutable evidence of his guilt.

I booked flights for the three of us to Antigua. I called Berscolini's boatyard and arranged to see the boat in three days time.

Then I met with Michael Staithe for an hour and kept my mouth shut about Tony and finally met Sylvie at four pm in a café on the harbour front.

A few stragglers from a late lunch were heading out of the door and we took our drinks to a quiet table in the corner. I lent against a cream-painted, brick wall. The music was loud jazz.

"How is Cluzon taking it?"

Sylvie smiled. "Badly." She delicately placed stray strands of hair behind her ears. "I can't believe we got so close to getting Captain Johnson's USB stick evidence and then we end up back here in France two thousand miles from it."

"If only we could get him back on side."

"Captain Johnson? He's terrified."

"The *Christina* has the answers," I said. "We can track it down and get back on board."

"The Brazilian police will have searched it." Sylvie's determined grey eyes were fixed ahead. "I hear they have searched Tony's house, too."

208

"His study?"

"I would guess so. We should tip them off that there are USB sticks to be found…"

The waitress brought our coffees. I took hold of Sylvie's slim, pale hand. "No," I said once we were alone again. "We can't lay the blame at Tony's door until we have concrete proof. If we do, he'll come after us and that could be putting Jenny and Rory at risk. The boat is the key. The police won't have done a forensic search of the boat. Why would they? The robber only got on deck before he was killed."

Sylvie nodded and put her hands to her rose coloured cheeks. "You want to go back to Brazil, then, to the *Christina*?"

"I have a plan for this Open 62 in Antigua. Have you crossed an ocean before?"

"You're kidding?" she said. The delicately pink lips turned up in a smile. "You want to take Rene and me to Brazil on a racing boat?"

"We'll go slow," I said.

"We won't!" she laughed. "It's time to live a little more wildly."

"I like your thinking." I smiled. I took in the tousled blond hair and the softness of her skin. Her laughter was a relief in the midst of the terrible bloodshed. The more I was with her, the more I liked her. Her grey eyes were full of renewed energy. She seemed like she wanted to live fully.

"No more the docile lamb, more the tiger," she said.

I laughed.

Although she was smiling, she shrugged as she said: "I'll probably lose my job taking all this time off."

I threw back the little espresso coffee in one swallow. The gritty, dark taste was strong. I thought about her expression, about the tiger and the lamb. It reminded me of Cluzon's statement back in the police station.

"Has anyone heard from Kate or Pete?" I asked.

"Nothing. They're still in Brazil. Amy said something about Pete filming Tony on the *Christina* when I was leaving to catch your flight."

"Really? Is Kate going, too?"

"I don't know." She wiped her pink lips with thin fingers and stared at me intently.

"I hope she is being careful. Listen Sylvie, will Cluzon still talk to you?"

"He's still pretty irritable. Why?" Sylvie took a sip from her own cup of thick, black coffee. Putting the cup down, she again brushed blond hair behind her ears.

"I want him to take a look at this." I held up my phone and I showed her the picture I had asked the houseboy to take of the four of us on the terrace outside Tony's house in Brazil.

"Email it to me now and I'll forward it on to him. Why?"

"Just to see what he thinks of the lambs. One last thing, Sylvie..." I started the email as I spoke.

"Yes?" Her grey eyes found mine as I looked up from the screen.

"I was going to stay in a hotel room tonight..."

She put down the coffee cup and placed her hand on top of mine. She leaned across the table so that her face was close. "Stay with me," she said, and she smiled warmly.

It was comforting to wake in Sylvie's heavy bed. A shaft of morning sunlight illuminated the white linen

210

sheets and, as I opened my eyes, I saw Sylvie's naked back curled away from me.

I shifted closer and placed my arms around her middle. She stirred and turned to kiss me with thick, sleepy lips and her head craned back to me so that her neck was exposed. I cradled her neck with one cracked hand and the other found the hollows of her hip bones and the smooth flesh of her rising stomach. I breathed in her perfume deeply and touched the belly button that pouted cheekily from the slight curve of her abdomen. The muscles tensed and relaxed as she swayed slightly; her buttocks softly undulated against me.

"What time is it?"

"Early," I said.

She slipped around and over me so that I felt the softness of her buttocks crossing me and then her stomach pressed against mine. Her breasts touched my chest. She placed her arms over and around my neck. Her brittle face came close to mine. "What time is the flight?"

"Later," I said. I kissed her delicate pink lips and she responded. The warmth of her body was radiant.

When we landed in Antigua, there was a man with a very stiff left leg and who was well past retirement age. He stood at an awkward angle with his knee locked out and he held up a card with my name on it. Luckily for us, the airport journalists had not yet descended on him. I grabbed the card and we followed him outside.

The man hobbled to his taxi with Sylvie, Rene and me giving his disability anxious glances. Not only did it look decidedly painful, but we couldn't imagine him driving with such a rigid limb. Rene followed him with his own, similar injury as if mimicking the driver.

As we darted through the traffic, we realised it was no impediment to racing through the back roads and over the top of the island at speed.

It was almost dark by the time we arrived at Berscolini's yard at English Harbour. The Open 62 was inside a big hangar, and as the lights went up, I saw immediately that the boat was in very good order.

I wiped the prickle of hot sweat from my dirty neck and walked around the underside slowly inspecting the hull which was currently an ugly and bright yellow.

From a first floor window, a set of steps descended to the hangar floor. Inside the room, an office of some kind, bright light spilled out.

Someone was in the office. He came to the door and peered through the window. It was a handsome and tanned man, Patrick Colt. He spotted me and came slowly down to the ground floor level.

"What do you think?" he asked in his west coast slur.

"Yes," I said. My eyes turned to the boat, avoiding him. "She's good. Has a surveyor been over her?"

"He's due tomorrow if you're satisfied with what you've seen. She is in great condition, though."

"I'll get up on the deck, but the hull seems solid enough from here. We need the expert opinion, but initially I'm happy."

Patrick Colt stopped walking. The others were momentarily out of sight.

"Look," he said abruptly. "I'm sorry about you and Amy."

I stopped and turned a grim face towards him.

Patrick Colt swayed back instinctively from my dark, ugly features. "I don't know what you think happened," he said. "I know you blame me but there's no reason to; you know it was her decision. I only encouraged her to do what she thought was best."

I felt my face flush and a hot anger burst over me. "I bet you did. It was what you wanted. There you are in your thousand pound suit and your six visits to the gym every week. Pristine hair and your tan." I waved an angry hand. "If that's what she prefers then..."

Patrick Colt didn't look abashed, in fact he smiled and then his face contorted into a strained expression of discomfort. He was laughing.

"What's so funny?" I said. I felt a red mist. The smarmy cheese ball thought I was a joke. I was this ugly brute and he was this handsome creature, all preened and elegant. I never could compete with that. I had fought for every moment of affection I had ever got. Women probably fell at his feet.

"I'm gay," he said. "I thought you knew. Phillipe said you saw him coming into my room."

I stopped for a moment.

"But Amy went off with you... She kept going on about what you said. 'Patrick says I should do this' and 'P. says I should do that.'"

"Look," he said, "it's none of my business. You obviously misunderstood, Amy confided in me and I advised her. That's all. I'm sorry if that upset you. In truth, she's been unbearable ever since. There's another thing, please don't tell anyone about me and Phillipe. No-one knows he's gay. There would be serious repercussions for him. The driving world, his father, it would be terrible."

I nodded dumbly.

"You hadn't made the connection, had you?" Patrick looked mortified. "I shouldn't have said anything. Phillipe will be furious."

"No," I said. I felt an idiot. How many little details did I not notice? I stammered to say: "Sorry. Don't worry, I'll keep it to myself. I'm more concerned with… other things."

"I understand," said Patrick. "Amy has gone wild."

"Yes, that, too," I said.

I wasn't sure what to think about Amy. It was true that I had assumed she was with Patrick because she kept talking about him all the time. I was wrong. Completely wrong. And about as observant as a newborn child. Another thing about it was also bugging me; the self pity had to go. I had been carrying around this sense of having been wronged. Amy could make up her own mind what she wanted from a man and if that didn't include me, I had to get over it.

If there was someone else in her life, then she had already gone. If there wasn't, it was still the same. It was over.

I stood on the balcony of a smartly rustic hotel over-looking the sea from a modern terrace. It was impressive. Rolling, green hills drifted down to a Caribbean Sea dazzling in hot winter sunshine. Below, in the tranquillity of a deep bay, expensive yachts, motor cruisers and vintage ships all lay to anchor. Big, lumbering pelicans dived on the water hunting for fish.

Sylvie stepped up behind me. She placed her hand on my shoulder and looked out at the harsh sunlight flashing back from the water.

"Does it never scare you being out there alone?"

I took another long look at the waves lapping against the sand and rock. The waves seemed docile now.

"It scares me a lot," I said. I watched as the pelicans circled the bay, hunting. "The worst thing is being scared. That's why I have to over-come it." She drew her fluttering scarf around her shoulders and I felt myself tense. "My dad said fear was an ally and to use it to my advantage against my enemies."

Sylvie thought about this, looking quizzically towards me as she re-arranged her scarf against the fluttering wind. "How old were you when he said that?"

"Seven or eight."

"Did you have many enemies when you were seven?" The grey eyes followed my lips.

"I guess he meant sporting enemies. That's the way he sees sporting rivals: as enemies. It took me a long while to realise the sailors out on the ocean aren't each other's enemies. We are in it together, fighting to survive. We want to win, but first of all, we want to be safe. We're a sort of family."

"So he was wrong?" Her delicate features were hit with harsh sunlight.

"He was wrong a lot of the time. We haven't spoken for five years," I said. A pelican on the water rose and swallowed a fish, throwing its head back.

"Why not?"

"Lots of reasons," I shook my head. "My first major offshore race, a competitor turned back to rescue me. I had hit something in the night, probably a submerged container lost off a big ship. It was Bernie who came back for me. He took me off my sinking boat and he lost time and maybe he lost the race despite the calculations they do for that sort of thing. Who knows if he might have had better wind?"

"But why did that cause you to fall out with your father?" she held my gaze steadily. She touched my hand with smooth fingers.

"He said I had called for help too soon and that I had been a coward." I turned to the seascape and the boats shifting minutely, never still. "I decided not to talk to him any more."

"I can see why…"

The successful pelican rose, shrugged off the cloying sea and began to circle again, studying the shadows.

I turned back to her. "You understand?"

"Of course I do. And that's why you were good friends with Bernie."

"That and a few other good deeds. He was my mentor that year as well."

"Bernie must have been proud that you won the *Vendee A Deux* race." She was scowling into the sunlight and she passed a slow hand across her face to draw back the fluttering scarf.

"I hope so because he was a good friend." Her hand found mine and I squeezed too hard. "That's why I can't ever believe he was involved in those photos."

"But they don't believe that," said Sylvie. The delicate lines of her skin were taut with determination. "They know he was gathering information and they know Josh was helping him."

"So why don't they arrest Tony now?"

"Because they still don't have the actual proof."

"No," I said. "Neither do I."

216

The pelican spotted prey and dived towards the water.

Sylvie was staring at me, grey eyes rudely intense. "What are you going to do now?"

I turned away from watching the prehistoric-looking bird and looked back into the pale, grey eyes.

"I'm going to sail this boat for him. When Tony's suspicions are at their lowest, I'm going to take another go at getting the proof from the *Christina*."

"But he must have ditched the USB sticks when the police came aboard in Brazil."

I relaxed my hold on her hand but searched in her eyes. "Why? Like I said, they probably never went down below for anything more than a brief inspection." The sun was hot overhead. I felt my scalp burning. The pelican came up empty-handed this time, feathers spraying salt water. "Our best hope is that he kept his nerve, believing the images are hidden where no-one can find them."

"Possibly…"

I stared out to sea, watching the pelican go round again.

I had to pursue Tony. It was the only way to stop him. I owed it to Josh and Bernie and to Stan Stosur. I wanted Sylvie's help to find the evidence. I wanted her help enough to lie to her. "I know where the USB stick is," I said. "Captain Johnson told me. And I know what has been doctored in those pictures."

"You do?" asked Sylvie turning back towards me.

In truth, Captain Jonhson had only told me that the evidence existed somewhere on the boat; that there was a safe that was so well-concealed only someone who knew where to look would have any chance of finding it.

I took Sylvie's slim hand in both of mine.

217

"I think I do know," I said. "So many people have been harmed over this. We must stop him. What will he do after this? I'm worried how far he will go."

Sylvie seemed committed. It took only a few words for the policewoman in her to emerge.

"I will help you, Tom," she said. Her thin, brittle features were serious with intent; the rose-coloured cheeks proud, the grey eyes serious and the delicate, pink lips were set straight.

I nodded and smiled weakly. "Did Cluzon get back to you yet?"

"About the picture? No, not yet. Why, what are you expecting him to say?"

"Whether there's anyone in that picture he recognises; his tiger masquerading as a lamb."

"It wasn't a good shot. It has made identification more difficult."

"Sylvie, we have to expose Tony, and soon. And where are Kate and Pete? Have you even heard from them?"

She shook her head slowly. "I haven't heard a thing."

Chapter twenty-seven

Rene and Sylvie eyed the boat with what looked like a combined mixture of wonder and dread. As the bright yellow hull of the replacement Open 62 swung out over the water, they stared at its sheer size. Sylvie had only ever been on heavy-displacement cruising boats no more than half its length and Rene was a dinghy sailor.

As soon as she was in the water and the lines were cleared by the three lanky marina hands, I threw my bag onboard and slipped on to the mast-less deck.

I held out my hand to Sylvie, squinting up into the dazzling sunlight. She gingerly climbed over the rail and stepped aboard as if she might tumble straight off. Rene followed. Patrick watched from the quay.

"Don't worry," I said. I had checked nothing and was going purely on the initial survey and my own instincts. "We're not racing," I said. "She will get us back to the UK."

But Sylvie knew I had no intention of simply delivering the boat home. The UK was a lie. I was going to Brazil and I was taking them with me, the two novice sailors who only dreamed from their armchairs of sailing on the ocean aboard a formula one sailing boat.

By the end of the day and three days after hastily signing the paperwork with Patrick Colt and Drax

Holdings as the guarantor, I had the boat under my command and filled with provisions.

By day two the mast was on and we were... acceptable. I had never prepared a boat so quickly before in my life.

Patrick Colt looked just as nervous as Sylvie and Rene as the new boat was dragged out of the harbour and towed into deep, clear water. I gave Patrick a list of things I needed him to do for me.

I waved once and then, patiently, I took the novice crew around the racing yacht. Luckily for them, it was barely a Force 2. We hoisted the sail high on the stream-lined mast that was raked back for speed, and up went the light-weather gennaker.

Sylvie gasped and Rene laughed with increasing delight as the racing sail boat glided away from the green of land and slipped forward as if water was no resistance.

"If this is Force 2, then I don't want to know what Force 8 might be like," said Rene.

I set the self-steering. "It's terrifying," I said and I stepped below to make tidy the great mess of stores that weighed us down.

After our dust-off sail, we made a return to Antigua. We found a corner in the crowded port of English Harbour. We took on water and more food and a lot of Rene's cigarettes. He had been complaining since the initial shake-down sail that he had forgotten to pack his supply. It was, by all accounts, the longest 24 hours of his life.

We checked in with Patrick Colt and I said on the phone, as the two, newly-hardened sailors watched me for signs of their immediate future: "We could be in Falmouth by the middle of next week. So, where's Tony? What's the boss up to?"

"He's still at home in Brazil. He's been spending a lot of time with Kate Hutchinson and Pete, that cameraman. They wanted to do some interviews with him."

So that was where those two were, still in Brazil.

"And Amy?" I asked.

Patrick Colt's voice sounded bleak. "Amy? She's been helping Pete with cameras otherwise she's by Tony's side, as always."

I could hear the irritation. Amy was a splinter under his skin.

"You've had a lot of correspondence," said Patrick, changing tack. "We've tried to keep on top of it. Lots of invitations to things."

"I'm going sailing," I muttered.

"I know," said Patrick in soothing tones. "There are a few you might be genuinely interested in, though; invites from famous sailors of the past, that sort of thing. I've forwarded the relevant ones to your private email address. Have a look and see."

"Very well," I said. "Anything else I should know?"

"I don't think so."

"What are Tony's plans for the next few weeks?"

"He tells me he is staying in Brazil to be close to Cecilia. She is unwell and has gone into a private hospital."

"What for?" I asked.

I thought the connection had gone, Patrick eventually said: "Helene takes her in and stays with her. She goes in periodically to… sober up."

"I see."

"Yeah, it all gets a bit tense round the house. Cecilia starts panicking, Helene goes moody because she doesn't want to go, and then they finally pack off to hospital. Tony usually does some sailing when she's in. She is often hospitalised for two to three weeks at a time so he goes out with Rex on the *Christina*."

That sounded like the sort of trip when they made films. Tony waited for Cecilia to go into rehab with Helene as chaperone and then he either took girls onboard or slipped ashore unseen to meet them in a hotel room.

Cautiously I said: "When do they leave for the trip?"

"Next weekend."

"The twenty-first?"

"Friday, the twentieth, why?"

"I was just curious," I said, thinking hard. "How long are they out for?" I bit at my nail.

"Three days. Is it important?"

"No. Is Amy going or is it just Tony and Rex?"

"Amy and Helene are going," said Patrick. "If Helene can leave Cecilia."

"Fine," I said, disappointed. If they were invited, there was clearly no way he would be filming with girls. "Remember what I asked you to do," I said. I broke the connection. I turned to Sylvie and Rene and said: "We've got ten days to get to Brazil."

"Can we do that?" In the heat, Sylvie sipped a cooling drink.

"Yes," I said. "If we sail through the night like we were in a race we can."

"What happens when we get there?" said Rene. He lit a cigarette and his moustache twitched so that the black ends rose and fell. Left of centre was a brown, nicotine stain.

222

"We get the USB sticks."

Rene took a long pull on what was his fourth cigarette, making up for lost smoking time. His intelligent eyes turned wide with addiction.

"I have to catch him. I am too dangerous to leave alive with what I know."

"What do you know?" asked Rene, and he relaxed now that he had the next hit. He bit at his moustache where the brown nicotine stain was.

"I know that Tony and Rex use that boat for their crimes. I know that the evidence is onboard."

"Yes, but Amy and Helene are going this time," said Rene. "He won't be making any movies." He sucked in smoke and removed a flake of tobacco from his lip.

"We can still find the films," said Sylvie twisting her drink in her hands.

"Get a search warrant." Rene's haze of smoke surrounded him. He flicked the stray tobacco leaf away and it fluttered off the boat.

"He'll know," I said. "He'll throw the films at the first sign of trouble. Truth is, I'm worried about Amy. I'm just not sure if Amy has got in too deep."

Sylvie put down her drink on the coaming of the yacht's topsides. "You can't think that Tony is going to kill Amy with Helene there?" She sounded shocked.

"Remember we said we didn't know how a billionaire gets to be one and how they operate? I think that those sorts of people do it by cornering their prey and convincing their victim to do as they are asked. They put people in positions that they can't get out of. He tried to convince us that he was a victim, that other people were the danger. He uses leverage where he can."

"And murder when he can't?" said Rene.

223

"Yes, and I think Tony is going to show Helene what happens to those who cross him."

Sylvie's expression turned dark; the thin wire of her cheekbones tensioned as her jaw muscles contracted stiffly. "You mean he will kill Amy? To scare Helene. As a warning?"

"To warn her and to make her an accomplice so he can keep her in line."

"But what has Amy done wrong?" asked Rene. He waved his cigarette across his body, intelligent eyes troubled.

"I don't know, maybe he just needs a victim. Maybe, she's becoming too demanding. Or maybe she knows everything and she asked for something too big to keep quiet about it."

"The apartment in France?"

The two French police officers said nothing darkly. Rene took a lungful of smoke and Sylvie sipped her drink, eyes staring at internal thoughts.

From Antigua, the long route down to Brazil is about one thousand nautical miles and then Brazil's coastline down to Rio is another three hundred. An Open 62 can cover a lot of ground in eight days, but that was a lot to ask with an inexperienced crew and a half-cocked boat. And we would need some decent wind.

We cast off from English Harbour and made our way out into a quiet Caribbean Sea. It was a fool's errand but I decided to go anyway.

Chapter twenty-eight

As night descended, Sylvie lent in against me and we added our body warmth to each other. Rene was asleep, ready to take the early shift on the four am watch. Sylvie was going to be taking the earlier twelve until four am watch and should have been in bed getting some rest, but she choose to cuddle up against me and enjoy the quickly disappearing sun.

"You know," I said, "that there's no such thing as the sunset, don't you?"

Sylvie turned towards me and the orange light caught her flushed cheeks. Her skin was fresh and alive from the days of exposure to the elements and the low evening sun at sea cast a healthy glow on her.

"You're not a romantic, are you, Tom?"

"It's the earth that rises as we spin around the sun," I continued. "As we spin, the sun appears to drop below the horizon. It should be called an earth-turn."

"I think you'd like to be a romantic but something beat it out of you."

I looked down at my arms that were around her and holding Sylvie to me, as if to point out that she was wrong.

She smiled weakly. "You make all the right noises," she said. "Like putting your arms round me now, but your heart isn't in it, is it?"

I sat back and my hands automatically fell away from her slim waist.

"Am I supposed to be in love with you, Sylvie, is that what you mean?"

"No," she said. "I just want to know what stops you from being with me?"

"I am with you."

"I mean emotionally. You're sitting here. You were holding me, but there is something stopping you from letting go of your English reserve."

"Maybe I'm just culturally different from French men."

"I don't think so. I think you are hurt. Is it Amy who hurt you?"

"Of course she hurt me," I said. I stopped and started again. "She left me. That is painful. Tell me the name of anyone who likes to be dumped." I drew Sylvie back to me and put my arms around her once more. I cooled my irritation. "Amy did surprise me. She left me on the day I won my first major race. That's quite a kick in the teeth."

"Of course," said Sylvie. "I'm sorry." We both gazed across the top of the ocean waves that lengthened beyond the racing boat's sharp nose.

The sun was dropping low and the light played on the water. A Force 2-3 drew the new boat towards Brazil. We were doing twelve knots and it wasn't enough. Beautiful as it was, we needed more speed.

"Maybe that's what's made me cautious," I said. "I did really care about Amy, I admit it. Even though there were things I didn't like about her."

One part of me was involved in the conversation, the rest thinking about how to improve our boat speed.

"What didn't you like about her?"

"Just, she was greedy for money. You know, always fantasizing about things she wanted to buy. And she got on a bit too well with my father."

Sylvie turned to look at me and raised an eyebrow. "I thought you hadn't spoken for five years."

"She thought we should make up. She tried to bring us together for a meeting. She spent a lot of time trying to convince him before telling me about it. I refused and it fell apart."

"That was kind of her."

I shrugged. "Maybe, except my father is worth a lot of money."

"I see." Sylvie stretched a stiff leg slowly in front of her. "You think she wanted to tap into that?"

"We were pretty skint at first, before Tony took me and Josh on. I don't know, perhaps she did." I took a long look down the boat. She moved like the thoroughbred she was, quickly slicing through a regular wave pattern, nose dipping keenly. The race boat was solid. "She liked older men anyway."

"Amy? What do you mean?"

"Her boyfriend before me was in his fifties."

"So what?"

"Nothing," I said. "It's just that when we met she was only twenty but she was seeing a man called Michael Hague who was fifty years old and drove a red Ferrari."

"Don't take this the wrong way, but why did she leave him for you, then? You only had a small flint cottage and a second-hand car."

"I asked myself the same question. At the time, I didn't care. Recently, I wondered if my dad's money had any hand in it. But, you know, Michael Hague was actually there."

"Where?"

"At the student party where Amy and I met. I danced with her half the night and we went home together. I found out later that he had been at the party the entire time. They had arrived together. She had dropped him about an hour after we met."

"Flattering."

"Not really. I've been going through my emails. Patrick insisted. I had one from Michael Hague, sent a couple of weeks after the race start. I traced him through Facebook."

"What did you find out?"

"It seems Michael Hague lost all his money about a week before I met Amy."

For a moment Sylvie said nothing. I could see her mulling it over. I felt the rise and fall of her delicate frame as her breath pressed her against me.

"What a bitch," she said at last. "You've been saved."

"There was another piece of news."

"What's that?"

"Michael Hague is dead."

Sylvie sat up and the semi-darkness surrounded us. The sun had disappeared as the earth turned away from it for another day and the boat continued to slice knife-like through the metre of swell. "How did he die?"

"Suicide," I said. "Two months ago. A couple of weeks into the race."

"Are they sure?"

I shrugged and stared out to sea and the increasing blackness. I should get up on deck and see what could be done to get more out of the boat. It was set up okay, but there were several things we would normally sort out before a race that had been left poorly prepared. The rigging needed tightening, stores needed shifting for better balance and the headsail had a small tear. All little things that turned a solid boat into a weak boat.

"You don't think Tony would have killed him, do you?" I asked.

"Why would he?" Sylvie touched the hair behind her ears.

"For Amy's protection." I checked the instruments, looking across the cockpit. "I mean, because Amy didn't want him bothering her."

"Did he - bother her?"

"Only once that I remember. About six months ago he came by and poured out his heart to her in front of me."

"But he wasn't dangerous, then. He was just annoying, still in love with her." Sylvie followed my line of sight across the boat.

"Except Michael also sent me an email the night he died. He said he would tell me everything."

"He told you he was committing suicide?"

I shook my head. "No, he didn't say that. And I didn't get the email because I was away. I don't know what 'everything' meant." The instruments showed no dangers ahead. "I'm going to prep the boat for the night. You should get some rest." I squeezed her hand. "I just have this horrible feeling," I said. I stood up.

"What's that? You said before you think she's in danger." Sylvie held on to my arm and pressed me to sit with her again.

"What if Michael Hague knew something about Tony, not Amy, and he was going to tell me."

Sylvie considered this for a moment.

"Michael Hague knew something about Tony two weeks into the race that he nearly told you about?"

"Maybe," I said. The sun's final orange rays dissipated quickly so that the night blackened.

"Oh, Tom," said Sylvie. "That's not what you think, is it? You think Michael Hague knew something about…"

"…About Tony and Amy," I finished. "And he was going to tell me."

Sylvie touched my arm. "That they were lovers? Tony and Amy."

"Yes, that's what I'm afraid of," I said. "The only odd thing about Amy as far as I knew was that she had an older boyfriend and that she was rough."

"Rough? What do you mean?"

"I mean she bit me a lot during sex and she could be aggressive about it. It put me off. I prefer the way…"

Sylvie took the failed sentence as a compliment and held her hand out to me in the darkness of night. "The way we make love?"

"Yes," I said. "I prefer… tender." I took her hand in mine and kissed her fingers. "Did you notice Amy's neck? She had on a scarf to cover up a bruise to her neck. I figured, quite wrongly, that that was Patrick Colt's doing. But what if it were Tony? He certainly seems to have more than just a mean streak sexually."

"Then she doesn't know about the young girls?"

"But what if she does?" I said. "What if she wanted his money so much that she doesn't care about his other… pursuits."

"If she knows, she is an accomplice."

"Which means he has control of her. But what if he has become tired of her? What if the way she tries to dominate him and her extravagance with money has gone too far? Amy is getting on everyone's nerves. That might just mean she is now in serious danger."

"Because she's a pain in the backside?"

"Because she's a pain in the backside with a brand new luxury apartment on the French Riviera who knows what Tony likes to do in his spare time."

I stood up to attend to the sails. I couldn't think about Amy with the old man any longer. I turned my attention to the boat. I looked at the set-up moodily; so many things were badly tuned. The speed was lousy and so was our attention to the details. We were dropping a good half a knot. It needed sorting.

Sylvie remained seated. "You want me to help you save your ex-girlfriend's life?" she called. "Is that it?"

"She's in danger." I walked up the boat, finding handholds.

"There is a lack of romance in this relationship that astounds even me," said Sylvie to my back.

I turned to her in the night. Under my feet, the boat moved smoothly across the shifting, unseen water. "I am a romantic, really I am."

"Maybe about your ex-girlfriend."

I held the shroud. "It's not like that," I searched for her shadowed face across the darkness of the deck. "I invited you..."

"You know, it's not romantic to catch a killer together." She helped me to harden up the sail plan to the freshening wind. On the boat, it was as if she were an old hand.

I clipped on.

"Almost romantic," I said. I took strides up the port side deck holding onto my harness. I felt my way along the boat until I reached the clew of the headsail. I touched the bowed edge of the sail, feeling in my finger's tips the amount of quivering tension. The bow rose and fell with simple regularity and the warm seas drifted by. The Open 62 cruised effortlessly through the black night and stars began to fill the sky.

I stared ahead, feeling the warmth of the wind against my face.

Chapter twenty-nine

The fresh breeze took us down the coast and stayed with us for twenty-four hours. I could see that Sylvie and Rene had enjoyed the passage so far. Then the barometer fell and the fresh breeze turned to a strong blow. Now we had a chance to get some speed over the water. We reefed the big main and the repaired headsail and the new boat sliced into blue seas, sending foam and spray scudding from under the bow. Cool, salt water showered us and I noted with satisfaction that Sylvie was getting just as much pleasure out of the big racing yacht as I was.

Rene prepared food whilst I did the navigation. Our passage plan was simple and we were doing as well as could be expected getting down to Brazil.

"What happens when you get to Tony?" Rene placed the pan over the hob's flame and poured in oil.

"Find the USB stick. He obviously took video so that he could watch it all back. I'm betting he is still keeping copies. I think he's still got the films somewhere on the boat."

"Why risk keeping it?" Rene, one hand on the frying pan, flipped a cigarette into his mouth and moved it around as if he was chewing it under the big Gallic moustache.

"Tony's a risk-taker, isn't he? He tried to have Captain Johnson murdered whilst we were all there, but the assassin was killed first. He had the trawler come out and run Josh and me down. He tried to shoot Josh through the hull of *Ocean Gladiator* the first time just as we finished the race. Tony isn't used to losing and he assumes he will come up with a solution soon enough."

"Maybe you're right. He certainly doesn't seem to be afraid of taking extreme action, but what makes you think the evidence is still on the boat?"

"Firstly, Captain Johnson said there was a safe on board somewhere in Tony's cabin. He said it was so well disguised the police would only find it if they tore the boat apart from the keel up. Secondly, that's where it all happened. He took girls there. He used the boat as cover when Helene and Cecilia were out of the way. He either went ashore or took girls onboard. We have to get inside the boat again."

"And you want to board them at sea?" asked Rene. He unbent his long legs as if stiff and cramped.

"At night, we could get to them in the rib and climb aboard."

"That's risky." Rene glanced at his aching knees as if to see any improvement. The unlit cigarette dangled from his lip.

"At sea, a stormy night would help. If he goes into an anchorage then we'll have more luck with good cloud cover."

"And who does what?" Rene relaxed his legs and finally lit the cigarette and took a long lungful with the pleasure of the addict.

"Sylvie steers the boat, you steer the rib and I'll go."

"I hope you know what you're doing." Rene turned back to his cooking. The meal seemed to consist of leftovers and hunks of meat. Rene was not a stereotypical French chef.

"I need evidence," I said. "The police will be too slow. If we jump early, he'll destroy the discs. It's the only way." I looked down at my bitten nails. There was little left to work on.

"Very well," said Rene. He turned out what he said was a meat and vegetable omelette that might in other circumstances have only enticed a hungry dog. He slipped it onto one large plate as the boat rolled.

"Dinner is served," he said, flicking ash from the stub of cigarette that dangled from his lip towards the pan.

Out on the ocean, we were ravenous and so we ate greedily.

Three days later and there were still two reefs in the sails. The wind remained fresh and the bow lifted and fell into the sparkling waves as we worked our way through the ocean's great swells.

We were making good progress and the intensity of the sailing had improved. Sylvie and Rene were getting to grips with the power of the Ocean 62. They worked diligently and hard. There is no escape from the constancy of the demands of the boat. It works the sailors, not the other way round. Twenty-four hours a day, the crew is expected to participate, think, and work and then grab food and rest where and if possible. Boat first, body second.

The short, dark blue waves were flashing past. Twice dolphins found their way into our bow wave and they powered through the water ahead of us, skimming in the surface spray, playing with us.

We drove forward, relentlessly sailing through day and night. There was little to do in terms of sail changes but there were always little tasks to perform to keep the boat true.

Through the doldrums, we motored using up half of our fuel in twenty-four hours. We gave thanks to Neptune as we passed the equator and I initiated the two French police officers into the sailor's inner sanctum with a brief ceremony.

On day five, we passed the port of Recife. We turned towards the southwest.

I checked my emails. Hundreds. I scanned down them, less and less interested. Then one caught my eye. It was from the old man, Johnnie Walter. It was another invitation to speak at the Royal Cruising Club, the dedicated band of offshore sailing enthusiasts. I made a note of his contact details in England and sent him a friendly and non-committal email in return. Without scaring him off, I really needed to know who had passed Josh's laptop with the doctored images to him.

"A few more days and we'll be there," I said to Sylvie across the saloon.

"I can't believe how long a few days at sea seems compared to normal life," said Sylvie. "It feels like a month and we've been away less than a week."

"Are you enjoying it?"

"It's fantastic," she said. Her salt-streaked hair was blond with dark roots. She wore bright yellow oilskins. Her face was tanned by exposure to sun and wind. She looked as if she was physically both exhausted and energised by the *real* use of her body. She looked newly alive. The fake tan she had had when we first met was gone, real life had touched her skin.

I leant over and kissed her and she clipped on her harness and went back out on to the deck as if she had been living as a sailor all her life. Her head reappeared at the companionway.

"Shouldn't we give this boat a name? We've been onboard a week." She was smiling, happy.

"How about *Rene's Rollercoaster*?" said the Frenchman, exaggerating his struggle to stay on his feet.

"I suggest we call her *Sylvie's Sweetheart*."

Sylvie nodded her approval. "I like that one. I take it back, you are a romantic; at least, you are when it comes to boats."

She disappeared from view and then she was back at the companionway again.

"I'll come offshore sailing with you any time," she said. She grinned and her head disappeared from view for the last time.

"Get back to work," I called.

Our luck ran out. The wind had blown northeasterly tradewinds that had helped us to the southeast along the north section of South America, exactly as we needed. Now we met the southeasterly tradewinds and these headed us as we turned the corner of the Brazilian mainland and tried to sail directly into it. Our only course of action was to sail upwind. We tacked every two hours and played the tide as best we could. Our speed remained impressive over the ground, but towards Rio our progress deteriorated as we tacked and crossed and re-crossed the direct line.

Once we got past the easternmost extremity of the land, the typical weather pattern should begin to push us southwest and into the path of a more northerly wind. The further we sailed south, the more it would push us on again.

Below Rio the winds turned westerly again, but we would not concern ourselves with that.

We tacked in close to the coast as the evening turned to darkness. I squashed myself into the seating behind the navigation station. I had the laptop on my knees. "I've got a connection. My emails are downloading. There are lots again. There's one from Kate." When it seemed there were no more I added: "We can tack out to sea again now."

"What is Kate saying?" asked Rene. It was cosy inside the lit cabin, a speck of warmth in the ocean and the night sky. We two men were taking a meal together. Sylvie was on deck. I could see her outside the cramped cabin, sitting in peaceful contemplation of the dark night, perched in an alert contentment high on the moulded deck of *Sweetheart*.

I peered into the laptop as the boat rolled and pitched. "She wants to know where we are. I haven't told her." I glanced up at Rene. "I still don't know if I can completely trust Kate. I feel sure I can't trust Pete." I turned back to the bright screen. "She says that Tony and Rex joined the *Christina* last night."

"Is it Friday already?"

"They were a day early," I said. "Apparently, they were keen to get going. Amy and Helene join later."

"So Friday's tomorrow? I'm losing track of the days. Where are they now?" Rene spooned bacon bits and rice in to his mouth and then washed it down with an inch of red wine in the bottom of a plastic beaker that floated across the saloon table to and from his hand.

"The *Christina* leaves in the morning. Helene and Amy are due to join them first thing. And yes, it's Friday tomorrow."

"That's a lot of people. You'll have trouble getting past the entire crew of eight and the four guests."

"I know," I said. "Can you suggest an alternative?"

"Wait for them to go ashore and then board the boat."

"The crew would have nothing to do but clean the bright work and then it would be all but impossible to get onboard. Besides, where do you park an Open 62 without people noticing?"

"We could drop you off."

"No offence, but you two wouldn't be safe alone on this thing if the weather turned nasty." I saw him flinch at the unintended insult. "No, I'll get you to put me onboard in the night. It'll be much safer."

"Does Kate say anything else?" asked Rene. He nodded towards the laptop and wiped his chin. He brushed away the accidental slight against his sailing skills.

"She says to get in touch. She says to keep safe."

"Ask her what else she's found out." Rene stood up and put on his foul weather jacket. "I'll relieve Sylvie for her dinner."

He placed a foot onto the exit steps.

"No offence," I said. "This boat becomes a submarine in strong winds. It's a lot to handle."

Rene turned and smiled. "It's okay, Tom," he said. "In fact, I had thought we had already experienced strong winds but when you said that, it just made me realise that we've barely been in a serious blow up to now." He zipped up his jacket. "Of course I'll help you, but I've learnt something: offshore sailing isn't for me.

238

If twenty-five knots of wind isn't strong, I don't want to see what fifty knots is like in this thing."

"You get regular gusts over eighty-five down south but I wouldn't recommend it."

"No," he said with a tight mouth. He rubbed his big Gallic moustache. "I just discovered that I like the sailing I do now; dinghy racing round the club buoys is plenty for me. I admire you for going to the South Pole, but I know I don't ever want to come with you."

I put a hand on the seat back as the boat rode a big wave. "You know what, Rene? I can't tell you why I want to go out and risk my neck down there in the Southern Ocean with the wind screaming at me and the rigging whistling as if it is going to shatter like glass. I only know the exhilaration of feeling alive that comes over me like electricity. As the temperature drops and the wind increases, suddenly I feel like life is really beginning, like I am only now truly living it. The intensity magnifies the experience. It's a distinctly odd sensation and I think I may be addicted to it."

Rene laughed. "As somebody who likes the comfort of my fireplace and a good yarn in the café, I can only admire you from a distance, and sometimes wish that I was there, too. But, like a man who does not take heroin, I cannot imagine why the addict would flirt with the inherent danger."

"I can't tell you that either," I said. "Why does anyone do anything? Why do some people do nothing at all? OK, let's put that tack in and then Sylvie can come down for her dinner."

Once the tack had been made, Sylvie was sent down. I joined her in the saloon. Sylvie placed her hair behind her ears in her characteristic way, and sat across the seat, feet up. She fingered her foul weather jacket that was on a hook by the companionway and stared absently into the the air. I handed her a bowl of the rice and bacon that Rene had cooked and she sank back into the seat opposite me, smiling wearily and broadly.

I took a long look at her. There was weariness, it was true, but there also was elation, there was tiredness but there was inspirational energy.

"How's it going?" I asked.

Sylvie spooned rice into her mouth, through the food she grinned and said: "Great."

I smiled and turned back to the laptop. I started a reply. I needed Kate to get me a passage plan for the *Christina*.

Chapter thirty

"Angra dos Reis."

"Where's that?" asked Sylvie. The early morning was already warm and the big waves bright with dappled sunlight. Sylvie had stripped off her night-shift jacket and stood in oily trousers and a thick fisherman's sweater.

"According to the chart, it's an inlet about one hundred miles south of Rio."

Rene took off his own jacket as the warmth of the day began to build. "How long before we can be there?"

"Tomorrow night," I said. "If they are at anchor, I can slip aboard easily."

"I thought they were due to go out on a long passage," said Sylvie. She drew the jumper over her head.

"One hundred miles is a long way." I patted her shoulder. "Just because you've sailed over a thousand miles this week, you've forgotten what a hundred is like."

Sylvie laughed. She stood in a white t-shirt with the black braces from the oilskin trousers over her shoulders. She dropped the sweater by her jacket and ran her fingers through her tousled hair. The wind still blowing strongly and the nights had begun to cool after the penetrating heat of the doldrums.

Rene rolled his eyes. "Don't you two ever get sick of being at sea?"

"No!" we both said.

Sylvie laughed again and Rene's big moustache twitched as he gave her an exaggerated frown.

Angra dos Reis tucks in just below Rio de Janeiro and just above Sao Paulo. It is a little haven of tranquillity on the long coastline of South America that faces the South Atlantic at twenty-five degrees south of the equator and forty-two degrees west of Greenwich.

My laptop showed it was a perfect spot for Tony to take a little sunshine and relax with his buddy. If Helene and Amy had not been there, no doubt they would have had girls shipped out to them from the nearby town.

I wondered how he managed to get rid of guests normally. Although Amy was a new addition, Helene must have been with him on several occasions in the past. Clearly, he also made legitimate trips to cover his tracks.

I handed the laptop to Sylvie.

"If they go straight, they will arrive tonight. We'll be there by tomorrow night if the wind holds good. It looks as if we might be able to sneak aboard while they are on anchor."

Sylvie looked up from her breakfast cereal and took hold of the computer. "What if they see you? You may well be shot as an intruder. Remember what happened last time."

"That's true. This way, I could row the dinghy the last part and stay silent."

"I don't like it. If you get it wrong, they will shoot and you *will* die."

"It's the best chance we have. Tony doesn't know we aren't sailing for the UK. I told Patrick to tell him we were still at sea until early next week." I saw her reaction was doubt. I said: "Anyway, what's the weather going to do over the next few days? Anything useful for our raid?"

Sylvie still didn't seem convinced, but she said: "It will be peaceful enough until Monday when there's bad weather coming." She glanced out through the companionway at the bright sky overhead. "We should expect the *Christina* either to hole up where she is or head back to port by Sunday night."

"Saturday is the night, then. Wherever she is, whatever the weather, Saturday is when we will have maximum surprise. After that, this boat will start drawing attention to itself and word will get round."

Saturday morning was bright once more. The wind had slackened to a Force 2-3 and we shook out the reefs for the first time in three days.

"I can't believe we've stolen into Brazilian waters on a racing yacht," said Sylvie. "It's a throwback to the pirates of old."

"No pirate ship hit twenty-two knots surfing down waves," I said.

Rene stuck his head up out of the saloon. He blinked in the bright sunshine. "There's an email from Kate." He handed me the laptop and I peered into the dazzling screen shielding the glare from the sun.

"They are in Angra," I said. "Kate seems to have made friends with Helene. She's feeding her back information about what's going on on the boat. Apparently, Amy is being a prima donna and annoying Helene. Otherwise, all is quiet."

"There's an email from Cluzon," said Sylvie searching her own in-box. "He says the picture you sent him might be of a Russian assassin."

"Might be?" I slapped my hand down on the seat. "We need to know for sure."

"Who's an assassin?" asked Rene.

"Pete Dunleavy, the cameraman," said Sylvie. "Cluzon says the picture is poor because he's looking away but it could be a prison-escapee called Petr Kryk."

"And who's Kryk?" said Rene. "What did he do to end up in a Russian gulag?"

Sylvie was reading from the screen. "Killed three men for money. Ex-Russian special forces. In Russia, he turned a politician's only daughter into a killer. She committed patricide to please him."

"And at the moment he dresses like a librarian," I said.

"Be careful," said Sylvie. "If it is him, he won't hold back. And be wary of Kate, she's been sleeping with him. You can't trust her, either."

"You're right, Sylvie; but the plan stands. Here's what we'll do: under cover of darkness we'll sail right into the bay. We'll turn off our AIS and pick theirs up. It's true they'll be looking out for intruders, so we'd better be mute. No doubt, there will be a guard on deck."

"Remember, mon ami," said Rene. "That guard has already killed. He, too, is also dangerous."

The darkness was complete as the Open 62 came to a gentle rest and Rene dropped the anchor. We could see nothing of the *Christina*, but her AIS signal was displaying. Although she was lost in the black of night, the chart plotter showed us the contours of the land and her position in the bay on the illuminated screen. She was a mile ahead of us, tucked into a safe-looking anchorage in a depth of about ten metres.

Other yachts were also anchored in the bay and some of them had AIS displays. Evening parties onboard should provide some background noise to cover our boat ride across the bay. Once we got close, we would paddle silently the last part to the *Christina* herself.

We stepped cautiously down into the rib and pushed away from the hull of *Sylvie's Sweetheart*. Rene started the outboard and we buzzed steadily through the anchorage and towards the *Christina* close in to shore.

A shaft of pale moonlight filtered through high cloud. It made us visible, a target. Rene cut the engine and we silently glided past a big, blue-hulled yacht. A party was in full swing and they ignored us. Rene pulled on the oars and we moved through the lapping water on silent paddle power and across the bay towards where the *Christina* was anchored nearest to the beach.

Onboard the handsome yacht, soft light glowed from the saloon portholes and in the half-light cast by the moon and the ship, I could see the watchman standing at the stern. He was taking his job seriously and sweeping the bay for intruders. He walked back and forth and kept his eyes open. No doubt, the killing of the bandit had made the crew extremely nervous in recent weeks.

I motioned to Rene and we paddled towards the bow, keeping away from the *Christina* until we were past, and then we headed back towards the boat and quickly sculled towards the bowsprit. I pocketed a screwdriver and a thin torch.

The little dinghy bumped silently against the wooden hull. I reached up for the netting hanging under the bowsprit and grabbed on. Rene sat back in the dinghy, released me, and then paddled swiftly out of sight. He was quickly lost in the shimmer of the water under moonlit blackness.

I clung upside down to the netting and worked my way towards the boat's hull. I placed a hand on the rail and lifted my head up to peer across the deck. All was quiet. Climbing over, I rested for a moment and then, in one quick movement, I slipped over the rail and onto the silent foredeck.

Cloud passed over the slither of crescent moon as I stepped onto the soft planks of the beautiful ship and the moonlight thankfully dimmed. I crept forward along the wooden foredeck, eyes darting from port to starboard side and down to the stern, looking for any movement.

Just then, I couldn't see the guard. He had been down at the stern when we saw him from the dinghy, and I prayed he had stayed where he was.

Light was streaming up through the glass of the overhead hatches. I crossed the deck and lay across the cabin and inched forward to peer down inside.

Tony and Rex were sitting to one side of the dining table and, as I turned my head, I could see Amy and Helene were opposite them.

They were starting what looked like the main course of their meal and were in conversation. Tony was talking, Helene was listening. Amy was taking small bites of her meal. Glasses of red wine were half-drunk and on the fine mahogany table. Rex Tourenasi, puffed up and too fat for his shirt, was listening and eating greedily.

I crept back towards the bow, staying low against the cabin top. The beautifully-crafted stairwell into the ship was in darkness. I crouched and scuttled crab-like over towards it as moonlight began to cross the deck once more.

As the cloud cleared from the moon, I drew back the wooden cover from the top of the forward companionway and it slid with a low rumble. I took a look around and seeing nothing, I slipped inside the ship and tiptoed down the short set of steps to the heavy timber sole boards. Light was breaking through a crack in the doorframe that led aft to the saloon. I could see Tony's left shoulder as he sat to the dining table. I could hear the hum of their conversation but not the exact words. I felt a dizzying euphoria. The mental and physical excitement was buzzing through me. The sensation of stealing into the ship was over-powering. I felt my throat close and as if I might cough.

Staying well back from the saloon, I cracked opened Tony's stateroom door and closed it behind me. I breathed slowly, calming my heightened nerves and resisted the urge to clear my throat. I flicked on the pencil-thin torch and began to search the room for the safety deposit box. Somewhere in this well-appointed little room, there was a secret compartment that was barely visible. Captain Johnson had told me it was almost impossible to find. He said that the dead crewman, the one knifed in a bar brawl, had said it was so well hidden the police wouldn't find it in a thorough search.

I looked around me. Built into the joinery of the yacht were the bed to my right and the chest of drawers to the left. I gave the bed an uncomfortable glance, aware of the appalling things that had occurred there. I closed my mind to the horror.

I knew the box had to be part of the structure of the boat, built into the wood itself. There were a dozen places where joinery met the frames of the great yacht. I felt around the edges, looking for something that might give under my hand. My breathing was more regular, sweat trickled down my temple. I felt my head pounding with blood. It blocked out all other sound. I doubted I would hear someone coming.

I lay under the bed and ignored the anxiety. I worked my hand along the seams. Nothing. I worked along the bulkheads aft and then forward. Nothing. I caught myself working too fast. *Calm down, and check carefully*, I thought.

I glanced at my watch. I had been in the room eleven minutes already; far longer than I thought possible. I wondered if Tony was already onto the dessert. I imagined Rex shovelling food into his purple, wine-stained lips.

I dared not open the door to check; better to continue my search as long as possible and then make a run for it. I felt along the underside of the in-built chest of drawers taking my time, the pounding in my ears filling my world.

Something protruded slightly from the chest downwards. I worked my hands under the wood of what felt like a box. This had to be what I was looking for. There must be a way in and surely the safe would be inside. It was smaller than I had imagined but it could easily be enough to hold two dozen of the small memory sticks.

I put down the torch, and with both hands, like a mechanic working under a particularly tight engine, I felt along the shaped wood. My hand came across an opening. I touched it carefully. It was a keyhole. The wooden box held something valuable.

I fished the screwdriver out of my pocket, excitement rising again. There would be nothing subtle about this break-in; Tony would know soon enough when he found the memory sticks missing. I dug the screwdriver into the box and rammed downwards. The wood shifted minutely and I rammed again and pressed my foot under the chest and onto the unseen screwdriver handle. I heard the splinter of wood.

I crept down and felt in the cracks. The front of the box was damaged but still effective. I dug away with the screwdriver and prised the front of the box away with my fingers. Another louder crack retorted from the chest as the front came away to my left. I looked up and waited but no-one came. I went back to my search. I felt inside. There was the familiar feel of metal. I crouched down and waved the torch along the front of the box. Inside the wooden casing, the grey metal of a safety deposit box was clearly visible.

I heard voices suddenly raised as if the dinner party had heard a good joke. I continued with my furtive task and edged out a second and the right-side piece of wood, cutting my finger on the splinters.

I worked the screwdriver under the metal edge of the safety deposit box and began to break it away from the underside of the chest of drawers.

Outside the room, it had fallen quiet once more. I listened for a moment and the soft sound of voices continued and the sound of my breathing was loud but my pounding head had receded, and then I continued with my efforts. After a while, I had to rest as my arms were beginning to burn with the exertion. I checked my watch. Seventeen minutes. I prayed they were drinking brandy; dinner must surely have been finished by now.

I shoved the screwdriver in fiercely. My sweaty hands were slippery with frustration and perspiration. I swiped my arm across my brow to dry it. The screwdriver skewed and rattled under the chest.

I lay down and placed my hand underneath the ornately carved piece of furniture as far as the bulkhead. I clasped the screwdriver with an inspiration from luck and desperation. I kept my arm out at full length, turned the screwdriver back towards me and inserted it between chest and box. I heaved. This time, the metal safety deposit box fell away and bounced on the floor.

I seized it. I pocketed the screwdriver and put out a hand for the door handle. I switched off the torch and opened the door minutely.

The door swung slowly and creaked loudly. I looked down the corridor both ways with my eyes blinded by the sudden absence of the torchlight. Down the faintly lit walkway, the saloon door was still ajar and a crack of light fell down the dark beams of the corridor's floor. I could see nobody at the table. They must have moved elsewhere. I prayed that if it was to go on deck, it was to sit in the cockpit and not to stroll on the foredeck where I was heading.

I put the safety deposit box under my arm and made for the stairway. The adrenaline was back in me and the euphoric feeling of being back in the boatshed, breaking and entering as a child with my little brother, Dan, was coursing through me. Except this time, I knew it wasn't just a child's game.

I put a hand on the railing. A sound alerted me. Behind me, the door from the saloon was opening. I placed a foot on the bottom step. I heard no more.

I slipped quickly up the stairs, throat burning. Then a voice shouted and I was bursting through the forward stairwell and onto the deck.

The black of night was still on my side, but what moonlight there was faintly illuminated the pitch pine and teak inlay of the deck. Sounds behind told me that the guards were coming. I would have no time to signal to Rene, just escape.

I ran to the port side bow rail. Somebody shouted in Portuguese. In one movement, I ran and dived over into the river. The safety deposit box was tugged by the strike of the water. I held onto it with a death grip. Swimming with it in my hand made it almost impossible to gain ground, and I side-stroked away awkwardly, box gripped tightly.

As I came up for air, shots hit the water. I could make out a guardsman firing down on me from only a dozen feet away. Tony was by his side shouting instructions and pointing. He grabbed at the gun, wrestled it from the guard and he took careful aim on me. Bullets hit the water and I expected any moment to be struck.

I swam until I was exhausted and then the purr of a motor could be heard in the distance.

Relief was momentary. I realised it wasn't Rene but the sound of a second dinghy. Somebody onboard the *Christina* had their own rib out. I lay back in the water too tired to swim further, exposed to any boat, hidden only by the darkness. I had to catch my breath, the shock of the cold water and the fear of capture had my nerves shooting overload into my brain.

All I could think was, *not as cold as the English Channel, I can survive it.*

"Rene!" I shouted hoarsely, mouth full of salt water.

Immediately, a response came from the night.

"Where are you?" he whispered hoarsely.

"Go south of the boat," I called, spluttering against the lapping sea. "Ahead of the bow."

Someone on the deck of the *Christina* had also heard the instruction and I could hear them relaying my position to their own dinghy.

With relief, I heard Rene's engine cut in. He was off to my left, near the shore and under some over-hanging trees. He gunned the outboard and came out of the gloom towards me.

I kept thinking about Josh being shot from the trawler when he had been in the life raft. I was the same; helpless in the water.

Across the bay, I could make out the other dinghy coming through the darkness from behind the *Christina*. Shots were zinging from the water and then I saw Rene weave alarmingly as more gunshots struck the water at his bow wave.

The two dinghies came towards me competing to be first, weaving and twisting. I took in a lungful of air and ducked as the *Christina's* dinghy came close and surged over me.

I came up for air gasping with over-worked lungs. They span the little boat around. They had seen me re-surface. They were coming straight back.

I swam away with heavy arms, making for Rene, desperate for salvation. Rene was closing on me, head down and jerking the dinghy forward. He looked up and powered the boat straight.

"Hang on!"

He hit me with the inflatable dinghy and I heard shots puncturing the chambers as I threw out an arm to grab on.

The dinghy was hit several times. We would sink in minutes. I grasped the lines attached to the outside of the dinghy and yelled: "Go! Go!"

Rene gunned the engine again and he span the front of the boat through ninety degrees.

We tore through the anchorage in the black of night with Rene ramming the throttle full and me in the water holding on to the starboard lines. Forcing my arm out of the water, I made sure the box was onboard.

The second rib chased us, shots were ringing from the water and one bounced noisily from the engine casing.

"Tell Sylvie to get ready to leave," I yelled.

"I already did," said Rene, head down by his knees. "She has pointed *Sweetheart* out to sea."

Shots hit the dinghy again and the air was now escaping more quickly. We were beginning to lose hull shape and tension and the speed began to suffer badly.

"To hell with this," said Rene. He pulled out his revolver. He turned and fired shots behind him at our pursuers.

The second dinghy stopped as the helm pulled up, avoiding Rene's gunshots. I rested momentarily as we lost speed and I held my head up for breath. A second later and the other rib was moving fast again.

We struck the Open 62 and bounced. Rene grabbed the wire stay. He leant down, put his large hand on my shoulder and hoisted me out of the water, first onto the dinghy and then in one powerful move, onto the hull. He yelled out with the effort like an old, injured bull.

I climbed over and onto the smooth fibreglass deck of the racing boat. I held up my prize for Sylvie to see and then threw the safety deposit box into the cockpit ahead of me. Rene climbed aboard clutching his knee. He dropped into the cockpit with a gasp for breath.

Sylvie, focused, gunned the engine and *Sweetheart* started to shift towards the exit from the bay.

The *Christina's* dinghy was closing in on us as *Sylvie's Sweetheart* struggled to get her bulk moving. Rene stood, holding one hand steady and he aimed his pistol carefully. He fired six shots into the bow of the advancing rib.

As *Sweetheart* began to get moving, the chasing boat sagged and I caught a glimpse of two people on board. Exhausted, I dropped onto the seat and stared back. I could see that Tony was standing in the bow of the rib wrestling a new cartridge into his rifle and behind him someone on the helm was lost in the darkness.

Then he looked up and I saw Petr Kryk for the first time.

Chapter thirty-one

The yellow-hulled Open 62 that we had christened *Sylvie's Sweetheart* made it to the entrance of Angra de Reis before the *Christina* had picked up Tony from the deflating tender.

We could make out the shape of the big yacht as it held station beside the floundering rubber dinghy. We stared backwards at its ghostly shape in the night, as we ourselves motored ahead at full throttle.

We kept all instruments off except for the depth sounder. I stood facing the rear and followed the dinghy's movements in the dark as it came back alongside the magnificent, old yacht.

"They'll still have radar," I said. "But let's not make it too easy."

Sylvie took my hand and gripped it. "Thank God you made it back, Tom. Are you alright?"

I kissed her, and relief at getting back to the boat washed over me.

"I think I just saw Pete..." I started. "Petr Kryk, I mean."

"I'll call the local police," asked Rene. He limped, his left knee held out straight, and his face contorted.

"Wait for the box. I must be able to prove it first." I took the screwdriver out of my pocket and worked it into the small opening at the lid of the heavy, metal box.

Darting glances behind me, I stood the metal container on its end and took a winch handle and hit downwards on the screwdriver, wedging it into the opening.

I worked at it. After a few minutes I looked up. "Where are they now?"

"There," said Sylvie pointing.

A hundred and fifty metres back, and the *Christina* was chasing us down.

"How are we going to lose them like this?" asked Sylvie.

"Once the box is open we won't have to worry about them."

Rene jumped down beside me, knee rigid. He took the winch handle from me and began to pound at the screwdriver's plastic end with heavy blows, his face screwed with pain.

"That's if the police can get here quick enough," he breathed.

A shot passed through the rigging.

"They're gaining," said Sylvie. "We've lost five metres since you asked where they were."

Rene smashed the box down on the cockpit floor. He twisted the screwdriver and the box split. Memory sticks skidded into the cockpit.

"We've got him," I said.

I ran below for the laptop and handed it back up to Rene.

Shots peppered the boat. Rene forced a memory stick in to the computer's driver. He waited with forced patience and glanced back over his shoulder.

I held the VHF, ready to turn on and transmit.

"Encrypted," said Rene. "Password protected."

Bullets hit the back of the ship.

"They are fifty metres behind us," said Sylvie.

256

"Try 'Helene'," I said.

Rene punched it in.

A bullet skidded past Sylvie's head and she ducked.

"No good," said Rene. "We only have two more attempts."

"Can't we decode them back in the lab?" shouted Sylvie. "You don't have to know first, Tom. Rene and I are witnesses to the gunshots."

"They'll say we are pirates and they'll be right. Rene," I looked up desperately at him. I thought, *What password would Tony use?*

"Rene," I said. "Try 'Amy.'"

Rene tapped on the keys quickly and hit enter. He drew his body up so that the leg could be eased. He dropped his head forward. For a moment, I thought he was concentrating on the screen, but then he fell forward and landed on the cockpit sole, smothering the laptop.

I climbed over to him and raised the heavy man's head, but he was dead. There was a single gunshot to the back of the skull. His empty eyes registered nothing. I let him down to the side carefully and he sagged to the floor; his peaceful face, large and serene with the flambouyant moustache, was oblivious.

I looked away from Rene's lifeless face and down at the laptop. A scroll of numbered files was listed on the screen. I tapped the first one and, as shots rang over the boat, the first images of a hotel room and a young girl began to appear.

Sylvie put a hand to her mouth and stared at Rene's spent body.

I kept watching the computer screen. I saw a hotel room with fire drill in Portuguese, then a man's feet appeared and the camera panned up his legs to brown corduroy trousers. It was the very film we had seen before.

The camera panned away from the man's face before it could be seen and turned towards the wall and the mirror on it. Somebody's hand came out to a white and black cover on a mobile phone. An iPhone 6.

The camera caught a glimpse of the person holding the camera in the mirror as they picked up the phone – Kryk - and then panned back shakily towards the crumpled bed. It caught an image of the man with the corduroy trousers full in his leering face. It was Tony.

This time he was getting naked and there could be no doubt what was about to occur in the film.

"It's them," I said. "I saw Tony."

Sylvie turned behind her. "They're almost on us," she said quietly. "I can't stay on the helm. Go!" Sylvie ran from the wheel and slipped into the darkness down the port side of *Sweetheart* as the *Christina* closed to within three metres.

I crawled inside the boat and over to the VHF radio to hit the transmit button.

"They've jammed it!" I shouted. Tony must be transmitting from the *Christina* to stop us getting through on the emergency channel, 16. I turned to 15, to transmit anyway, in the hope someone was listening there.

The *Christina* hit the starboard side on the Open 62's rear. Someone jumped and landed aboard *Sylvie's Sweetheart*.

His gun raised, I turned to the companionway and stared into the bland, blue eyes of Pete.

"You're Kryk," I said.

He stared down on me.

"That name signs your death warrant," he said.

258

He motioned me out of the saloon with the automatic weapon. I climbed up the short steps slowly and stood up fully.

For the second time in a month, someone cracked me across the head with a blunt instrument. This time I saw my assailant, it was Petr Kryk with the butt of a rifle.

Chapter thirty-two

When I came round, my wrists were tied so that the circulation was cut. My hands were swelling. I tugged at the ropes and found I was attached to the wheel pedestal. Kryk was helping someone down on to the boat from the *Christina*.

"Amy," I said. "You're helping them."

She knelt beside me.

"What do you mean?" She twitched her neck to one side, a fresh bruise was visible.

Amy picked up the memory sticks and placed them into her trouser pockets. Kryk stood over her searching beyond us, down the boat.

Amy, on her knees, stretched back and threw the empty safety deposit box over the side.

"You've got to help me," I said.

"Help you? Steal Tony's accounts?"

Amy knelt down further so that her breath was warm against my cheek. Her ashen face, pale and black around the eyes that were wide and haunting, whispered: "What's wrong with you?"

"You wanted a rich man to cling on to, Amy. Why didn't you wait? I would have been rich."

"You could never be rich like Tony." Her black eyes gleamed with avarice even now. "Tony is a genuine billionaire. He can buy anything he wants."

"Can he buy you?" I stared up at the paleness of her skin close to my face and the bruised neck.

Amy picked up every one of the memory sticks from the floor of the cockpit and then jerked the one in my laptop free. She tossed the laptop over the side of the boat into the black water.

I shot a glance down the boat in the hope of spotting Sylvie but she was out of sight. I turned back as Amy looked up once more, her white features the same, her expression strangely unfamiliar.

"You know they're not the accounts, don't you, Amy?"

There was a hint of doubt and her black eyes shifted to mine. "He said to throw them over the side."

Petr Kryk had been standing behind her and watching Amy collect the USB sticks. Now, he looked beyond us and down towards the bow of the boat searching for Sylvie. He stepped forward with a cautious black boot and climbed onto the cabin top.

"Call me when you've finished." He left us in the cockpit and stepped lightly into the darkness.

I said: "Keep one of the sticks, Amy. Hide it."

Amy watched Kryk go and we heard him call in a low voice: "Hurry up. I'll be back when I've found the French bitch."

Amy's black eyes took careful stock of me. "Very well," she said. She quickly tucked the memory stick from the laptop into her sock, hiding it. "I can't promise anything."

"Just look at it. Your name is the password, Amy."

"It is?"

"On there is a film, Amy. You need to see what he is."

"Billionaires do what they want." She breathed warmly on me, eyes nervously darting back towards the *Christina*.

I indicated Kryk up forward. "Pete Dunleavy, you know he's really an electronics expert from the Russian Army. He's called Petr Kryk. He's a killer."

"Look, this is insane," said Amy. "I'm stuck in this, Tom. If something is wrong, you must think of a way to…"

The faint blush of colour on her cheeks fixed the waxy beauty of her youth. There were no lines, no age spots. Only the grey-blue bruise on her neck was the same colour as those dark, sunken eyes.

"Since very recently," she whispered. She stared around her, conscious that Kryk would come back any moment. "Since Kryk got here, people started dying."

"Amy, that's what I'm telling you. You're not safe."

"This will protect me." She stood by the rail, and one by one she dropped memory sticks into the sea. She glanced down to the one in her sock. I couldn't tell if she meant dropping the data or holding onto the one at her ankle.

"Are you staying with him?" My hands were beginning to burn with the restricted blood flow and they were beginning to go numb.

"I…" She turned her cold, white face away from me.

I could see over Amy's shoulder that someone else was walking towards the bow of the *Christina*. It was unmistakably Tony's rotund waddling gait. He climbed over with some difficulty; his plump body unused to climbing across obstacles at sea. He landed on the stern of *Sweetheart* and caught his breath.

Kryk also came back. He moved quickly, agile and strong. As he turned, I saw the difference between Pete's placid face and Kryk's assassin's features. The slick hair and the intensity completely changed him.

Gone were the glasses and the air of meekness. Just the simple fact of a facial expression, a haircut and other clothes made him someone else. Kryk glanced towards Amy and seemed to smile greasily. Amy turned away from him and back to me.

The Russian went to the stern to help Tony down on to the deck.

"I've finally seen the evidence for myself," I said in a low voice. "How will you protect yourself? He's killed so many people, Amy. He's employing assassins. He will tire of you and kill you, too."

Amy glanced behind at Tony and Kryk. She turned back to look straight at me.

"Is the money really worth that?"

"I'll survive," she whispered. "That's what we both do best, isn't it? Two survivors. I'll just keep moving on."

"You can only move on if you are free. Don't you see? We followed the wrong money this time. You're taking such a terrible risk... I don't think you're as important to him as you imagine."

Amy clutched my arm. They were coming towards us. "Come after me," she said. "Where is Sylvie? I can protect her."

I stared up at Amy, mouth open. I didn't know what to say. She stared back at me and nodded her head, imploring me.

Tony was suddenly there. He indicated to Amy that she should go and she stepped away, eyes still burning into mine. Amy passed Kryk at the stern and they exchanged a flat look between them. She climbed back onboard the *Christina*.

Kryk, the Russian assassin, took in the unmanned wheel that was jogging from side-to-side in the flow of the current.

He looked ahead of the boat. It was still moving forward with plenty of speed.

"What happens now?" I asked. I felt my forehead where the new injury was by bending down to my bound wrists. A thin trickle of blood came away against the back of my hand.

Tony came to stand beside me and for a long time he simply gazed ahead as if into the distance.

Kryk looked down the boat once more, an absent expression of disinterest on his face. "Where's the French tart?"

"I don't know," I said. "If you mean Sylvie, she fell overboard."

Kryk laughed with a short bark. He came to stand in front of me. He looked behind him and then swiped his hand across connecting with my jaw. I knelt and tasted the sweet, metallic blood.

The *Christina* rode against *Sweetheart* with a grind of wood on plastic. In the darkness, I caught a glimpse of Amy standing on the bow of the beautiful, old vessel.

I nursed my face with the back of my bound hand.

"I'll take it from here," said Tony.

Kryk stood back. He handed Tony the automatic rifle and said in a low voice: "Make sure."

Tony stood in front of me; he wrung his hands together like he was some cartoon villain, a fat pantomime despot full of nervous discomfort. He frowned. He sagged. He whined.

"I am not a bad person, Tom." He spread his hands and his plump stomach fell to protrude forward. He might have been comical if he wasn't about to kill me. His face had fallen like a scolded child's. "I have been trying to protect you."

I could only feel a knife-like pain in my hands, and a dead sensation. The ropes were knotted against my

264

wrists and I struggled to release some tension but they wouldn't give.

"Youth is renewal," said Tony as if continuing a previous conversation. He watched me twisting my bound wrists together. His face clouded with dismay, the big eyes were doleful and sad. "You don't understand the impermance of youth. It disappears in a moment. And everything to you is new. Exciting. Me, I've seen everything." Tony turned towards the bow of *Sweetheart*. "I tried to save you a dozen times, you know. We all did. I gave you every possible chance to walk away from this." He hunted around with his eyes, as if seeing this alternative universe. "Now, I have no choice. *You* have given me no choice." He was searching around the boat. "Where is Sylvie Melville?"

"Look, Tony, forget Sylvie. Between me and you only. Me, you and Kryk." I glanced past the two men and back towards the *Christina*. I searched in the darkness for Amy. I could see her outlined shadow standing unmoving on the bow of the ship, a dark shape in the night.

Petr Kryk was standing almost below her on the stern of *Sweetheart* where he waited for Tony. Now, Kryk said: "Let's go."

"Not until we have Sylvie Melville, as well. Where is she, Tom?"

Truthfully, I said: "I have no idea."

With impatience, Kryk said: "Just let the boat hit the rocks."

Tony glanced towards him. "Wait."

Kryk said nothing but he tensed in irritation at the command.

"Why did you kill Josh and Bernie?" I said. "Couldn't you have stolen back the evidence?"

Tony suddenly was with me, out of the dream world he was imagining in which he was a force for good. He smiled warmly. His round face, with the soft, dimpled cheeks, was delicate and filled with tenderness.

He patted my cruel face. "Young people are so easily confused. You think all this world is just for you. Old people deserve some respect. We deserve to take something, too." He seemed helpless. His loud voice was imploring. "But you're all so black and white. Youth good, middle-age bad. Just ungrateful children in an adult's world. But why can't adults join in the fun, Tom? So what if I cross over? I'm flesh and blood. Why should anyone else care? Why steal my tapes?" He flashed quick eyes at me. "You kept coming back to the films, Tom. Josh and Bernie made themselves quite clear, too; they were going public. Too many people knew."

Tony set the boat's course with quick hands on the wheel.

"Up ahead," he said, "is a shoal of rocks. I'm sure they'll find the boat in the morning. You never know, you might survive it. If you do, remember I am only doing what I have to do. Killing is not in my nature."

You've killed so many people…you're delusional."

Tony started. "No, Tom. I am not a killer, I told you. I am misunderstood. There are things, I admit, I like to… do and to get them I have to use particular types of people to help me."

"Like using Russian assassins."

"A useful inheritance. He told me you were after Patrick Colt. Of course, I never believed that's what you thought." Tony laughed quickly as he felt along the coaming, searching for a loose rope. "Jenny and Rory were my insurance," he said, "but this time you've

266

shown your true agenda. Luckily, we have stopped you before it's too late. Jenny and the child can be protected."

"Leave them."

"Children need adults, Tom. They just don't know it."

I looked out into the night, and seeing the faint outline of the *Christina* and Amy's dark shape on the foredeck, I yelled: "Amy, help me!"

Tony glanced back to the *Christina* as it silently shadowed our progress.

I could see that Amy had placed one foot on the rail and that she was watching us. She said nothing; her facial expression was lost in the darkness. If she was thinking how to intervene, I could not tell. I knew it was useless; Kryk was there.

Kryk said to Tony: "The rocks. Come now."

Up ahead, the jagged outline of the coast seemed to be advancing on us more quickly as *Sweetheart* motored steadily forward.

Tony fired the automatic rifle into the bottom of the boat. The damage would be fatal. He lashed the wheel with a short strop of rope.

I could see the cockpit knife more than a metre away from me hanging from its lanyard and swinging to the boat's roll.

"Amy!" I shouted again.

Tony turned towards me. Pained, he said: "Amy won't help you now, Tom. She is fully with me. We're getting married."

"*Married*? You and Amy? What about Cecilia?"

Tony twisted his body. He held the automatic up and pointed it at me.

"I love her," he said. "I want to marry her."

He looked ridiculous with his sagging, plump apple-shaped stomach and his round, puppy-dog face. I couldn't imagine how Amy could be with him. "Does she want to marry you? You're so old. Has she seen your movies?"

Tony stepped back, lowering the gun. His big, round eyes fell and his chubby face darkened. I think he would liked to have been able to, but I realised that he couldn't pull the trigger. He climbed out onto the deck coaming and across to the stern. He put hands up into the bow mesh of the *Christina*. Kryk took back the automatic rifle and pushed him up, hands under his fat bottom.

A flare, like a shooting star, seemed to descend from the heavens and it struck the *Christina* at the bow. It descended under water still shining brightly.

On *Sweetheart's* stern, Kryk turned in confusion to the black sky. He peered up to where the flare seemed to have come from and he fired the automatic into the empty air.

Tony, hanging from the mesh at the yacht's bowsprit, had failed to climb. His hand slipped. He shouted fearfully: "Kryk!" but Tony fell into the waves between the two boats.

A second flare came down from the air. It came from the top of the mast. Sylvie must be up there, I realised.

Kryk had turned to Tony in the water and the flare struck him in the back of the knee. He yelled in pain as the intensely bright projectile sliced into the top of his calf muscle. Without thinking, he threw himself into the water.

From my position, tied to the wheel, I craned to see over the ship's hull. Somewhere, the two men were both in the cold water in the black of night.

I could see Amy was also staring down from the *Christina's* bow. There was a crewman beside her – the immature boxer. He was pointing and relaying back to Captain Johnson.

The Open 62 was already beginning to falter in the seas. Water would be pouring up from the wound inflicted by the dozens of bullets fired into her hull.

A wave slammed at the two boats, and the *Christina's* great planks groaned with the fresh injury to her bow as she sheared against *Sweetheart*. And then the old, wooden yacht was drifting free, leaving us to our fate.

I stared back at Amy, hoping she could do something and confused that she had allowed Tony to influence her, to drag her down this deep. I remembered the bruised neck. He had done that. She was his possession. I shook my head with guilt. Surely, I should have stopped him getting control of her. She was with me when they met. I had introduced her to a monster. He wanted to marry her…

A moment later, we hit the rock.

Sweetheart shuddered into the underwater obstacle with a ripple of unquiet. The engine, still stuck in forward, whined, and, together with the wave action, the racing yacht continued to drive itself forcefully onto the shore.

The *Christina* was only a few metres back from the jagged rocks and holding station. *Sweetheart* began to crumple.

I reached out for the cockpit knife. It was impossibly out of my grasp. The boat rose and fell heavily and I crashed against the wheel. If it had been Dan, he could have wriggled out of it, but my brother was somewhere safe. My hands screamed pain at me.

I saw a movement, Sylvie was climbing down from the mast. She scrambled past the boom and over the cabin top and threw herself against the bucking wheel to put her arms around me.

"That was a risky place to hide," I said. "Please, my hands." I held out my burning wrists and the ropes.

Sylvie turned and yanked the knife from its clip. She slit the lines and the fire in my wrists seemed to race up my arms as the blood began to flow again. Sylvie kissed my face with tears running down her cheeks. I felt the fear in both of us, and the relief.

"When we hit the rocks, I thought I would be thrown clear," she said.

"It's okay," I said. "You did everything right." I held her to me, soothing her, soothing myself.

I rubbed my wrists, staring back. Life was returning to my hands. Painful pins and needles stabbed at my palms.

"Where's Kryk? Where's Tony?"

Sylvie held the flare gun ahead of her. "I've got one more flare," she said.

I went inside the cramped cabin. The VHF was smashed with everything else, bullet holes through it. I couldn't see any more flares.

"Do you have a phone?" I shouted.

"It's gone," she called back from the deck.

The *Christina* had remained on station, a few metres from the rocky shoreline.

Sweetheart was smashing against the rocks, dashing herself bodily against the shore.

"There!" yelled Sylvie. She fired the flare gun into the water. Petr Kryk's head appeared in the orange light before he dived down out of sight.

"Where's Rene's gun?" Sylvie was searching in the cockpit in shadow as the boat began to collapse into sections, wide gaps growing in her beams. The mast was already at a crazy angle and the shrouds loose and flailing.

The *Christina* seemed almost silent. The crew were nowhere to be seen. It was as if the ship was deserted and proceeding ghostlike.

"The rib's out," said Sylvie.

Behind the *Christina,* their deflating rib, damaged in the gunfight, had been lowered into the water on a long line. It moved with awkward shudders because the chambers were soft and undulating in the seas.

"We have to get over there while Kryk and Tony are in the water."

We took the two rigid lifebelts from the stern pushpit.

"Now!" I said.

We jumped into the sea. The water was a shock of cold even in the warm climes of Brazil.

I held Rene's gun high above my head, hoping to keep it dry and Sylvie did the same with the flare gun although she had no more ammunition for it.

We swam pushing the lifebelts ahead of us. Ten metres, no more.

I could see Tony being hauled into the rib by two of the ship's crew. His heavy body was difficult to roll over the softened rib's side.

I couldn't see Kryk.

We were close to the bow.

I threw out a hand to catch the bow mesh. Now I could see that they had located Kryk. He too was being dragged over the rib's floppy starboard tube.

A crewman hauled on the long line and the rib slipped back towards the *Christina*.

Sylvie had a hand on the mesh. We climbed together.

The rib was closing on the stern of the *Christina*.

I held Rene's gun in my right hand and felt out for the pitch pine woodwork with my left.

I indicated the foreward hatch to Sylvie. She stepped forward and dropped down inside the boat. The darkness inside was complete.

Sylvie held up a hand for silence and to rest. Water dripped from her tense face.

We heard the big engines begin to shift the *Christina*. We knew that meant that they must be back on board.

"She's moving forward," I said.

We stared up and heard feet crossing the deck overhead. Our eyes began to adjust to the dim light. The *Christina* shuddered. Now, they had brought her to a halt.

Without warning, gunfire sounded loudly over our heads.

"They must be firing on the 62," I said.

A few moments and the gun must have been emptied of bullets. I heard Kryk swearing and then the sound of someone crossing the deck above us, limping heavily.

I shot a glance to Sylvie. She wiped her face of the salt water.

"Ready?"

We heard the engines and felt the *Christina* moving astern.

272

Gunfire sounded again. This time from within the saloon.

"Who was shot in there?" asked Sylvie.

I shook my head.

We kept eye contact and the sound of firing stopped as if fading away.

"On deck," said Sylvie. She waved the empty flare gun upwards.

I went first up the dark staircase and I raised my head out on the deck.

It was silent.

The rocks were disappearing from view as the *Christina* motored astern.

We slipped on to the lovely deck and crawled on our bellies down the port side. At the cabin top, I crawled to a port hole and peered inside. The crew were laid out, dead. I could see them side by side and sprawled. Captain Johnson lay, mouth open as if staring and so did his crew.

I heard voices.

Down in the cockpit, Kryk and Tony were there in the dark.

I stood and fired the gun.

Sylvie followed me, pointing the flare gun with its empty chambers ahead. Her wiry body tensed, ready.

I heard shouts.

Kryk fired. Sylvie stumbled on the deck. Another shot from the cockpit and Sylvie fell, hit the rail and went overboard in a sudden rush.

The *Christina* was turning. No-one was on the wheel and the yacht's helm had locked over to put the ship into an arc that would send it backwards so that it too would eventually strike against the shore.

Sylvie was alone in the water but I could not see her. I was shocked at how quickly she had disappeared into the blackness of night and how insignificant she had become in the shifting waves.

I turned back to the boat. I couldn't see Kryk or Tony. I fired and ran down into the cockpit. The night gave me no clue where they were.

From behind the mizzen mast, I heard a sound. I turned. I thought I saw someone there. A man.

Kryk came from the shadows to my right. I fired into his chest but the gun was empty.

Kryk had his pistol out. I lunged towards him.

Kryk fired and I felt the thud of a bullet hit my leg.

I fell, stunned with a pain like a deadened leg, not the sharpness I had imagined I might feel, and I noticed the warmth of the wooden deck as I lay panting like a dog at Kryk's feet.

"That's for the flare," he said. He limped closer.

I put out a hand to grasp his ankle. He aimed the gun down on me. This time, he did not speak.

I stared up. A gunshot rang out.

Kryk fell to his knees in front of me. He dropped the gun and his eyes rolled in pain as he fell to the deck.

I grabbed the weapon from the floor and stood up fighting against my injured leg.

It took me a moment to realise what had happened. I looked up and around. Tony had disappeared, Kryk was down.

I span round to the saloon entrance with the automatic raised to my eye.

Helene came onto the deck. She was holding a rifle and she lowered the gun as I watched her. Her beautiful features creased into tragedy as she began to cry.

Chapter thirty-three

I lowered the automatic and grabbed Helene's wrist. Staring into her eyes, I shouted: "Where's your father? Where is Tony?"

Helene dropped her rifle onto the deck. She darted a glance towards Kryk's limp body.

"Is *he* dead?"

I didn't know. Kryk wasn't moving and was curled in a loose ball. I had to find Tony first.

I threw the spare rifle into the saloon and held onto Helene's hand. I shot a quick sideways glance at Kryk and went down into the saloon. I could see the VHF. I needed to call the Coastguard. Someone had to go after Sylvie in the water.

"Where's your father?" I asked again, urgently this time. I dragged my injured leg down the companionway steps.

I heard an engine flare into life.

"He's gone in the rib with Rex Tourenasi," Helene said and she pointed off the ship. I could hear the rib was moving away in the dark.

"He left you here?"

"I wouldn't have gone with him." She had regained composure. She wiped her streaming nose.

"Where's Amy?"

She shook her head. "I don't know."

I ducked inside the companionway and headed to the VHF radio.

As I had imagined, the VHF was taped down to broadcast static on channel 16. Then I saw up close the horrible sight of the dead crewmen. Shot and laid out like victims of a war.

I could barely glance the way of the ghostlike ashen, anguished faces on the eight angled bodies, set out like a gruesome morgue. Captain Johnson was at the far left of the lifeless group, his brightly sea-distant blue eyes were directed towards the bulkhead and emptied of life. The young boxer was lying with almost peaceful features at his feet, his muscle slack and bloodied.

I ripped the tape off the VHF and said breathlessly: "Mayday, Mayday, Mayday. This is sailing vessel *Christina*, *Christina*, *Christina*, we are two persons on board and one casualty in the water. Repeat: a casualty in the water. Our position," I read off the GPS co-ordinates eyeing the corpses as if they might suddenly rear up and avenge their untimely deaths.

Very quickly the VHF response came. It was the blue-hulled Brazilian party ship that had also been in the anchorage. They were coming to help. They had seen flares and had already alerted the Coastguard.

Behind me, Helene sat down. Her little cocktail dress was flimsy and she needed something to keep her warm, to protect her. She held her knees close to her, eyes fixed on the dead crew. There was a jacket by the companionway and I placed it around her shoulders.

"You okay?" I asked.

"No," she said gently. "Oh, my God, no."

I pointed up the stairs and we silently headed up on deck again away from the bodies. She glanced behind her once with wide eyes back at the awful scene and I dragged her arm and pulled her away.

When we got on deck, Kryk had disappeared.

Chapter thirty-four

The Coastguard vessel took Helene and me from the *Christina* at three am.

I was greeted inside the safety of the ship by Patrick with an unaccustomed five o'clock shadow on his chin and he looked exhausted.

"How is Sylvie?" I asked.

"She has been airlifted to hospital with exposure and medical shock," he said. His eyes were dark. Quickly he added: "But the medics seemed to be positive; hopeful of a full recovery."

I nodded wearily.

"What happened to Tony?"

"He got away in the rib," I said, "with Rex Tourenasi. Petr Kryk – I mean Pete - has disappeared."

Patrick winced. "And Amy?"

I shook my head this time. "I don't know. They must have taken her with them."

I lay back, leg strapped heavily. The bullet had been removed and the wound cleaned.

Patrick took a blanket from one of the Coastguardsmen and wrapped it around Helene. The big ship began to surge forward. A second Navy ship had arrived to take responsibility for the *Christina*. The Coastguard took us away from that terrible shore. We left the grey frigate behind as the sailors began the dangerous manoeuvre of putting hands on the swaying deck of the *Christina* from their own gun-metal grey rib. The rocks of the shoreline tore *Sylvie's Sweetheart* apart a few metres away.

"I can't believe what you've just told me," said Patrick.

We were standing on the dockside waiting for Helene to come ashore. The sun was already hot. The light too bright.

"You had no idea?" I said. I shielded my eyes.

"I promise you," said Patrick. "If I had known what they do, I would have gone to the police myself."

It was what anyone would have said but somehow I thought it was the truth.

We waited on the dockside. Patrick was there to bring Helene to Cecilia and we watched as she stepped down the short gangplank from the Coastguard vessel with the grey blanket around her shoulders and helped by a young guardsman.

"Patrick," I asked. "Have you ever lost your phone?"

Patrick gave me a sideways look.

"A couple of months ago," he said. "How did you know?"

"But you got it back, right?"

"Yes," he said. "Rex Tourenasi found it."

"Rex did. And did you ever upset Rex?"

Patrick shot a glance towards Helene.

He leaned in so that only I could hear him. "Rex doesn't like me because of Phillipe," he said. "It upset him. A lot. Look, I knew they had private parties and I admit I was discreet about because I thought it was just women that they paid, not…" he trailed off.

Bright morning sunlight streamed over the hills.

Patrick put on his sunglasses as Helene arrived on the dockside. He didn't finish the sentence but gave her a tight smile.

The overweight Brazilian Police Chief, Romana, was heading our way across the uneven concrete. Behind him, the city was alive. The journalists were already standing three deep at the perimeter fence. They had cameras trained through the linked chain taking long-range footage.

"We have to save Amy," I said to Patrick. "And we can't let Tony and Rex escape."

Chief Romana stopped in front of us. He shifted his over-burdened belt under his enormous round stomach. He blew out his cheeks and tidied his shirt tails. He stood with his feet facing ten-to-two.

"Mr Shepherd," he said. "What has happened now?"

"Chief Romana, I want to report Tony Drax and Rex Tourenasi to be paedophiles." At last the truth was out. "I had proof but… I don't know where it is now." I wouldn't put Amy in more danger.

The policeman's eyes appeared to flip and blink at the same time. He leaned forward and his big belly seemed as if it might topple him over. "Do you know what you are saying? These are two of Rio's most powerful men."

"They are very dangerous," I said.

"And the proof. What sort of proof do you have?" His eyes remained wide.

"Video film."

Police Chief Romana gave a fleshy smile that showed a row of big and very clean teeth. "We really need to see it. Where is it now?"

"I can't say. They have also kidnapped his assistant, Amy MacKintosh."

"Are you sure?"

"She might have got away," I admitted.

"These accusations cannot be spoken lightly, Mr Shepherd. Do you know it is true, or not?"

I hesitated. "I can't prove that," I said. "But I did see the film."

"Look, I am trying to help you, believe me, but only the facts. If Ms MacKintosh got away, where would she go?" He tucked his hands into his belt and pulled upwards. He puffed out his cheeks.

"Last I saw her, Amy was on the *Christina.* She has a new apartment in France," I said. "If she can, she might try to go there."

"I will speak to M. Cluzon," said the chief.

"But you must find her. She is in incredible danger."

"I will put my best men on it." His fat cheeks bulged as smiled sympathetically. "What will you do, Mr Shepherd?"

"I need to find a friend of mine, Kate Hutchinson."

He spread his hand. "I'll have a car take you wherever you need to go."

"I'm grateful," I said. "I think I should take Helene home to her mother first."

The chief's extended hand retreated. "I understand from the Coastguard that Miss Drax was a witness to the murder of the yacht's entire paid crew. We need to interview her."

"Then you had better come up to the house," I said.

The police Chief considered this.

"Very well, Mr Shepherd, I can do that." He turned towards the building and the crowd of reporters at the perimeter fence.

"Follow me," he said.

I put my arm around Helene. She pulled the sailing jacket over her head to protect her face from the photographers, and we walked towards the waiting police cars. The sunshine was already powerful over our heads.

"I can't believe we let them get away," I said.

Kate paced across the large, sunlit room and back towards the bookcases. I watched her from the window of the library. It was calm now. Patrick sat across from me, hands across his lap but Kate was still twitchy and she smoked as she walked.

"Where would they go?" said Kate.

"Tony and Rex must have contingency money and a bolthole somewhere," said Patrick. He had shaved and he was wearing an expensive and different blue suit. He appeared pristinely groomed once more.

"What about Amy?" asked Kate. "Does Tony have her with him?"

I stood by the French doors. I had showered and patched up my new head wound. This one was less significant than the first. My fearsome features were this time unsullied, I thought, as I caught a glimpse of myself in the mirror. I still looked the devil. But my leg wasn't so bad; the bullet had come out cleanly and I could move quite well.

Helene was in the lounge giving evidence to police officers. Cecilia sat with her, and her mask of make-up could not hide the astonishment and horror that she obviously felt at the story she was hearing.

Patrick, Kate and I had been sent into the library to keep out of the way of the investigation.

Kate waved the cigarette smoke. I watched her for signs that she was, like Pete, really working for Tony.

"We don't know where any of them are, do we? Look, I know you told me what happened," she said, "but tell me again, why is Patrick here?"

"He's helping us."

"But I thought you didn't trust him," said Kate without embarrassment.

I shot a glance his way, unsure how to explain to him how my attitude had changed or explain to Kate what I now knew about Patrick that made me trust him. And then there were my new doubts about Kate; she was after all, Petr Kryk's lover.

"Thing is, I found out why I should be able to trust him," I said. "Patrick's iPhone was in the film we saw. I think to implicate him."

"Why?" asked Kate.

She exchanged looks with Patrick who smiled awkwardly.

"You'd better tell me," she said. "I'm none the wiser."

"P. wasn't Patrick after all," I said cautiously. I kept the matter of Phillipe and Patrick to myself. Regardless of whether I could trust Kate, it wasn't public knowledge.

"Who's P., then?" said Kate.

"Amy seemed to be saying that she's been having an affair with Tony. Tony says he wants to marry her. Tony must be P.," I said.

"With Tony? I thought she didn't like old people."

"Er, no, that was me, I'm afraid. Her last boyfriend before me was fifty. She obviously does…"

"It's the money," said Patrick cutting in. "Amy likes the money."

"Christ," said Kate breathing out smoke.

I glanced between them. "She's in terrible danger. Helene has said that Pete and Rex also killed the crew. Eight people, all shot. Essentially, simultaneously."

"That's awful…," said Kate. "Unthinkable."

"Helene said that Pete showed them how to kill the men, but that Tony couldn't pull the trigger when it came to it so Rex and Pete did it."

"Pete actually helped kill the crew, Helene said that?"

"Pete," I said, "is not who you thought he was. He has been working for Tony all along. I'm sorry, I saw him coming out of Tony's study when we were staying here. He didn't tell us about it. Did he tell you?"

Kate blanched so that for once her warm, smooth colours seem to dim. "No," she said. "He didn't."

I pulled out my mobile phone. "There's more. This came from Cluzon just before we boarded the *Christina*. It's an email in reply to a photo I sent of the four of us. I sent it through Sylvie. Cluzon put Pete through the Interpol files. It took a while because Pete turned away when the houseboy took the picture. But he's not who he says he is. His real name is Petr Kryk. He's a Russian assassin and his forte is turning women. He trains them to kill." Kate struck her chin high and then hunted round the room for an ashtray. "And Sylvie shot him with a flare gun," I added.

Kate couldn't find a suitable place to stub out her cigarette and eventually threw a magazine on the floor and used it as a base to grind out the cigarette with her stiletto shoe. Something in her defiant, animal expression as she crushed the stub showed what she was really thinking about Kryk.

She waved away the cigarette smoke energetically and colour returned to her face.

"Is there," she said, stopping only once the magazine was in shreds, "is there any possibility that they have gone to England?"

"What for?"

Kate winced and her handsome animal face shone with perspiration. "The one thing that you were most afraid of – that they would go after Jenny and Rory."

Chapter thirty-five

This time, I called the police. Now that Sylvie and I had both seen his face in the film, there was clear evidence that he was a paedophile. And a murderer, or at least he had ordered murders even if he couldn't pull an actual trigger. Now, there was no reason to keep my fears about Tony to myself. I spoke to a very understanding detective in Cornwall. He gave me his word that a 24-hour protective custody would be placed on Jenny and Rory.

I wanted them to be moved, but he insisted that keeping Rory at the hospital and protecting that location would be better. I accepted his solution unhappily and got into a taxi for the airport.

Kate and Patrick followed me out of the door.

"I'll come with you," said Kate.

"And I'll find out what I can here," said Patrick.

I saw Helene's face at the window of the main reception room. She glanced my way and gave a flicker of recognition before turning back to the policewoman inside the room.

"Make sure Helene gets some trauma counselling, I don't think she can bare the image of those dead bodies in her mind."

"Good luck," said Patrick. He smoothed his neat tie and I noticed that some of his self-confidence had returned. "I'll see to Helene. I know her mother can take care of her."

I called ahead. The first flight back to the UK was in five hours time. It was a forty-five minute drive to the airport. I banged on the glass partition of the taxi.

The driver glanced back.

"Take me to the city hospital first."

The warmth in the hospital room was oppressive. Sylvie was lying on her back, staring at the ceiling and asleep. Her breathing was calm and controlled with shallow intakes and her lip seemed to tremble minutely on each exhale.

I had sent Kate ahead. I wanted some time alone with Sylvie, even if it was to wait quietly by her side.

For two hours I sat and watched her breath in, seem to hesitate and then exhale without force. I scribbled a brief note on the bedside table. I kissed her forehead. As I left, she stirred a little but then she went back to a medically-induced sleep without seeing me.

I arrived at the airport, paid for a hotel room and visited a store.

For thirty minutes, I stood in the shower and rinsed away what I could of the filth of the last few days. Then I re-dressed the leg bandage, put on entirely new clothes, threw my others in the bin and headed for my flight to London.

I found Kate at the airport ticket desk. I pulled a cap down low over my head and buried myself amongst the crowd. The journalists missed me as I darted through security, limping as I did, and finally I slipped into the safety of a plane seat.

I left Kate in London twelve hours later.

Six hours after that, I arrived inside the grounds of Truro hospital, Cornwall.

I was greeted by a single police officer at the doors of the premature baby unit. One sole police officer wasn't enough. I would have to do more, like get Jenny and Rory away.

As I stepped up to take the handle of the door, I could see Jenny through the window coming towards me. She was smiling grimly. The hollowed eyes of widowhood stared out from her under-nourished face.

"Hello, Tom."

"How is Rory?"

"He can go home in two weeks," she said. Then quietly she whispered, smile vanishing: "What the hell is going on?"

Chapter thirty-six

"…So it's really unlikely that they would come here. It's just an insurance policy against it."

Jenny was watching the policeman standing in the hall outside the little family room where we sat. She followed my words whilst her eyes followed the policeman and they filled with tears and what looked like a mixture of distrust, horror and incredulity.

She said nothing but turned away, pulling down the sleeves of her Breton-striped jumper. I noticed it was the top that she had been wearing in the photo Josh had kept pinned up in *Ocean Gladiator* as we sailed around the world together. Amy's photo had been on the wall on my side of the boat until a wave had doused it, running the colours. Jenny's photo had miraculously remained dry throughout, much to our amusement. No matter what weather we hit and what objects had become salt-water encrusted, Jenny's photo remained dry.

She said: "If Tony knows that you have seen the evidence and Helene can identify the murderers, what use would it be to come here now?"

"None," I said. I wanted to believe that, too. I wanted to believe that I had come here for no good reason other than to see that they were safe. Jenny was right; there was no reason for Tony and Rex to come after her and little Rory. Why would they do that?

I picked up a cup of coffee from the sideboard above the little fridge in the tight and shabby family room.

Jenny shot a glance back towards the ward, eager to return to Rory.

A shadow caused me to look up; the policeman was coming into the room.

"Mr Shepherd," he said with the measured tone of policemen everywhere, "my governor says to tell you that they've picked up a man in Argentina who saw Rex Tourenasi and Tony Drax escaping."

"What did the man say?"

"That they got into a light aircraft and headed south."

I turned to Jenny. "I don't like it," I said.

She smiled wanly, touched my arm and flicked her dark hair behind her ear in a way that reminded me of Sylvie. She stood up. She had lost all the baby weight so that she seemed terribly thin and the white tinge of her make-up free face showed anxiety and doubt.

The policeman had been watching her and he dropped his gaze and went back outside.

"Jenny, I'm sorry, we have to get Rory away from here."

"He's got two more weeks in hospital…"

"I don't know what Tony might do."

"You just said he'd do nothing."

"But who does he blame for having nothing?" My leg was aching and my head pounding. Adrenaline was trying to tell me to get her away, anywhere but here.

"Why don't you have a break?" said Jenny. "You know you look like hell."

"What do you need?" I asked her.

"My God, Tom, you're serious."

Chapter thirty-seven

I checked my emails; still nothing from Amy. I lay back against the mahogany cabin in the cockpit of a thirty-six foot 1968 Sparkman and Stevens-designed yawl and it was a very pretty boat.

The sun was blinking through low cloud that whispered across the skyline in the windless evening. The yawl, *Arabella*, swung to a lazy tide on a private buoy on a backwater river, not much more than a muddy creek, called the Deben.

The pub on the riverbank was quiet but for a few stragglers, despite the glorious sunset that stretched over the west and the low hill. The turn of the river allowed for a west facing riverbank on the east coast of the UK and I surprised myself by being impressed by this simple place and the pretty public house nestled amongst trees by the tiny red-sand beach. Not the rugged beauty of the great cliffs of Devon that thrust down into a pounding Atlantic Ocean, but the soft, slippery, deep mud of the shelving coastline of the east, a lost sleepy grey-water world.

Six days after breaking Rory out of the hospital and we rested doing nothing but gathering mud and cockles in amongst the curlews and heron, and listening to the plaintive calls of the oystercatchers bickering in poetic cries over the lugworms and shellfish in the deep, oozing and thick, black mud of a forgotten river.

A voice called me.

"Dinner is ready."

I put down the laptop, halfway through another email from Johnnie Walter asking yet again if I was free to talk at the Royal Cruising Club, and went to help.

"Don't worry," said Jenny, "it is all done. Just take these things up on deck."

After the meal, my phone rang. It was Cluzon.

"Chief Inspector, how may I help you?"

I was in the cockpit. The light on the water came through patchy high cloud. The wind had fallen to a whisper. Jenny was below decks washing up the dinner things.

Cluzon sounded weary. I checked my watch. It was an hour later in France and would be nearly ten pm there. "I thought you might like to know, we found the trawler," he said. "It sails out of St Nazaire. The owner – the fisherman - rented it to a man, and a woman he didn't get a good look at."

"Do you know who they were?"

"His description matches Petr Kryk's. The fisherman only glimpsed the woman going onboard and from behind. She wore a long summer coat. Not much use."

"That's a hell of a boat to lend to a stranger…"

"Paid ten thousand Euros for one day's charter, cash upfront. When he heard what had happened, the fisherman kept very quiet because he knew that this must have been the real reason for the charter, that his boat had caused the sinking of *Ocean Gladiator*. He was scared. He said he fixed up the scars on the boat and said nothing to anyone."

"That tells me something," I said noncommittally.

"Are you sure you didn't see the gunman?"

I looked out across the water, the phone soft against my cheek.

"I didn't see their face," I said, "but I think it was a woman."

"And the woman," said Cluzon. "Who is she?"

"I don't know," I said.

"Be careful," said Cluzon. "You upset some pretty big plans. Remember, Petr Kryk isn't the only tiger ever to be mistaken for a lamb."

Jenny came on deck and I terminated the call.

The *Arabella* rocked peacefully in the night time and the sound of the bird calls drifted away to silence. I could hear the faint sound of Jenny's breathing.

She had, at first, told me that I was entirely insane to want to take Rory out of hospital and then when I had said I wanted to get him on a boat, she knew I was. But Rory had done okay. He was a fighter like his dad and he was beginning to put on weight. Other than crying in the night, he was as good as gold now he could cuddle his mother properly.

I opened my eyes wide. How long had I been asleep? I couldn't tell from the still darkness.

I turned to my phone. Three am. Dousing the glare of the light, I lay back thinking, what was it that had woken me from a deep sleep?

I sat up, crossed the saloon and stood to look down on Rory and over at Jenny. We slept on either of the two saloon berths, one on each side of the boat, with

292

Rory in the forward cabin in his moses basket. Jenny could feel the protection of someone near her and get some sleep and Rory could have a private place to keep him from waking when we made dinner.

I checked my phone, so far there was very little information about Tony Drax and his lawyer, Rex Tourenasi.

Three days on the river Deben had seemed like a lifetime away from the mad circus of chasing them. To her credit, Jenny didn't spend the entire time telling me how much she hated me for dragging her into this mess.

I got up and walked through the boat, stepping up the soft, wooden steps of the companionway and into the handsome, mahogany cockpit.

Although she wasn't mine, I liked the feel of *Arabella*. Touching her wooden beams and planks was like a home-coming. There was a tenderness in her care-worn, handled parts. She belonged to my cousin, a native of the east coast, who tended to her soft, wooden needs diligently.

Casting a long look around the boat and beyond to the moonlit, muddy shoreline, with water cascading in on the flooding tide, I saw nothing but stillness and drifting water.

I turned back.

"Oh," I said. "You made me jump."

Jenny said nothing but eyed me with fear.

"It's okay," I said. "We're alone."

"Did something wake you?"

"No, it was nothing," I said. "I just woke up."

Jenny touched my shoulder.

"I'm going back to bed," she said.

Sylvie called me the next morning. We spoke most days. She was finalising her work schedule. She had given notice to the French police.

"When do you leave?"

"Only ten days to go," she said. "But it's unbearable. I tried to get back into work, but too much has happened."

"What are you going to do?"

"I am emailing you a picture right now. Take a look."

I fiddled with my phone, coming across the email from Johnnie Walter again and then the picture.

"Very nice," I said. "Two weeks in Fiji?" The photo had been taken from a brochure and showed the ubiquitous palm trees on a deserted beach.

"You've got me wrong," said Sylvie. "Hold on a minute... I'll call you back."

She went and I looked up at Jenny who was playing with Rory, holding him up above her head. Sunlight glimmered from the white tray. It was like being a family.

The phone rang again.

"Yes, Sylvie?"

I motioned to Jenny that I wouldn't be long on the phone.

I sat up, alert. Jenny instinctively clutched Rory to her. He sensed the change in his mother and he began to cry.

"What is it?" she asked.

"They've been spotted," I said. I relayed back to Jenny as Sylvie spoke quickly into my ear. "They have been seen in France. They think Tony went to his house for something."

I felt Jenny's calm exterior, covering that terrible conflict. Here she was with me playing families but her husband was dead, killed by the father of his mistress.

She rocked Rory and bounced him on her knee and smiled to him. A tear ran down her cheek.

Weak British sunlight reflected from the water. Jenny said nothing, Rory yawned and his head dropped to one side, and I tried to think what to do.

Chapter thirty-eight

A cool, east coast breeze off the land drew the pretty yawl, with her cut-away stern and slender beam, through the grey waters of the North Sea. The flat landscape, with its shingled and deserted beaches, gave way to the grey and white scatter of waves.

Seagulls followed a little fishing boat that chugged relentlessly towards the river Alde. The miniature trawler swayed from beam to beam as it crossed the shingle bar and turned upstream into the flooding river.

Jenny, in a thick woollen jumper, tucked herself behind the warmth of the wooden cabin with Rory in her arms swaddled against the cold. I steered for the entrance, lining up the short row of houses on the shingle with the grey Martello Tower, built to keep out Napoleon's untested invasion.

The river accepted us, and the fast-flowing current took us quickly in through the slim entrance and into the dog-leg and winding, canal-like river entrance. After following beside the sea as if transfixed, the river eventually cuts inland towards the fertile soil of East Anglia.

We dropped the hook in a small anchorage in view of Orford Castle and the pretty, little village quay. It was Monday morning. I put the kettle on and I checked the time. Six am. A three hour sail at dawn on a breezy, early summer's day; it was a good way to start the day.

"Where can we go?" said Jenny.

"We just need to be patient here. We'll be okay. He'll be caught soon enough."

"And if he isn't?"

I shrugged. "I honestly don't know."

The phone rang.

This time it was Helene.

"I want to see you."

"Okay," I said. "When?"

"I'm in London from the fourth. Meet me there?"

"Okay," I said. "I can come on the fifth, I have a meeting with Kate. What's it about?"

"I've heard from my father…"

"What did he say?"

"Not over the phone," said Helene. "Where are you?"

"I'm sailing in East Anglia."

"Just watch out. Petr Kryk is still on the job."

I smiled to Jenny.

"What is it?" she said.

Sylvie rang me a little later. I asked if she had any news about Amy but there was nothing new.

Sylvie found my constant worrying about Amy an irritation; but I couldn't stop thinking about her. Why would she agree to marry Tony when she knew what he had done? But I had found nothing. She had gone to ground or been taken. I felt guilty that I was not searching for her but I had to keep Jenny and Rory safe.

According to Helene's testimony, Amy had not taken up a rifle and shot the crewmen in cold blood with the others. Helene had sworn to the Brazilian police that Tony had failed to fire although he held a gun to the crew and that Rex killed two and Petr Kryk six men. Captain Johnson had pleaded for his crew's lives unsuccessfully. The killing had been co-ordinated. They turned on the crew together, taking them by surprise. There were a few seconds when Tony choked and Captain Johnson begged and then Petr Kryk opened fire.

I took tea to Jenny and felt the coolness of the breeze over the cabin top flutter through my hair. White clouds puffed through the blue sky on a quick course to seaward. Offshore the wind turbines rolled, clustered on the sand banks. The wind was rising now that the day was full but we were safely at anchor behind the shingle and the mud.

"The backwaters of England?"

"Yes," I said. "We're going down to the Walton Backwaters this afternoon." It was Tuesday. "Following Maurice Griffith."

"Who?" Sylvie didn't seem to be impressed.

"Maurice Griffith, a writer from… never mind. What are you doing about Fiji?"

"I'm glad you asked," she said. I could hear that she was walking in the town, probably at a French market by the sounds of loud chatter in the background. "Can I send you some details?"

"Yes," I said. "Of what?"

"Of my boat, of course."

I opened the email attachment. There was a picture of a blue-water cruising boat. It was big for one person to handle. It looked strong and I could well imagine it getting to Fiji. I knew Sylvie was tough enough to get there.

I called her back.

"On your own?"

"No," she said. "With a friend."

"It'll be perfect," I said. Perhaps my indecision between forgiving Amy and thinking about a future with Sylvie did not matter, Sylvie already had someone in mind for her trip. She was leaving for the Pacific Islands. I always did think about my love life at the strangest times and just as it fell apart.

I walked down the side of the boat, raised the main, and we tore out of the Alde into the North Sea, on our way to the Walton Backwaters.

I read my emails. Johnnie Walter, again. He was persistent. Would I come to a talk for the Cruising Club at Greenwich Maritime Museum?

Jenny stood in the companionway with a bottle for Rory. The yawl was on an anchor in thick mud up a lonely creek in the Backwaters and the tide was ebbing fast and opening up the salty mud flats for the wading birds.

"It's peaceful here," said Jenny. "I don't mind sailing on the rivers."

"Less daunting than the sea," I said.

I had a meeting with Kate and I could go down to London for a day. Johnnie Walter's talk was the fifth, Helene wanted to meet me and two days later Sylvie was planning to leave Brest. I could see Kate, go to the talk and then travel on to wish Sylvie and her travelling companion good luck and be back in two days.

I just needed somewhere safe to leave Jenny and Rory.

"I have to write an email…"

"Ok," said Jenny. Rory was sucking eagerly on the bottled milk.

Jenny descended into the boat holding her son carefully to her.

I wrote to Johnnie Walter and he replied within minutes. I would be top billing, he said. I quickly replied that I only wanted fifteen minutes and was greatly looking forward to his talk and his exploits in the Atlantic during the war years.

After a short battle, we agreed that I would be the warm-up to introduce him.

"Jenny," I said. "I have to go to London…"

"What about us?"

"I'll leave you here on the boat and be back before you know it," I said.

Jenny gave a dark frown. She wiped her hands on a tea towel and shrugged, putting her chin down.

"You'll be okay," I said.

"I want to come with you," she said heatedly, her face suddenly thrust forward and imploring.

"You can't," I said. "I have to go but you must stay."

"Why do you have to go?"

"Johnnie Walter knows something about the computer files Josh was guarding."

Jenny turned and fled into the boat, tears welling in her big, brown and intense eyes.

It was cruel, but I couldn't take her with me.

I arrived in London on the fifth.

300

I met Helene at the Savoy Hotel.

We took tea.

"How have you been coping?"

"Not very well," she said. She was still the most gorgeous sight in the room but she had covered herself in a plain summer coat even whilst we sat in the warmth of the morning room and she had dark eyes that only intensified her beauty.

"Where is your father now?"

"He's in France, I believe." Her eyes were lowered to the table with its complicated array of cups and tea things. She spoke in a low voice.

"What did he say?"

Helene leaned in across the table. The room was half full but no-one was near us.

"He said to remind you of the deal you made." She stared at me from below, just over the tea cups.

"What deal?"

"That's what I want to know."

"Helene," I said. "I made no deal with Tony." I searched her own face.

"A deal you made on the *Christina*." Her shoulders tightened, closing her up.

"I never made a deal with him…" But I remembered what he had said. "He doesn't mean the deal he made with me. He means the one he made with Josh."

"What deal was that?" She sat upright alarmed at the mention of her dead lover's name.

"'Ruin my child's life and I'll ruin yours.'"

Meeting her in such lavish surroundings made me think nothing bad could really come to harm Helene, although it was pure illusion. Of course, she was no safer there than anywhere else.

The timid eyes seemed anguished. "Old people are sick, Tom. Don't you think?"

I made an excuse to go the gents.

I called Jenny.

"Are you okay?"

"We're fine."

"What's that noise?"

"It's just a helicopter going over. Is anything wrong, Tom? What did Helene say?"

"She said that Tony's in France. Just keep out of sight until I get back. Listen, I won't go to Sylvie in Brittany but I do still need to see the old man. I've got to ask Johnnie about the computer. I'll be back around midnight tonight."

"Don't tell anyone where the boat is."

"I won't."

Cecilia came in to the lounge. I had to leave.

Cecilia appeared sober. Suddenly, as if she had required such adversity to begin to live in the real world, Cecilia seemed transformed from extravagant lush into an intelligent, devoted mother.

Cecilia said she had taken it upon herself to care for the families of those who had been murdered. She was taking on the responsibilities of the great house, Tony's businesses, and the world he had so long controlled. She had tracked down the young women damaged by Tony and Rex and helped them in ways that were not discussed publicly.

"I couldn't do that an alcoholic, Tom," she said.

We drank tea and she told me that Drax Holdings was to be sold off and dissolved and every penny was going into a charitable organisation that she would run to help victims of sexual crime.

Helene, the collapsed, frightened little girl sat up as her mother spoke to us. Her shoulders drew back, her spine straightened and the dull eyes that had followed me across the cucumber sandwiches and tea full of despair, brightened into intelligence.

"May I help you, Mama?" she asked.

Cecilia beamed. Her thickly-lined face broke into a grisly smile of foundation and lipstick.

"We two will be the antidote," she said.

Helene turned to me and smiled. "No more hospital visits," she said with pleasure.

"Lets hope not," Cecilia said and patted her leg softly.

"It will be alright now," I said.

I stepped out into the sunshine, my head spinning. The change in Cecilia was amazing, old age had improved her; adversity had stunned her into purposeful action. Sobriety had transformed her. Like that, she could genuinely protect Helene.

My appointment with Kate Hutchinson at three pm was nearby. We were to go over the documentary before it was sealed and *Race Sailing TV* had an office in Soho.

At lunch, I sat outside a café in Covent Garden and watched the people going by. I spoke to my brother. He was in Sydney, Australia, working his gap year, which was now extending to his gap second year. He was difficult to understand because he was both drunk and standing on the balcony of a noisy pub on the boardwalk of Manly Beach. He sounded like he was having a good time.

The young and beautiful were out in the square. I couldn't help but notice the vibrancy and the attractiveness of youth. There were the old, the middle-aged, the grey and the indistinct, too. They carried the bags, they opened their wallets and they kept a protective eye on the young. They were there, too, I acknowledged, doing the things the youngsters didn't want to, making it possible. I had learnt something, I realised. I had learnt that I missed my mentor, the man who had helped me to become a race winner. Bernie was in my thoughts. He had gone out of his way to save me, literally on one occasion out on the high seas. Old people did earn respect after all, I thought. I felt good about acknowledging that.

I felt a strange sense of peace, and then the phone rang.

"Hi, Sylvie. I'm just enjoying the sunshine in Covent Garden. I'm watching the young hipsters at play. There are some very nice fashion ideas this summer – mostly, without a lot of fabric to get in the way."

Sylvie interrupted my prattling. "Tony and Rex are in England."

I sat up.

"Are you sure?"

"Yes," she said. "Cluzon said they're with Kryk. He brought them in by helicopter."

"Does Cluzon know where they are now?"

"No-one seems to know."

"How can you lose a helicopter?"

"Planes go missing all the time." Sylvie paused. "Will you still come to see me off? I go Tuesday."

"I can't," I said. "I'm going back to Jenny straight after I see Johnnie tonight."

"Of course," she said. "Tom, there was something else…"

"Yes?"

"I… I'll call you tonight."

"Nothing urgent?"

"No. Pas de tout."

Chapter thirty-nine

At three pm, I met with Kate. I hadn't spoken to her much. The documentary had fallen flat as I was no longer planning a race. She was now piecing together the final cut of what they did have, which was quite a lot of background on me and some footage of Josh that I had never seen. Inevitably, the programme was more about murder than sailing.

We sat in the dark room of her edit suite watching silently.

When it was finished, Kate stood up.

"What do you think?"

She turned the lights up in the little room. Her richly cream complexion and bright red lipstick illuminated.

"It's fine," I said. I wasn't really interested although seeing Josh again was welcome. There was a brief excerpt where they interviewed Bernie about me which had been touching.

"Do you have any more footage of Bernie or Josh that you've left out?"

"Not much," she said.

"I haven't been able to trace Amy," I said. "I've tried everything but she has disappeared." Kate was fiddling with the dials of the edit suite but she was listening. "Have you tried to locate Pete - Petr Kryk?"

She shook her head quickly. "I have tried but nothing. Only background."

"Which is?"

"Just what you already know. A paid killer. He was in Russian special forces and was an expert in electronics; he's good with cameras and computers, as we know. You said you actually saw him in one of the films?" I nodded. "And he likes to use women. He has been known to get them to kill for him."

"That's an ugly trick. Do you know where he was after the race?"

Kate frowned and the tiny lines near her eyes appeared. "The night Bernie was killed he went out to film *French Foundations* coming in… but there's no film of it here."

"So he could have gone to kill Bernie instead. And when Stan and I were attacked, where was he then?"

"Then, he was with me all night; first we were both with Tony and Cecilia, later, just the two of us. He never left my sight."

I said nothing. Unless Kate was lying, there must be another assassin.

"He could have doctored the images on Josh's computer, too? If he's an electronic's expert?"

"I guess," she said. She threw back her head so that the long dark hair resettled. "Someone did."

"You know, Tony and Rex were spotted today."

"Where?"

"Here. In England."

She flicked a look my way and stopped fiddling with the edit suite controls.

"Why would they come here?"

"He's after Rory."

"But Why?"

"Because he blames me and Josh."

She sat back. She crossed one shapely leg over the other and lit a cigarette. The smoke curled past her red lips and the warm coffee of her skin.

"Where is Rory?"

"Safe," I said. "Is that allowed in here?"

"No," she said. She drew in cigarette smoke, defiant as ever of the rules.

"What do you think?"

"I would have to say be very careful." Kate blew out a long stream of cigarette smoke that streamed to the ceiling.

There was a tension in her. She seemed edgy.

"Is everything alright?" I asked.

"Yes," she said slowly, sounding like she might say something she would regret.

"What's wrong?"

"Do you trust Sylvie?" she asked. Her long, animal face was suddenly serious.

"Sylvie? Why?"

"Forget it," she said. "No reason."

I left the edit suite in Soho and walked briskly to the tube station. I called Jenny as I walked. She sounded sleepy but she said that they were okay. The reception was quite poor.

I had to be at Greenwich where the talk was being given for seven pm. It was already six and I didn't want to be late as I was first to speak.

I was still mulling over Kate's question when I arrived. Why had she asked if I trusted Sylive? Whatever it was, she had said no more.

The crowd of attendees had already gathered. I spotted the old man, Johnnie Walter. He was in amongst them and laughing.

He was bent forward, gnarled and smartly dressed in his dress uniform from his Navy days, presumably re-cut for his ancient and reduced frame.

"Mr Walter," I said.

He beamed a smile. "Johnnie, please," he said easily but he had that hoarse, thin voice of old age. "I'm ninety-seven, no time to stand on ceremony." He laughed as he glanced at our surroundings in the magnificent hallway of the Greenwich Maritime Museum. "I will introduce you to the chairman, Admiral Sir Alan Peasegood." As they had once before when we had spoken in France, his false teeth wobbled at the difficult name. "He is to compere for us tonight. Quite a crowd. Come to see you, really."

"Come to hear the murky story of murder and the like."

Johnnie Walter walked towards the entrance to the hall at a snail's pace. Standing outside the hotel in France, I hadn't appreciated just how frail the old man was. Despite it, his mind was obviously still clear enough.

"Come with me," he said.

An Admiral was walking towards us and I assumed this must be Peasegood.

"I heard all about the terrible murders, of course," said Johnnie. "Did they ever mention the computer I handed in?"

"No. Tony lost it to the police. That always seemed strange to me."

"If they ever catch him," said Johnnie. "I heard about the escape in the light aircraft. And the girl who handed me the computer, what happened to her?"

309

"The girl?" I said. I still didn't know who had handed Josh's laptop to Johnnie Walter. "That's what I wanted to ask you."

"Yes, blond, pretty girl. A day or two after we spoke a girl handed me the computer and asked me to give it to the police. It was the day after you were attacked, you and the other sailor – Bernie Gramm's partner... Sorry, I tend to forget names these days more than anything else."

"You mean Stan Stosur."

"Yes, yes. Stanley, dear me."

The Admiral was closing on us with a chubby hand out-stretched. It reminded me of the friendly way Tony had entered a conversation.

"Do you mean the blond girl I was seeing?" I said before the Admiral could speak.

"I don't know," said Johnnie. "I get confused."

We shook hands with the sturdily built Admiral Peasegood whose expression told me he found the tail-end of our conversation baffling and we followed his pristine, blue-uniformed figure through to the backstage. He explained the procedure to us as I tried to take in what Johnnie Walter had said.

"Do you mean Amy?"

"I don't know her name," said Johnnie. "I was confused, you see." He smiled wearily. "I had already thought she was in the police."

We sat side-by-side and faced the audience of three hundred in the great hall.

Admiral Peasegood was speaking at the dais. The crowd looked on expectantly.

"What made you mention her now?" I whispered.

310

Johnnie smiled at me with watery eyes. "I saw her this morning," he said brightly. "Yes, charming girl as I recall. I didn't speak to her today, mind, but I saw her walking in the grounds at eleven this morning when I was practising my speech. She had done something to her hair." He smiled again and his eyes shone. "Very shapely legs." He giggled boyishly.

I stared at the old man. He had seen her, seen her here. I called Jenny. I was checking on her every twenty minutes. This time, there was no reply.

"You're up," said Johnnie and I suddenly noticed that there was loud applause from the hall, reverberating from the high ceiling.

I got to my feet, unsteady as if I was falling down a wave. Ahead of me was the dais and I put both hands out and clasped hold of it firmly. The oil paintings of the great, and many of obscure, sea Lords looked down in disapproval.

"Thank you," I said hoarsely and, without thinking, I launched into my speech.

I sat down to another burst of loud applause. Normally, I'm a pretty decent public-speaker; I don't buy into this "I'd rather die than speak" thing. Now that I'd seen death up close, I couldn't equate the two anyway. This time, though, I had no idea what I had just said. If it was rambling or coherent, my mind was on Jenny and Rory and Johnnie Walter's testimony that he had seen the blond girl here.

I tried Jenny again – nothing.

Johnnie was up and speaking. He had a big scoliosis in his spine, I noticed, now that I saw him from the side. It shrunk him so that he could barely see over the speaker's podium. He had a twinkle in his eye and playfulness in his manner that meant despite how he looked, the audience warmed to him quickly.

I scanned the room, something that I had found impossible when speaking. I started going through the faces, mostly men.

There were only two blond women in Brest who could have had the computer. That was either Amy, or was it Sylvie he meant? She was the only blond policewoman.

I would describe Amy as a girl; she was twenty-five, and Sylvie as a woman; she was over thirty. But Johnnie might describe them both as girls at age ninety-seven. He hadn't mentioned the Nordic features of Amy, and Sylvie, to my mind, was quite French-looking. Although they were both blond and attractive, Amy's hair was straight and Sylvie's unruly and they were quite different facially. He had said she had good legs. They both did, that was true, but so did Kate.

The question that most confused me was how Johnnie could have thought Amy, if it had been her, was a policewoman.

I tried Jenny again. She must have fallen asleep. I got halfway through scanning the room, the crowd was laughing at one of Johnnie's anecdotes. I glanced his way; he was a natural story-teller. He turned and winked. I guessed the story must have involved me but I had been far too distracted to take it in.

I smiled. As Johnnie turned back to the audience, he raised his head indicating the back of the room. I followed his line of sight. I scanned the faces. Second row from the back, blond hair under a cap, there was no mistaking. I sat bolt upright as she buried her head in her coat.

There was no question, though. It was Sylvie.

Chapter forty

As Johnnie finished speaking, the crowd stood to applaud him, and I stared down the aisle.

The standing ovation continued as I hunted through the back of the room, and the crowd turned to stare in the same direction. I could see at the end of the column, second row in, Sylvie had gone.

Confused faces watched me as the audience came to order and began to sit down once more.

A hush descended then followed quickly by whispers in the crowd.

Admiral Peasegood, standing at the lectern, said: "We have time for questions."

"Johnnie, was that her?" I said. "Was that the policewoman who gave you the computer?"

"I'm not sure," he said, his voice wavered. "I can't see that far without binoculars these days."

"She's not Nordic-looking, she's French."

"She had a long winter coat like police officers often wear... oh, dear, I'm sorry, perhaps I am confused."

"Come with me," I said. I helped him down the steps amongst the audience.

The crowd murmured and Peasegood started to politely object to our leaving.

"Excuse us," I said. I pushed forward.

A blast knocked me off my feet. I felt Johnnie being thrown forward alongside me. Instinctively, I put

313

my arms around the old man and we fell amongst the crowd together.

I turned. From the floor, I could see the dais was shattered, the podium exposed. Admiral Peasegood was lying where he had been thrown. Whatever bomb had exploded, Admiral Peasegood was the victim.

A cloud of dust was rising from the mangled wreckage of the raised platform. Several of the front row were holding injuries.

The crowd of sailors surged through the doors and into the corridor. Johnnie was pulled from me and dragged along.

I let go of the old man's hand and ran out of the conference room. The big entrance hall was empty but at the back, looking over the grounds, the heavy curtain was fluttering in the light breeze. I ran across to the window and looked through to the outside.

Sylvie was standing in the garden in the late evening sunlight. One hand was in the pocket of her summer coat. With the other, she beckoned me outside.

I climbed through the window, jumped down into the garden and Sylvie took my arm.

"Come with me," she said.

We found a bench in the park. The spring sun was drifting down towards the horizon and the last light dazzled behind the trees. It was still warm. An almost delicate plume of smoke drifted through the shattered window of the museum's hall.

Sylvie took off her cap and stray hair fell.

"Are you ok?" she asked.

"Yes, I'm fine," I said. "what are doing here?" I looked up at her with doubt. "I was coming to see you."

314

She was well-dressed, elegant. Her brittle, rose-delicate beauty was evident to me. Something was wrong.

I pressed redial on my phone as I watched her lips.

"I came to see you," Sylvie said. "I wanted to ask you about... my boat. When I got Kate's message..."

"What message?"

"She texted me. Told me to come."

"When?"

"Right after you called. She said it was urgent. I just got here." Sylvie placed her cap in her lap with a clumsy hand. "I was going to ask you to consider... That's not important now. Look, Kate must have called us here for the bomb. She must be the one working with Kryk."

I stared at Sylvie. The grey eyes were guarded. I watched her hands moving nervously on the summer hat. I had only seen Kate a couple of hours ago. And I had only spoken to Sylvie an hour before that.

There were two killers. An efficient one – Kryk – who had killed Bernie and left no trace. And an inexpert one. One who failed to kill Stan and me. Someone covered in blood as they struck out with a winch handle. I struggled to understand.

Behind Sylvie, I could see Johnnie down on the grass being escorted away. I wanted his help.

"Come with me," I said. "I need to ask Johnnie."

"He's ninety-seven, Tom. Even if his faculties are pretty good, he can be mistaken."

"Anyone can be mistaken. No witness is totally reliable. Why did you come all this way when you must have so many things to take care of on the boat? I was due in France, to see you, tomorrow."

"You said you weren't coming. I wanted to ask you…" She smiled awkwardly. "And I'm here because Kate texted me, she said to surprise you."

"Kate did? What did she say?"

"That we should support you tonight."

That didn't sound like Kate. She knew I could take care of myself.

Below us, the majority of the people had spilled out onto the museum's neat lawn. The plume of dust that had followed the explosion was settling towards the grass and many of the people were covered in a grey layer of soot. I realised I was, too.

"Johnnie's down there," I said. I walked purposefully through the crowd many of whom suffered from shock and deafness. "I should go check he's okay. Come on."

"Yes," she nodded towards the old man. "Let's go down and clear things up."

As I hurried down, I rang Jenny. My phone said I had tried eighteen times unsuccessfully.

I took hold of Johnnie's arm and tugged him away from well-wishes who seemed concerned, but they reluctantly let him go with me.

I turned Johnnie to face Sylvie.

"Is this the woman who gave you the laptop?"

Johnnie looked at Sylvie for a long moment. He was covered in the fine dust from the explosion.

"No," he said. "That is the policewoman I gave the laptop to."

I fished out my phone and found a picture of Amy on it. I held it up and Johnnie took hold of my hand

316

with his own shaking fingers. He squinted into the picture on the phone.

"Ah, yes," he said. "That is the Nordic-looking girl."

He smiled at us as if he had done something rather clever.

"That's the woman who gave you the computer?" I could hear the distant wail of a siren.

"No," he said smiling. Clear as mud, now. "Although she was in France, wasn't she? She ran into me and nearly knocked me off my feet that night when you and...Stanley... were injured. I was out walking. I don't sleep well at night and I was out strolling. Although I do fall asleep at the drop of a hat in the daytime..."

Who else is there? I thought. Johnnie was still talking.

I pushed through my photo collection. The picture of the four of us together in Brazil outside Tony's – the one I had given to Cluzon to identify Petr Kryk.

"This woman? With a blond wig maybe?"

Johnnie smiled again, his bent little frame exuberant through little mannerisms. "Yes," he said. "That is the girl. She said she was from the British police."

I nodded. "And you say you saw her today, here?"

Sylvie saw the photo and glanced up at me sharply.

"Oh, yes," said Johnnie, "this morning; out here in the gardens."

"What here?" said Sylvie. "Kate was here?" She placed her hair behind her ears, pressing her face forward towards the bent, little man.

"Come on," I said. "We have to go. We're putting Johnnie in danger." I turned to him. "Johnnie, I'll see you soon. That was quite a speech!"

317

He laughed. "Goodbye, Tom." He turned to well-wishes. "I haven't been bombed for seventy years..." he said. He sounded more excited than concerned.

I took Sylvie's hand and we ran through the crowd towards the main building of the museum. At the door, we barged our way through the crowd and then we ran through the museum's echoing hall and out through the grand entrance.

We began to run towards the tube station.

I checked behind me. Nothing. We ran. Sylvie nervously turned back to search behind us every few steps. My phone rang and I ignored it.

At the station, we ducked inside and waited for a train. There were a handful of people waiting and it was beginning to get dark. Several more sirens could be heard as emergency vehicles sped towards the museum. Onboard, we sat together in an almost empty carriage heading in the direction of central London.

"What is going on?" I asked Sylvie.

My phone was ringing and I looked to the screen.

"It's Kate," I said.

"Are you going to answer it?"

The train was ducking through tunnels. Light and shadow reflected from the windows. I had phone signal and then it disappeared.

"Kate testified that she was at dinner with Tony and Cecilia and Petr Kryk the night you were injured," said Sylvie, "the night she handed the laptop to Johnnie."

"Yes, Tony's alibi. The first time when Bernie was killed, he says he was with Helene, the second time,

318

when Stan and I were attacked, he was with Kate, Petr and Cecilia."

"And Kate was sleeping with Petr Kryk whose resume says he is a multiple killer and his favourite trick is to turn women he finds into assassins on his behalf."

"Are you saying that Kate tried to kill me and Stan because Petr Kryk asked her to?"

"They were sleeping together. You've been in hiding since Brazil. Today at the speech, it's the first time you have made a public declaration of where you will be and when. Someone could have been waiting for you to come here tonight..."

The phone rang again.

I answered, staring at Sylvie.

"Yes?" I said. "What is it, Kate?"

The line was crackling, the sound indistinct. I couldn't make out what she was saying.

"What's she want?" asked Sylvie.

"I don't know; she's gone."

I stared across the train at Sylvie. I had been blind. Sylvie stared straight back at me.

"Do you have your gun?" I asked.

She nodded stiffly.

The train pulled into a station. A crowd of people descended and walked swiftly towards the stairs. As the doors began to close, I grabbed Sylvie's hand and we ran from the train.

I pulled my phone out of my pocket.

"She's trying again. I have to get outside to get a signal. Come on." I ran towards the exit, pushing through the crowd.

Sylvie stumbled on the stairs.

"Go on," she said. She had stopped. "I'll catch you up."

319

Dozens of passengers were already between us in the stairwell. I ran on ahead.

"I'm getting signal. There's an email," I yelled back. "It's downloading…"

Outside, I stood in the darkening street behind the tube station entrance. The crowds quickly dispersed.

I could see Sylvie making her way towards me. I held up my phone hunting for unseen satellites.

The phone rang.

"Is Sylvie with you?" asked Kate down the faint phone line.

"Yes."

"Check your emails," said Kate.

I found and opened the email from Kate. There were attachments. I opened the first, a photo of a woman's back.

"What does this mean?" I asked.

Kate said: "Have you seen who they are? Look at all the photos."

I scrolled down through a series of photographs. The man in them was walking towards the camera on a beach. A woman with slender legs and shapely hips had her back to the lens.

I glanced up. Outside the tube station, Sylvie was walking towards me very quickly. She had her hand inside the pocket of her light overcoat, probably clutching her gun.

I couldn't understand, Amy was with Tony, Kate was with Petr Kryk, Sylvie was with me, but which one of them had planted a bomb hoping to kill me and Johnnie? Sylvie continued towards me.

I looked down at the phone again. The next photo was a poor quality shot. Except, there was no disguising, the man in it was Petr Kryk, standing on what looked like a Mediterranean beach. The woman, face peculiarly difficult to see under a big hat, that was Sylvie Melville.

It was a miracle that she had come to London to help me in time. Why hadn't she told me she was coming? Had Kate really asked her to come? Kate had implied something wasn't right in her edit suite, but I had ignored it.

Sylvie continued walking straight towards me with deliberate steps.

Which of them was the second assassin? Who was lying to me? I saw Sylvie's hand move inside the coat pocket. She walked straight, steps measured.

"Tom, Tom…" she said.

I broke the connection to Kate.

Sylvie came to me.

I felt two quick, dull thuds and Sylvie pushed against me.

"Sylvie…?" I began, but the blood on my hand stopped me mid sentence.

I dragged her towards a large gap between buildings and dropped down behind it. The little white tiles were grubby with mud where somebody had wiped a boot and I worried that Sylvie might catch something.

I looked at the wounds. Sylvie had been shot twice.

"Sylvie?"

She murmured. At least she was alive.

"My pocket," she said.

I felt inside the long coat she was wearing, careful not to press on the two bullet wounds. Under the flimsy material, I felt the heaviness of a weapon. I dragged the pistol from her pocket and, the way she had shown me on the boat, I unclipped the safety catch and held the gun out in my right hand, and clutched Sylvie to me in my left. We knelt together outside the station, darkness had begun to fall. Sylvie lay against me, immobilised.

"Help!" I shouted to anyone. "Help!"

The empty chug of a bullet thwacking into the upright of the building answered.

It had come from my left. I saw a black-suited woman. She was across the road, alone. I wondered if a security camera had spotted us. No-one seemed to be at the station now except for us three.

"Help!" I shouted again. "Help!"

I fired Sylvie's gun. It's retort echoed loudly from the buildings.

I saw a woman in a black outfit and hat pass across the other side of the now deserted road. She had a handgun with a silencer. She ran quickly. I saw that she had long, slender and shapely legs. She was all in black with her head covered. She crouched low making herself small in the shadows.

She reminded me of the gunman I had seen before, the one on the trawler out at sea. The one who had shot and killed Josh. It had been a woman holding the weapon and I could see it was the same woman.

"Kate!?" I shouted.

A volley of shots hit the thick upright that supported the station's roof.

"It's only a matter of time before someone spots you on the station CCTV!" I yelled.

The next link uploaded on my phone and I stared down on it. It was a picture of a blond woman from behind wearing only bikini bottoms. She was on a beach. She was embracing a man in a pair of high-fashion shorts and sunglasses. Without doubt, they were intimate. Underneath, the caption read.

"Nearly there, baby."

I switched to the phone and dialled Kate back.

"What does this mean? Where are you?"

People were walking towards the tube station entrance. The assassin across the street had disappeared down an alleyway.

Kate's voice was clear. It didn't sound breathless like that of someone running. "Have you looked at all the pictures?" she asked.

"Yes," I said, "most of them."

On the screen, Petr Kryk turned towards the camera and removed his sunglasses to put them down on a table before turning back to put his hands around the semi-naked woman with broad hips and long, powerful thighs on slender, long legs.

The next image and they were kissing, their faces obscured. Then they were apart and faces clear. The woman's face oddly pale.

I put the phone to my ear.

"That's Sylvie. The guy in the cool shades, that's Petr Kryk, isn't? What the hell's going on?"

Passengers began to descend the stairs. No shots had been fired for several minutes.

I called out nervously and a young man in plimsolls came towards us. I hid the gun as he knelt down.

"Are you okay?" he asked.

"She's been shot," I answered.

The young man, black stubble on his chin, pulled out a phone.

"Ambulance, please," he said.

Chapter forty-one

At the hospital, I sat and drank coffee outside a door marked "no admittance." The smell of floor cleaner and antiseptic was pungent. I had a text from Jenny. We had agreed any text would include a codeword – we had chosen *Nappy*. 'We're fine. Rory was asleep and I tried to get some. I'll call you later.'

Jenny wouldn't have forgotten the codeword. I rang the police in Suffolk. The police would go to the boat.

An hour after we arrived, Sylvie was still in theatre having an emergency operation to save her life and I had lost Jenny and Rory.

I heard the door open and close. I peered up at the dull corridor. I stood up. Kate walked towards me, heels clicking against the oppressive echo of the hallway. She wore a light-weight green overcoat very similar to the light brown one worn by Sylvie.

They all wore these coats, I thought.

Kate had her hands deep in her pockets.

She stopped in front of me.

"Any news?"

I scowled with absolute confusion. Had Kate just shot at us whilst I had spoken to her on the phone and then coldly walked in here to question me? She seemed cool, detached. Surely, it was impossible. She had hardly sounded out of breath on the phone. She was calm then as now.

"In theatre," I said carefully. "Bullet one passed though her lower intestine, bullet two lodged in her left lung just below the heart. They don't know yet if she'll survive."

I scrutinised the impassive features of her face through the thick make-up and the creamy-warm complexion to the dead-pan expression.

"It sounds survivable," said Kate, matter-of-factly.

"What do you know?" I asked.

"Sylvie is tough," said Kate searching my own face with brown eyes that dealt in scrutiny.

"Kate," I said. "Did you know Sylvie was coming to England?"

"No." She looked momentarily confused. "Why?"

"She told me you had texted – invited her to come."

"That's not true."

"It must have shown your number on her phone."

"A trick – some sort of electronic intervention," said Kate quickly. "Kryk perhaps."

Had she just shot Sylvie and now come here to kill me? She seemed too cool, too impassive, too… Kate.

"Where did you get the photos you sent me of Sylvie with him - with Kryk?"

Kate put her hands back into her pockets and pulled the light coat close to her. "From a friend of mine who works for Reuters. He took the shots in the South of France three days ago. He emailed them, said that the girl was French-looking."

"But Kryk shot at Sylvie so that she fell from the *Christina*. Was that something they planned? How could they have done that?"

"I have no idea. How long were they together? It could have been since the race ended in France, or even before."

325

"But now she has been shot…" It made no sense.

"Maybe they fell out…"

"I can't believe that." I glanced at my watch. It was only ten pm but the day felt a month long. It seemed an age ago that I had had the appointment with Kate in Soho. And hours since I had called out to the person I had thought was her in the street.

Kate tossed her long, brown hair aside with a shake of her head. Her Italian features were too vital for this ugly green hallway. She seemed out of place. "My friend was on an assignment in St Tropez filming the Classic Sailing Regatta."

"Your friend from Reuters?"

"Yes, he was taking stills for promotional work, a side line of his. He thought he recognised Pete, my cameraman. He went over to say hello and then he realised something was wrong. So he took some shots and made a note of what he heard them say."

"He told you this?"

"In an email he did." Kate took a hand from her coat and gestured towards the operating theatre. "Who shot Sylvie?"

"A woman with a gun dressed in black. The same woman who shot Josh from the trawler, I'd say. Do you know any possibilities? Johnnie Walter says he saw you earlier in the day at the museum. What were you doing there?"

"I came to meet you. I got the wrong time." Her eyebrows were raised with only minute expression even now.

"Why didn't you tell me?"

"I didn't think it was important."

"Why didn't you tell me this afternoon about these photos?"

326

"I was embarrassed. He tricked me…" Kate sat down on one of the cheap plastic seats bolted to the wall. She fished in the pocket of the overcoat. "I had no idea it would come to this…" She indicated the door to the operating theatre. "I started to tell you but it made no sense to me. Like you, I just really couldn't imagine that Sylvie was helping Kryk."

Kate paused and looked up. A white-suited doctor walked through the doors and down the long hall.

"I only got the photos today," she said under her breath, even so the doctor glanced her way as he passed. "How come Sylvie was at the museum?"

"She said you asked her to come," I said.

"It's not true."

"She told me in the ambulance that she had wanted to ask me to sail to Fiji with her – but she said she didn't want to stop me from going back to sail racing and was doubting asking. So when I said I couldn't come to France because of Jenny and then you texted to invite her here, she decided she would come and ask me in person."

"What did you say?"

"I said that we'd better plug the holes in her stomach before we go."

"This is a mess," said Kate.

I shook my head. "I don't know who to trust. You didn't just shoot Sylvie, did you? Maybe you thought she was the killer? You shot her to protect me?"

Kate shook her head. She pulled her hand out of the long coat and clutched a packet of cigarettes.

"That's not it," she said.

I started to object and she stopped midway to her mouth. She held the unlit cigarette in her hand.

The doctor had disappeared at the other end of the long corridor and the door swung closed with two dull thuds.

"Look," I said. "There's something I have to ask you." I was looking at her trying to see the fakery but she seemed too real. "Look, I need to know why you put on a wig and handed Josh's computer to Johnnie Walter."

Kate shook her head as if in shame. "It was Pete's – Petr Kryk's - idea. He said he had stolen the laptop and that we needed to get it back to the police as if we hadn't had it. He asked me to give it to a bystander to hand in."

"So you gave it to Johnnie Walter… but why the wig?"

She laughed awkwardly. "To protect my identity in case anyone saw me. It's not journalistic good practice to steal evidence. I assumed Johnnie Walter would be an unreliable witness and that he would probably forget my face quickly at his age. I told him I was a British police officer and to hand the computer over to Sylvie Melville."

I nodded. "Johnnie's more canny than he looks, though. He recognised you. Did you ask Petr how he got the laptop in the first place?"

Kate's smile disappeared. "No," she said. "I didn't want to know. I just assumed he had stolen it before the police could take it in."

I said: "What did you see on the computer?"

"Nothing. Kryk must have already doctored the images because it was the same stuff Sylvie showed us on the plane; just a glimpse of male legs."

"It kept Josh in the shit but hid the true identity of the man in it – but that was risky. What if something had been left in that did provide proof?"

"That's the risk-taking billionaire," said Kate. "You've got to be prepared to gamble big if you want to win high stakes. He must have thought he could turn it back on Bernie and Josh."

"You told me that Kryk was with you interviewing Tony and Cecilia that night, it was Tony's alibi for the attack on me and Stan. Is that right?"

"Yes," she said. Her make-up, perfect as ever, hardly creased as she said: "I was there. So was Petr. I can't get used to calling him that."

"So who attacked me and Stan if Petr Kryk was with you?"

My phone rang. It was the Suffolk police. There was no sign of Jenny or Rory on the boat.

Kate's phone also rang and she put the unlit cigarette back in the packet. She listened and walked away from me.

The police had found nothing. I had to go. I knew Tony had Jenny. And I hadn't told Kate in case she was with him. In case she was the female assassin.

Kate also came off the phone.

"I just don't understand," I said.

"Sylvie's in good hands, right?" Kate stood in front of me, defiant. The coat fluttered open.

"I hope so," I said. "Because I have to go."

I started to walk down the long tunnel-like corridor.

"Wait for me." Kate followed, staring into her mobile as she walked. "I have one more call to take and then I'll come with you – I'll help."

Her phone rang before I could answer her. Kate took the call. She followed me along the green hallway listening without speaking.

"You're sure," she said into the mouthpiece. She glanced at me. "No mistaking?" She put the phone in her overcoat's deep pocket as she took long strides down the corridor. "That was my technician," she said. "I asked him to check on the voracity of the photos."

"And?"

"The photos were doctored. Sylvie's face can be pulled straight out of them. That's why she looks oddly pale. Apparently, it wasn't a very good job. I don't think it was even intended to be. And something much worse… my friend from Reuters – he's dead. Strangled in his apartment this morning."

"Before you received the email."

"Long before."

"This was planned, then," I said. "Somebody wanted you and Sylvie to be suspicious of each other."

"And they wanted us together and dead, even now. I just checked my texts." She held up her phone. "Here's a message apparently from you asking me to be at the talk."

For a moment neither of us spoke as we walked. I opened the door and pushed through. I began to run through the sickly-coloured corridors.

"Where are you going?" said Kate.

"Chist, I don't even know," I shouted.

"Come with me," she said. "We must go to the airport - now."

Chapter forty-two

A private flight to Madrid was due to depart at eleven-thirty, one of the last to leave the airport that night.

When we arrived, there were still a lot of people in the terminal building despite the lateness of the hour. We headed for airside and took the long route through a nervous security line. They didn't like the look of us but eventually our unwanted tickets persuaded and we ran to the private room.

Kate called out. Cecilia in her large tinted glasses and Helene in her little brown dress turned to see us.

Cecilia appeared to be embarrassed. She scratched at the back of her hand with long and painted nails. Helene stood up and her mother patted her arm so that she sat back down.

We crossed the room as if infiltrating the upper classes. Kate sat down sweeping the light overcoat around her knees as she did. I smiled to Helene who made tight lips.

"I'm surprised at you, Mrs Drax," said Kate. "My question is 'why?' after what he had done?"

I shot a glance between them.

Cecilia had recovered her composure.

"My dear," she said calmly, sipping from a bottle of mineral water, "when you discover something as terrible as I did, you can go only one of two ways."

Helene and I stared between them.

Kate said: "So you played both parts."

Cecilia's eye twitched. She twisted the bottle in her hand. The perfect red nails dug into the plastic. She raised her tinted glasses and her lined face was painted in heavy make-up. She peered at Kate with eyelids low on her eyes.

"You are disappointed in your boyfriend?"

Kate took a second to reply. "Not really," she said. "When I found who he really was, I didn't think of him as anything other than a criminal who had lied to me. It didn't seem like he'd ever been my boyfriend at all."

Cecilia waved a dismissive hand. "Not as disappointed as I was in my husband," she said ignoring Kate's explanation. Then she softened. "Try finding out your husband of thirty years is a paedophile. That's beyond 'lied to by a criminal'. And for you, too, Tom. It must have been disappointing."

"Yes," I said. "But different."

Cecilia looked at each of us as if appraising our capabilities.

"You don't have anything for me, do you?" she said. "Nothing new, I mean. Because you still don't know what happened, do you, Tom?"

"No," I admitted. "I don't."

"Nor do I," said Helene, the anxious look had returned to her eye. She shot glances between Cecilia and Kate and then at me as if her vision had suddenly clouded.

"Don't worry, my dear," said Cecilia. She patted her daughter's leg, touching her slender thigh with a calming hand.

The airline staff were beginning to become agitated waiting for Cecilia and Helene to board their jet but they didn't feel confident to come forward to speak to her.

The four of us were silent for a moment.

"Very well," said Kate because Cecilia only stared straight ahead and clutched the bottle of mineral water. "Cecilia discovered that her husband was a paedophile." Kate blushed and shot a glance towards Helene. "I'm sorry, Helene, but we all know that this is the truth…"

Helene stared down at her hands. Her shoulders moved in a tiny shudder of anguish but she said nothing.

Cecilia continued to stare ahead.

"She turned to drink," said Kate.

"I'm an addict now," said Cecilia defensively.

"Then she came up with a plan. She would expose Tony and Rex Tourenasi and take over the company. She employed Petr Kryk to seek out the evidence and bring it to her."

Cecilia laughed.

"My dear," she said looking straight into Kate's eyes. "My foolish journalist. Wrong." She waved a hand in front of her as if clearing fog. "I will tell the story. You are unreliable."

Helene blinked and moved a little closer to Cecilia.

"Go on," I said.

Cecilia let the dark glasses fall back over her eyes. "I've never had surgery," said Cecilia. "I was always proud of that fact. I was quite something years ago, you know. When I was young, I was a model." She raised the glasses once more, holding them above her eyes. She stared hard at me and her wrinkled lips pursed. "Of course, it was foolish of me to think Tony would love me forever..."

Kate looked irritated.

Cecilia noticed her impatience. She continued: "Well, anyway, I found out, like you said. I turned to drink like you said. It's got so bad, Helene had to take me to a psychiatric hospital at least twice a year to try to sober me up. One day, when I was too drunk to think straight I went into Tony's study and stole one of the memory sticks. I watched the pictures. Oh, dear God.

"I was so incensed that I posted it to a friend. Someone I knew could be trusted. Someone I had known a long time."

"Bernie Gramm," I said.

Cecilia nodded.

"When I sobered up, I realised my stupidity and I rang him. He had not looked at the photos. He had been sailing in an offshore race. I begged him to throw the package away without looking at it and he agreed. He was a good man."

"Go on," said Helene in a soft voice so low it took a moment to register what she had said.

Cecilia patted her daughter's arm tenderly.

"I got drunk again – there had been another one of these, these terrible... parties... on the *Christina* and so I asked Bernie to open the memory stick this time. He hadn't even been home and his post was lying there when he got back. Before I could change my mind again, he had looked at it.

"Bernie said he would go to the police. I am afraid I was sober again by this point and I convinced him not to. I said I would take care of it."

Cecilia gave Helene a tragic look.

"It was a mistake. I told Tony what I knew. He became enraged and said it was lies. I had a drink, of

334

course became drunk, and I admitted that Bernie had the downloaded images on his computer.

"Tony went quiet. He realised then that he was in serious trouble."

There was a pause as we considered this information. The stewardess came towards us, preparing to ask them to board perhaps.

Cecilia waved her away and the young woman turned with a scowl.

The former model with the heavy make-up and dark glasses took a sip from the bottle of mineral water.

"Tony said he had recruited two people from his firm to keep an eye on me. He didn't say who they were. He said if he couldn't fix it…" Cecilia stopped and finished her drink in one. "The rest you know; Petr Kryk was recruited to help Tony salvage this. They helped him make a last video that looked doctored to confuse his enemies in the hope of creating an illusion. They could show it was faked. They wanted to blame others. Rex even stole Patrick Colt's iPhone and filmed it before handing it back to him later."

"So Petr Kryk could share it publicly?"

"It was risky, but Tony thought he could show faked video stills and collapse the case against him, if it came to that. Clever, old bastard, he was." Cecilia raised her empty bottle in salute.

"He just tried something similar with us, faking pictures of Sylvie," I said.

Cecilia scratched the spot on the back of her hand with the sharp nails, she drew a trickle of blood. She drew up her thinly-painted, black eyebrows and her mouth turned down.

"Petr Kryk's talents with a camera?" she said. "Tony used that to his best advantage." She wiped the blood away.

Kate said: "Why didn't you say any of this? It could be important to any trial."

"Will they ever catch him? Besides, I hadn't worked out who the two people were. I knew one was a woman. It was clear from the way she had started to control Tony. They were merely sleeping together at first. Then he lavished ever more expensive gifts on her," she eyed us. "He didn't normally buy more than trinkets for his girlfriends; a necklace, maybe, but not much more. The other person, I thought that was Patrick Colt. He seemed to be in Tony's pocket but then later he seemed to be pushed aside and when they filmed his phone in that video I realised they wanted him implicated."

"Patrick was out of favour," I said.

"He had upset Rex over something," said Cecilia.

Rex had found out about Phillipe, I thought, that's why he never liked Patrick. He didn't like the idea of the two of them together.

"So then you realised Petr Kryk was the assassin?"

"No," said Cecilia. "I thought it might be you. Helene told me you had threatened her…"

"Threatened?" I said. "That was a mistake…"

Helene seemed almost startled and then she smiled to me thinly.

Cecilia put the empty drink down. "I know, I know. We know that now, of course. I accused Tony of hiring you after you scared her at the party and I could see by his dumb-puppy expression it wasn't you."

So that was how Tony knew Helene had had words with me, I thought. Cecilia had confronted him.

"I know it was just your clumsy way of getting Helene to tell you what she knew. I just didn't know it then." Cecilia smiled grimly. She patted Helene's arm as if unconscious of doing it. "No, it was only when

336

Helene said Petr Kryk had killed the crew of the *Christina* that I finally discovered he was the second killer."

"So how did Kryk hit me and Stan with a winch handle when he was with you, Kate and Tony that night?" I asked.

"He couldn't have," said Kate. "He was with us the whole time."

"You're sure you don't know the answer?" asked Cecilia. She peered at me and waved to the attendant at the same time. The stewardess came back looking irritated to be summoned.

Kate had been with them that night. She may have given Johnnie the laptop but she was the alibi for both Petr Kryk and Tony that evening.

I was thinking everything through as Kate said: "I'm sorry, I really thought that you had ordered the killings, Mrs Drax. It just seemed logical because Tony can't do it himself."

"Ordered murders for Tony?" Cecilia took an involuntary glance towards the stwewardesss but she was out of earshot. "Because he's not a killer? Not even for the love of my life. No, don't concern yourself, my dear. Tony employed killers to take care of the things he couldn't do for himself. I was just glad when I thought that it was over. That Helene and I could go back to normality."

We watched the stewardess cross the room. She stood leaning her weight on to her right leg and smiled irritably.

"There's nothing normal," said Helene in a weak voice.

Cecilia raised one pencilled eyebrow.

"No," she said. She patted her daughter's arm and ordered a second drink of water from the bemused-looking attendant.

"Will you be boarding soon because…?" asked the woman.

"Very shortly," said Cecilia. She gave a brief flick of her hand and the stewardess turned on her heel with flushed cheeks.

Once the stewardess had gone, Kate turned to me. "You told the police that you saw a woman running away before you were struck with the winch handle, Tom. And you said you thought it was Sylvie Melville, the French policewoman."

"I had slept with her and I thought she was coming to meet me but Sylvie can't be the killer because someone just shot her twice in the stomach."

Helene flinched. "They did? Is she okay?"

I realised what I had been trying not to believe for a long time. Cecilia and Kate were looking at me as if waiting for me to speak.

"And if you were all together and Sylvie cannot be the one, then that does only leave Amy," I said. "And Amy has a brand new apartment on the Cote D'Azur."

"I needed to find out if you were trustworthy, Tom, but I already knew she was one of the killers." Cecilia impatiently looked around for the returning stewardess but she was still looking for the bottled water out of sight.

"How so?"

Cecilia patted Helene's arm again. Helene gave her a small, weak smile in return.

"I saw Amy come back from the boat that night," Cecilia said. "She was covered in blood."

"What did Petr Kryk tell you?"

Kate and I were in a hire car and driving to Suffolk. Kate turned to me with the fixed expression, the impassive journalist.

"Only what he wanted me to know, obviously." She thought back. "We met at *Race Sailing TV* a few months into your campaign. He was sent to be my cameraman. Very quiet, very good at his job. He was good at keeping his mouth shut which is why I trusted him."

"Did he meet with Tony often?"

"Not that I was aware of."

"You know I saw him in Tony's office when we were there. They were talking; it was the night I walked in on the two of you together."

Kate's eyes flickered. "I know, you said that. But why didn't you say so at the time? We might have stopped the murders at Angra…"

"I wasn't sure who I could trust." I rubbed my tired eyes with stiff fingers and tightened my hold on the wheel. "I guess Cecilia felt the same. You know, even now Sylvie still thinks it's you because of your text and the explosion at the museum."

"Do you still believe it was me?" The journalist in her seemed curious more than anxious.

I shook my head and concentrated on the road ahead. "I guess not," I said. "Cecilia tells the same story. I'm the idiot, I believed in Amy despite everything that I heard against her. I am such a fool."

"Kryk and I were lovers for almost six months," Kate said, "but I didn't suspect a thing."

"You never suspected he was holding anything back?" I turned to look at her.

"He always said it was me who was holding back. That I was too closed…" She smiled with embarrassment.

The smile disappeared and Kate closed her eyes. I turned back to the on-coming white lights and the black road.

I couldn't help but wonder about Cecilia, trapped as she was in a marriage to a psychopathic paedophile. What must it be like living with a man who had employed two people to watch over her? Two unnamed people who could have been anybody in the organisation. It was no wonder she had turned to drink.

And then she had tried to expose him by turning to Bernie. Cecilia had always been the sailor. It was Cecilia who had got Tony interested in the first place. Of course, Cecilia had only been a leisure sailor, but Tony had needed to invest in a major sponsorship deal. He had to do it big and with the best sailors. He couldn't just dabble – in anything.

Good for Cecilia that she was now sober. And good for Helene that she had her mother to help her to deal with so much that was mentally disturbing about her father.

Petr Kryk made sense to me; a violent enigma, the unknown assassin.

But Amy made no sense at all. Cecilia had told me that Amy had tried to kill on Tony's behalf. That she had tried to kill me. And she had admitted that she had been with Tony. And I had seen the photos of Sylvie's head pasted onto Amy's body that was pressed against Petr Kryk on a beach. Amy had moved on again and again.

Kate searched on her phone for news.

I called Suffolk police. They knew nothing. I called Cluzon. He had nothing either.

The press were all over the story. There were diagrams and routes from France to England. A helicopter had been identified as heading across the Channel from Le Touquet with three men and a woman on board. Eye witnesses had seen the helicopter going towards the east coast. Journalists considered the likely options. But I knew exactly where they had gone: to a small wooden yacht on the river Deben.

Grainy pictures made out a group, heads covered, crossing tarmac to a helicopter pad. There was no way to distinguish who they were. One of them could have been Petr Kryk, it was unclear, and there was one who might have been a woman but she was surrounded by the men. It could have been Amy or anybody else.

Kate spoke to contacts, but nothing new came up about the whereabouts of Tony or Rex. Nor did we find anything on Jenny and Rory.

Chapter forty-three

I couldn't think too closely about what they might be doing to Jenny and Rory. I needed to focus only on getting them back.

I spoke to the hospital. Sylvie was in ICU. She had lost the lower one of the two lobes of her left lung and her bowel had to be stitched back together. In six weeks, she could be breathing almost normally, they said.

On the drive, I explained to Kate that Jenny and Rory had been on the river with me and were missing.

"It can only be Tony," I said.

She stared ahead. "Yes," she said.

When we arrived back in Suffolk, the *Arabella* seemed peaceful and untouched.

"There must be something here," said Kate. We entered the saloon quickly.

It had been almost thirty-six hours since I had left Jenny and Rory quietly playing together on the yacht. We searched the boat. I placed Sylvie's gun inside the starboard-side cockpit locker. I found nothing to tell me where they had gone.

My phone rang.

Kate looked at me. It was an unknown number.

I answered.

And it was Tony.

"Here's what you'll do," said Tony. There was no preamble. "Bring me back what's mine or Jenny and the boy die and the assassin comes for you again."

"What are you talking about, Tony?"

"I want it back. Don't play me a fool, Tom."

I searched my memory for what it was he could want back. I had nothing of his. He had lost but he had destroyed everything. The tapes had gone over the side in Brazilian waters. Only Amy had one. He had what I wanted: the safe return of Jenny and Rory.

"When?" I asked, stalling.

I heard Tony take a quick breath down the line.

"Tomorrow. North Sea. A mile south of the Cork Sand Buoy. At six am. Come alone."

"I need to know Jenny and Rory are safe."

There was a pause.

A small voice spoke. Jenny sounded hoarse and desperate down the phone line. "Please…" she started.

Tony cut in.

"Bring it and they are yours. I'll transfer Jenny and the child."

I said: "What about Petr Kryk? And Amy?"

"What about them?"

"Are they with you?"

But the line was dead.

Kate turned around in a circle and headed out on deck with her pack of cigarettes.

"I don't get it," she said.

It was dark and the quay was difficult to see. The lights along the pontoon lit only dim patches in a fine drizzle. Kate's cigarette lighter lit her face momentarily

343

so that the warm coffee cream of her complexion lit up in a flicker.

"No," I said. "What do I have that belongs to Tony?" I ran both hands through my hair and rubbed at my eyes as I did. "Whatever it is, I must go to them."

"When do we leave?" asked Kate.

"In an hour." She stepped over the guardwires and onto the floating pontoon.

She walked towards the washrooms smoking. She passed through the light patches and into the fog of darkness and stopped under a lamp post. A fine mist had formed around its glow.

"Don't leave without me," she called.

"Deal," I said.

Back inside the boat, I tugged a wedged bottle of my sponsor's mineral water from under the bunk. I took a long slug. I thought about what Cecilia had said about Amy being covered in blood and wondered why my ex-girlfriend would want to kill me. It wasn't as if I had run off with Sylvie. Amy had left me. She had followed the money. And the only thing I had that Tony wanted was my youth.

"Shit," I said. "But that's it."

I threw the water bottle through the companionway and it skidded into the cockpit. I found my phone and called Cluzon.

"Bernie's computer – was it ever recovered?"

Cluzon took a moment to realise who it was on the line. "No," he said. He sounded cautious.

"Could you access his email account?"

"We have. The password was written down in his notebook. Why, Tom?"

"Did you see any correspondence from Cecilia to Bernie?"

"Yes, several. One asking him to keep quiet…"

"About Tony?"

"No," said Cluzon. "About going into hospital with Helene."

I climbed one-handed onto the deck. I untied my lines with the phone wedged between ear and shoulder.

"When was that?" I dragged the mooring ropes onboard and dropped them in through the companionway in loose coils.

"A week before your race began."

I climbed inside the cockpit and turned over *Arabella's* engine and it broke into a steady rhythm. I said: "What hospital does Cecilia use when she goes in for her alcoholism?"

"A private psychiatric unit in Rio. Very expensive. Why?"

"I'll call you back."

I checked that I had the lines onboard and re-dialled, this time to Patrick.

"Is Phillipe with you?"

"Yes..." he said.

"Put him on... Phillipe, what happened the week before the race? My race. Did they go into hospital?"

Phillipe's words were thin and stuttering down the line. "There was a lot of... crying," he said. "They should have gone in. It would have been better..."

"But they didn't, right?"

"Tony made it worse. He was trying to help in his own way, but it just turned her wild."

"Phillipe, Cecilia's favourite drink?"

But there was no answer.

I dropped the phone into the glory-bag on the bulkhead.

When Kate came back, she shouted across the pontoon because I was already heading out of the marina's tight fairway leaving her behind.

"Tom, you can't go alone!"

"It's better this way, Kate. It's too dangerous. Kryk is there. Amy must be, too. Look what happened to Sylvie. I'll see you tomorrow when I get back. I'll bring Jenny back safe."

"But what does he want?"

"Blood and water."

"What do you mean?"

I held the tiller with a tight grip. "And we missed youth. Look, Cecilia told us that Amy was covered in blood but she ran into Johnnie in the night. He didn't mention any blood. Johnnie would have seen it. And Sylvie said that she used to fill coke cans with vodka. You can do that the other way round, can't you? With water, I mean. Meet me here tomorrow at ten pm. Okay?"

Kate walked so that she followed the contour of the pontoons until she could go no further. She held one of the uprights and leaned out over the placid water. "Where's the pick-up, Tom?"

"Sorry, Kate. Tomorrow."

Arabella cruised effortlessly out of the harbour's tight entrance and took the ebb tide out of the river. I saw Kate's confusion as I left her on the shore.

A Force six was blowing and there would be a big tide.

I would easily be there by six am in this wind.

And now that I realised my mistakes I had to finish it. I had to go to Jenny.

Chapter forty-four

I could see a big motor launch in about the right place: south of the Cork Sand Buoy and holding station in the relative deep water east of the hazardous slab which is the Cork Sand – a vast strip of innocuous danger just below the surface. There was nothing else nearby and so I crept closer under a reduced sail plan. The waves were big and rolled heavily, crests breaking and foaming. The wind remained strong, gnawing at the coast.

The cruiser was about sixty feet long and white all over. It held station bucking in the breaking swell as I neared, and I knew it must be them.

All I could think was, *For some the deal is money and for others the deal is blood.*

I doused all sail and ran the engine on low. The boats dipped and pitched into the uncomfortable sea.

Through big windows, I saw Tony was moving from inside. He scrambled out on to the aft deck clumsily and I realised that he had Jenny and Rory with him.

I drew in as close as I dared to the other ship and kept working to keep them on station four metres apart.

"Where is it?" yelled Tony.

"Safe!" I called back, lying. I had to hope they were all there. "Send Jenny and Rory over first."

I could see Petr Kryk up on the helming deck, one level up. He was holding the motor launch steady. His black polo neck and slicked-back hair made him seem lean and athletic. And dangerous.

"Show me!" shouted Tony. "Or I'll have someone shoot you on the boat like I did on the finish line in Brest."

"But you didn't, Tony. Whatever sick things you do do, you're not a murderer."

"Come on, Tom. I don't have all day," shouted Tony but he was nervous.

I could see Rex inside the yacht and he had Amy with him. His angry purple-blotched face and long nose were thrust down to the deck. Rex had hold of Amy's arm. He shoved her forward and she stumbled into the doorway. Behind them was Helene, small and doll-like.

They came out onto the bucking platform that was the aft deck.

Tony put out a chubby hand to Helene as if to wave her back inside. In his hand was a gun.

"Helene," I said. "Weren't you supposed to be flying to Madrid and on to Brazil with your mother?"

"I was," said Helene, her wild and dark beauty tempestuous in the storm. She stood to Tony's left side. "But I thought dad needed me here."

Amy, on Tony's right, had said nothing and I looked towards her. Her pale and cold neck was exposed and her hair roughly tied back. She dropped her head to stare at her feet. And then she stared directly back at me with black eyes as if trying to convey a message.

I thought: *I'm right: blood left, money right.*

Rex growled from behind them. "Come on, for God's sake," he said, blotched face and sagging eyes violent. "Give us the USB stick or they get it."

348

Chapter forty-five

"You were so cool at the airport, Helene," I shouted. "Cecilia sat there drinking pure water and she asked if I had brought anything with me – because you both knew about the deal."

"That's not important now," said Tony. He staggered as a wave crashed the motor launch down at the stern and his soft belly tensed. "I just want my film back. The money you asked for is already in the account."

"The money…" I started. I dared not catch Amy's eye. Yes, I thought, that was the deal that Helene had asked about when we met in the Savoy in London. I had thought she meant the deal Tony said he had made with Josh. But it wasn't that, it was another deal. One they thought I had made for money. And Cecilia had asked if I had brought something to the airport. When I said I had nothing, she had told me a pack of lies. I caught sight of Amy's expression. I knew it wasn't my deal they meant but hers. One she had created.

"Before we do this deal," I shouted. "First I want to hear you say it, Helene." First I needed to hear about the blood. "It was you who shot at *Ocean Gladiator* to kill Josh – that's the real truth, isn't it? Then, when you failed you came out looking for him when he was actually in Truro and you hit me with a winch handle and brain-damaged Stan. But you were always hoping to kill Josh."

Jenny was holding Rory against her and she stared at Helene. She gasped and staggered as the cruiser fell heavily into a trough.

"I thought it was Tony trying to save himself," I shouted. The wind tried to swallow my words. "But it was Helene trying to cover up for him by killing Bernie and then going after Josh because he wouldn't come back to her."

Helene spat. "He wouldn't leave daddy alone. I warned him."

"You had an argument…"

"You told Jenny he was with me when you came back from the race practice a day early and he said he had to choose. He said he wanted to stay with Jenny. That baby made up his mind." If she had been beautiful to me once, she was ulgy now.

"And he knew all about your dad's nasty habits."

"Bernie was going to tell the world and that would have been the end of the family. I couldn't let him do that. I hired Petr Kryk. I wanted Josh to understand that I was serious. He would see it when Bernie died. I gave him the fake photos. But Josh betrayed our love - for her."

Tony was between them as Helene lunged towards Jenny holding Rory.

Tony held her back, straining against her power.

"Cecilia's not an alcoholic," I said. "She was drinking water every time. She pretends to be a lush to cover taking you into hospital. Not the other way round. You're the patient. A week before the race Josh and Jenny got married and Cecilia tried to take you into hospital again. You're a psychiatric patient. You're the one covered in blood."

"She's…she's not well," said Tony.

"No," I said. "Not well at all. That's probably because she's your daughter, don't you think, Tony? Because she's a sick child amongst dangerous adults." I shot a look towards Amy. *Now, for the money*, I thought. "Let's do the deal. Let's do it now. Send Amy over and I'll give her the USB stick." I would continue that lie. I would play out Amy's deal and she could hand over the actual data stick that she still held on her. "Amy can make the swap," I said.

"Very well," said Tony.

"And then she comes with me."

"Amy stays," said Tony. "We're getting married."

"No," said Amy. "I told you I won't go through with it. Tom, please!"

I knelt down to the locker and drew out the pistol unseen. I stood and without hesitation fired at Tony.

Tony fell as the bullet hit him in the right shoulder. Behind him, Rex caught hold of the gun that fell from his boss' hand. I fired again and Rex was hit in the chest. He slipped backwards, knocked from his feet and he too dropped the gun.

Helene ran back inside the boat.

I saw Petr Kryk pulling an automatic up from the floor on the bridge deck above.

I weaved *Arabella* in close and jumped aboard the motor launch as he fired down. *Arabella* crashed against the cruiser and span away into the jumping waves abandoned to the force of wind and tide.

I saw Helene crouching to a gun inside the saloon. Jenny and Rory were behind me outside and Amy was to my right side.

I fired into the saloon and Helene slithered away as the boat lurched down the back of a vast, smooth wave.

"You've still got the USB?" I asked.

"Yes," said Amy. She was more pale than I had ever seen her and her eyes were hollowed black and grey. She was stick thin. There was what looked like an old injury behind her right ear.

"And you blackmailed Tony for cash in my name? That's the deal Tony thinks he made with me: cash for the original film. You're the money."

I crouched low, staring into the saloon with the gun out-stretched.

She turned a haunted face to me so that we stared at each other. Her black eyes were wild in the turbulence of the sea. Her neck muscles were tensed as if she were unable to swallow.

"But now I know everything he did." Her eyes seemed to plead. "I'm sorry, Tom. You've got to believe that I didn't know before Angra de Reis. You didn't tell me. Of course he didn't either. How could I have known what he was really like?"

"You were already sleeping with him by the time I knew anything," I said.

"Until Angra we were together," she said. Another wave rolled through and the ship rose and fell with a lurch. Amy put out a hand to steady herself, touching me. "But I stopped. Once I saw the whole film, I stopped. He lied to me and he beat me. I've been a prisoner since then."

I resisted the urge to flinch away from her hand. "What about Petr Kryk?"

"No," she said. "Those photos of Sylvie's face on my body – they were fakes that Kryk made. Helene wanted you all at the museum."

"You wrote me a letter saying Bernie touched you, Amy…"

She knelt alone, steady now. On my other side, Jenny sat down against the bulkhead shielded from the saloon. She held Rory to her, pressed in.

"Tony told me Bernie took sick photos. He showed me – said they were Bernie's legs. I didn't see very much. He said Josh and maybe even you were involved. I believed him. So I did it – I added it to the letter for him."

"And he bought you an apartment on the French Riviera in return."

"Tom," she said. "I'm sorry."

I saw Helene pressed back against furniture inside the boat and she fired. We ducked away and I shot back. Helene slithered further into the interior of the boat.

I glanced down at Tony and Rex on the deck's heaving floor. Rex was dead. Tony was groaning and holding his shoulder. His chest rose and fell with staccato movements.

"Cecilia swore to me that she saw you covered in blood that night."

"She lied to save Helene," said Amy. "It was Helene who sent the original video to Bernie. She had been horrified by what she saw in St Tropez and she wanted to punish Tony. He interfered when Josh got married before the race and it just made things worse. Then, she wanted the films back because she realised what would happen to him if they got out. But Bernie wouldn't give. So she hired Kryk and took matters into her own hands to save her father."

I took the dropped weapon. I looked deep into Amy's black eyes. Her gaze was steady. I could see the injury behind her ear. It looked like she had cut her head badly. It looked a few weeks old.

"When did you get that?"

"Angra," she said touching the skin. "Twenty-three stitches."

Her eyes were old. Her skin fresh and pale. The purple bruise and stitching looked badly repaired despite being partially concealed under her straight, blond hair. Her neck was cold and exposed.

"How long have you known all this?"

She swallowed. Perhaps she felt seasick from the violent slamming of the boat into the heavy seas. "Since Angra," she said. "You're right about Helene."

I turned to Tony, writhing on the deck in pain. He saw me watching him.

"You don't know what it's like to touch youth when you are my age…"

"Shut up, Tony," I said.

"Youth is beautiful stupidity – begging for money even now. Wanting something from the old but not prepared to give anything." He shifted but the pain speared him and he gasped.

"It's tantalising…" I said because my thoughts had turned to cold murder.

"I made you a winner. Number one. That's all you wanted…" Tony wheezed. And I realised that he was only trying to slow me down to give Kryk the chance to come after me.

I turned away and handed Amy the dropped gun. Whatever she thought of me, I knew she wasn't the killer.

"Cover Tony. Protect Jenny and Rory." I looked down on the panting body. "Tony, you're right – I did win. And it doesn't mean what I thought."

I headed inside.

Automatic gunfire speared through the ship. I fell under a table and covered my face as splinters flew from the tabletop.

I turned and crawled after Helene into the boat.

Inside the main cabin was dark. Forward there was a glitzy bar for cocktails. Directly above me, there were steps leading up to the bridge deck.

I heard someone descending, feet dancing to cope with the irregular pattern of the big waves.

I pointed the gun towards the sound waiting for the feet to come down. I hid beneath the stairs. I had to be sure who it was. I assumed it was Kryk.

The boat heaved. A shot rang out. Across the boat at the bar I saw Kryk was hiding. He must have come down first.

I fired.

There was more gunfire, both from Kryk and from above.

Amongst the retorts of the bullets and the sound of shattered glass crashing from the cocktail bar, I heard a yell.

Brown shoes quickly descended the stairs. It was Helene coming down from the bridge and she crossed to the sliced portions of mirror from the bar. She pulled something. It was Kryk. She dragged him free of the long glass shards but his head sagged. She had shot him by mistake.

"He taught you too well," I said. I had my gun trained on her back. "Drop the weapon, Helene."

The ship lurched in the heavy seas as the ship fell into the empty hole that lay east of the Cork Sand and Helene staggered.

She turned slowly to me. Her petite, womanly frame on slender legs struggled to stand as the boat hit another big wave. Kryk's automatic was at her feet. The handgun she lowered in compliance as she turned to me.

"It was you that your mother saw covered in Stan's blood," I said. "Not Amy."

"I thought he was Josh…" she started.

There was one thing that made no sense. "I don't understand why you shot Kryk on the *Christina*." I said.

"I didn't. Amy was about to shoot him. I clubbed her from behind." That explained the gash to Amy's head. "It stopped her from killing him but the bullet still hit him in the stomach. And then I stepped up on deck with the gun. You assumed it was me who shot Kryk because I had the weapon. But you had Petr's automatic rifle and I knew right then that I couldn't outgun you so I dropped my gun. Dad smuggled Amy away. He really loved her, you know. Just like I loved Josh."

"And you pretended to be traumatised. But really you were the killer. You killed Bernie to stop him going public with the video that you yourself gave to him."

"I paid Kryk to kill Bernie for me. I came for Josh myself but I hit you and Stan by mistake. I did finally shoot Josh from the trawler. I had to. He had betrayed my whole family. He had betrayed me. You must see that. The only other person I have killed…" she said.

A big wave unsteadied her and she dropped to one knee. She raised the gun as she fell, and together we both fired.

Chapter forty-six

The heavy displacement yacht shuddered down from a wave. I felt the pain in my ribs where they had been broken.

I tried to steady myself by jamming in against the galley's sink.

"What are you doing up there?" I shouted.

A head appeared at the companionway.

"Mon pauvre cherie. Je m'excuse," said Sylvie.

"Yeah, well, just because we're close to French Polynesia doesn't mean you can start bouncing the English out of their bunks."

I put an arm across my belly and rubbed the thick scar that covered the missing ends of ribs ten and eleven. It had been a long and painful six months for Sylvie and me. She with bullets in her lungs and me with a bullet through my liver which I now know lies protected underneath my tenth to twelfth ribs on the right.

"Seulement deux ou trois jours de plus jusqu'a ce que les isles, mon petit lapin..."

"Now, I know you just called me a 'little rabbit' which in English is closer to an insult than a compliment," I said.

"Tom, will you ever learn French properly?"

"Probably not," I admitted.

We had been sailing for eight months. Sylvie's strong, new boat was just right for our trip – a heavy displacement vessel with a long keel for a circumnavigation at a restful pace. Together, we could recuperate. And if I wasn't mistaken, Sylvie had just said we were two or three days from the Islands.

"I've finished the manuscript," I said.

"The whole thing?" she asked.

I put down the laptop, squeezed through the galley and climbed up the companionway of *Sprinter* in newly energetic strides. I broke out into the dazzling light to join her on deck. The sun was shining with piercing depth and the temperature was balmy warm. A breeze behind us was surging the beamy forty-foot yacht along through a calm sea with a long swell.

"All murders accounted for." I held up my hand and knocked off fingers. "Bernie Gramm in France, Rene Pignol in Brazil and Admiral Peasegood in Greenwich down to Petr Kryk. Josh Lewis and the attempted murder of Stan Stosur to Helene Drax. Here, I'll read the last bit."

I collected the laptop and returned to the reflecting deck. I stripped off my shirt so that the sun added to my already bronzed colour. The large scar on my abdomen was cross-shaped like a thick and ulgy pink star-fish.

I read: "*Rex Tourenasi died on the boat from a single bullet through the chest that ruptured his aorta.* Down to me," I added. "*Tony Drax survived. He received multiple sentences for kidnapping, financing murder and for paedophilia and rape. He recovered from his injuries and went to gaol for 'at least' one hundred and thirty-nine years and where he would stay until he died.*

"*Petr Kryk also died on the motor launch, mistakenly killed by Helene.*

"*Cecilia Drax remained free. She had known that her daughter was the second assassin and had lied on*

358

her behalf more than once but she had money enough to pay lawyers to keep her untouched.

"*Kate Hutchinson later married a US Marine named Steitly who she met on holiday in Thailand. Patrick Colt and Phillipe Tourenasi were outed by a newspaper although they were publicly lauded for their dignity throughout. Despite his association with Rex, Phillipe continued his racing career and won two Grand Prix the following season.*

"*Jenny took Rory home healthy.*

"*Amy Mackintosh was never caught. I doubt now that she ever will be. Her French apartment has been confiscated in abstentia. No-one knows how much money Tony paid anonymously to Amy for the USB stick he never received – money he erroneously believed was buying my silence. People have speculated that Amy was involved with all of Tony's nefarious affairs and that she may well have been planning to marry him despite what she knew about his activities.*

"*It has never been followed up. It is believed she escaped from the motor launch on the Arabella with the USB stick still on her. Some say she sold it a second time; this time back to Cecilia Drax.*

"*I got myself healthy again, at least healthy enough. Sylvie and I took her boat and sailed it to Fiji, both coughing painfully all the way. We plan to meet my brother Dan there for a proper holiday.*

"*Helene Drax died on the motor cruiser. She had killed Josh, her one-time lover, and she had severely injured Stan Stosur. She said that Petr Kryk had been her teacher. She told me she had also killed one other.*

"*People have speculated who that might be. Some said she meant in London; that she thought she had killed Sylvie outside the tube station. I have always thought that she was in fact talking about the immediate crime she was hoping to commit: to kill me."*

Sylvie twisted her mouth into a French pout. "You should put: 'By Tom Shepherd, the exceptionally talented, devilishly good-looking winner of the inaugural and subsequently dissolved sailing race, the *Vendee Globe A Deux.'*"

"I might have done once," I said. "But Sylvie?"

I watched as she lay back against the teak inlay of the forty-footer's cockpit seats. She wore only an indiscreet yellow bikini and she stretched out one leg so that her toe curled in the air. Her hair had turned from straw-blond to bleach blond in the beating sunshine. She looked vibrantly alive.

"Yes?" she said.

"I'm no longer a dinghy sailor racing round the buoys. I know there's more to life than first place and how I look."

"Is that so? So you're a man now, are you?"

"I know what I love – long distance sailing. And I know why. I love it because it has depth – literally and psychologically – it goes further regardless of the effort required."

Sylvie smiled doubtfully. She tucked stray strands of hair behind her ears. Her healthy, delicate skin radiated warmth. She brought her face close to mine and the rose cheeks and pink lips were smooth, the grey eyes steady.

"And *who* do you love?" She stared at me intently from too close.

"Vous, ma cherie," I said.

"Not enough to learn proper French." She moved away to sit with upright posture. "You mean 'tu.' Also, you mentioned 'why' you love so much. Please don't try to answer in French – I don't wish to be translating all day."

"It's because we have matching scars," I said.

Sylvie stood and twirled so that her twin gunshot wounds were displayed. She smiled. "You're such an idiot. You only see the earth-turn and not the beauty of the sunset."

"My darling, Sylvie," I said. I had the laptop on my knees. "That is no longer true. I have moved on."

"To someone new?"

"To permanence."

"Moved on to permanence? What on earth do you mean by that?"

"I mean longevity: the promise of old age."

"The promise of old age? Is this *the* Tom Shepherd I'm sailing with? The ageist free spirit who knows no earthly ties? He who sees only parties in his immediate future?"

"You have to admit it beats dying young," I said. The boat was nicely balanced so that we barely looked up. *Sprinter* beat into the swell dipping and moving in the expanse of an empty ocean. No other vessel was in sight. The horizon hazed into blue in all directions. "Longevity is something that I would like to see out with you," I said.

Sylvie only watched me without speaking. She rotated oddly. She turned in front of me, holding eye contact as she did. She span round three times and pointed to her scars and to mine jigging her body like a merry hippy at stonehenge. I pressed 'save' on my computer and closed the lid.

"I expect ever more romance if we are to stay together permanently," she said once her odd dance was complete.

361

"For a stuck up, hard-nosed French detective, you're pretty soft on love," I said.

She eyed me critically for a moment.

"And for an ugly, Anglo-Mexican schoolboy with no sense of love's meaning, I guess you'll have to do."

She leaned across the cockpit in a measured descent.

I was about to protest that at least the last part of the label no longer fitted, but she kissed me so that my lips were held and I fell silent and closed my eyes. The blinding sunlight behind Sylvie's mess of bleach-blond, straggling hair dazzled my closed eyes. Without breaking the kiss, I put out a hand and tucked the stray strands of blond behind her ear. I stood up in an awkward embrace and drew her slim body against mine so that her soft belly and scars intermingled with my own.

There were two or maybe three more days before French Polynesia.

Tom Shepherd, en route.

The End.

Also by Jez Evans

Sea Thrillers
Waypoint, 2012
Watertight, 2015
Coming soon
Offshore, book one, 2015
Offshore, sanctity 2016
Corsican Gold, 2015

Science fiction
Planet Fall, 2012

Fiction
Coming soon
Children of the Abel Tasman, 2015

With Anna Evans
The Lost babies, 2014

Lightning Source UK Ltd.
Milton Keynes UK
UKOW04f0953140415

249604UK00004B/162/P